WILD CARD

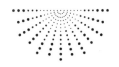

KELSIE RAE

TWISTY PINES LLC

Dear Reader,

As of January 9, 2021, the updated eBook for *Wild Card* (the version you are reading at this moment) now includes *Dark King,* (the original Book Two in the Advantage Play Series) and does *not* end on a cliffhanger.

I hope you enjoy Kingston and Ace's story!

-Kelsie

ACE'S RULES

- Rule #1: Keep your head down and your eyes up. It makes you invisible but not stupid.
- Rule #2: Always be aware of your surroundings.
- Rule #3: If something feels fishy, it probably is. Trust your instincts.
- Rule #4: Never say never.
- Rule #5: Be a machine. Don't allow distractions. They'll only break you.
- Rule #6: Never reveal your true identity and don't get personal.
- Rule #7: Never leave something of value out in the open.
- Rule #8: Don't discuss private shit in public. It's bound to screw you over.

PROLOGUE

ACE

"**L**ook, you have no legal right to detain me," I argue. "Let me cash out my chips, and I'll leave, okay?"

With his heavy hand on my shoulder, the pitboss chuckles behind me. His pudgy fingers dig into my collarbone. "You do know whose casino you're in, right?"

A lump the size of a golf ball lodges in my throat, so I don't respond.

I'm so screwed.

"That's what I thought." He stops me in front of a door on the right before opening it and roughly pushing me inside. Other than a folding chair in the center of the room, it's empty.

I turn around as soon as he releases me, only to be greeted with the back of his hand.

With the force of a wrecking ball, my head swings to the side.

"Fuuuck," I mutter to myself, gingerly touching the side of my face to find the skin already hot and angry.

Shit, that hurt.

Ears ringing, I struggle to find the willpower to focus on

my attacker, but I know that if I curl up into a ball like I want to, I'll be screwed.

"Enough!" a gruff voice barks from the doorway. The sound is almost muffled, but I search for its owner anyway. When my gaze connects with the stranger, I nearly swallow my tongue.

"Fuuuuck," I repeat on a breath. The guy looks pissed. Sexy as hell, yes. But *pissed*.

The pit boss must feel the same anger radiating off him because he takes a cautious step away from me before tucking his hands into the front pockets of his charcoal slacks.

"Sir—"

"Out," the stranger growls, cutting him off while striding over the threshold and into the room. The room that feels like it's shrinking with each of his steps. My heart rate spikes.

I feel like I'm made of granite as he comes closer to me. Even if I wanted to, I'd be unable to move a muscle. Not a damn one.

With hurried steps, the asshole who hit me disappears through the door, leaving me alone with...*him*.

I've only seen him once or twice on the upper floor of the casino. But with the power he exudes, it's hard to miss him. No matter how hard he tries to blend in with the crowds, it's impossible. I've never bothered to find out his name, but I'm really wishing I had done my research now that I'm alone in a room with him in the basement of a casino.

I'm so screwed.

My attention is glued to the stranger as he relaxes right before my eyes. His broad shoulders soften. His clenched fists release. But his pinched brows stay in place, making the uneasiness in my lower gut flair in anticipation. I'm positive he can hear my heart pounding in my chest as he assesses me.

Still frozen, I watch him circle me like a shark, and a single thought whispers through my mind. *I'm about to get eaten alive.*

"Do you know who I am?" his low voice rumbles.

I hold my breath, but don't respond.

"Answer me, Acely Mezzerich." With a knowing smirk and a few choice words, he nearly knocks me on my ass.

Shit. Shit. Shit.

"Surprised I know who you are?" he pushes.

Again, I'm silent.

How the hell does he know my real name?

"Do you know why you're here?"

Yup. I keep my lips zipped.

"Answer me, Ace. I won't ask again." His authoritative tone does weird things to me, but I don't have time to assess them now, so I shove them deep down in a little box labeled: Do Not Open.

"Yes," I whisper as I watch him continue to circle me in his expensive loafers. The guy is built like a freaking panther. I can see his muscles bunching beneath the tailored suit he wears like a second skin as he slowly inches closer with every step.

He pauses at my voice. With a quirked brow, he asks, "Yes, you're surprised I know who you are? Or yes, you know why you're here?"

Licking my chapped lips, I hold his gaze. "Both, I guess."

"And do you know how much money you've taken from me and my casino?"

I nearly grimace before schooling my features. If I had my notebook that's not-so-safely tucked away in my backpack by the blackjack table upstairs, I'd be able to tell him *exactly* how much money I've taken from him. Even without it, I think I can still ballpark the number off the top of my head. That is if I wanted to get backhanded. *Again.*

3

A cocky grin tugs at his mouth. "So you *do* know, I take it. Interesting."

Shit. Shit. Shit.

"Do you know who *I* am?" he continues his probing while slowly closing the circle he's been surrounding me with. The shrinking proximity is giving me heart palpitations, and my hands sweat as they hang by my sides, bunching up the black material of my dress.

When I remain silent, he pushes a little harder with a sharp tongue and an icy stare. "Better start talking, Ace. I'd hate to see that pretty little face get any more bruised than it already is."

Asshole.

Part of me doesn't believe he'd actually hit me, but the other part doesn't want to risk any more damage. Getting hit hurts no matter how many times it happens.

Lifting my chin, I find the courage to answer. "I have an idea."

He laughs dryly. "You have an idea of how much you've stolen from me, or you have an idea of who I am?"

"Both." My lips tilt up on one side, and I find it ironic that any of this situation could possibly be found amusing to me.

"This is starting to feel an awful lot like déjà vu, isn't it?" Again, I catch him reading my mind.

Rule #3: If something feels fishy, it probably is. Trust your instincts. The only problem? My instincts aren't telling me to run in the other direction. The longer I'm in this room, the less threatened I'm beginning to feel, which is weird. And foreign. Thanks to my past, I always feel the need to run.

His forest green eyes flash as soon as the thought enters my mind. Instead of continuing his predatory stalking, he stops in front of me, leaving only a foot of room between us.

Tilting his head to the side, he states, "You're not afraid of me."

My poker face slips, revealing my confusion at his narrowed eyes. How can he tell when I just figured out the same thing myself?

"Excuse me?" I ask.

"Let's play a game."

I feel like I have whiplash from the turn of events, and I'm having a hard time keeping up.

Shaking my head, I utter a single word. "What?"

A husky chuckle reverberates from him before he inches closer while my feet are still glued to the same spot. "Let's play a game, Ace. After all, you're good at games, aren't you." *It's not a question.* "I mean, that *is* what got you here in the first place, isn't it?"

HE HAS NO IDEA...

CHAPTER ONE

KINGSTON

A little while earlier

"Take a seat." I motion to the chair in front of my desk while keeping my face void of any expression.

The pathetic fucker in front of me plops into the chair, and I watch as his beady little eyes dart around the room, desperately searching for anything that might give him a clue as to why he's been called here.

He'll find out soon enough.

I let the silence feed his anxiety until a light sheen of sweat collects along his forehead. My mouth twitches at how easy this is going to be.

Looking at his watch, Diece quirks his brow, and the action reminds me that I have more important shit to do than interrogate a rat. Diece is my right-hand man, and if I'm being honest, one of the few men I really trust, especially when I find myself surrounded by traitors like the one in front of me. Diece and I have been friends since we were little. He was groomed for his position as much as I was, though I don't think either of us is comfortable with our new responsibilities.

Leaning forward, I rest my elbows along the top of my desk. The movement makes the rat in question gulp thickly.

"So...uh...B-Boss? There a reason you called me in here?" he stutters, trying––and failing––to look me in the eye.

"Have you ever been in this office before, Vince?"

"N-no, sir."

"Do you know who this office belongs to?"

"Your father?" It comes out as more of a question than an answer.

I shake my head. "It *did* belong to my father. Just like it belonged to his father before him and my great-grandfather before that. This office belongs to the head of the Romano family, Vince. So let me ask you again...who does this office belong to?"

With a quick glance in my direction, he mumbles, "It's yours."

"A few of your associates have told me you feel differently than that," I explain before pushing myself up from the seat and walking around the desk. "That I haven't earned the position. That I'm not strong enough or smart enough to lead the family. That I'm too soft."

Diece laughs, grabbing Vince's attention before his neck snaps back toward me.

"W-what?" he asks, feigning confusion, though that same soft stutter makes it clear he understands the shitstorm he has created for himself. With his eyes wide, it's as if he's surprised by my audacity to voice such a ludicrous accusation.

"I know. I found it quite surprising, as well. I mean, who did you expect would take over the Romano family after my father died when I've been groomed for the position since I was six years old?"

His index finger starts tapping against his upper thigh, and my gaze shoots to Diece. Stepping forward, Diece drops his burly hands onto Vince's trembling shoulders, making him flinch while simultaneously keeping him in the chair when I know he's contemplating bolting from the room. He wouldn't have gotten far, but still.

"I asked you a question, Vince. I suggest you answer it."

Raising his chin, he looks me straight in the eye, and I know he's putting on his bravest face. "I don't know what my associates have told you, but they're lying."

I shake my head. "Let me ask you something else, Vince. Were they lying about the fact you've been in contact with Burlone Allegretti?"

His Adam's apple bobs up and down before Diece leans over him and digs his fingers into Vince's wrists. Vince starts to struggle when my cold voice freezes him in place. "I suggest you cooperate. I have a few questions, and if you can answer them truthfully, then you have nothing to be afraid of."

His lower lip quivers, but he stops fighting long enough for Diece to restrain him to the chair with a set of zip ties around his forearms and wrists followed by his ankles around the legs of the seat. Vince might think he's fooling me by his compliance, but I'm not the idiot he thinks I am.

Once he's secured, I continue my interrogation as the sweat that'd been collecting around his hairline finally drips down the side of his face before gathering along his chin. Unfortunately, he can't wipe the moisture away, so it just hangs there, threatening to finally fall while still clinging desperately to the sniveling asswipe it belongs to.

Blinking slowly, I snap my focus back to the traitor in the room.

"Tell me, Vince. Why did you reach out to Burlone?"

"W-what? I didn't—"

I cut him off. "Now, now, Vince. We both know you're lying to me, and I think you'd be wise to change your strategy if you want to get out of this situation in one piece. Answer the question. Truthfully, this time."

"I'm not—"

"Do you know who I am?" I probe.

"Kingston Romano?"

"Yes. Do you know what I specialize in?"

He gulps. Again. If that's not a tell, I don't know what is. Growing frustrated, I reach for the letter opener lying on my desk and run the pad of my thumb along the dull edge before dragging it up to the pointed tip. *Yes, this'll do nicely.*

"You specialize in torture," Vince mumbles, his gaze glued to my hands.

"I *specialize* in getting answers. How I get them depends on the individual I'm interrogating. Now, you're trying my patience, Vince. Let me be clear. You won't be walking out of this office. You said goodbye to that possibility the moment you gave sensitive information to my enemy. However, Diece can carry you out of this office in one piece...or multiple. That's the only control you have here. And even that decision is given to you because I'm feeling generous." Again, he eyes the letter opener in my hand warily, and I reply with a dry laugh. "No. This can't slice through dry bone, but it can still poke you full of holes before I decide to send Diece for my kit that holds the fun stuff. Now, tell me why you betrayed the Romano family."

When he remains silent, I count to three in my head before lunging forward and driving the letter opener into him an inch below his left collarbone, and he screams in pain. After twisting it clockwise, I tug the weapon back and wipe the crimson blood along his ashen cheek as he sobs like a baby. Satisfied with the war paint I've gifted him with, I growl a single word, "Talk."

Through his sniveling, he starts, "Y-you don't understand. He approached me. He asked about the warehouses near Harbor Drive. Wanted to know how heavily they're watched. I-I didn't mean to say anything—"

"Wrong. You approached him because you weren't happy when I took my father's position and wanted to get into Burlone's good graces. However, only a fool would trust someone from a family other than their own, and Burlone isn't a fool. That being said, he did take advantage of the situation by asking for information concerning his enemies. What does he want with our warehouses?"

"I don't know!" he weeps, tears streaming down his cheeks.

Tilting my head to the side, I assess him before nodding, satisfied he's finally telling the truth.

"And what did you tell him?"

As he squeezes his eyes shut, I can tell he's going to need a little more persuasion, and I drive the letter opener into his opposite side but in the same spot near his collarbone. Again, he squeals in pain; then the truth begins to spill out of him just like the piss that's soiled my chair.

I'll have to get a new one.

Dammit.

By the time I'm finished prying the answers I need out of the little weasel, my shirt is splattered with the traitor's blood. Looking down at the soiled clothes, my fingers slowly unbutton the white dress shirt at my collar. D's voice distracts me from inspecting the dead body slumped in my office. It's a shame he squealed so quickly that I had to put him out of his misery before getting to the fun part.

"Seems you haven't lost your touch," he notes. "And the sulfuric acid? That was new."

I laugh dryly, observing the marks along his skin where it was eaten away by a clear liquid I keep in my liquor cabinet.

11

"I dunno. I'm a little disappointed I didn't need to pull out my hunting knife."

He joins in with a deep chuckle. "And *that* is why your enemies call you Dark King."

"If only I didn't have to remind the Romano family," I sigh before pulling my arms out of the sleeves and dropping the stained shirt onto the lifeless body hunched in the chair. "Have you heard anyone else who's disappointed in the transition?"

"No. Vince was the only one. You heard him. He wasn't conspiring with anyone else."

"Yeah, but not before he passed along valuable information to Burlone," I argue bitterly.

With a shrug, Diece pulls out his phone and sends a text to someone before looking back at me. "Doesn't matter how well we do our job, there's always going to be someone with a stick up their ass. We'll figure out what Burlone is trying to do with the information about the dock, and when we do, we'll eradicate the issue like we did with Vince. I just sent a text to Stefan to clean up this mess. We've got more important shit to do anyway."

I nod. "You're right. I guess I shouldn't expect anything less."

"Not when you're the head of one of the most powerful mafia families."

"One of?" I jest with a quirked brow.

"For now."

2

ACE

Rule #1: Keep your head down and your eyes up. It makes you invisible but not stupid.

It's quiet at this time of night. I'd almost consider it peaceful if it weren't for the homeless guy pretending to sleep on the sidewalk. I can feel him watching me as I take each purposeful step toward my destination. Or maybe I'm just paranoid because I'm carrying around fifteen hundred bucks in my worn, blue backpack, and I feel like every Tom, Dick, and Harry knows about it. Being a twenty-two-year-old female in this part of town always makes you feel like you have a target on your back, but being a twenty-two-year-old girl with a shit-ton of money? That brings on a whole other level of anxiety.

Which leads me to Rule #2: Always be aware of your surroundings. Hence why the creeper is giving me goosebumps.

I grip the nylon straps a little tighter before turning the corner and spotting my destination, Dottie's.

"Finally," I mumble under my breath.

Grasping the cold metal handle of the fifties-themed diner's door, I swing it open and bask in the smell of bacon grease and burnt coffee.

"Hey, Dottie!" I greet the owner as she wipes down the chipped Formica countertop.

Her curly, red-dyed hair doesn't move an inch as she lifts her chin in my direction. "Hey, doll! Let me finish cleanin' up this mess, and I'll be over in a minute."

I make my way toward a corner booth that's currently occupied by my best friend, Gigi.

"Man, I'm starving," I announce as I approach. She grunts her reply while shoving another bite of pancakes into her mouth.

After I slide into my seat, I slip off my backpack then place it between my feet under the table.

Rule #7: Never leave something of value out in the open.

"Sorry 'bout that, doll. What can I get ya?" Dottie asks in her thick Southern drawl.

I don't bother opening my menu because I have the whole thing memorized, anyway. "Scrambled eggs. Extra crispy hashbrowns. And…" I tap my finger against my chin. "A side of sausage, please."

Dottie doesn't bother to write down my order, either, because I almost always ask for the same thing. "Comin' right up."

She turns on her heel to put my order in.

"Really? Scrambled eggs again? We've been meeting here for like three months, and you always order the same thing. Don't you get sick of it?" Gigi's brow is quirked from questioning.

"Meh. It's all I ever ate as a kid, so I guess it kinda stuck. They're cheap and were the only thing my mom could cook, which is ironic because she somehow found a way to screw those up too."

"So how'd it go?" Gigi talks through her mouthful of food as she tilts her head toward my bag under the table. I scoot my feet together an extra couple of inches, making sure my black ankle boots are deliberately pinning the straps to the floor.

"Not too bad."

Her lips tilt up in amusement. "Not too bad for you? Or not too bad for the average Joe?"

I snort before reaching for her cup of coffee and bringing it to my lips. After taking a sip of the lukewarm liquid, I set it back down in front of her. "Not too bad for *me*," I clarify. "I'm getting close. Only a few more nights, and I'll have enough for the buy-in."

"Ah." She leans back in her seat and folds her arms. "Then I see it was a relatively good night. Which place did you hit up?"

Shrugging, I lick my lips then casually toss a glance over my shoulder to make sure we're alone. "The Charlette."

A dry laugh escapes her as she shakes her head. "That's perfect."

The Charlette is a casino. One that I frequent often. For some reason, Gigi's amusement is always amplified whenever I count cards there versus a few of the other locations I like to hit up. "I think you should try hitting up the Charlette more often. Just sayin'," she adds with a grin.

"It isn't safe to go to the same casino too often. You get flagged by the pit boss pretty damn quick when they notice you're regularly leaving with a bagful of their money instead of empty-handed."

"But you never get caught."

"Rule #4: Never say never." I rap my knuckles across the table––even though it isn't wooden––as a silly superstition. But when your life could possibly be on the line, you don't mess with jinxes. "The only reason I haven't been caught yet is because I have a solid rotation, a foolproof game plan that helps me get by without any issues, and my rules."

Gigi huffs a breath of laughter before probing, "Ah yes. How could I forget *the rules*? Where did you come up with those anyway?"

"Some of them I picked up on my own. Some of them were little pieces of advice from my mom. Some of them were tiny tidbits of wisdom left by her *friends*." I lift my fingers and dramatically place air quotes around the term. My mother was a druggie, and I'm pretty sure she was paid for sex on multiple occasions––scratch that. I'm positive about it.

"What do you mean her *friends*?" With a teasing smile, Gigi mimics my air quotes from seconds before.

"I've told you what my mom was like before she disap-peared. Must've been stuck in the eighties because all she loved was sex, drugs, and rock and roll." A scoff slips past my lips. "Unfortunately for both of us, she didn't have the money to support that lifestyle, which meant she had to find alterna-tive ways of earning income including, but not limited to, sex with strange men in our little trailer." My eyes go wide at the memories before I sarcastically add, "That was *a lot* of fun. No wonder having sex is about as appealing as getting a colonoscopy."

"Depending on who you're with and how kinky they are, it's probably pretty similar," Gigi quips with a grin.

Gripping my stomach in laughter, Dottie interrupts us by planting my food on the table with a solid thud.

"Thanks, Dottie!" I yell to her retreating form.

Ketchup in hand, I squirt a generous portion of red sauce over my food. "Speaking of family, how's the family life?"

She snorts. "Shitty, as always."

Her words act like a wet blanket, sobering me instantly.

Gigi's a very private person, but she broke down a few weeks ago and told me that her family is falling apart, and she feels helpless. *Hopeless.* I held her as she cried before she wiped under her eyes with a napkin and pretended her little breakdown never happened at all.

"I'd say I can relate, but since my only family went missing when I was twelve…."

"Sometimes, I wish *I* could be the one to disappear." Gigi's confession is said under her breath, and I doubt I was meant to hear it. Regardless, it hangs in the air with a weight I can't disburse.

Clearing her throat, she reaches for a sausage link off my plate. "I'm jealous you get to go have fun and live on the edge, Ace. I think you should let me tag along one of these days."

"Ya think? No offense, Gigi, but you would stick out like a sore thumb." Scooping up a forkful of scrambled eggs, I bring it to my mouth and chew slowly.

With a gasp, a mock offended Gigi chucks her crumpled napkin at my head. "What the hell is that supposed to mean?"

"It means you're drop-dead gorgeous, and every guy will notice you as soon as you step foot onto the carpet."

Gigi tosses her thick, dark hair over her shoulder in outrage. "Whatever. You're just as gorgeous as I am, so cut the shit."

Laughing, I pick up the second link of sausage and take a bite. "Sorry, G. But I'm going to have to disagree with you on that one. I,"—I point to my chest— "am girl-next-door cute. You," —I motion to her— "are runway-model cute. There's a difference. I can blend in at the blackjack table. You can't."

With a shake of her head, she tries a different tactic. "Then let's skip the blackjack table. I need to get out. I need to live. The slots look fun."

I balk, pointing my utensil at her and talking through a

mouth full of food. "Don't waste your money on slots. They're designed to make you lose."

"And what would you suggest I play, then?" She leans forward and rests her elbows on the table, clearly intrigued.

After taking another bite of eggs, I reply, "Blackjack." She snorts. "Or poker. Hell, even roulette has better odds than the freaking slot machines. Especially when the gaming commission turns a blind eye and doesn't audit their machines since they're owned by the freaking mob. Just sayin'."

She quirks her brow. "Then you should teach me black-jack or poker. Just sayin'," she mimics with a teasing smile.

"We've already discussed this."

"I know, I know. What if we play just for fun, then? No counting. No crazy strategies. No rules. Just *fun*." She bounces her brows up and down suggestively like it's a preposterously genius idea, and it's a little pathetic that I can't remember the last time I played for fun. I guess, with my history of the game, the answer would be *never*. And I can thank Burlone for that.

The same worn deck of cards that I learned how to count with is sitting in the front pouch of my backpack, burning a hole in the pocket as I consider using them for fun instead of an outlet for revenge.

I release a sigh then pull my backpack out, unzip the compartment, and grab one of my most prized possessions. The cards have swirling gold ink on the back with a cursive 'A' woven into the colors. Though they've definitely seen better days, I push my plate aside then deal her in.

We continue to shoot the shit while playing cards for a few more hours when dawn finally breaks, and we go our separate ways with the promise of meeting again tomorrow night.

Just like always.

And, just like always, I make the trek back to my lonely apartment in a bad part of town by myself, praying it'll be nighttime soon, so I'm one step closer to my revenge.

3

ACE

S wirling my straw in the watered-down vodka tonic, I shift awkwardly in my seat.

Damn, this dress is uncomfortable.

It's red. And short. And about two sizes too small.

Casually, I glance to the blackjack table a few feet below. The bar is set up in the center of the casino on a platform that gives me a crazy good view of the entire floor plan–– including the blackjack tables.

My gaze zeroes in on the dealer as he lays down the cards face up. They're playing with six decks, which means I can lazily count the cards as he puts them on the table instead of waiting for the players to throw them in once the round is over. Regardless, my focus is wicked-sharp as I watch from my perched position.

Rule #5: Be a machine. Don't allow distractions. They'll only break you.

Two. Two. Seven. Four. I watch as he slowly turns over one low card after another. The deck is hot.

Hell, it's *scorching*. The more low cards that come out of

the deck raise the probability of high ones begging to be played, which means it's go-time.

Without thought, I pull out my phone and set a timer then slide off my stool and stumble down the steps, making sure to splash a little of my drink for good measure.

I can feel the dealer's eyes on me as I set the scene.

Perfect.

Looking around the room without a care in the world, I stop when our gazes connect and give the dealer a dopey-eyed smile. "Hi. Ooo…" I step closer to the table. "Blackjack. Mind if I join you?"

"Not at all." He scans me from head to toe before remembering he's at work and checking out the players is slightly frowned upon. His neck snaps to the player on his left as I take a seat and fumble with the clasp on my clutch like a pro. Pulling out a roll of fifties, I toss ten onto the table.

With a smile, the dealer exchanges the cash for poker chips. "Here you go, miss."

"Why, thank you," I quip, making sure to keep track of the cards he dealt from a moment before.

Nine. Three. Five. Six.

Seriously, this couldn't be a better time to play.

I can almost feel the heat radiating from the scorching deck as I wait for him to finish collecting the used cards then discard them into a pile.

Tucking a strand of hair behind my ear, I lean forward and motion to the empty chair next to me. "Mind if I play two hands? My boyfriend loves blackjack, so I like to play a hand for him too." My red-tinted lips tilt up flirtatiously while the little tidbit of information I just dropped makes it clear I'm off-limits.

He deflates a few inches at my mention of a fake boyfriend then offers a quick, "Sure," before motioning to the table.

"Perfect." With a wink, I place the chips in two separate piles to show I'm playing two hands––two hundred each.

The dealer furrows his brows. "Miss, the minimum bet is fifty. You're welcome to play that much, but I just want to make sure you're aware of the rules."

It's far from appropriate to question how much a player gambles, but I must be nailing the scatterbrained sorority chick act because he takes pity on me.

Chewing my lower lip, I take a second to look at my watch before giving my attention back to the dealer. "I lost track of time at the bar and only have time for a couple of hands. Am I allowed to play more than fifty? My boyfriend said I could go crazy, so...." Batting my lashes at him, I channel my inner Gigi and give him my best puppy dog expression.

He caves like a champ.

"Of course, miss."

The dealer starts making his way around the table, laying a card face-down in front of him before turning to his left and placing them face-up to everyone else.

Nine. Four. Six. Ten.

My turn.

A king of clubs is placed in front of my first hand, and I dig my teeth into my lower lip to contain my excitement. For my second hand, he turns over an ace of hearts. The dealer places a six of diamonds in front of him before he goes around again. I couldn't ask for a better set-up. It's practically a card counter's wet dream.

Ten. Six. Three. Eight.

Again, it's my turn.

A rush of adrenaline spikes through me as I watch it unfold.

Ten of spades for my first hand, which means I'm at twenty. It's damn-near perfect. The only thing that beats a twenty in blackjack is twenty-one. Any more than that, and you bust.

I nibble my fingernail to contain my anxiety before glancing at the dealer's face and smiling nervously.

It's an act. I'm not nervous. I'm *going* to win. Hell, if I could put another five grand on the table, I would. But I can't, so my measly four hundred bucks will have to do.

Next, the dealer slides a card off the top of the deck to pair with my ace of hearts. With bated breath, I watch as he flips over a king of spades.

Yes!

"Yay!" I clap my hands in front of me while bouncing in my chair. After all, I'm playing a peppy ex-cheerleader who loves spending her boyfriend's money. Might as well have fun while I'm at it. "That's good, right? I mean…it's twenty-one!"

The people surrounding the table laugh.

"Yeah. That's really good, miss," the dealer confirms. "As long as I don't beat it, then you'll get paid three hundred for it."

"But," I play dumb. "I thought I put down two hundred?"

"If you get dealt blackjack, then you get paid out three to two, so it looks like it might be your lucky night."

Or it's statistics. But sure, we'll go with luck.

I grin widely.

The dealer flips over his card on the bottom, displaying a six to tag along with his other six. He takes the top card from the deck and turns it over to reveal a queen of spades.

He busted.

"Yes!" With a squeal, I clap my hands again as he hands over five hundred dollars worth of chips.

I risk another hand and win another six hundred bucks when the alarm on my phone vibrates.

With an innocent smile, I lift my forefinger to the dealer and silence the alarm before pretending to read a text.

"It's my boyfriend. Apparently, he had too much to drink and needs me to take care of him." I roll my eyes. "You know boys. Thanks for the fun night!" I wave my fingers his way then gather my chips up from the table and head to the information center to cash out.

It feels super crowded for a Thursday night as I weave between sweaty bodies toward my destination. When I'm shoved from behind, I stumble forward, nearly twisting my ankle.

Damn heels.

"Shit," I mumble under my breath. With a clenched jaw, I look over my shoulder to find the culprit with his hands in the air.

Asshole.

4

ACE

"**I**'m so sorry. Are you okay?"

The guy looks to be a few years older than me, and he's built like a swimmer. Tall and trim with a tapered waist. I'd probably punch his chiseled jaw if he didn't look so damn apologetic for almost mowing me over.

"Yeah," I murmur, taking a wobbly step back with my chips still in hand. "I'm fine."

"You sure?" His brows are pinched in concern as he looks me up and down, searching for any bumps or bruises.

"Um...yeah."

"I'm Jack." He offers his hand to me, and I take it. His palm is warm; his fingers long and calloused.

"Ace." My real name slips past my lips before I can stop it, and frustration quickly follows.

Shit.

He knocked me off guard when he ran into me, and now I'm going to pay dearly for it.

Rule #6: Never reveal your true identity and don't get personal.

I'm an idiot.

"Nice to meet you, Ace. Seems you were meant to play cards with a name like that," he teases with a playful smirk. His chin drops to my left hand that's still clutching my fat stack of chips.

Clearing my throat, I search for a response but come up empty.

The only thing going through my mind right now is *shit, shit, shit*. I need to get out of here. I'm supposed to be invisible, or as invisible as possible in a casino full of cameras at least, and right now, I feel like I have a glaring spotlight pointed right at me.

Holding my stare, a curious Jack asks, "Do you play often? I feel like I've seen you before."

The hairs on the back of my neck stand on end, though he doesn't appear aggressive in any way. His hands are relaxed at his sides; his smile seems genuine. Maybe it really is a coincidence, and I'm not seconds away from being dragged to a dark room and backed off by a scary pit boss. Or worse. If I played at legit casinos, I wouldn't worry, but when I'm dealing with mob money, things can get sticky. Fast.

Breathing in through my nostrils, I look at the situation from every angle, searching for the optimal response before going with a classic excuse. "My boyfriend and I like to party. I should probably go hunt him down, though. He's looking for me." To soften my blow, I smile innocently at him, then take a step closer to the information desk.

"That's too bad. I think we could've made quite the pair," he shamelessly flirts.

With a snort and heated cheeks, I cover my face in embarrassment.

A jack and an ace in blackjack give you twenty-one.

"Very clever," I laugh, though the tension in my body is still very present.

"Why, thank you." He winks.

I need to get out of here.

"Maybe I'll see you around, Jack." With a swift turn on my heel, I plan to make my escape when his smooth voice makes me pause.

"I hope you will, Ace."

Digging my teeth into my lower lip, I press forward and ignore his parting comment. My hips lazily sway back and forth as I continue on my way, making sure to keep the persona I've chosen for the night by being confident even though I'm freaking out inside. I was supposed to be invisible. It's one of my main rules. Yet tonight, I was the opposite. I just hope it doesn't come back to bite me in the ass.

I refuse to acknowledge how shaky my hands are as I give my chips to the casino clerk. Within thirty seconds, he hands me my cash, and I look over my shoulder in search of Jack, but he's gone. Slipping the money into my clutch, I make my escape.

Rule #1 is fresh in my mind as I scan the parking lot and head to Dottie's where I stashed my backpack.

The sooner I get out of this dress and back to myself, the better.

5

ACE

"**I** thought you said you're not supposed to draw attention when playing blackjack, Little Miss Red Dress," Gigi notes before shoving a bite of pancake into her mouth as soon as I step inside Dottie's.

Rolling my eyes, I walk into the break room, grab my ratty backpack from an unassigned locker, then head to the bathroom. Changing into a baggie hoodie that swallows me whole and a pair of jeans, I stand in front of the mirror and take in my appearance. A stranger's gaze meets mine before I bend at the waist and splash water from the faucet against my face in hopes of erasing a woman that looks way too similar to someone I used to know and grew to hate.

My mom.

Peeking into the mirror again, I deem myself regular ol' Ace then pat my face with a paper towel.

The bathroom door squeaks as my feet carry me toward the same corner booth from the night before.

I was hoping Gigi wouldn't see me in the red dress, but it looks like I'm about to get a tongue lashing if her pursed lips are anything to go by.

"Something you wanna say?" she starts. Her arms are crossed, and her back is pressed against the vinyl booth as she waits for my response.

"Well—"

"No, no, no. You're not allowed to come up with excuses. Not when you told me *yesterday*," she drags out the word to emphasize her point, "that I couldn't come 'cause I was too pretty. You. In that dress? Girl, I'm surprised you were able to walk here without getting picked up by a few lonely men looking for a good time."

My cheeks are on fire as a huff of laughter escapes her. "Wait! You *did* get hit on, didn't you?"

With a scrunched up face, I search for a few words that will shut her up. "Look, the red dress is a good persona when I need to bet big and quickly. People think I'm too stupid to actually count cards, and that I'm playing with someone else's money, which means I don't care if I lose it or not. I don't use it often, but desperate times call for desperate measures."

"Desperate measures as in…you haven't been laid lately?" she razzes.

I haven't been laid *ever*, but that's beside the point.

"Shut up." I reach for her plate and finish off her pancakes since Dottie's too busy with other customers to serve her most loyal one.

Brat.

"For real though," G continues. "What do you mean by desperate measures? I thought you were close to saving up enough for the buy-in."

"Shh." My gaze shifts over my shoulder.

Rule #8: Don't discuss private shit in public. It's bound to screw you over.

With a sigh, an apologetic Gigi leans forward and releases a hushed whisper. "Ace, you're being paranoid. Everything is

29

fine. Plus, no one knows or cares what we're talking about. And let's be honest, you haven't seen any advertisements for the tournament yet, anyway. You've only heard rumors."

With the mention of the tournament, my appetite disappears. I put Gigi's fork back on the table and rest my elbows on the solid surface before tangling my fingers in my long hair and groaning in frustration. "I know, but it might be my only shot."

"You're only shot at what, Ace?" Gigi probes.

This is the part she doesn't know. The *why*. The *who*.

Rule #6 is obnoxious as it flashes to the forefront of my mind. Never reveal your true identity and don't get personal.

Not even to your best friend.

My silence is palpable; my lips forming a thin line as the truth begs to slip through.

Gigi cuts me some slack and asks another question. Well, two, if her forefinger and middle finger that are raised in the air are any indication. "One. Why are we dealing with desperate measures all of a sudden? And two. Who hit on you, and was he hot?" Her lips stretch into a grin of epic proportions, and I grab on wholeheartedly.

"One." Mirroring her, I lift my forefinger. "I may have slipped some cash to Eddie last night. He's the homeless guy that hangs out by my apartment. Remember? Anyway, he needs it more than I do, and it's not like I can't scrounge up some more money with a little lipstick and a red dress." She scoffs as I raise my second finger. "And two, a guy named Jack. He stumbled into me while I was cashing out, and we talked for a second. He said I looked familiar, though. I think he might've noticed me in the past."

"When you were counting?"

My teeth dig into my lower lip. "Probably."

"Hmmm…." With a pucker of Gigi's lips, she voices the

same thing that's been running through my mind all night. "Is he going to be a problem?"

With a wicked grin, I reply, "Probably."

6

KINGSTON

A knock on the door breaks my concentration as I attempt to go over the same damn files for the thousandth time today.

"Hey, Boss?"

The patience I try to muster is abysmal. "Yeah?"

With a creak, the door opens a few more inches, and one of my soldiers comes into view. "Your sister just got back."

Grasping my neck, I squeeze the tense muscles in frustration. "Is she getting into trouble?"

"Well, not really, but—"

"Then I don't really care. My father's death is affecting Regina's life as much as it's affecting mine. We all have shit to sort out," —I motion to the stack of papers in front of me— "so I would suggest you let me get back to it."

"Of course, sir."

As he grabs the handle to close the door, I stop him. "Stefan."

"Yeah, Boss?"

"Are you shadowing her like I ordered?"

"Of course."

I nod. "Then give her the time she needs."

"Yes, sir." He hovers near the doorway until I dismiss him with a quick wave of my hand as the phone on my desk rings.

My jaw clenches at another interruption. Hastily, I pick it up. "Yeah?"

"Hey, Kingston. We need to talk," Diece's voice rings through the phone. His brusque tone makes me sit straighter in my cushioned office chair.

"What's going on, D?"

"Burlone is an ass. That's what's going on."

I laugh, dryly. "Burlone Allegretti has always been an ass. Usually, that doesn't constitute a phone call." *Unless it has something to do with our warehouses that Vince squealed about,* I think to myself.

"Well, this time, it does. Burlone has the Feds up his ass and is getting twitchy."

With a clenched jaw, I grit out, "And how is that my problem?"

"Because Burlone decided the best way to get out of being prosecuted for human trafficking is to frame our guys instead. He thinks that our little transition of power"—*i.e., me taking my father's place as head of the Romano Mob*— "is the perfect time to get the Feds sniffing someone else's ass instead of his own."

"Shit." My hand slams against my father's oak desk. The sound echoes throughout his office. *My* office.

"Yeah. *Shit.* What are we gonna do?"

Dropping my head back, I look toward the ceiling before closing my eyes. "What do we know?"

The other end of the call goes quiet for a few brief seconds before D's voice rolls through the speaker. "We know that he's planning on doing an exchange near one of our warehouses outside the city."

"Let me guess…the ones near Harbor Drive?"

"Yeah. The ones Vince talked about," Diece replies.

"Do we know when?"

"No."

My fist clenches around the phone, my nostrils flaring. "And how do we rectify that?"

On a sigh, D continues, "I dunno. Burlone's men are pretty tight-lipped, King. The only thing I can think of is to get eyes inside his casino. Supposedly, that's the only time his men let loose. But I think we both know that's pretty fucking impossible. As soon as any of us step within a mile radius, we're flagged."

"Which is why they aren't tight-lipped when they're on their own property," I finish.

"Exactly."

Tapping my forefinger against my chin, I weigh my options. "Then it looks like we need to find someone who can get close, now don't we?"

7
ACE

My pulse spikes as I enter Sin, a casino that lives up to its name. Strippers in cages are peppered throughout the vicinity, along with big-busted women in lingerie carrying trays. With the low lighting and thumping base, I can tell I'm going to have a migraine before the night is over.

I've only counted at this casino a handful of times. The rules for blackjack aren't as good here, and the male dealers don't keep their hands to themselves, but I need to keep making the rounds, which includes Sin. I've put off coming here for too long. It doesn't matter that Burlone owns the place and makes my stomach churn anytime I see him. I need to find out if the opportunity I've been anticipating is happening or not.

Scanning the walls, I search for an announcement of the tournament I've been prepping for but come up empty. With a sigh, I approach a blackjack table and get ready for a long night of counting while praying I don't run into Burlone while I'm here.

Not yet.

~

THE DECKS HAVE BEEN SHIT ALL NIGHT. I CAN'T GET A SOLID streak of low cards played in order to justify raising my bet. Hell, I've been bleeding chips for the past three hours, and it's been driving me insane.

In order to follow Rule #5: Be a machine, I need to bet the minimum until I see the deck get hot. That's when I bet big. Unfortunately for me, it hasn't happened yet.

Sucking my lips into my mouth in frustration, I watch the dealer shuffle the deck one more time.

"Fancy seeing you here," a vaguely familiar voice calls from my right.

My head swivels in its direction before my jaw almost touches the ground.

Jack.

"Uh...hi?"

"Seems you and I share a similar interest." He gives me a knowing smirk before dropping some cash onto the table for the dealer to exchange for chips.

My back is ramrod straight, as I consider my options.

Rule #3: If something feels fishy, it probably is. Trust your instincts.

He doesn't feel threatening, just...*smart.* And *observant.* Like me.

"Seems we do," I mutter under my breath. Refocusing on the dealer, I watch as he begins flipping cards.

The hands go by in a blur until a series of low cards start popping up. My gaze darts to Jack as he flips a chip between his knuckles like a seasoned pro. Glancing back at the table, I see a few more low cards revealed.

Slowly, my lungs expand to full capacity as I give myself a mental pep talk. *Ace. If you're gonna make up for the chips you've bled tonight, then you need to bet big on this next hand.*

Again, I give Jack the side-eye. He seems pleasant enough. Doesn't give me any vibes that he's an undercover pit boss looking to drag me away. That's a good sign, right? If I'm going to follow Rule #5, then I can't let my emotions get in the way. Be. A. Machine. The statistics work, but only if I play without my emotions. However, if I tip Jack off to me being a card-counter, and he turns out to not be as friendly as he seems, I'll be screwed.

With a gulp, I push the rest of my chips forward.

The dealer quirks his brow but doesn't comment.

"Feeling lucky, Ace?" Jack teases by my side.

I toss a look his way before shrugging innocently. "Go big or go home, right? Plus, it's getting late. I need to get going."

Throwing his head back, he laughs. "I like your thinking." With a casual flick of his wrist, he puts the rest of his chips onto the table.

The dealer ignores our banter as he starts placing the cards around the table. First, he puts a card face down in front of himself, then deals to his left, which is Jack's card. Ironically, a jack of diamonds is shown. My turn. Nine of clubs.

Not bad. Not great. But not bad. It'll calm my nerves when I see the dealer's second card. A ten. In the blink of an eye, I'm running the probability of me coming out ahead, but it doesn't look great.

Next, another ten for Jack. He's in the clear. Now it's my turn. Again. A queen. I can work with a queen. I'm at nineteen, and as long as the dealer doesn't show a face card or a ten, then I should be good. My head bobs up and down on its own accord as the dealer flips over his bottom card to reveal an eight of clubs. With a fishy face, I release the gust of air I'd been holding in my lungs.

"Damn, Ace. If that's not luck, I don't know what is." Jack

winks for good measure as I laugh off his lame joke, relief pulsing through my veins.

"Thanks. I'm just glad the cards were in my favor tonight."

The dealer collects the rest of the deck then pushes a separate stack of chips each for Jack and me. Tossing one back to the dealer as a tip, I collect the rest and stand from my chair before the pit boss catches on to me.

"Calling it a night?" Jack follows my lead, stacking his chips before rising to his feet.

"Yup."

"Want me to walk you out or anything?"

Placing my hands, and subsequently the chips, into the front pocket of my hoodie, I shake my head. "Nah. Boyfriend is waiting for me so…."

"Boyfriend?" With a quirked brow, a knowing Jack smirks down at me.

"Yup. Boyfriend."

"Does *boyfriend* have a name?" he teases.

Of course, it's at this moment that my brain short-circuits, and I can't come up with a masculine name for the life of me.

After a chorus of crickets, my voice squeaks, "Yup. Bye!" I turn on my heel to make my escape from a guy who's becoming way too familiar with me then rush toward the cashier to exchange my chips for bills. Thankfully, only Jack's laughter follows me.

After I collect my cash and intending to head to Dottie's, I freeze when the sound of a voice that's haunted my dreams since I was a little girl floats through the smoky air.

"I'll be here with a thousand witnesses as I play in the tournament. It's foolproof."

My breath catches in my throat, making me feel like I'm choking as I glance over my shoulder.

It's him.

He always did have a big mouth. After all, I learned the importance of Rule #8 from him in the first place.

Rule #8: Don't discuss private shit in public. It's bound to screw you over.

Idiots.

Swallowing thickly, I let Rule #1 and #2 flash like a neon sign in my mind as I pull out my phone and pretend to text someone. Keep your head down and your eyes up. It makes you invisible. But not stupid. And always be aware of your surroundings.

I listen closer while hiding in plain sight.

Again, I peek up to see the man whom I hate more than anyone else in the world. He looks older than I remember, but I guess that makes sense since it's been almost ten years. His hair is thinner and tinted with gray. His once muscular build has turned into a few layers of extra fat that hang over his polished belt buckle. But his hands are the same. Decorated with gold embellishments. Strong. Able to break things with a lazily clenched fist. Like my mom's nose. Or our family picture that once hung on our wall. Or a twelve-year-old's arm.

I squeeze my eyes shut and push the memory away before gaining the courage to open them and assess the rest of his crew.

Standing next to Burlone is a clean-cut guy with a massive 'X' tattooed on his forearm and another man with a diamond tattoo printed below his right eye on his cheekbone. I purse my lips for a split second, committing them both to memory before turning my gaze back to the blank screen on my phone. My thumbs slide across the glass as I listen closely.

"I'm just saying we need to be careful. I think the Romanos know something's up," argues Mr. X as his gaze scans the casino in suspicion. "And I would suggest we take this conversation upstairs, Boss."

Shit. Looks like we found someone with a brain.

"Stop being a pussy, Dex. They can think whatever the hell they want," diamond guy states before pressing the elevator button. "The fact is, they don't know shit. Let's keep it that way."

Burlone sets his big burly hands on their shoulders before shoving them into the lift. "Gentlemen, stop being so dramatic. I've designed this plan to be foolproof. And my plans never fail—"

The doors slide closed, cutting off his confident remark and leaving me with more questions than answers. The only useful bit of information was the mention of the tournament. The one I plan on winning so I can get out of this hellhole while simultaneously hitting Burlone where it hurts.

His pride--and his wallet.

8

ACE

With sweaty palms, I grip the handle of Dottie's door and enter one of the few places I feel comfortable.

"Hey!" I greet Gigi as I slide into my seat.

"Hey, you. What's going on?" She scans me up and down before her eyes land on my face. "You look spooked."

My brows furrow. "Really? Is it that obvious? Apparently, my poker face is shit."

On a laugh, a laid-back Gigi argues, "Naw. I just know you too well. What happened?"

My teeth dig into my lower lip for a few seconds before ignoring Rule #6 and telling her the truth. "I saw him."

"Him?"

"Burlone. The guy who used to beat my mom and me. The one who introduced her to drugs in the first place. Hell, when I look back, I'm pretty sure he was my mom's pimp or something." Gigi's jaw drops as I reveal something so personal. It's not like me, but right now I need someone else's perspective or else I'm going to go crazy.

Swallowing my doubt, I continue, "He owns a casino and

is one of the big players at the tournament I'm wanting to enter. Actually,...he's the *only* big player. Burlone has never lost a tournament before. Sure, he's lost a few hands here and there, but he always comes out on top. *Always.*"

"Then how the hell are you going to beat him?"

My lips tilt up on one side. "Because I learned from the best."

A very confused Gigi leans forward, resting her elbows on the table. "But I thought you just said...."

"Yup. And I know every single one of his tells."

"How the hell did that happen?"

Reaching for Gigi's cup of coffee, I take a quick swig in hopes of it washing away the bitter memories of Burlone and my childhood. Unfortunately, it only adds to them. "After he'd finish with my mom, she'd stay cooped up in her room, and he'd light a cigar. He'd sit at our old kitchen table and shuffle a deck of cards. Over and over again, I'd watch through the crack of my bedroom door, waiting for him to leave while praying he wouldn't see me. But he'd stay for hours, shuffling those damn cards, and I'd watch because I was too terrified to do anything else."

Gigi's face is blank, but I can tell she's absorbing every word. "Why would he stay?"

"I don't know, but I think it's because he liked proving he owned my mom. It was just another way to show her she was helpless. That she couldn't control what he did. Even in her own home."

With a nod, G silently urges me to continue, so I do. "And then, one day, he invited another guy over. Pretty sure this was the first time my mom was pimped out but...." I shrug like it isn't a big deal when in reality, it's one of my most scarring memories as a kid. "After he finished with my mom, they played a hand of poker. Then two, then three. They stayed the night, and I watched from my crack in the door. I couldn't see the cards, only his face. Every muscle twitch. Every pursed lip. Every brush of the cards. Everything."

"But if you couldn't see the cards...."

I laugh dryly before offering, "I didn't *need* to see the cards. Not in the beginning. I needed to learn how to read people. And I did. But you're right. At one point, I needed to learn the basic rules other than figuring out people's tells. Which is when I met Joe."

"Who was Joe?" Gigi probes.

"He was a regular of my mom's. For years, I thought he was her boyfriend. But looking back, I think he just had a soft spot for her and me." My eyes glaze over slightly, taking me back to those times in my trailer.

Shaking my head, I keep explaining, "Anyway...on the nights Burlone didn't come over, Joe *did*. He didn't hit my mom or me. He was actually a pretty good guy. I'd seen him play cards with Burlone, so I began to get braver. It started with me getting a glass of water while Joe was leaving the trailer, then changed to me shuffling a worn deck of cards when he'd step out of my mom's room. He'd smile kindly, tip his head in my direction, then leave. That was it. And then... one day, I got the courage to ask him if he played. *I* knew he played because I'd seen him with Burlone, but he didn't know that. His eyes softened when I caught his attention, and he pulled out a chair. From there, he taught me everything he knew. And between all of it, I figured out how to play. How to keep my emotions in check. And how to read my opponents better than your average Joe." I laugh. "No pun intended."

With my story finished, I lean my back against the cushion. Normally, I'd be annoyed that Dottie hasn't come over to take my order, but tonight, I'm not exactly hungry.

"So what makes you so sure you can beat Burlone?"

"I'm not." I shrug. "But it's the only way I can think of to hurt him the way he hurt me."

"What do you mean? I mean…" she rushes. "I know he hurt you, but why do you have this long vendetta?"

Closing my eyes, I take a few deep breaths before opening them and addressing Gigi's question. "The day my mom disappeared, I found Burlone's old deck of cards on the table. They're the ones I carry in my backpack."

"The gold ones?"

"Yeah. I know he took her. I know he probably killed her. And I know that he has no remorse for tearing my family apart. My mom and I might not have been on great terms, but she did the best she could even if that meant spreading her legs for any guy that contacted Burlone for a ride. And then, Burlone made her vanish into thin air, leaving me a sad, pathetic little twelve-year-old to fend for herself in the foster care system."

Raising my arms, I give her a set of sarcastic jazz hands. "Ta-da."

A dry laugh escapes her before she sobers slightly. "You're pretty screwed up, Ace."

I chuckle. "Thanks for your assessment."

With a grin, she adds, "I'm pretty screwed up, too."

"Two peas in a pod?" I tease her.

"Yeah, Ace. Two peas in a pod."

9
ACE

Charlette. Oh, Charlette. My favorite casino ever. Walking into the classic hotel, I breathe a sigh of relief. After Sin a few nights ago, I couldn't be happier to be on more comfortable turf. Hell, this place is practically my second home. Other than Dottie's, of course.

Tugging at the hem of my black dress, I head for the blackjack tables.

The night passes at a snail's pace when the deck finally starts to get hot. Betting big, I can barely contain the grin that spreads across my face when the dealer places a shit-ton of chips in front of me.

Going for another round, I keep the stack on the table for the next hand. Again, it pays out.

Moments later, a set of strong hands grab my upper arms when a husky voice laced with smoke fills my ears. "Excuse me, miss. I'm going to need you to come with me."

I hold my breath then peek over my shoulder to see the pit boss hovering a few inches away as his fingers dig into my bicep.

Shit. Shit. Shit.

With a thick swallow, I murmur, "Umm…sure."

I reach for my purse and chips, but the pit boss shakes his head. "You can come get them when we're finished." I look toward the dealer to see his eyes shining with pity, and I know I'm in deep trouble.

I've heard these horror stories before. They're rare, but they happen, which is why I've always had my rules in place. My heart is pounding against my ribcage as I force my legs to hold my weight. With a tip of his head, the angry pit boss guides me to the elevators and presses the down button.

Shit.

We're going to the basement. Nothing good happens in basements.

When the doors slide open a few seconds later, the big gorilla loses a bit of his chivalry and shoves me inside. After a stumble, I glare over my shoulder but don't say anything.

Other than the boring elevator music, a heavy silence encompasses the small space as I dig my teeth into my lower lip, chewing the flesh anxiously.

Shit, shit, shit, I repeat in my head over and over again. It's kind of my mantra when I'm in crappy situations, and boy are the warning bells ringing right now.

This is all my fault. I'd completely discarded Rule #2 as soon as I entered the Charlette. I was comfortable. Too comfortable. I should've seen this coming. I know better than this.

I have my damn rules for a reason!

When the door slides open, I find myself being dragged down a long, dark, windowless hallway with closed doors lining each side. The fluorescent lights cast shadows along the blank, gray walls, and I feel like I've just stepped into a horror movie. The likelihood of me getting out of this situation without a few bruises is slim to none, and my mind scrambles for options.

Unfortunately, I doubt any of them will help me.

"Look, you have no legal right to detain me," I argue. "Let me cash out my chips, and I'll leave, okay?"

With his heavy hand on my shoulder, he chuckles behind me. His pudgy fingers dig into my collarbone. "You do know whose casino you're in, right?"

A lump the size of a golf ball lodges in my throat, so I don't respond.

I'm so screwed.

"That's what I thought." He stops me in front of a door on the right before opening it and roughly pushing me inside. Other than a folding chair in the center of the room, it's empty.

I turn around as soon as he releases me, only to be greeted with the back of his hand.

With the force of a wrecking ball, my head swings to the side.

"Fuuuck," I mutter to myself, gingerly touching the side of my face to find the skin already hot and angry.

Shit, that hurt.

Ears ringing, I struggle to find the willpower to focus on my attacker, but I know that if I curl up into a ball like I want to, I'll be screwed.

"Enough!" a gruff voice barks from the doorway. The sound is almost muffled, but I search for its owner anyway. When my gaze connects with the stranger, I nearly swallow my tongue.

"Fuuuuck," I repeat on a breath. The guy looks pissed. Sexy as hell, yes. But *pissed*.

The pit boss must feel the same anger radiating off him because he takes a cautious step away from me before tucking his hands into the front pockets of his charcoal slacks.

"Sir—"

"Out," the stranger growls, cutting him off while striding over the threshold and into the room. The room that feels like it's shrinking with each of his steps. My heart rate spikes.

I feel like I'm made of granite as he comes closer to me. Even if I wanted to, I'd be unable to move a muscle. Not a damn one.

With hurried steps, the asshole who hit me disappears through the door, leaving me alone with...*him*.

I've only seen him once or twice on the upper floor of the casino. But with the power he exudes, it's hard to miss him. No matter how hard he tries to blend in with the crowds, it's impossible. I've never bothered to find out his name, but I'm really wishing I had done my research now that I'm alone in a room with him in the basement of a casino.

I'm so screwed.

My attention is glued to the stranger as he relaxes right before my eyes. His broad shoulders soften. His clenched fists release. But his pinched brows stay in place, making the uneasiness in my lower gut flair in anticipation. I'm positive he can hear my heart pounding in my chest as he assesses me.

Still frozen, I watch him circle me like a shark, and a single thought whispers through my mind. *I'm about to get eaten alive.*

"Do you know who I am?" his low voice rumbles.

I hold my breath, but don't respond.

"Answer me, Acely Mezzerich." With a knowing smirk and a few choice words, he nearly knocks me on my ass.

Shit. Shit. Shit.

"Surprised I know who you are?" he pushes.

Again, I'm silent.

How the hell does he know my real name?

"Do you know why you're here?"

Yup. I keep my lips zipped.

"Answer me, Ace. I won't ask again." His authoritative tone does weird things to me, but I don't have time to assess them now, so I shove them deep down in a little box labeled: Do Not Open.

"Yes," I whisper as I watch him continue to circle me in his expensive loafers. The guy is built like a freaking panther. I can see his muscles bunching beneath the tailored suit he wears like a second skin as he slowly inches closer with every step.

He pauses at my voice. With a quirked brow, he asks, "Yes, you're surprised I know who you are? Or yes, you know why you're here?"

Licking my chapped lips, I hold his gaze. "Both, I guess."

"And do you know how much money you've taken from me and my casino?"

I nearly grimace before schooling my features. If I had my notebook that's not-so-safely tucked away in my backpack by the blackjack table upstairs, I'd be able to tell him *exactly* how much money I've taken from him. Even without it, I think I can still ballpark the number off the top of my head. That is if I wanted to get backhanded. *Again.*

A cocky grin tugs at his mouth. "So you *do* know, I take it. Interesting."

Shit. Shit. Shit.

"Do you know who *I* am?" he continues his probing while slowly closing the circle he's been surrounding me with. The shrinking proximity is giving me heart palpitations, and my hands sweat as they hang by my sides, bunching up the black material of my dress.

When I remain silent, he pushes a little harder with a sharp tongue and an icy stare. "Better start talking, Ace. I'd hate to see that pretty little face get any more bruised than it already is."

Asshole.

Part of me doesn't believe he'd actually hit me, but the other part doesn't want to risk any more damage. Getting hit hurts no matter how many times it happens.

Lifting my chin, I find the courage to answer. "I have an idea."

He laughs dryly. "You have an idea of how much you've stolen from me, or you have an idea of who I am?"

"Both." My lips tilt up on one side, and I find it ironic that any of this situation could possibly be found amusing to me.

"This is starting to feel an awful lot like déjà vu, isn't it?" Again, I catch him reading my mind.

Rule #3: If something feels fishy, it probably is. Trust your instincts. The only problem? My instincts aren't telling me to run in the other direction. The longer I'm in this room, the less threatened I'm beginning to feel, which is weird. And foreign. Thanks to my past, I always feel the need to run.

His forest green eyes flash as soon as the thought enters my mind. Instead of continuing his predatory stalking, he stops in front of me, leaving only a foot of room between us.

Tilting his head to the side, he states, "You're not afraid of me."

My poker face slips, revealing my confusion at his narrowed eyes. How can he tell when I just figured out the same thing myself?

"Excuse me?" I ask.

"Let's play a game."

I feel like I have whiplash from the turn of events, and I'm having a hard time keeping up.

Shaking my head, I utter a single word. "What?"

A husky chuckle reverberates from him before he inches closer while my feet are still glued to the same spot. "Let's play a game, Ace. After all, you're good at games, aren't you." *It's not a question.* "I mean, that *is* what got you here in the first place, isn't it?"

Our gazes are still locked together as I search for a proper response. Part of me wonders what would happen if I refused, but the other part is dying from curiosity.

He must see the moment I decide I'm willing to play because his wicked mouth tugs into a knowing grin. The mysterious man in front of me has piqued my curiosity. He's like a puzzle I'm dying to put together, and his smile is just the tip of the iceberg.

"Perfect," he mutters under his breath before saying more loudly, "You seem as curious about me as I am about you, so let's make it interesting. You can ask me anything, and I promise to answer. The trick is, I'm allowed to lie if I choose to do so."

With a question on the tip of my tongue, my brows pinch together, and he calls me out on it. "What's your question, Ace?"

I don't like how easily he can read me, but I ask it anyway. "What's the point in playing a game where you don't need to tell the truth?"

The sound of his masculine laugh has a weird way of making my heart pick up a notch, and I push away the butterflies that swarm my insides when I realize I might like the sound.

Focus, Ace! I yell at myself.

Inching closer, he answers, "What's the point of poker without a solid bluff? And you didn't let me finish. The object of the game is to see how well you can read me. If you call me out for lying, then I have another chance to tell you the truth. But," —he lifts his finger— "if you accuse me of lying when I'm telling the truth, then you aren't allowed to ask me any more questions. Understand?"

I nod.

"Perfect. We each get to take turns asking each other questions until we both lose, or I decide I'm done playing."

Sensing my agitation, he gently lifts my chin with his forefinger, forcing me to look up at him. "My game. My rules, sweetheart."

My teeth dig into my lower lip as I watch him get distracted by the throbbing bruise on my cheekbone. Clenching his jaw, he softly drags his fingers down my sensitive skin, making my eyelids flutter for a split second. "Does it hurt?"

"Is that your question?" I bite out.

With a smoldering look, he volleys, "I suppose it is."

"Then, no."

His mesmerizing green eyes flare with amusement before shifting back to my swollen cheek. "Lie," he murmurs. "Give me the truth."

"Why would you ask a question when you already know the answer? Of course, it hurts. I just got backhanded by a damn gorilla. What's your name?"

"Kingston."

Searching his face, I mutter, "Truth," calling it like it is.

He nods his approval before taking his turn. "How long have you been counting cards?"

"Professionally?"

"And recreationally," he clarifies.

"Not long."

"Lie."

I grit my teeth. "As soon as I could afford a fake I.D."

"Which is…?"

"Six years. Why did you bring me down here? This isn't exactly normal behavior for a casino." I leave out *even for one run by the mob.*

He drops his hand from my face to his side but doesn't step back. "Maybe this is normal casino behavior for the Charlette."

"Lie." My voice is absolute, brooking no argument.

Kingston grins before adding, "I've been looking for someone to help me with something, and you fit the bill."

"And what bill is that?"

Tapping his tongue against the roof of his mouth, he tsks me. "Uh-uh, sweetheart. My turn. How often do you count at other casinos?"

"Often enough."

"That's not an answer."

"Depends on how badly I need money."

He tilts his head as he inspects me, making me feel like I'm beneath a microscope with the intensity of his gaze. "Half-lie. You like counting. You might play more often when you need a little extra cash, but there's more to it than that. You like taking the power from the casinos who swindle innocent gamblers on a daily basis. Am I right?"

"Not your turn, sweetheart," I mimic his condescending tone from moments before.

With a laugh, he lifts his hand to silently offer me the floor. "My apologies."

I circle back to my question from a second ago. "What makes me a good candidate for whatever you need?"

Scrutinizing me, he answers, "You're a pretty little advantage player. Did you know that?"

What the hell? First, he used the term advantage player, which refers to a person who uses legal methods to gain an advantage while gambling, such as counting cards, but it can also be attributed to poker. No one knows I play poker. No one.

And second, he called me pretty. The word does weird things to my insides, making them turn to Jell-O in the blink of an eye. Subtly, I shake my head once in an attempt to focus and zero in on his face. His mouth. His eyes. His chiseled jaw. I'm looking for a twitch. An itch. A flicker of something that tells me he's lying.

"That's a non-answer," I accuse.

He furrows his brows. "Excuse me?"

"It isn't exactly a lie, but it isn't really the answer to my question. You're not playing by the rules, Kingston."

Throwing his head back, he laughs. Hard. Apparently, Kingston must find me pretty amusing because, for a guy so cold, he does that a lot around me. "I like playing this game with you. Fine. I need someone to be a set of eyes and ears for me. Someone who can go where I can't. Someone who can fly under the radar." He motions to me with his hand. "You fit the bill. Why do you like sticking it to the casinos so much?"

An image of my mom flashes before my eyes. "I won't answer that. Pick another question."

"Fine," he relents. "How often do you visit Sin?"

"Not enough, yet far too often."

With a heavy silence hanging in the air, he inspects me. "Truth. And I know it's not my turn, but would you mind expanding on that since I was a gentleman and chose another question?"

A smile tugs at the corner of my lips before my face pulses in pain, reminding me that I'm definitely not here by choice. "Sin's rules are pretty shitty, but their dealers are sloppy, and their pit boss is pretty oblivious."

"And what about Burlone?" he presses.

"Excuse me?" The name alone is enough to make my palms sweat.

"Well, with your history…."

My tone is defensive when I ask, "What do you mean *my history?*"

"Lie. You know what I'm talking about, and I need you to answer the question right now. What do you think about Burlone?"

Running my fingers through my long, dark hair, I tug at

the roots before tucking the strands behind my ears. "It's not your turn."

"Answer the question, Ace."

"But it's not your turn," I repeat.

"Answer the fucking question," he growls with an icy cold stare.

Digging my teeth into my lower lip, I search for a way out of this. Out of this situation. Out of this room. Out of this whole freaking conversation. *Everything.*

"Now!" His tone is sharp, making me jump.

It's just enough to snap me out of my panic attack. I tell him the truth, spewing my disdain like word vomit across the basement floor. "I hate Burlone with every fiber of my being, and I would do anything to see him buried in the ground."

The silence hangs heavy in the room, and I just pray to whoever might be listening that Kingston isn't friendly with Burlone. Because if he is, I might've just dug my own grave by admitting my hatred for the man who ruined my life.

"Truth." The word is nothing but a whisper as it leaves Kingston's mouth before he divulges a piece of honesty I haven't asked for. "Burlone is trying to frame my family for something. All I need you to do is frequent Sin for the next few days and see if you hear anything."

"Hear anything? Like what?" My chin dips to the toe of my shoe as I drag it against the linoleum floor and wait for him to answer.

"I need a time. A day. I know the what and where. I'm looking for the when."

The conversation I overheard a few nights ago buzzes in the back of my mind, tugging at my memory. Looking up at Kingston, I ask, "And what if I already know it?"

He locks down any expression from his face, leaving it

nothing but a clean slate. "And how would you already know it?"

"I was there the other night. I overheard him talking to two men." I close my eyes and try to remember what they looked like. "One had a small diamond tattoo on the side of his face. He had long, greasy hair that he slicked back, and his teeth were stained yellow. The other one was cleaner cut with a giant X tattooed on his forearm. I might even call the guy good-looking if I didn't know who he was acquainted with." Opening my eyes, I find Kingston's attention glued to me. I clear my throat and continue describing Burlone's guy. "He seemed smarter than the others. He kept looking around the room, practically begging them to shut up until they got somewhere private."

"What were they talking about?" Kingston probes.

"Burlone mentioned something about a tournament and having a solid alibi. It sounded like something was going down that night, and he'd be safe from the repercussions of whatever it was because he'd be at the casino with a ton of witnesses."

Kingston's expression remains indifferent, though I know I've just given him whatever he's looking for.

"Am I free to go?"

With a shake of his head, my feet remain glued to their spot on the concrete floor.

"Did they see you listening?"

I shrug before looking around the room and searching my memory. "I don't know. I don't think so."

His expression is blank as he reaches into his pocket and pulls out a business card. "I need you to memorize this number then throw it away. If you hear anything else, call me."

I take the piece of paper and attempt to focus on the jumbled numbers.

"That's it?" I ask, feeling confused. I'm missing something, but I can't quite put my finger on what it is. Something about the way he asked *did they see you listening*, irks me. What if they *did* see me listening? Am I in trouble? Should I even be here? It's obvious I stepped into something that I shouldn't have, but am I going to be okay?

"Ace." My head snaps up at the sound of his thick voice. "I'll be in touch."

He goes to take a step toward the door, but I interrupt his departure, feeling the unfamiliar need to keep him close.

"Wait!" I call out, shocking the hell out of both of us.

He glances over his shoulder. "Yeah?"

"What did I step into?"

Scrubbing his hand over his face, he releases a heavy sigh that tells me more than any words he could possibly say right now. "Something an innocent girl like you should know nothing about."

"That's not an answer." I fight the panic that threatens to spill over.

With a forced smile, he murmurs, "My game. My rules."

I drop my eyes back to my feet as I hear his footsteps echo in the tiny box of a room as he retreats.

After a few minutes of silence, I'm convinced that he really did leave me down here by myself, and I must be free to go. The hallway is just as empty as it was before, and I can't help but wonder what's on the other side of the doors lining the walls. Is Kingston in there? Is he watching me? The thought brings a shot of anticipation with it, though I refuse to address why.

Exiting the elevator onto the casino floor, I feel like I'm in a daze. My ears are buzzing, my vision is foggy, and my breathing feels out of sync.

What the hell just happened?

I came in here to play a few hands of blackjack and walk

away with a few more dollars than I came with, but instead, I'm leaving with my world turned upside down.

Mechanically, I turn toward the blackjack tables. I need to grab my things and cash out my chips. When I see the gorilla of a pit boss hovering in the vicinity, I resist the urge to run in the other direction. Instead, I force one foot in front of the other until I see him holding my stuff.

"Miss. I believe these belong to you."

Looking contrite, the pit boss gives me my worn back-pack along with a fat stack of chips. His hands are jittery as he pulls away before taking a large step backward, giving me a wide berth.

With furrowed brows, I add up the total of my chips. My eyes nearly pop out of their sockets when I find the total. There's got to be almost ten thousand dollars worth of chips right here.

Is this a trick?

"Umm...I think—"

"Miss," he interrupts with a quick look to the camera hidden on the ceiling then rocks back and forth on his feet like a recently disciplined toddler. "I'd like to apologize for any inconvenience I may have caused. I-if you need anything, p-please let me know."

What the hell?

I glance over my shoulder and look up at the ceiling camera the pit boss had been fascinated with from only a moment ago before shaking off the feeling of being watched.

Turning back to the asshole who hit me earlier, I notice he's acting like a skittish little squirrel instead of the brooding giant gorilla from an hour ago. Hell, I'm pretty sure if I took a step toward him, he'd flinch.

"Don't worry about it," I mumble under my breath. I don't have time for this. I need to get out of here. Giving him my back, I rush toward the information desk and cash out my chips. Once I'm handed the money, I tuck the bills into my backpack then race to the door like a bat out of hell. I've almost escaped the smoky haze, and I'm seconds from breathing fresh air when a hand comes out of nowhere and grabs my forearm. The foreign touch scares the shit out of me, making me simultaneously jump and squeal at once.

Rule #2: Always be aware of your surroundings.

Dammit, I'm screwing up left and right tonight.

Instead of paying attention, I was in la-la land analyzing the last hour of my life, how the hell I just got handed almost ten thousand dollars, and if it's a test of some sort that I'm miserably failing.

My heart is pounding frantically as my fingers dig into the straps of my backpack, hanging on for dear life as my head snaps in the direction of the culprit.

"What the fu—" I take a step back in shock. "Jack?"

"Yeah, are you okay? What the hell happened to your face?" He lifts his other hand that isn't touching my forearm and brushes his long fingers against my swollen cheek.

Though it's futile, I untuck my hair behind my ear in an attempt to hide the damage. "It's nothing. What are you doing here?"

With his gaze glued to my partially hidden wound, a frustrated Jack clenches his jaw before gritting out, "I think we both know that you and I have a common fascination with numbers and like to visit casinos to cash in on it. Now, what the hell happened to your face? Who touched you?"

"No one touched me," I lie.

He scoffs. "Sure, they didn't. Did you run into a door?" His voice is dripping with sarcasm as he looks closer and adds, "And was the door wearing a ring?"

My lips form a narrow line, but I don't bother arguing.

With a sigh, he slumps forward and looks me straight in the eye. "Listen, despite what you think, I feel a sense of camaraderie with you, and I just want to know if you're okay. Can I help with anything? How'd you get caught?" As he peppers me with questions, I make a point to enforce Rule #1, glancing over my shoulder for any mysterious spectators witnessing this conversation.

You don't talk about counting. Especially not in the middle of a damn casino. Rule #8, remember? Don't discuss private shit in public. It's bound to screw you over.

When I see Kingston watching me from the shadows, my breath hitches. He looks pissed. Looking down, I notice Jack is still touching me, and I slowly twist out of his grasp. I can't explain my actions, but I know it's the right decision regardless.

"I'm fine, but I gotta go." I sneak another glance at Kingston, who appears to be made of stone. His eyes are a green inferno, pinning me in place. His muscles hidden beneath his tailored suit are coiled and ready for confrontation. And his fists are clenched at his sides in anger. If I hadn't been analyzing him so closely for the last hour, I probably wouldn't notice how upset he looks in this moment, though it's obvious to me now. Or maybe he wants me to see his disapproval. Regardless, I add, "If I were you, I'd find a different casino to play at for a little while. Bye, Jack."

And with that, I rush toward the parking lot to make my escape.

10

KINGSTON

"**R**eggie," I call to one of my soldiers as he sits with a bag of Cheetos in his lap while watching reality television on a laptop in the security room. The walls are lined with monitors that display different views of the casino along with a few choice rooms in the basement. One of which is the room I just left Ace in. I watch in fascination as Ace tucks a strand of her long, dark hair behind her ear before looking around the empty room. The disbelief painted on her face tells me how surprised she is that I'm letting her go. Rubbing her hands along her bare arms, she takes a few cautious steps to the door before peeking down the hallway to find it empty. Like a little mouse, she scurries to the elevator and presses the up button.

The sound of Reggie munching another Cheeto snaps me out of my reverie, and I turn to him.

"Acely Mezzerich."

"What about her?" he asks, looking at the screens to see her talking with the pit boss who hit her once she's back on the main floor. My hands clench into fists as I remember the swelling along her delicate cheekbone. He'll pay for that. The

Romano family doesn't hit women. We're taught to treat them with respect, and apparently, he needs another reminder. I see him hand her a fat stack of chips, and my mouth lifts in approval. The asshat knows he screwed up and is rectifying it the only way he knows how. If only it were enough to get back into my good graces.

I catch Reggie assessing me curiously and tell him, "I need you to follow her. There's a possibility she's being watched and doesn't even know it. We need to keep her safe until she's served her purpose."

"And after that?"

My throat tightens. "We'll see."

11

DEX

"Why you worried, man? Stop being a pussy," Sei mutters while balancing an unlit cigarette between his lips. Reaching for his lighter, he brings it to his mouth and lights the end.

The warm glow reflects off his face and makes Sei look even more sinister than usual.

"I'm not worried," I argue. "I just want to make sure we have everything in order. With the Feds sniffing around, we can't afford to make any mistakes."

He blows the acrid smoke from his mouth as he gets ready to give me the usual talk. The one where he says I have a stick up my ass, and I need to let loose every once in a while. The one that grinds on my gears. "Naw. I think you're full of shit. How do we even know the Feds are sniffing around anyway? We haven't seen 'em. Ever since Burlone took us under his wing when we were kids, you've always been the one with a stick up your ass."

Aaand there it is.

I don't bother to respond. It's the same shit, different day.

"What? Nothing to say, Dex? Cat got your tongue?" He squeals in laughter like he's a fucking comedian.

Keeping my mouth shut, I lean back in my chair and wait for our boss to finally show up. We've been sitting in Burlone's office for almost an hour, ready for him to give us our orders for the night. But he better hurry up because I'm ten seconds away from strangling Sei.

Again...same shit, different day.

"So, you gonna take the new shipment in for a test drive before we hand it over? I mean, Burlone says we're gonna have to lie low for a while after. This might be your last chance to finally lose your virginity." He smirks widely, showcasing his stained teeth.

It's these types of conversations that make me feel like the star in *Groundhog Day*, living the same shitty existence over and over again. By some miracle, I ignore him, choosing to stare at the back wall instead, but he keeps pushing. "Dude. For real, though. How come you never have any fun? We're fucking untouchable, man." I watch as he raises his arms from his sides to emphasize his point.

"We're not untouchable. If we were, we wouldn't be using the Romanos as a scapegoat."

"Aw, come on. We're not using them as a scapegoat. We're just putting them in their place. That's all."

I release a sigh of frustration, feeling like I want to pound my head against a brick wall in lieu of continuing this conversation. Both options will do about the same amount of good.

Thankfully, Burlone storms into his office, saving me from further explanation.

"Sei. I need you to pick up two more apples by the end of the week. I don't care what they look like, just get them to the drop off point by Thursday."

Apples are a code name for any common girl off the

street. Grapes mean someone younger; watermelons mean a woman with curves. Passion fruit means that they need to be attractive. You'd be surprised how rarely Burlone orders passion fruit. He's more of a quantity versus quality kind of guy.

"Why do we need more apples? I thought we already had some for delivery?" I don't know why I ask. It isn't any of my business. I don't deal with the women, but curiosity gets the best of me.

With a wicked grin, he answers, "One was overripe, and the other's already been purchased and transported."

Overripe means he's already tasted the goods and either kept her for himself or killed her already.

The thought makes my stomach roll. For a guy who raised me since I was ten, I don't have a whole lot of respect for him.

Leaning against his desk, he addresses me. "Dex, I need you to go for a collection run."

A collection run. *That* I can do. "Okay."

"Did you get the plates registered for the Romanos?" he continues.

"Yeah. It'll be on the truck for the delivery."

Burlone turns to Sei who's busy lighting another cigarette. "Sei, did you contact the buyer?"

"The one who fucked us over on payment last time? Yeah. He'll be there. He was a giddy little school girl when I told him we'd still do business." Feeling pleased with himself, Sei puts his hands behind his head and props his feet on Burlone's desk.

Seconds later, Burlone slaps his hands against them. "Get your fucking boots off my desk, Sei."

"Yes, sir."

"Good," Burlone grumbles before addressing me. "Dex, did you find a good little soldier willing to drive the truck?" I try to ignore his condescending tone. After all, the guy is taking a bullet for us. Even if we *are* paying out the ass to keep him quiet.

Clearing my throat, I sit a little straighter in my seat and reply, "Yeah. Marty is drowning in debt. If we pay it off and give his wife and kid a little cash every month, then he'll tell the Feds he was working for the Romanos."

With his beady little eyes shining at me, Burlone grins. "Perfect."

"When are you going to announce the tournament?" I ask, crossing each mental note off as we discuss it.

"Already did while you sons of bitches were sitting in my office."

"So we're good?" Sei coughs, the smoke from his cigarette going down the wrong pipe.

"Yeah." Unbuttoning his suit jacket, a satisfied Burlone takes a seat behind his desk and starts flipping through various shipment documents scattered along the top of it. "We're good. Now, get out of here. I need to get some work done."

12

KINGSTON

"**H**ey, asshole!" my sister shouts, storming into my office.

Slowly, I look up from my computer screen. When I confirm it's Regina, I pinch the bridge of my nose and squeeze my eyes shut. I don't have time for this.

"Hey, Regina."

"Don't *hey, Regina* me, Kingston. What the hell is up with Stefan following me?"

With a sigh, I motion to the chair across from me. Angrily, she stomps the rest of the way into the room then plops down into the seat and folds her arms.

Does she not understand how important her safety is? She's the princess of the fucking Romano family. She needs protection, yet she's acting like an ungrateful toddler, and I want to shake her for it.

Digging deep, I pray for patience. "Look. Just because Dad died doesn't mean there aren't men looking for you. I understand you want to get out of the house because you're hurting, and you think you've hidden long enough that no one will be able to recognize you as the princess of the

67

Romano family, but I'm not okay with you disappearing on your own. Having Stefan follow you was the best compromise I could come up with." My voice is soft yet commanding. The sound reminds me of my father, and I see her eyes darken in front of me, confirming that I'm right.

"Screw you, Kingston. Just because you took over Dad's role here,"—she waves her hand around the room that showcases her point—"doesn't mean you get to pretend you're my father. I can go wherever the hell I want, so back off!"

With gritted teeth, my gaze narrows. "Careful, Regina. I've had a shit day, and I'm not in the mood for you to challenge me right now. You want to leave this place and do whatever the hell you want? Fine. But only under my conditions. One. You go with a guard. Two. You keep your legs crossed. And three. You come home when I tell you to. If you can't meet those conditions, then I lock you in your fucking room until I find you a suitable spouse that benefits the family. Do you understand?"

She flattens her lips to keep them from quivering before hastily wiping at the tears threatening to spill beneath her eyes. I've pissed her off, and a hum of guilt quickly follows.

"Did you really just go there?" she whispers.

"Dammit, Regina!" I slam my hands against the desk. The sound makes her flinch.

With a sigh of frustration, I squeeze the back of my neck and take a second to breathe. How can I be expected to lead this family when my own sister looks at me with so much misery and disdain? "You're right. I know how much it pisses you off when I talk about you like a pawn instead of a person. It was a hit below the belt, and that's on me. I'm sorry, okay?" Grudgingly, she gives me a jerky nod, accepting my apology before I continue. "Listen, I know how much you miss him even though he was a shit father sometimes. I miss him too, but that won't bring him back. You don't remember when Mom passed, but I do. And it sucked. Just like this. We'll get through this. But I need you to promise me that you won't try to ditch Stefan every time you try to sneak out. If you want to leave, fine. But leave from the front door and take someone with you. I'm really close to pissing off the Allegretti family, and I don't want you to become collateral because of it. Understand?"

"What do you mean, you're really close to pissing off the Allegretti family?"

I frown. "You know I can't tell you that, Regina. It's—"

"Business. Right." She pouts.

"Don't be like that—"

"Like what, Kingston?" she argues. "For a guy who claims to respect women, you sure know how to put them in their place."

"Regina—"

"No," she cuts me off with an icy glare and a wave of her hand. "I'm going out. Bye."

Knowing it'll piss her off but left with no choice, I yell to her retreating form, "Don't forget to take Stefan!"

"Asshole," she shouts back. Seconds later, the front door slams, and I pull out my phone to text Stefan.

Me: Regina just left. Follow her.

13

ACE

After my surreal encounter at the Charlette, I almost head to Dottie's before remembering my busted up face. There's no way I can get by without an inquisition from Gigi and Dottie herself, so I choose to go home early tonight, instead.

My backpack is thrown over one shoulder as my feet scrape against the gravel, taking me to my humble little apartment. When I see my dingy building, a wave of relief rolls through me.

Sliding between a cut in the chain-link fence, I enter the parking lot and keep my head down but my eyes up.

Eddie, one of the sweetest old men you've ever met, is curled up into a ball near a set of trash cans, and I decide to go say hi.

"Hey, Eddie," I greet him. Checking my pockets, I find a crumpled-up ten-dollar bill and hand it to him.

His toothless grin makes my heart ache. "Thanks, Ace. You know you don't have ta do that."

With a shake of my head, I argue, "Yes, I do. You keep my place safe, remember?"

A light blush peeks through his weathered skin at my compliment, but it isn't a lie. In a roundabout way, he *does* keep an eye on my apartment in case anything fishy goes on while I'm away. I couldn't be more grateful for an extra set of eyes.

"Don't mention it, Ace. You know I'm happy ta help." Tilting his head to the side, he covers his mouth in shock when he looks up at me. "What happened ta your face?"

I lift my hand to touch the sensitive bruise. "Ran into a door." The lame joke slips past my lips, followed by a dry laugh and the memory of Jack's concern. "I'm okay. Promise."

"Ya sure?"

"Positive. Goodnight, Eddie. I'll talk to you later, okay?"

"'Night, sweet girl. I'll keep an eye on the place. Won't let no more monsters get to ya, I swear!"

With a soft smile, I reach down and grab his frail fingers with my own before squeezing them softly. "I know you won't, Eddie. See ya!"

THE REST OF MY NIGHT IS SPENT IN MY RUNDOWN LITTLE ONE-bedroom apartment near the railroad tracks. After I stuff a granola bar into my mouth, I jump into the shower and let the hot water run over my skin. Memories of my first meeting with Kingston run through my mind as fresh questions surface. Am I in trouble? Did I make a deal with the devil by helping him? Who is Kingston, anyway? The power emanating from him was potent––with a side of danger with a capital D. But I didn't feel threatened. He was right when he voiced the fact that I wasn't really scared of him. I just can't figure out *why*.

Rinsing the shampoo from my hair, I let my unexplained questions swirl down the drain with the shampoo suds, coming to the conclusion that I won't receive the answers I'm looking for by spending any more time in the shower, no matter how much I dissect my night.

After drying myself off, I put on my sleep shorts and a tank top then slide under my covers. The comforting hum of the steam engines nearly lulls me to sleep when I hear a muffled noise coming from the kitchen.

What was that?

My eyes snap open, but I don't move a muscle.

Did I imagine that?

I lie in wait, my ears straining to hear anything other than the damn trains that I found so comforting from only a minute ago. Now, they're potentially covering up sounds of an intruder in my house.

Shit. Someone might be in my house.

Breathing out a stilted breath as slowly as I possibly can, I roll to my side and face the door leading to the hallway. It's empty.

See? You're probably imagining things.

But I still need to check out the family room to be sure.

At a snail's pace, I sit up in my bed and gently press my feet to the cool hardwood floors before standing to my full height. Shakily, I breathe in through my nose before releasing the air out through my mouth, attempting to hear anything out of the ordinary. I'm greeted with an eerie silence that puts my senses on high alert. Again, my rules scream at me. Rule #3: If something feels fishy, it probably is. Trust your instincts. And right now, my instincts are flashing like a damn strobe light, causing a soft buzz in the back of my mind.

With a slow squat, I reach for the baseball bat tucked under my bed. Keeping my eyes on the open door leading to the hall, I search for the makeshift weapon while trying to keep myself from having a full-blown panic attack. When I feel the comforting wooden handle under my sweaty palms, I breathe a sigh of relief.

It's okay. You're not a defenseless woman living alone in a bad neighborhood. You have a bat and...and that's about it. I'm practically a sitting duck, for shit's sake. But I will not *go out without a fight.*

As quietly as I can, I take a step toward the hallway, trying to convince myself it's all in my head, and nothing is wrong. One step after another, I creep past my door and into the hallway with nothing but a baseball bat for protection. Lifting the thick piece of wood into the air, my eyes slowly adjust to the dark, only to see a shadow sitting on my second-hand couch tucked away in the corner of the family room.

I'm frozen in place from absolute terror as I blink rapidly a few more times to dispel the dark cloud in my living room. Unfortunately, it doesn't work.

"You gonna hit me with that bat?" a vaguely familiar voice rumbles throughout my tiny apartment.

I know that voice.

The sound shocks me to my core, making the item in question slip through my fingers. After a loud thud, the bat rolls a few inches away and leaves me defenseless.

"Apparently, not. No offense, sweetheart, but I think we need to work on your self-defense." I dive for the light switch in the hallway and flip it before snapping my neck toward the culprit. My jaw hits the floor when I see the intruder. With one hand thrown haphazardly across the back of the couch and one foot on his knee, a very pristine Kingston gives me a cocky grin and says, "Fancy seeing you again."

14

ACE

"**W**hat are you doing here?"

His grin widens for a split second before softening to his usual smirk. "I told you I'd be checking on you."

"Well, yeah, but I didn't think it would be tonight. It's been what...six hours?"

With a shrug, he leans forward until his elbows are resting on his knees. "I thought of another question, and it couldn't wait."

"And what's that?"

He licks his lips, catching my attention before he answers. "I was unaware you were dating someone, and I'm curious if he'll be an issue."

I open my mouth, but nothing comes out. Stuttering, I ask, "I-I...uh...I'm sorry?"

"Your boyfriend. Is he going to be an issue?" Kingston's gruff voice speaks slowly like he's talking to an idiot. The condescending tone instantly ruffles my feathers, but I'm still trying to figure out who he's talking about when my conversation with Jack comes to mind.

"Oh," I pause, shaking my head. "That's not my boyfriend."

Pressing his hands to his thighs, he pushes off from the couch and swaggers over to me, his entire body practically oozing sex and confidence and every other attractive trait a guy can have. It's annoying. When he reaches my frozen position, he keeps stepping forward, and I mirror his movements with steps of my own until my back hits the wall behind me.

Caging me in with both hands on each side of my face, he leans forward. "Say it again."

"I think you heard me just fine," I argue. "And I think you're close enough."

With a deliberate shake of his head, he continues, "Answer me again. I want to see if you're telling the truth or not."

"And you need to be an inch away from my face to decide if I'm being honest?"

The right side of his mouth tilts up in amusement. "Something like that."

"He isn't my boyfriend," I repeat, straightening my spine. I won't let him intimidate me even if he's doing a damn good job at trying.

"Then, who was he?" His green gaze is like fire as he voices his question.

"Just an acquaintance."

"Lie," he murmurs. His gaze slides down to my mouth for a split second before returning to my eyes.

I clench my jaw in frustration before flinching in pain, feeling the soreness from Mr. Gorilla earlier today.

"Answer the question. Then I'll give you a little present."

"What kind of present?"

He doesn't budge. "Answer the question, Ace."

With a huff, I purse my lips. "His name is Jack. He's a counter who recently appeared out of nowhere. I'm not sure

I'd call him a friend, but I *do* think he's trying to look out for me. He noticed I went missing earlier today then popped back up with a bruise the size of Texas taking up half my face and was concerned. Is that a good enough answer?"

Again, Kingston assesses me, inspecting me with laser focus before pushing off the wall and sliding his hand into his pants pocket. "Yeah." He pulls an emergency ice pack from his slacks and breaks it with his hands, forcing the chemicals to combine and create a cold compress.

With a gentleness I didn't expect, he presses it against the side of my face. I sigh as soon as it comes into contact with the bruise, resting my cheek against it and simultaneously his hand.

"Better?" he asks, nearly holding my head up as I soak up the cold bliss radiating from the compress.

"Yeah," I whisper with a smile. "Thank you."

Peeking up at him, I hear him mumble, "Don't mention it."

We stand in silence for a few long seconds, and I'm hesitant to admit the comfort I feel with him being so close. He's an impenetrable wall, yet I feel like he's keeping the dangers *out* instead of keeping me caged *in*.

I watch with rapt attention as his Adam's apple bobs up and down in his throat before he steps away and slowly drops his hand from my face, making me hold the cold compress instead.

"I also wanted you to know that you weren't followed, which means Burlone doesn't suspect anything. You're safe."

Relief swells in my gut as I process his words. *I'm safe.* With a nod, I lightly press my teeth into my lower lip, trying to muster the courage to voice my appreciation. "Thank you. Again. First, the compress, and now this." I laugh to break the silence, and he follows along with a low chuckle.

"Don't mention it. *Again*," he adds with a teasing smile.

The silence is almost palpable, and I awkwardly tuck my hair behind my ear before feeling his gaze slide down my body, heating me up from the outside in. It isn't unusual for me to feel someone checking me out. It kind of comes along with the territory when you're a young female card counter and spend your days in grimy casinos. But my reaction to it *is* unusual. It makes me...curious. And with my history, I don't know how to handle it. Within seconds, I find myself squirming from his intensity, chancing a glance at his clear green eyes that are scorching.

When he knows he's been caught staring, Kingston clears his throat and tops it off with another sexy smile. "Get some rest, Ace. We'll talk later. And don't worry about anyone else breaking in. I'll leave someone outside to watch the place." He turns around and grabs his suit jacket that was laid on the arm of my couch as I try to recuperate from his whiplash.

He's leaving? Okay....

"How did you get in?"

Glancing over his shoulder, he responds, "The fire escape."

"But I locked my window?" It's voiced as a question more than a statement. Maybe I'm going crazy?

"Yeah, you did. 'Night, sweetheart." He slides open the window and steps into the darkness, disappearing from my sight in the blink of an eye.

"Goodnight."

15

ACE

I feel like my legs are seconds away from giving out as I step into the lobby of Sin. Chewing my lower lip, I scan the surrounding area for Burlone or either of his men before heading to the bar.

As I make eye contact with the bartender, I yell, "Vodka tonic, please," in order to be heard over the noise from the slot machines. With a lift of his chin, he gets to work, and seconds later, my drink is placed on the counter, accompanied by a friendly wink before he whisks away to help another customer.

Grabbing the fresh drink, I bring the straw to my lips and take a generous sip in hopes of numbing my anxiety. I need to find the date of the tournament. As soon as I find it, I'm out of here. Where would I find the date?

With a wandering gaze, I tap my finger against the icy glass.

"Looking for something?" a voice asks to my right. Swiveling in my chair, my gaze narrows.

"Are you following me, Jack?"

He raises his arms into the air defensively. "What? Of course not!"

"You sure about that?" I push. Raising my brows and pursing my lips, I wait for his response.

On a sigh, he admits, "Alright. I haven't been following you, but you freaked me out the other day, so I have been keeping an eye out for you. Is that fair?"

Watching him closely, I look for any minor facial twitches or avoidance of eye contact but come up empty. "Truth," I mumble to myself, lifting my glass and taking another sip.

"What was that?"

"Nothing."

"Your face is looking better," a sympathetic Jack offers.

I snort, nearly spilling my drink. "Are you insinuating my face has looked worse?"

Balking, he defends himself. "Not what I meant, Ace, and you know it. For real, though, your bruise is almost gone. I'm happy you healed so quickly. Has the *doorknob*,"—he rolls his eyes—"been giving you any more problems?"

Just ten grand in my pocket, I note to myself with a smile.

"I take it that's a *no* with the sly little grin you're sporting." He lifts his hand and brushes it against my lower lip, mirroring my expression with a smile of his own. The unexpected touch shocks me, reminding me of when I was little and stuck my finger in an outlet. Not exactly what I'd call pleasant. Shifting back in my chair, I pull away from his touch and tuck a strand of hair behind my ear as an uncomfortable silence envelops our little section of the bar.

"Sorry," Jack apologizes.

"It's okay. So..." I let the word drag out, attempting to find a solid subject change to save us from the awkwardness.

"So...," Jack mimics. "Do you play anything else? Or are you a blackjack girl through and through?"

Rule #6 and Rule #8 whisper in the back of my conscience before I decide his question is relatively harmless and give him an answer. "I play a bit of poker too. How about you?"

"Naw, blackjack for me. Poker brings in too many variables. But did you see the tournament they just started advertising? A shit ton of big players are flying in from all around the states to get a piece of the action."

No freaking way.

Schooling my features, I lean forward in casual interest. "Really? That sounds interesting. Where will it be held?"

"Here at Sin. I heard the owner is going to participate, too, which is crazy. I didn't even know that was legal."

When you're a mob boss, you'd be surprised what you can get away with.

"Yeah, that's crazy," I agree with a smile. "Do you know when it is?"

Jack remains silent, his brows pinching together in concentration. "I can't remember, but they have a billboard over there announcing it. Come on."

With an excitement I didn't expect, a friendly Jack grabs my hand from the bartop and pulls me with him, leaving my drink forgotten. After we round the corner, weave through copious amounts of slot machines, and take another left near a bunch of shops, I'm greeted with a big ass sign revealing exactly what I've been searching for.

October 15th.

"Do you see how much money the buy-in is?" Jack says, breaking the silence. "Fifty thousand dollars. Can you even imagine having that much cash lying around?"

"Yeah," I hedge. "Crazy. Hey, I gotta go. It was good seeing you, though, and thanks for keeping an eye out for me. We'll talk soon." Spinning around, I make my escape while the numbers on Kingston's business card gleam in my memory.

Seems I have a call to make.

16

ACE

Fun Fact: Pay phones are almost non-existent nowadays. However, Dottie is a gem and hasn't renovated her diner in almost forty years, which means I'm still in luck.

Rushing into my home away from home, I slide my hand into my pocket in search of change before putting the quarters into the phone and dialing Kingston's number.

"Ace! I'm over here!" Gigi calls, waving her hands up in the air.

I lift my forefinger to motion for her to give me a second.

With pinched brows, a confused Gigi slides back into her seat, waiting for me to finish whatever I'm up to. I'm sure she'll interrogate me in a minute, but I'll deal with that later.

The ringing stops echoing through the earpiece, and I wait to see if he's answered. "Yeah?" a voice barks on the other end.

"Um, hey." The diner is practically empty at this time of night, but it doesn't stop me from looking over my shoulder while remembering my rules. I can't believe I'm actually calling him.

There's a soft rustling on the other end of the line before Kingston murmurs, "Ace?"

"Yeah. It's me."

"You okay?" His tone is softer now--or maybe I'm imagining things--but the sound of his voice doesn't stop my heart from racing.

"Yeah," I whisper before twisting my finger around the phone's cord and scanning the empty diner for the thousandth time. "I just wanted to tell you—"

"Shh," he interrupts. "I'll meet you tonight."

Meet? Again?

There's a heady pause as an angel and a demon on my shoulders give their arguments for whether or not this is a good idea. Maybe some distance would be a good thing. When I'm around Kingston, he tugs the control from my grasp whether I want him to or not.

Blowing out a slow breath, I mutter, "I don't think that's--"

"It wasn't a question, Ace."

"Hmph." I look around before tugging on the cord and gritting my teeth. "Fine. Where do you want to meet?"

"At your place. You can leave the bat under your bed though, Babe Ruth." I can hear the smile in his voice, and it brings a grudging one to my own.

With a snort, I murmur, "Whatever. See you then."

After the call is disconnected, I head to the corner booth when Dottie stops me. "Usual order, doll?"

"Yeah. Thanks, Dottie."

"No problem, darlin'. I'll bring it over in a few."

I take a seat across from Gigi and prepare for the inquisition in three...two...one....

"So, who'd ya call?"

My teeth dig into my lower lip in hopes of containing my smile at the predictability of the conversation. "No one.

French toast today, huh? Are they all out of pancake batter? Ya know, with how much shit you give me for ordering the same thing, I've never seen you eat anything that isn't drenched in butter and syrup. Just sayin'."

"Well, maybe I need a little something sweet in my life. Ever think of that?"

Raising my hands in surrender, I nod my thanks to Dottie as she places a hot plate in front of me. "Thanks, Dottie. That was fast."

"I put in the order when ya walked in, doll." With a wink, Dottie moves along to her next task for the evening, leaving Gigi and me alone in our booth.

"Ha! Now *that's* what I call perfect timing," Gigi teases. "So how'd tonight go? You're here earlier than usual. Was it bad?"

My face nearly splits in two from my grin as I remember why my night was cut short.

"I take that as a no," she quips.

"It's a definite no," I reply, feeling giddy. "The tournament is official. They must've announced it in the last few days, but I just saw the billboard tonight."

The realization that my plan is finally coming to fruition is enough to make me dizzy with anticipation. It's so close that I can almost taste it. The revenge I've been plotting for years is in reach. I just need to finish strong and grab onto it with both hands.

As I take a giant bite of eggs and hashbrowns, G starts probing, "So, are you going to make the buy-in? I know you were worried about the deadline..." her voice trails off.

After swallowing my bite, I lean forward and keep my voice low. "Yeah. I'll have enough. I can't believe it's only a week away, though. I thought I'd have more time to mentally prep."

"I thought you've had years to mentally prep to face him again."

"Yeah, but this is different. Initially, I was simply counting to get by. It's the only thing I knew how to do, and it was fun sticking it to the man. But then I saw Burlone and pieced together he owned the place during the last poker tournament a few years ago, so I started saving up." The memory surfaces as if it were yesterday, making my stomach churn with anxiety. I know I'm not the little girl he abused all those years ago, but it doesn't stop the fight or flight response from flaring up every time I think about him. Shaking the feelings off, I continue. "I never felt like I'd actually have a chance to take him down, ya know?"

"Yeah, I get that. Do you think you're ready?"

Now *that's* the question. I don't know what else I could've done to prepare for this tournament. I've practiced. I've watched. I've learned. I've put in enough hours to last me a lifetime. Now, I just need to pray it's enough to make him hurt.

"Ready as I'll ever be." I shrug, taking another bite of eggs.

As Gigi watches me devour my breakfast, I can see the wheels turning in her head before she works up the courage to ask me something. "Do you think he'll recognize you? I mean, you've said you're the mirror image of your mom."

The eggs nearly get stuck in my throat as I contemplate the answer. "I've been dying my hair for years, and my arms are track-mark free. Other than that? I don't know what else I can do to keep it from him."

"To be fair," Gigi offers, "he probably doesn't even remember her. The guy's a slimeball and has been doing shady shit for a long time. I mean, we've all heard rumors of what he does even if no one's able to prove it. I doubt he recalls everyone he's screwed over in the past. And like you've said, you usually hid out in your room when he was there, anyway. Maybe he doesn't remember that your mom had a daughter in the first place."

I stare into the distance as visions of his fist connecting with my face as a kid--and the night my mom wasn't home--scream their rebuttal, but I choose not to voice it.

After a few heavy seconds, I murmur, "Maybe."

The eggs and hashbrowns I'd eaten a few minutes ago roll in my gut, so I push my plate away.

"Do you want me to come to the tournament? To show some support?" Gigi's smile is hesitant, and I think she knows it isn't a great idea, either. We both have our reasons for only ever meeting at Dottie's even if neither of us has voiced them out loud.

"No, it's okay. Meet me here, though. We'll celebrate with a kickass waffle smothered in butter and syrup." I grin, and she returns it with one of her own.

"Deal."

17

ACE

I'm anxious. I don't want to admit it to myself, but it doesn't stop the way I keep tossing and turning in my bed, my heart skipping a beat every time I imagine hearing a sound in the house, only to find it empty.

I can't believe I actually agreed to this. The guy is breaking into my apartment for Pete's sake, and I'm allowing it? Just because he's the sexiest man I've ever seen doesn't mean he should get a free pass for breaking and entering.

Fidgeting with the sheets, I finally sit up and head to the kitchen for a glass of water. There's no way I'm going to be able to sleep tonight when I know I'm going to be woken up by an intruder any minute now. As I open the cabinet and reach for a cup, I nearly jump out of my skin at the sound of the window latch being unlocked.

With barely restrained anticipation––though I refuse to admit it to myself––I turn on my heel to see a very sexy Kingston grinning at me.

"Fancy seeing you here," I murmur while folding my arms and popping out my hip.

He ignores my snarky tone and replies, "Likewise.

Although I think I prefer the other pajamas." I look down at my baggy hoodie with threadbare sweats that nearly swallow me whole.

"And why's that?" I ask with a quirked brow.

His deep laugh reverberates through his chest, softening a bit of my prickly demeanor.

"Skin, Ace. Guys like when you show it off."

A smile cracks on my face before I join in his laughter.

Dammit, he's charming.

An ass. But a charming one.

"Well, maybe I want a guy to like me for my mind instead of my body. Ever think of that one, Sherlock?"

"Is this your way of trying to find out if I'm still attracted to you or not?"

"Are you saying you were attracted to me in the first place?" I counter.

With another deep laugh, he asks, "Are you fishing for a compliment?"

"Are you going to give me one?"

Shaking his head, he stalks closer. "I wouldn't have pegged you for being so feisty."

"I wouldn't have pegged you for being so stubborn."

"Lie." He grins, calling me out.

With my eyes crinkled in the corners from smiling so hard, I admit, "Touché. I definitely pegged you for being stubborn." My voice is light. Airy. The opposite of how it should be when addressing a mob boss. Especially when he just broke into my freaking apartment. But right now, in a pair of low sweats and a t-shirt, he appears to be the furthest thing from it.

"Where's the suit?" I ask, lifting my chin at his attire.

"A suit doesn't exactly blend in, and when I'm trying to be discreet—"

"You go for ghetto. I like it."

"Ghetto?" A mock-offended Kingston clutches at his chest. "I was going for casual. Are you saying I look like a thug?"

Casually, I check him out from head to toe, turning the tables on him and enjoying the power that thrums through my veins. When I'm away from Kingston, I can almost convince myself I'm imagining his good looks, but nope. Here he is, in the flesh, and I definitely can't argue with the fact that Kingston is sexy as hell.

For once, I notice that he looks his age. Only a few years older than me, instead of the man I met who let his experiences age him right before my eyes.

The tension in the room spikes as he scratches the scruff on his chiseled jaw, but it doesn't stop me from blatantly checking him out.

"So that's what it's like," he notes.

The huskiness in his voice distracts me, and I catch myself peeking up into his hypnotic eyes.

"That's what *what's* like?" I ask.

"Being checked out."

I laugh while covering my face as my cheeks heat to epic proportions. "Yup. How'd you like it?"

With a shrug, he offers, "Meh. Not too bad. I don't know what you women are always complaining about."

Again, I just shake my head as another fit of giggles rolls through me.

"You're ridiculous."

"And you're gorgeous. Even with no skin showing," he compliments. I'm positive I'll burn up from embarrassment as I drop my gaze down to my bare feet, speechless. Taking a step closer until we're nearly chest to chest, he changes the subject. "You wanted to tell me something?"

Clearing my throat in hopes of breaking the spell, I look

back up at him and reply, "Uh, yeah. I wanted to let you know that I found out the date of the tournament."

A smirk tugs at the corner of his lips. "Yeah. We already figured that part out."

"How?"

"The casino has been advertising the hell out of the tournament since the night you and I talked. It was even on the news, Ace. How did you *not* know about it as soon as it was announced a few days ago?"

Well, that's not embarrassing.

My cheeks are on fire as I admit, "I don't exactly watch the news."

"I figured."

I open my mouth to respond before closing it again, and he watches with amusement as I stumble along. "S-so why'd you come if you already knew the date of the tournament?" My voice is laced with confusion, and Kingston hears it loud and clear.

"I didn't know that's the information you were going to give me."

"But you suspected it," I counter.

"Yeah." Lifting his hand, Kingston tucks a few dark strands of hair behind my ear, then confirms my suspicion. "I suspected it."

Frozen, I let his calloused fingers brush against the shell of my ear before he drops his arm back down to his side. But he doesn't back away. Nope. That would be way too convenient for me and my muddled feelings.

I've never felt more confused in my entire life, but a question tugs at the back of my mind, and because I'm begging for punishment, I voice it aloud. "Do you always touch your informants like this?" My chest squeezes with curiosity, though I refuse to admit why I'm anxious to hear his response.

With a flash of a smile, his tongue sneaks out between his lips to moisten them before his piercing gaze pins me in place.

"Not usually," he rumbles.

"Then, why me?"

The question hangs in the air, making his silence speak louder than words. I can't believe I just said that out loud. It's not like I'm special or anything. He probably just thinks I'd be an easy lay, and since he's using me for information, I bet that he assumes he could pass the time with a solid screw too, right?

My head screams this is a terrible idea, while the rest of my body is shouting the opposite. I mean, is there anything wrong with a solid screw? I wouldn't know from personal experience, but I've heard good things. Things that have made me wonder if the entire world is smoking something when it comes to the idea of sex, or if my childhood has screwed me up to the point that I'll never understand what it's like to enjoy a solid orgasm unless I'm alone in my bed with an itch that needs to be scratched.

As I stare at the tan skin along the column of his throat, that same insistent curiosity threatens to take over again. What would it be like if someone else scratched that itch for me? Chewing on my lower lip, I can't seem to find my voice, but I don't know what I would say, anyway, so maybe it's for the best. Hell, I can't figure out how my body betrayed me by rubbing up against his as I find us standing so closely together that I can feel his warmth radiating through my thin hoodie. However, at least leaning closer to him is the only thing my traitorous body did when the possibilities running through my mind are endless.

"I should get going." He steps back, taking his heat with him. "Let me know if you hear anything else."

I nod but don't move another muscle as I watch him go. Once the window is securely closed behind him, I whisper, "Okay."

What the hell was that?

18

ACE

"Hi," I squeak. My voice is high and mousy as I address the hotel concierge, who also happens to be the one handling the tournament registration.

"Hello." His voice is a stark contrast to mine. Low and monotone that would put me to sleep in minutes. "How can I help you?"

Wiping my sweaty palms on my skinny jeans, I clear my throat in hopes of keeping it from cracking. "I'd like to sign up for the tournament, please." I probably look like I'm about to pee my pants as I catch myself shifting from foot to foot in front of him, but I can't stop the need to bounce up and down in excitement that this is actually happening. I'm registering for the tournament. *The* tournament.

With furrowed brows, the concierge gives me a look of disinterest. "Which tournament, exactly?" His tone is dull, bordering on annoyed.

Pulling my shoulders back, I stand to my full height and look him straight in the eye. I'm not going to let some stranger push me around just because he's standing in the way of me fulfilling my dreams. I'm not a little girl anymore. I'm stronger than that.

"The high-stakes poker tournament. I'd like to register," I state clearly.

"I'm sorry, ma'am,"—*he's not sorry*—"I think you're confused. The buy-in is fifty thousand dollars."

"Yes, I understand that." Without meaning to, I catch myself mimicking his tone as if I'm speaking with a toddler. By the way his eyes narrow, I don't think he appreciates it.

"We don't take credit card payments."

In an attempt to keep my patience, I pinch the bridge of my nose then I grit out, "I understand that."

"Then how, exactly, do you plan on paying the registration fee?"

Pulling out a thick envelope that's nearly bursting from my backpack, I put it on the counter and push it a few inches toward him and his polished fingers. "In cash." The sweetest smile I can muster nearly splits my face in two as I secretly pray he chokes on the sugar I'm throwing at him.

With pursed lips, a very disapproving concierge named Phillip reaches for the envelope and takes his time counting the hundred dollar bills. To be fair, it *is* a lot of cash, so I don't blame him for double-checking the amount. My sneaker-clad feet tap against the tile as I push my hands into my back pockets and look around the premises. When my eyes land on a very intrigued Jack, they narrow in suspicion.

What the hell are you doing here, Jack?

"Seems we have everything accounted for." Phillip breaks my little staring contest with my fellow card counter, and my head whips back around. "And what name would you like to play under? Aliases are accepted. However, if you end up winning," he says the word as if it leaves a sour taste in his mouth, pursing his lips before continuing, "then we'll need you to fill out a few forms."

"Can I fill them out right now?"

Again, there are those pursed lips. "Of course."

Turning around, he sorts through a stack of papers before handing me the necessary ones.

"Why, thank you, Phillip."

His mouth goes from puckered to a flat line that vaguely looks like a smile if I squint my eyes and tilt my head to the side.

"Of course," he offers.

I fill out the forms in record time, triple-checking I've written the information that matches my fake ID before handing them back over to Phillip. There's not a chance in hell I'd write my real name on this thing. Gigi might be right about Burlone not remembering my mom, but that doesn't mean I'm stupid enough to put a spotlight on the fact we're related––or that my participation in the tournament is not a complete coincidence.

Taking the completed papers from my sweaty palms, Phillip does a quick scan to confirm my competency at filling out a few forms before giving me his back, clearly dismissing me.

Wow.

I turn around and take a step toward the exit when I'm stopped by a familiar voice.

"Hey, you."

Tossing a look over my shoulder, I nearly roll my eyes. "Hey, stalker."

Jack gasps in faux shock before dramatically clutching his chest. "Ouch. That hurts, Ace."

"Sure it does," I tease. "What are you doing here?"

"Making the rounds, like always." He shrugs. "What are you doing here?"

"Making the rounds, like always."

Scratching his chin, he shakes his head. "You sure about

that? I didn't see you at the tables, but I did see you talking to the concierge."

With a smirk, I quip, "See what I mean? Stalker."

"Whatever. You saw me at the blackjack tables, not hiding in the shadows. It's not my fault you stick out like a sore thumb, and I noticed you were here."

"What's that supposed to mean?"

"Sorry, Ace," Jack apologizes. "But a pretty girl like you was never meant to blend in."

I'm taken aback by his compliment, recognizing that Kingston used the same one to describe me the first night we met. Chewing my lower lip––it's a bad habit––I let the awkward silence swallow us both. Only the constant buzz of slot machines breaks it.

"Anyway…" he changes the subject, sensing my discomfort. "Why were you talking to the concierge?"

"No reason," I bluff.

He doesn't believe me. "You gonna play?"

"Play what?" Batting my lashes up at him, I go for innocence, yet he sees right through me.

"Don't play dumb, Ace. It doesn't suit you."

Breathing a sigh, I push Rule #6 aside. "Yeah. I'm gonna play."

I can't believe I just admitted that out loud. Telling Gigi is one thing, but talking about it with a casual acquaintance makes the truth more real. I just signed up to play in a tournament against Burlone. I just put fifty *thousand* dollars of hard-earned cash on the table in order to compete against the man who stars in my nightmares. *What the hell am I doing?*

"And you know what you're doing?" Jack's expression is filled with concern as he waits for my reply while making me want to laugh at the fact that he just read my mind.

Sobering, I reply, "Yeah. I know what I'm doing."

Or at least I sure as hell hope so.

With a nod, he offers, "If you ever need anything, just let me know, okay?"

Lifting my thumb, I chew on the fingernail and glance around the room before I give Jack my attention again. "Yeah. Thanks. I should probably get going though...."

"Yeah, of course. I'll see you around, Ace."

"See ya, stalker," I razz, causing him to laugh at my attempt to lighten the mood.

Shaking his head, he turns back toward the blackjack tables for another round while I head to the parking lot with the intention of going home.

I've had enough casinos for one night.

19

KINGSTON

My phone rings, pulling me out of the chaotic jumble of export documents sitting on the top of my desk.

With my focus on a mass of numbers, I answer it. "Yeah?"

"Hey, Boss. You got a sec?" It's Diece.

"Not really. What is it?" My tone is sharp. To the point. I've got shit to do.

"Lou just gave me an updated registration list for the tournament." Lou is a fucking computer guru. If I need something that can be found on the internet, he finds it.

Tugging on the tie around my neck that feels like a noose more than an accessory, I ask, "And?"

"As far as I can see, there aren't any traffickers other than Burlone who are planning on participating, which means he's only trying to cover his own ass with this stunt and not anyone else's."

"Good," I grunt. "So there's no one of interest who's registered so far?"

With a subtle clearing of his throat, an uncomfortable Diece continues, "A few rich boys from the South, a bigshot entrepreneur from the East, a professional poker player who thinks he stands a chance against Burlone from the West, and…." His voice trails off, piquing my curiosity.

"And?" I sit back in my chair, giving the conversation at hand my full attention.

"And your little spy. Is there a reason she registered an hour ago?"

With flared nostrils, I try to maintain a semblance of control. "Can you repeat that, D?" My white knuckles squeeze the phone in my hand, threatening to break it.

"Yeah. Acely Mezzerich registered for the poker tournament an hour ago at Sin. She used an alias, Macey Johnson. But the fake name wouldn't hold up for more than five minutes for anyone who was looking. She must've bought the fake ID from an inexperienced junkie, though I doubt she could afford a good one. Anyway, I had Lou pull up the security tapes, and sure enough, it's your girl. By your reaction, I assume you didn't know she was planning on participating?"

A low growl rumbles in my chest as I grit out, "No. Seems my little wild card and I need to have a chat."

With a click, I disconnect the call.

20

ACE

With a pep in my step, I round the corner and duck under the chain-link fence before tossing a few twenties at Eddie.

"Yer in a good mood today." His voice is slurred, making me pause.

"Eddie, did you have something to drink?" With a tilted head, I assess him. He's nothing more than a crumpled mess on the pavement. His jaw is slack, and his eyes are glassy.

Shit.

"Just a bit, Ace. Just a bit."

"Where'd you get it from, Eddie?" Squatting down, I gently press on his shoulder in hopes of encouraging him to lay down. Thankfully, he obliges, resting his head against an old backpack with his personal stuff tucked inside of it.

Eddie gives me a grin, showcasing his stained teeth. "The liquor store, Ace. The man at the counter said they were overstocked, so he gave me a discount. Ain't that so great of him?"

I see three giant bottles of alcohol nestled between his things as if they're his most prized possessions, and the sight makes me want to cry. I'm always careful to give him just enough cash to buy him a burger here or there, but not enough to give him the opportunity to save it for a rainy day because I always knew how he'd prefer to spend it. Looking down at the bottles of alcohol, it confirms my theory.

Stupid discounts. Stupid addictions. Stupid vices.

"Ya look sad, Ace. Here, have a drink. It'll turn that frown upside down in no time." Raising his arm, he offers a nearly empty bottle, and I take it before setting it back onto the asphalt.

"Oh, Eddie." The defeat weighs heavily on my shoulders as I grab his threadbare blanket and toss it over him. "Get some rest, okay?"

"Okay, Ace. Night, Ace. That really is a weird name, Ace."

A strangled chuckle slips past my defenses as I watch him drift off to sleep.

Wiping a tear from beneath my eye, I release a sigh then search his things for any more alcohol. When I find two bottles of bourbon and one of whiskey, I confiscate them with a heavy heart.

My body feels like I've gained an extra fifty pounds as I carry the bottles up to my apartment. *Dammit, Eddie! Why do you have to ruin your life like this?* My grip tightens around the bottles, my feet pounding up the stairs until I reach my floor. After I enter my tiny apartment, I head straight for the sink and pour the liquor down the drain. The potent stench of alcohol burns my nostrils as I watch it disappear.

When I'm done, it takes me a second to notice the cold, disconnected presence behind me.

"Finished?" a harsh voice barks, making me flinch.

Spinning around, my mouth open in shock, I clutch the empty bottle to my chest when I find a scrutinizing Kingston staring daggers at me.

"Shit, Kingston. You scared the crap out of me!"

"Didn't take you for an alcoholic." He turns his glare to the bottle in my hand before bringing it back to my puzzled expression.

"I'm not. If I were, do you think I'd be pouring it down the drain?"

"Maybe you found a moment of strength," he offers, pushing himself up from the worn couch in the corner and stalking closer.

"I have many weaknesses, but alcohol isn't one of them," I reply bitterly.

"Truth," he acknowledges with a lift of his chin before clenching it in frustration and crowding me against the wall. "In a way, I was hoping you were inebriated tonight. That was the only possible explanation I could come up with to explain *why* you did what you did."

I pull back, my spine straightening. "Excuse me? Did *what* exactly?"

I'm not in the mood for this right now. Not after I found Eddie wasted when I was so sure he was getting better. I don't think I can handle a lecture, and I *really* don't think I can handle having a mob boss mad at me, either.

His eyes heat with fire, showing me he's beyond pissed right now. In the blink of an eye, he puts one hand on each side of my face, caging me in before slamming his palm against the wall behind me. "I gave you one fucking rule, Ace. *One rule.*"

"What are you talking about?" I whisper, losing a bit of my earlier frustration and replacing it with defeat. Apparently, I failed again, though I don't even know how.

As I peek up at Kingston, a tremble races down my spine because the beast in front of me is terrifying. He's nothing short of a nightmare. But the part that really freaks me out is that I don't want to wake up from this particular dream. If I focus on Kingston, I'm able to put my own issues on the back burner and forget about all of my problems. Seeing him like this makes me want to understand and soothe the monster in front of me who's clawing to get out, though the fact that I'm *not* scared out of my mind makes me question my own sanity. It's obvious he's pissed, and that rage is completely centered on me and my mistake.

"I told you to stay under the radar. I told you to keep your head down. And what do you do?" he growls. "You sign up for the fucking tournament." His anger is palpable. I can touch it. Taste it. Feel it seeping into my pores.

My lower lip trembles. "You don't understand—"

"You're wrong," he spits, cutting me off. "You're the one who doesn't understand, Ace. You don't know what he does to random women on the street, let alone someone who pisses him off. He kidnaps. He rapes. He beats. He maims. He twists them up like a dirty dishrag, squeezing whatever the fuck he wants from them before tossing them aside, usually to another asshole who buys them from him and does the exact same thing. And that's *if* you cooperate. If you don't? He shoots heroin into your veins to make you more compliant, but only after he's beaten you within an inch of your life."

A breath catches in my lungs, making me feel like I can't breathe. Like he's sucked all the air from the room, keeping it hostage until he sees fit to gift me with some.

"Is that what you want, Ace?" He leans forward until I can feel his cool, minty breath on my cheeks. "Do you want that kind of future? Do you want to be on his fucking radar? Because, if you participate in that tournament, you will be." His jaw tightens until I'm sure he'll crack a molar as he grits his teeth. "I think you already are."

Panic blossoms in my chest, taking over any rational thought. "What do you mean I'm already on his radar?"

"You think he doesn't check the roster for the tournament

whenever someone signs up? That he doesn't do background checks on every motherfucker who shows interest? You screwed up, Ace. You screwed up big time."

"I'm being careful," I start.

He scoffs. "Not careful enough."

"What's that supposed to mean?"

"What the hell do you think it's supposed to mean?" His brows pinch in frustration, trying to understand why I would put myself in this position. With staggered breathing, he tries to get ahold of himself.

Squeezing my eyes shut, I admit, "I wanted to have a chance to make him hurt." My voice is nothing but a whisper, nearly getting lost in the heavy silence that follows it.

"And how exactly were you planning on doing that?"

In a daze, my fingers toy with the hem of his shirt, rolling the starched fabric back and forth between the tips of my fingers until I realize what I'm doing. Eyes widening, I look down to see my hands playing with the material. The action catches his attention. With flared nostrils, a mesmerized Kingston watches my fidgeting hands before bringing his gaze back to mine, shocking us both by allowing my inappropriate touch.

"Tell me, Ace." His tone surprises me. If I didn't know any better, I might even consider it to be gentle. But that can't be right. This is Kingston Romano. He's never looked more the part of a badass mob boss than he does right now. There's a fire in his eyes and a crisp suit covering his muscular frame. The combination screams power, making me feel like an insignificant little blip on his radar.

"Tell me," he repeats, reminding me of his request.

Breathing deep, I push forward. "If you know my history like you say you do, then you know he took my mom. That he likely did all those things you just explicitly mentioned *to her*. And that he left me alone and without a mom for my teenage years, only to be raised by a bunch of assholes in the foster care system who only cared about their monthly paycheck." I swallow, dropping my gaze to his mouth because I'm a coward and don't have the courage to hold his stare as I finish. "The only way I could figure out how to exact an ounce of revenge on that sonofabitch was to wound his pride before I stole some of his pocket change and disappeared into thin air. *That* was my plan."

Kingston's arms drop to his sides, releasing me from my prison. But he doesn't step back, and his menacing presence is still enough to cage me against the wall behind me. "You're brave, Ace, but it won't work. You don't know who you're dealing with. Burlone has never lost a game of poker. Sure, a hand here and there, but that's it. He always comes back."

If only he knew that I've done my research. That I know every tiny detail about the guy. I'm not stupid, and I've taken every precaution I can to succeed.

"No offense, Kingston, but I know exactly who I'm dealing with. He's never played against me."

"Truth," Kingston admits. "But that doesn't change the fact that you just put a big ass target on your back. And that's the last thing you want with a guy like him. The alias you gave the concierge was shit. My guy was able to see through it in about five minutes. He created something a little more solid for Macey Johnson's background, but you need to be careful."

The thinly-veiled concern in his voice makes me pause. No one cares about me. Sure, there are Dottie and Gigi, but even they don't know the details of what I've been through, and why my walls were built in the first place.

Raising my chin, I ask, "Why do you care?"

The silence is palpable as his penetrating eyes bounce around every inch of my face. I can feel him searching for something; I just don't know what it is. Honestly, I don't know if he knows what he's searching for, either, but I don't cower under his scrutiny. I stand to my full height until there's less than an inch of space between the two of us, leaving only enough room for my fingers to continue their fidgeting.

After a moment, he murmurs, "You're able to get through Sin's doors without anyone suspecting a thing."

Bullshit. He could find plenty of people who could walk into Sin without anyone batting an eye.

Licking my lips, I push, "So that's it?"

"Yeah." Again, his tone is laced with indifference as his minty breath brushes against my cheeks. And for some reason, the response grates on my nerves. I go to release the fabric from my fingers that I'd been playing with when he grabs my wrist to keep me from letting his shirt go.

"Let me go," I grit out.

Ignoring my plea, he asks, "Do you trust me?"

With furrowed brows, I ask myself the same thing. *Do I trust him?* I barely know him. But that doesn't stop the way I feel when I'm around him. When I think about him. Hell, as soon as I feel his presence in my tiny apartment, an overwhelming need to press his buttons, to peel back every layer that makes up the man in front of me, and to dissect every single word that comes out of his mouth consumes me.

"No," I admit quietly. "But I think I want to."

Silence.

That's all I get in reply as he doesn't move a muscle. Not a twitch. Not a flinch. Nothing. Until seconds later, the word, "Truth," slips from his mouth before his lips connect with mine.

My entire body is frozen, my mind trying to catch up to what the hell is happening. And then it hits me. His mouth-- *Kingston's* mouth--is on mine. And for the first time in my life, I don't feel indifference toward physical touch. I feel heat. And passion. And lust.

I feel *everything*.

From the top of my head to the tips of my toes, I feel it all. And I don't want it to stop.

As soon as the realization hits, my body jolts into action as he guides me through the kiss. My eyes slide closed, and I part my lips on a sigh. *I'm kissing Kingston Romano.* A satisfied Kingston takes the lead by dipping his tongue into my mouth like I'm a decadent dessert before slipping back out and repeating the motion all over again.

I never would've guessed Kingston would taste this good. I never would've guessed *anyone* would taste this good. But he does. And I want more. Parting my mouth farther, I decide it's my turn for a taste and mimic his movements. With a slide of my tongue, I come to the obvious conclusion that I like kissing Kingston, and I should definitely do it more often. How the hell we got from him yelling at me, to me defending myself, and back to him asking if I trust him or not before finally landing on a toe-curling kiss, I'll never know. But I like it——a lot.

With a groan, he crowds me against the wall before I feel his hands slowly press into my lower back. The heat from his palms nearly brands me through my hoodie before he lifts the hem and brushes his calloused fingertips across the sliver of skin from my jeans to my top. The unfamiliar touch nearly brings me to my knees, creating goosebumps that pebble my skin.

With a triumphant smile, Kingston pulls away and peppers kisses along my jaw and neck. "You like that, Ace?" he murmurs against my skin. "You like when I touch you?"

"Yes," I moan, not caring how desperate I sound. Twisting my fingers into his shirt, I tug him closer until my front is plastered to his, then wrap my arms around his lower back. I feel like I've run a marathon with the way my heart is racing, but I don't care.

He chuckles then dives in for another heated kiss, our tongues dueling for dominance. Pulling away, he looks down at me with a cocky grin that's been stripped of his usual armor. "Truth."

"Shut up and kiss me." I tug him closer before wrapping one of my legs around his and tilting my hips toward him. I'm desperate. I know I am. But I've never felt like this before. Not when I'm around anyone else. It's not a *want*. The feeling pulsing through me is so much stronger than that. I need some relief, and I need him to give it to me.

Thankfully, Kingston complies without argument, shoving me back against the wall before grabbing my ass and picking me up. With an open mouth, I nearly scream with relief as soon as he grinds into me. His fingers bruise my thighs as he holds me in place, taking me to a height I've never known. The realization that my clothes are still on, yet he's still zeroed in on the perfect spot is enough evidence to prove he knows what he's doing.

How he's that talented, I'll never know, but I sure as hell won't question it, either.

"I'm close," I whisper, my tone laced with disbelief.

"Let go, Ace." Diving in for another kiss, I pull his tongue into my mouth, sucking on it for dear life as I finally fall over the edge with a few more thrusts.

My mouth is opened wide, desperate for oxygen when Kingston stops grinding and slowly puts me back on solid ground. Resting his forehead against mine, he stares into my eyes. The intimacy in his gaze is enough to keep me on cloud nine for a few more seconds before reality brings me crashing down.

"You a virgin, Ace?" Kingston asks, watching every tiny movement to see my reaction.

With my face on fire, my mouth opens then closes like a fish out of water, but I don't know how to respond.

"Answer the question."

Squeezing my eyes closed, I pray to all that is holy that I'll disappear into the wall behind me, but it doesn't work.

Rule #6: Don't get personal feels like a freaking joke right now. This is as personal as it gets, and I know that Kingston won't let me out of answering his question no matter how hard I try.

"Do you want me to be?" I return.

A low growl reverberates through his chest, and the sound hits me in all the right places. Mainly my lower gut. "Hell, yes."

Truth.

21

ACE

Kingston left a few minutes after my little *moment*--as I like to call it--when he received a call on his cell from someone named D. I didn't hear the details, but it didn't really matter. With a soft kiss against my forehead and a muttered, "Talk soon," he was out the window, and all I was left with was the memory of my first big O. With another person, anyway.

I slept like the dead in my lonely twin-sized bed, only to wake up with a giant grin on my face before doing some quick grocery shopping, then searching the internet for a Macey Johnson.

When I see a fake Facebook profile pop up, along with a fake family, fake friends, and a few fake status updates, I catch myself nodding in approval. *Not too shabby, Kingston. Not too shabby at all.*

Closing my laptop in satisfaction, I peek through my window that Kingston escaped through. The sun is starting to set in the sky, and my stomach rumbles.

Dottie's, here I come.

~

"You look chipper," Gigi quips while sipping her coffee. Her piercing green eyes are narrowed as she assesses me before pushing a plate of fresh eggs toward me. "Here. Mama Gigi ordered your eggs. You're welcome."

With a grin, I reach for the plate and dig in. "Thanks," I say through a mouthful of food. "And what kind of a word is *chipper* anyway?"

She waves me off. "I grew up in a weird family. We use words like chipper and darlin' and sip Old Fashioneds on the weekend. So, sue me."

With a grin, I ask, "Now, Gigi, it almost sounds like you're describing a rich family who vacations in the Hamptons. What are you not telling me?"

"Trust me, you couldn't be further off," she corrects me before rolling her eyes. "But we do say, 'chipper.' So what's with the smile and the pep in your step?"

"Pep in my step?"

"Yes. There is a definite pep in your step."

"And, how does one step with pep?" I razz.

"Oh, shut up and spill it."

Rule #6 makes an appearance before I shove it away, pretending I'm a normal girl who's allowed to have normal gossip with one of her normal best friends.

Smiling softly at the memory of Kingston from earlier, Gigi interrupts before I have a chance to utter a single word.

"You met someone, didn't you?" With an accusatory tone, a curious Gigi plants her elbows on the table and leans forward in rapt attention as I consider her comment. *Have I met someone?* It feels so weird to have someone say those words to me. Meet someone? Me? Not possible. I don't meet people. I don't have flings. I don't do what I did last night.

Ever. But then memories of Kingston and me resurface, and my grin nearly splits my face in two.

"Maybe…."

"Don't maybe me…you met someone!" she practically screeches, "Oo…give me the details. Who is he? How did you meet? And has he given you the big O yet?" Suggestively, she bounces her brows up and down while my face lights on fire.

"Gigi! Will you shut up?" My voice is high-pitched and squeaky enough to make my face even redder as it cracks on the last word.

With a laugh, a satisfied Gigi shakes her head. "Nope. No deal. Girl code, Ace. It's a rule. And we all know how great you are with those. Now, spill."

I scrunch my face before I finally give in.

"Yes,"—I look around the empty diner—"I did kind of meet someone."

"Kind of?"

"Well," I hedge, "it's a weird situation. But I think I like him."

"You think?" She grins, challenging me.

Throwing my hands into the air, I huff out, "Oh, will you shut up? I don't know how I feel, okay? It's complicated."

"How is it complicated?" As if she doesn't have a care in the world, she takes another sip of coffee while she waits for me to explain.

Shifting in my seat, I try to do just that.

"He's…," I pause, trying to find the best way to make her understand. "He's not someone I would normally date. We aren't exactly in the same social circle, and I don't really think he's what most people would consider boyfriend material." I grimace as soon as the 'B' word rolls off my tongue. Plus, using the word *date* to describe what we're doing feels wrong too. He's using me for information then snuck into my apartment a few times before kissing me. If that's not the definition of unconventional, I don't know what is.

"Boyfriend, eh? Sounds like it could be serious if you're considering a relationship."

"I don't know what I'm considering anymore. Boys, in general, have never been part of the plan. But—"

"Shiiiiit," Gigi interrupts me, fidgeting with her cup, her shoulders slumping until she's almost a lump in the corner of the booth.

"Wait, what is it?" I ask in confusion, looking around the diner.

"Look, I gotta go. But I'll see you later, okay? How 'bout we meet here after the tournament? What do you think?"

Rule #3: If something feels fishy, it probably is. And my warning bells are clanging like crazy right now.

Grabbing her wrist, I stop her from running. "What's going on, G?"

She's always kept her life hidden from me, and I've always respected her privacy, but right now feels different. Like I need to step in. Like I need to know why she looks so freaked out even though I know she won't let me get close enough to find out.

"Nothing. Promise. Everything is fine, but I really gotta go. See you tomorrow! And good luck!"

With a twist of her wrist, a panicked Gigi disappears out the back of the diner in the blink of an eye as I mumble a single word under my breath.

"Lie."

22

ACE

My hands are shaky as I dial Kingston's number. Part of me wonders if the anticipation I feel whenever he's involved will ever go away, and the other part of me hopes it doesn't.

"Yeah?" his gruff voice greets.

I let the silence hang on my end for a second, wondering if his tone will soften like it did the last time we spoke on the phone when he found out I was on the other end.

"Hey." My tone is far breathier than I'd been hoping for, but I can't change it.

"Hey, Ace." A soft smile graces my lips as I hear my name roll off his tongue.

Releasing a sigh, I get to the point of why I called. And no, it wasn't in a desperate attempt to see if he's still thinking about what happened last night the same way I am. Or maybe it is, but I refuse to admit the unsettling truth to myself.

"I have a weird question."

His throaty laugh echoes through the speakers, making me smile even wider.

"Yes, I did jack off to you in the shower. No need to be shy."

"Kingston!" I squeal, my cheeks heating to epic proportions. "That's not what I was going to ask!"

"Hey, don't feel bad for being curious. You were great, by the way. In my head, it was crazy hot."

"Kingston!" My eyes nearly pop out of my head as I look around the diner. I want to kick myself for giving into temptation and calling him under the guise that I need a favor from him when, in reality, I just miss the guy. Sure, I'm anxious about Gigi, and when I'm anxious, I use counting to clear my head, but I shouldn't try to fool myself that my reason for calling him is completely innocent. I wanted to hear his voice. His laugh.

Gah! Gigi was right. I like the guy. This is ridiculous.

With a laugh, an unapologetic Kingston continues, "Alright, alright. What can I do for you, Wild Card?"

Wild card?

"Um…" *I can't believe I'm actually asking this right now.* "I was just wondering if I could possibly swing by the Charlette for a game of blackjack?" Grimacing, I rush on, "I know that sounds terrible, but I'm feeling anxious about some stuff right now, and the best way for me to calm down is to count cards. That probably sounds ridiculous, or like I'm using it as an excuse to see you after what happened, but it really does help—"

"Ace," he interrupts.

I stop to catch my breath from all my rambling. "Yeah?"

"I'll see you in a little bit."

A big, dopey grin spreads across my face. "Okay."

KINGSTON

I've been going through the motions since my dad died a few months ago from liver failure that threw my entire world from its axis. I guess all that alcohol finally did him in. After he passed, I stopped caring about life in general, let alone the family. But as I left a satisfied Ace last night, her pheromones still lingering in the air, I found the potential for a new reason to get up in the morning. And it's scary as hell.

With my knuckles taped, I pummel the punching bag as visions of Burlone filter through my mind. In the basement of my father's estate—*my* estate—there's an in-home gym where I can usually be found when I need to work off a little steam. And after my time at Ace's, I need to work off a little more than that.

Diece and I are dripping in sweat as he holds the bag and yells at me for another cross, jab, hook combination. Finishing the move, my chest inflates for some much-needed oxygen while my knuckles flex and release to ease the tension in them.

"Not bad," D notes. "You seem awfully chipper today."

I quirk my brow but refuse to admit it's because of my

conversation with Ace on the phone an hour or so ago. "Chipper?"

"You get laid?" he continues, ignoring my ribbing.

D doesn't give a shit that I'm the boss. That I could have him in the ground with a snap of my fingers if he ever offended me.

But as I roll my sore shoulders up and down, I shake my head.

"No?" he pushes. "Did Burlone fall into a vat of acid?"

A dry laugh escapes me. "Wrong again, D. You going soft on me? Losing your edge?"

With a narrowed gaze, an intense Diece considers me. "Oh, so you want me to play hardball?" He squares his shoulders and stands to his full height, stepping around the heavy bag hanging from the ceiling. The guy is built like a fucking grizzly, but it doesn't stop me from lifting my taped knuckles to goad him.

"You *are* in a good mood." Mirroring my position, he brings his fists from his sides up near his chin. "We haven't sparred in months. You've been too much of a pussy to take me on."

I snort before sending a half-assed jab his way. The big bear doesn't bother dodging as I connect with his forearm.

With a laugh, he continues, "No wonder she wouldn't sleep with you. With a punch like that? My grandma could take you down."

I join in his laughter as D throws a cross hook. Squatting low, his fists graze nothing but air before I cut upward with my clenched hands, connecting with his stomach. A gush of air escapes Diece, but it doesn't stop him from throwing a punch at my unprotected face and hitting me on my left cheekbone.

"Going soft, my ass," he grumbles under his breath.

Seeing stars, I blink rapidly to center myself while raising my hands up protectively to block another shot. He does a quick cross, jab combination, bruising the shit out of my forearms when I see an opening and uppercut him in the jaw.

"Who said she wouldn't sleep with me?" I throw out as he rubs his chin.

"You already told me you didn't get laid, and it doesn't take a genius to figure out you're interested in Ace. No offense, King, but you're not exactly a hard one to read. Not for me, anyway. What happened after you had your little chat about her entering the tournament?"

A frustrated groan echoes throughout the room as I rub my hand against my swollen face. D's mouth tilts up in amusement before coming back to the conversation at hand. "Cat got your tongue, King? Or maybe it's your little wild card that has you tied in knots."

"Something like that," I mutter. "She's got history with Burlone. Some of it was in the file you dug up for me before I hired her. Some of it was new information. Hell, I'm not even sure she's told me everything yet. Regardless, she has her own reasons for wanting to go after Burlone, just like we do. The only problem is that we have the means to do it. Ace, though? She's up shit creek without a paddle and has no idea."

"So what do you suggest?"

"Did you put eyes on Ace like I asked you to?"

"You mean the text at two in the morning, demanding she's protected or you cut off my balls? That request?"

Laughing, I nod. "Yeah. That one."

"Yeah. I got it done." He walks toward the fridge in the corner of the room and grabs a couple bottles of water before tossing one my way. When I catch it, he continues, "So you found out part of her history and have decided she's worth one of your soldier's time to keep her safe. But you *haven't* explained the chipper attitude."

"You and that word."

He rolls his eyes. "Just answer the fucking question, King."

His stare is pointed, but I don't really know what to say. Why *am* I chipper? Because I got to second base like a kid in middle school and almost came in my jeans from a twenty-minute make-out session? What the hell does he want me to say?

"You care about her," he accuses.

Dropping my head back, I look up at the ceiling. "I don't care about her. I just…."

"Care about her," he repeats. "Then let me lay this all out, King. She put herself in a fucked-up situation by putting herself on Burlone's radar. I need to know where your head will be if she gets caught in the crossfire."

My hackles rise as I give him a glare. "What the hell is that supposed to mean?"

He returns it with one of his own. "I need to know if this mild interest in her is something that's going to be happening for the foreseeable future, or if she's just a fling when we both know you don't have those very often. Let's be honest…when you do get laid, you sure as hell don't wind up grinning for hours afterward. We both know that men like us aren't capable of real relationships, yet it looks to me like you might be toying with the idea. I'm asking if it came down to her or the family, which would you like me to protect?"

Shit. Count on D to call it like it is.

Steeling my gaze, I look him square in the eye. "Family first. Always."

"Good. Because whether you like it or not, shit's about to hit the fan in a few days. I know I'm your right-hand man, and that I'm the only reason this family stays together,"—he smirks— "but I can't be everywhere at once, King. No matter how hard I try. And with the screwed-up situation Ace put herself in, I can't guarantee her safety––along with Regina's *and* our family––when we're already spread thin as it is."

"I know you like to think the fate of this family lies on your shoulders, but it doesn't. We're going to figure this shit out. We're going to take down Burlone. Regina's going to stop throwing a fit and acting like a sullen teenager. And I'm going to get laid." Diece throws his head back laughing, and I give him a few seconds to give me shit before I ask, "Do we have everything lined up for the drop-off?"

With a towel thrown over his shoulder, a serious Diece responds, "Yeah. We should be good to go. Any chance you could convince Regina to stay home that night? It'd be nice to have Stefan there for backup and shit. We could use him."

Nodding, I reach for a towel of my own and wipe the sweat as it drips down my face. "Yeah. I'll talk to her. Any other issues with our men?"

"You mean since Vince wound up dead? Nope. Everyone is perfectly content with the current set up in the family, and I don't see that changing anytime soon."

"Even though we might go to war with the Allegrettis?" I push before flipping the switch on the lights and blanketing the exercise room in darkness.

"Those pussies?" He waves me off as we walk down the hall. "Nah. They're practically chomping at the bit to finally put those overconfident assholes in their place."

"Good. Because their chance is just around the corner."

"And they wouldn't have it any other way."

24

ACE

Anytime I walk into a familiar casino, I always get a weird sense of déjà vu. Sometimes it's euphoric if I left with a fat stack of cash. Sometimes a little bitter if it was a bad night, and I lost. This time, however, that same sense of déjà vu is followed by a dull ache in my cheek from getting smacked around, and a wave of anticipation in my lower gut at the potential of seeing Kingston again.

Walking straight to the blackjack tables, I pull out five hundred bucks to start my night. I always keep my extra money tucked away in my backpack for when I need to cash in a bit more. It makes me look like a gambling addict instead of a strategic counter who's planning on sticking around for the evening.

With puckered lips and a platinum blonde wig, I settle into my persona for the evening––a wannabe grunge rock-star who's looking to score some cash for her drug addiction.

My eyes are rimmed with thick charcoal-colored eyeliner as I watch the cards being dealt.

A few hands later, I'm practically yelling at the poor

beginner to my left, feeling guilty as hell for making her feel bad, but I can't break character.

"Fuck this shit. You're not supposed to hit on a sixteen, Lucinda. Ever heard of basic strategy?"

The poor girl's cheeks are on fire as the dealer hands her another card, resulting in her total number being twenty-three.

She busted.

With a sigh, the girl gets up to leave, and I don't stop her.

I might've been harsh, but I wasn't lying. If she doesn't know basic strategy, she's practically handing the casinos her hard-earned cash, and they don't deserve it.

"Basic strategy, huh?" the dealer quips, grabbing my attention.

Casually, I lean back in my chair, giving him a bit of attitude while still keeping the count in my head.

"Yeah. Basic strategy. You got a problem with that?" Basic strategy isn't illegal. Hell, it's almost common knowledge at the tables, so it's not like I'm divulging any sensitive information.

"Nope."

We stay this way, mainly in silence with the occasional shout of profanities from my mouth when I lose a big hand until the count starts to get hot and I clean up like a seasoned pro.

When the chair squeaks on my left, I look to see the asshole who hit me the last time I was here and lose the triumphant smile I'd been wearing seconds before.

What the hell?

I've never been caught, and now it's twice by the same gorilla? I thought Kingston would've known to call off his dogs, but maybe the idiot doesn't recognize me.

"Ma'am, I'm going to need you to come with me."

Narrowing my gaze, I bite out, "I don't think so."

I'd rather get thrown out the front door than be taken to the basement again by this jerk. With a curse on the tip of my tongue, I scratch the top of my wig and consider pulling it off for a split second before restraining myself. Although, part of me wishes I could reveal my true identity because I'm pretty sure if the pit boss knew it was *me*, he'd be quaking in his boots.

However, when he subtly tilts his head behind him, my gaze follows only to connect with a satisfied looking Kingston standing near the back wall. The heat in his eyes is scorching as he folds his arms over his broad chest and smirks from his partially hidden view near an empty corridor.

Sneaky bastard.

"Are you going to cooperate?" the pit boss pleads.

"Yup."

Swallowing, I stand from my chair and subtly tug on the ripped Rolling Stones crop top I'm wearing in hopes of covering the exposed skin on my stomach and back. I'd been fine with the outfit when I walked into the Charlette, but now that I'm mere inches away from this guy, I wish I hadn't dressed so vulnerably.

With a sullen expression, the pit boss raises his hand to guide me where I need to go. When his palm brushes against the bare skin along my lower back, I flinch away, and I'm surprised when he drops it back to his side.

"This way, ma'am."

Shocked that he didn't take advantage of making me feel uncomfortable, I glance over my shoulder to see his face an ashy gray color.

"Everything okay?"

I don't know why I'm asking. The guy's an ass.

"Of course." His gaze shifts back to the corridor where I know I'll find Kingston. Curiously, I follow his subtle glance to see the guy I can't stop thinking about practically made from stone. His anger is almost palpable from all the way over here.

I nearly stumble from its intensity, but the pit boss urges me forward.

"Go on."

With a grimace, I do as I'm told and scurry toward the same hallway I'd been guided to when I met Kingston for the first time. When I reach Kingston's side, he presses the elevator button then leans forward and whispers something to the pit boss while completely ignoring that I exist. My ears strain to hear what's said. Even though the slot machines are loud, and Kingston is talking quietly, I can still make out his comment.

"Touch her bare flesh again, and you lose a hand. Understand, Charles?"

"Yes, sir," the pit boss, who's apparently named Charles, mumbles. "It won't happen again."

With a cold, hard nod, Kingston turns to me and clearly dismisses Charles with the sight of his back before gently running the tips of his fingers along the hem of my shirt and across my belly button.

"This,"—my stomach quivers under his touch—"is a new look."

"You said you like skin."

"Did I say I liked it when you showed it around others?" he counters, referring to the pit boss from seconds ago.

Pursing my lips, I reply, "I'm going to ignore the caveman comment that deserves a knee to your balls." He smirks as I continue. "Do you like *Punk Rock* Ace?"

Lazily, he scans me up and down before tugging on a blonde strand of hair. "Blonde suits you. It's different, though. I can't decide what I prefer."

Of course, blonde suits me. It's my natural hair color, but

he doesn't need to know that. I open my mouth to give him a snarky reply about his barbaric views on my ensemble when the elevator dings behind us, interrupting our innocent flirting.

He guides me inside with his hand pressed against my lower back. The heat of his palm scorches me as I follow his orders and step inside. We've only been together for a couple of minutes, but I can't help but notice how he hasn't been able to stop touching me since the moment I was escorted into the hallway where he was waiting for me. Whether it was my stomach, my hair, or my back, he's kept me close. And I kind of like it. It makes me feel powerful. Strong. Like maybe one day, I just might be able to own this man the way he owns everyone else around him.

But that's scary thinking for a girl like me. I don't want things. I've never allowed myself to. Yet, as I glance behind me at the man who's stolen all my thoughts, a few dreams start to take hold.

Shaking off the desire that floods through me at something I can't have, I quip, "Then I guess it's a good thing my hair color isn't up to you, now is it?"

The elevator is lined with mirrors on all sides, and it gives me a perfect view of the man who's way too far out of my league. His hair is mussed as if he's run his fingers through it one too many times this evening, but his red tie is perfectly knotted around his neck, and his jaw looks freshly shaved. But I bet it would still be prickly against my fingertips if I dared to turn around and brush them against it. My hands itch to do exactly that, but by some miracle, I keep my arm at my side and my back pressed against his front.

"Careful," he growls, leaning forward until I can feel his breath against the shell of my ear as he stands behind me. "If I decide I want something, I can be very persuasive."

I watch him in the mirror-lined walls of the elevator.

The power that emanates from him is almost enough to bring me to my knees, and my palms grow sweaty at the thought.

"Is that right?" I ask, holding his gaze through the reflection.

"Yeah." With a slide of his hand against my waist, he spins me around then pins me between his groin and the cool wall behind me. "Would you like me to give you a demonstration?"

"For someone who rules with an iron fist, you're quite accommodating to my wishes," I murmur as his lips graze my ear, sucking the lobe into his mouth.

A soft moan escapes me while my eyes roll into the back of my head.

Shit, he's talented. And he didn't even do anything.

"Only with you," he admits quietly. His fingers flex into my bare skin along my hips before releasing it. Stepping back, he continues talking like he didn't just rock my world with the potential of another encounter like the night before. "So, did you get what you came for?"

My brows furrow. *Uh, no?*

"The money?" he clarifies with a tilted smirk.

"Oh." *That.* "Umm, yeah. Although it feels a little weird to admit that to the casino owner."

A deep laugh is pulled from him at my honesty, bringing a light blush to my cheeks. "If you didn't tell the truth, I'd just call you out on it."

My face scrunches up before agreeing with a roll of my eyes, "You're probably right about that."

"I'm always right," he teases. "Were you able to work out your nerves? What had you feeling so anxious that you needed to call me in the first place?"

"No reason."

"Lie. Tell me the truth. If I'm going to let you come in

here and swindle money from my dealers, then you need to tell me why."

"Let me swindle your dealers? My dear friend, I believe I've swindled them in the past without your permission. Just sayin'."

"Truth." He shakes his head. "But you asked to come to my casino earlier today, and I think it had more to do with seeing me than the loose rules I have for my blackjack tables."

He's right. Even though I hate to admit it to myself, let alone him, I can't deny the truth. I wanted to see him. I just can't decide how stupid I am for following through with it.

When the elevator doors slide open, he ushers me into the same hallway from where we first met before crowding me against one of the gray walls.

"Start talking, Ace."

Why his Neanderthal ways are a turn on, I'll never know, but it doesn't stop me from digging my teeth into my lower lip and clenching my hands at my sides to stop them from pulling him closer to me and putting both of us out of our misery.

Rule #6 takes a second to scream that I'm an idiot before I lick my lips and reveal to him the truth. "It's nothing crazy. I just have a friend who was acting weird. We're close, but our relationship isn't exactly conventional."

He quirks his brow in interest, and I laugh. "Not like *that*. I just mean that even though we'd kill for each other, we're pretty quiet about our personal lives. It's hard to explain. She was acting weird today, but she disappeared before I could ask what was going on. It left me feeling helpless, and when I feel helpless—"

"You search for control in any way you can."

"Yup. Which includes—"

"Blackjack," he finishes for me. With the gentlest of touches, Kingston lifts my chin and places a soft, open-mouthed kiss against my lips. Sighing, I close my eyes and soak up his touch. The knowledge that I'm slowly becoming addicted to his mouth is troubling, but I push it aside.

"I'm glad I could give you the control you were craving," he admits.

"You sure about that? I would've pegged you for a guy who doesn't like to give up control to others."

He takes a step closer until the toes of his loafers brush against my beat-up Chucks. "You have no idea. In my profession, giving up control is giving up power, and I think we both know I don't relinquish it without getting something in return."

I laugh. "*That,* I can believe."

"And what do you think I want?"

Biting my lip, I drop my gaze to our shoes and hedge, "I think I can guess."

"I think you can too." His breath fans across the top of my head as I dig up the courage to look back up at him.

"Come on, Kingston. Show me a little of that control you were just boasting about. Patience is a virtue, isn't it? Or would this be more of a self-discipline kind of thing?" I ask while tapping my chin in thought.

"Why, Ace, I don't know if I should be offended or proud that you've questioned my self-discipline."

"And why's that?"

"Because you've willingly stepped into a private elevator with me while knowing I could have my way with you. I'm currently displaying the self-discipline of a saint by not pushing you up against this wall and taking what you so innocently revealed to me last night."

Clearing my throat, I mutter, "I didn't reveal anything."

"Lie. I can practically smell the innocence on you, Ace, and it's a lethal scent."

With a smile, I ask, "Are you saying that if I won't let you have me, you'll die?"

"Possibly," he mutters, bending down and hovering near my lips. "Now tell me, Wild Card, will *Punk Rock Ace* knee me in the balls if I kiss her again?"

"Possibly," I tease, my gaze bouncing between his hypnotic eyes and tantalizing lips. "Are you willing to risk the future generations of the Romano lineage to find out?"

A wicked grin spreads across his face as he inches closer. "Possibly."

Closing the last millimeter of distance between us, he presses his lips against mine then tugs the wig off, dropping it near my feet as my brunette hair pools around my shoulders. Smiling, I return his kiss and wrap my arms around his neck then lace my fingers through the short hair on the back of his head.

With a groan, a sexually frustrated Kingston tugs on my lower lip with his teeth, pulling a light laugh from me in return.

"I like you," I admit on a sigh as he teases me with his mouth. My fingers unlace themselves from his hair before brushing against the jaw I'd been drooling over earlier. When the five o'clock shadow grazes my fingertips, I smile softly in fascination.

Looking down at me, Kingston wraps his thick forearms around my waist and drags me into him. "Then you should show me, Wild Card."

He's called me that before, but I didn't have the guts to ask why. Maybe I'm still drunk from his kiss, but I'm curious enough to voice my question.

"Wild Card?"

"I never know what to expect with you." Lightly, he tugs on my messy curls, mimicking his motion from a few minutes ago. Only this time, it's the real me instead of a wig

I'd been using as a disguise. The girl in front of him is stripped bare. She's the girl I normally keep locked away in an attempt to protect myself. But as he peers down at me, his gaze shining with lust and intrigue, I like that he can see her.

"Truth." Smiling up at him, I reach onto my tiptoes and plant a soft kiss against his lips before murmuring, "So is there a reason you brought me down here?"

He shrugs. "We still can't be seen together, even in my own casino. I think we both know what would happen if Burlone found out we were...."

As his voice trails off, I catch him studying me like an abstract piece of art. The intensity is almost bruising, and my body presses back into the wall behind me to escape it. There are so many ways he could finish that sentence, and I'm dying to know what was on the tip of his tongue before he thought better of voicing his statement aloud. What are we? Working together? Passing the time with each other? Possibly sleeping together? Dating? I have no idea what I want, let alone what the man in front of me is interested in. If only I could read minds as easily as he can read faces.

Clearing my throat, I tuck a stray strand of my hair behind my ear. "I should probably get going. Thanks for letting me feel a bit of control for the night, though. I really appreciate it."

The silence that follows is enough to shine a glaring light on our unconventional...whatever this is, and he takes a step back to give me a little breathing room.

"Anytime, Ace. Anytime."

25

JACK

A s I pace the floor near the lobby entrance, my imagination coming up with the most gruesome of possibilities for what Ace could be going through. I attempt to take a few slow, deep breaths in through my nose and out of my mouth.

Calm down, Jack.

Convinced I look too suspicious, I take a seat at a slot machine with a perfect view of the corridor Ace disappeared through and start wasting quarters.

My foot is thumping against the carpet like a damn jackrabbit, and my gaze is continually shifting from the digital screen in front of me to the dark hallway.

Where is she?

With a glance at my wristwatch, I do the math, only to realize she's been missing for nearly thirty minutes. I saw the pit boss hand her off to the motherfucking head of the Romano family before he took his spot back on the floor like it was just another day at the office. I saw the way Mr. Romano touched her bare skin. The way she trembled under his touch. Bile floods my mouth, and I swallow it back.

I'm two seconds away from blowing everything I've worked so hard for, but I can't. Not even for an innocent girl that seems to be caught in the crosshairs of something she knows nothing about.

In the corner of my eye, I see a flash of black, and I'm gifted with Ace in a blonde wig, ripped jeans, and a black t-shirt that's been torn to reveal her toned stomach. The same stomach I saw him touch.

She walks my way, completely oblivious to my presence until I reach out and grab her forearm.

With a squeal, she rips herself away from my grasp before her eyes widen in surprise.

"Jack?"

"Hey. Are you okay?"

"What the hell? What are you doing here?"

I can't tell her the truth, yet I'm sick of lying too. My mouth forms a thin line.

She senses my hesitation and pushes, "Tell me, Jack. Now."

"Answer me first," I return. "Are you okay? I saw you get escorted again. I saw you talk to Kingston Romano. Did he touch you?"

Please say no. Please say no.

She gasps in shock. "What? What are you talking about? And how the hell do you know Kingston?"

Fuck. Seems they're on a first-name basis. That seems promising.

Seeing it's apparent she isn't half as terrified as she should be for having been alone with the Dark King, I try a different tactic. "Listen, I need to talk to you in private. Can we go somewhere?"

She takes a step backward, her brows pinching in confusion. "I don't think that's a good idea."

"I need to talk to you," I repeat. "Please?"

"No offense, Jack, but I don't exactly know you well enough to go somewhere with you in private." I can tell she's put up her walls. I just don't know how to get her to take them down for me. *I'm not the bad guy.*

Lifting my arm toward the corridor she just returned from, I argue, "But you're good enough to be alone with Kingston? Do you know him at all? What he's capable of?"

I watch as she swallows, chewing on her lower lip as she assesses me. "How do you know Kingston or what he's supposedly capable of?"

My hands dig into my short blonde hair before tugging on the strands in frustration. "It doesn't matter. All that matters is that you need to know who you're dealing with."

Her gaze is wary as it shifts around the casino before coming back to me. "I don't think we should be talking about this out in the open."

"That's why I've been begging you to go somewhere with me," I insist.

Crossing her arms over her chest, she releases a deep sigh. "Listen, Jack. I don't think you're a bad guy, but I *do* think you've stuck your nose where it doesn't belong. If you know Kingston as well as you say you do then you also know that you should probably back off right now. Look, I gotta go." She steps toward the exit, but I reach for her again only to pull her close into my chest.

She's practically a marble statue in my arms as I lean down to whisper in her ear, "Do you do drugs, Ace? Is he your dealer? Is that it? I can help you—"

"You need to shut up right now, Jack." Her voice is low but lethal. "I have a set of rules, and you're breaking every fucking one of them as we speak. If you don't let me walk out that door in the next ten seconds, you're going to regret it."

"Ace, I'm just trying to hel—"

A large hand slams onto my upper shoulder like a slab of meat, interrupting me. "There a problem here?"

I squeeze my eyes in defeat before letting my arms go limp at my sides. *I'm so screwed.* Ace steps back, leaving a solid three feet between us as her attention bounces between me and the guy digging his fingers into my collarbone.

"No problem," I reply as I slowly raise my hands into the air in surrender.

"Hey," Ace seethes while snapping her fingers in the guy's face. "I'm fine. Everything's fine. It's allll fine." She drags out the word while bouncing on the balls of her feet. "See?" Raising her hands into the air, she does a cute little twirl like a ballerina. "It's all good, so you can let Jack go now. I was uh…I was just going now, so…."

With a tilt of her head, she motions toward the exit. "See ya around, Jack." Her gaze is glued to the guy behind me before he lets out a low grunt and releases his hold. Satisfied, she turns on her heel and disappears through the exit, leaving me alone to fend for myself.

Cautiously, I glance over my shoulder to see a guy the size of a bear with a curled upper lip.

Diece. Motherfucking Diece.

"Yeah. See ya around, Jack." Diece's voice is laced with venom as he spits out my name like it's a curse, and I know I've just put myself on the Romano's radar all because I was trying to help a girl who looks like she's knee-deep in an organization I assume she knows nothing about.

I'm so screwed.

26

ACE

"So, are you the one that's been following me today?" My voice sounds rusty. It's probably from the nerves. A few feet ahead of me is the giant who confronted Jack in the casino. The giant whose hands are inked as they swing by his sides. The giant who has a cold stare as he scans the area like it's a natural habit. The guy who, I have no doubt, has killed before. Probably more times than I can count. I cough softly in an attempt to clear my voice as the cool night breeze brushes across my cheeks. I'd rushed out of the Charlette like a bat out of hell only to turn around thirty seconds later to find the giant following behind me while adjusting his suit.

"Naw." The behemoth shrugs. "That'd be Reggie."

Who the hell is Reggie?

"Oh, I thought you looked a little familiar." Looking closer, I take in his eyes, mouth, and nose, but I can't put my finger on where I've seen him before. It's probably just from my time at the Charlette. That's all. "So, where's Reggie?"

"He was on break when the fucker started bothering you, but Kingston refused to wait a second longer before rescuing your ass, and he's not ready to put a bigger target on your back by claiming you in front of so many witnesses, which left me to save the day." His sarcasm is thick as though he can't believe the ridiculousness of the situation he just found himself in––namely babysitting me.

Grimacing, I tuck my thumbs into my back pockets while following my new bodyguard toward Dottie's. However, there's one term there that made my ears perk up like a little bunny.

Claiming me? Is that even possible? He won't even tell *me* what he's feeling. I can't imagine him making a statement like that in front of every eye witness in the casino. Diece is probably just blowing things out of proportion. He seems like someone who might appreciate the occasional dramatic flair, right?

However, curiosity is still getting the better of me, and I can't help but ask, "So, Kingston saw that, huh?"

That same cold stare connects with mine. "Are you asking if he witnessed that asshat touching you?"

My cheeks burn, along with my forearm where he touched me, as I give him a single nod.

"Yeah. He did. You're lucky your little friend is still breathing."

A lump the size of a golf ball gets lodged in my throat, but I suck my lips into my mouth and keep walking on my merry way like he didn't just scare the crap out of me. Like Jack's nickname for Kingston didn't just flash through my mind. Like the fact that I'm kind of, sort of, *maybe* dating a mafia boss isn't a big deal at all.

Nope. Just another day in the life of Acely Mezzerich.

Due to my new bodyguard's massive size, I can barely see around his ripped back as I follow in his steps. His feet slapping against the cold pavement is the only sound that accompanies his not-so-subtle threat.

"He's not my friend," I mutter under my breath, feeling the need to defend myself.

"Sure he isn't," the giant returns before giving me a quick glance over his massive shoulder. "He likes you, ya know."

"Who?"

Jack or Kingston? The guilt swirls in my stomach that I even have to ask that question. If Gigi could see me right now, she'd be laughing her ass off. Two good looking guys who might be interested in me? Especially when I'm only interested in the mob boss who could kill the other guy with a flick of his wrist? I shake my head. *Ridiculous.*

"Both," he grunts, answering my question. His legs eat up the distance with ease while I struggle to keep up with his pace as he adds, "I'm Diece, by the way. You can call me D."

"Ace," I return, speaking to his back. "Nice to meet you, D."

"Wish I could say the same."

With furrowed brows, I mutter, "What's that supposed to mean?"

"It means that I have a feeling you're going to be trouble."

Should I be offended? I mean, who says something like that? I don't even know this guy, yet he's already made up his mind about me?

I march forward.

"How am I going to be trouble? No offense, Diece, but I wasn't the one who approached either of those guys." I point back to the casino where I assume Jack and Kingston are still at. "Jack is a fellow blackjack player, and Kingston asked if I could help him with something. That's it."

Diece huffs out a deep breath but doesn't bother to reply, so I press on as I stomp closer to him.

"Don't you huff at me! It's not like I'm toying with either of them or planned on starting anything in the first place. Jack is barely an acquaintance, and Kingston is--"

My mouth slams shut.

Shit. What is Kingston? I'd kill for an explanation, yet I know I won't get one no matter how hard I try to dissect our situation, let alone confiding in his soldier in hopes that he might know something I don't know. Squeezing my eyes shut, I scrunch up my face and bite out, "You know what? Never mind. Forget I said anything."

My silence seems to be enough to finally grab the jerk's attention. Lazily, he scans me up and down.

After a few seconds, he lifts his chin and says, "I can see why they like you."

Feeling exasperated, I joke, "Then can you tell me? 'Cause I don't get it. And who says they like me anyway?"

With a dry laugh, he stops walking long enough to let me catch up to him. Once I've reached his side, he continues heading to our destination at a slower speed, and I appreciate the opportunity to catch my breath instead of chasing him around.

"People don't talk much in this line of business," he confides. "If they do, they wind up dead. Instead, we use our instincts, and we watch. From what I've seen? You're smart. Cute. Sarcastic. And you scream innocence louder than a damn siren. It's no wonder you have Kingston wrapped around your dainty little finger."

"I don't know about the whole innocence part," I mumble, keeping my head down while completely ignoring the *having Kingston wrapped around my finger part*. Apparently, Diece is delusional.

He scoffs. "What? Because of your past? No offense, sweetheart, but just because you had a shitty upbringing doesn't make you a cynic. In fact, I think that's why you appeal so much to him."

Heart racing at the mention of my upbringing, I whisper, "What do you know about my past?"

"Who do you think wrote up most of your file, sweetheart?" His brow is quirked in a silent challenge, leaving me speechless. He can't know everything. If he did, he would've told Kingston, and Kingston wouldn't have asked if I was a virgin. He would've already known the truth. My hands are shaky as we round the corner, but I can't find the drive to continue a conversation I wish could be wiped from his memory.

Sensing my uneasiness, D stops near the lower steps of Dottie's Diner and slides his palm into his suit pocket before pulling out a cigarette.

"Mind if I wait outside?"

The step almost brings us to the same height as I look over at him. "Nope." I take the stairs two at a time before turning around and adding, "And thanks for not killing Jack."

With a wink, he gives the cigarette pack a tap against the palm of his hand. "The night's still young, sweetheart."

There's something about him. I don't know what it is. Maybe it's his crooked grin. Maybe it's the big burly arms that make me *almost* feel safe. Maybe there's a sense of camaraderie I feel toward him. That he didn't write the gory details of my past for his boss to read with a glass of whiskey in his hand. I don't know, but I come to a conclusion regardless. One that would probably kill him if he knew what I was thinking.

"What are you thinking, sweetheart?" he asks, reading me like a freaking book while placing a cigarette into his mouth and reaching for the lighter.

I shake my head. "You don't wanna know."

With a laugh, he takes another pull from his cigarette before saying, "Well, now I gotta know."

"You really want to know?" I press in disbelief.

Please say no. Please say no.

"Yeah."

Rule #3: If something feels fishy, it probably is. Trust your instincts. And my instincts are humming on low right now. There's no threat. No malice toward me. There might've been a smidge of it when we left the casino, but after our conversation, I think he came to a conclusion about me just like I did about him.

With a grin, I confide, "I think you're nothing but a cuddly little puppy in a Doberman's body."

He throws his head back as a deep laugh tumbles out of him. "Puppy, huh? Well, don't tell Kingston, alright?"

Winking, I quip, "The night's still young. Will you be out here when I get back?"

"No. It's not a very good idea for people to see you hanging around the Romano's second in command. Reggie will keep an eye on you though, okay?"

Disappointment sits in my stomach at the thought of missing another one of these conversations, but I nod anyway. "Okay. It was nice to meet you, D."

"You too, sweetheart," he grunts before releasing a puff of acrid smoke from his mouth. Obviously, I've been dismissed, and if I didn't know any better, I might be offended because of it.

Good thing I can see past his gruff exterior, right?

"HEY, DOTTIE!"

"Hey, doll! Your usual?" Dottie asks while wiping up an empty table littered with plates, used napkins, and half-empty glasses of juice.

"Sure, thanks." I take a seat at Gigi's and my corner booth before glancing out the window to see Diece hidden in the shadows.

A few minutes later, Dottie places my order on the table.

"Thanks, Dottie. Has Gigi been in yet today?" I want to give her crap for disappearing last night, and maybe even beg for a few details about why she left in such a hurry.

Unfortunately, Dottie shakes her head. "Sorry, darlin'. She disappeared out the back a few minutes before you walked in. Said there was an emergency she forgot about. Told me to tell ya she'll see ya tomorrow, though."

Shoulders slumping, I reach for the ketchup and squirt some onto my eggs while trying to hide my disappointment.

"Thanks for letting me know."

"Anytime."

As she leaves me to enjoy my eggs alone, I can't help the questions that arise.

What the hell is going on with you, Gigi?

"You sure?" I murmur into my cell. My stomach twists with anticipation.

"Yeah, yeah, I'm sure. I almost didn't believe it, but I'd recognize her anywhere."

Clearing my throat, I snap my fingers to get Sei's attention as he plays Candy Crush on his phone. Looking up at me, he mouths, "What?" I lift my finger to my lips to motion for him to stay quiet before I wrap up the conversation with an unexpected ally. "Alright, thanks for reaching out. We'll let you know how it goes."

"Good, good. If you find her, let me know. Her bastard of a father ended up pulling out of the deal, but that doesn't mean I wouldn't be willing to pay for her." His desperation is embarrassing. You have to be a special kind of filth to pay for a woman. But it's these kinds of men that keep my pockets lined, so I guess I shouldn't judge them too harshly.

"No offense, Dominic, but I doubt you'd be able to afford the heiress to the Romano family fortune."

"Yeah, but—"

"We'll be in touch." Ending the call, I push my cell into the front pocket of my suit then tilt my head toward Burlone's office. Sei follows without a word.

Tap. Tap. Tap.

I rap my knuckles against Burlone's door, then we wait.

Seconds later, I'm greeted with his muffled voice, yelling, "What?"

"I just got off an interesting phone call," I speak through the closed door.

Straining, I listen for his response but only hear muffled crying, and it definitely isn't coming from Burlone.

After a brief wait, the door swings open to reveal a half-naked girl with mascara running down her cheeks. Sniffling, she slips past us with her top clutched to her chest then disappears down the hall.

I turn to Sei to see him watching as she goes, his eyes shining with interest.

"Get the fuck in here." Burlone's deep voice breaks Sei's trance, and I follow him into the office.

Plopping down onto the corner chair, Sei lifts his chin while a lit cigarette dangles from the side of his mouth. "Hey, Boss."

Burlone's frustration is almost palpable, but I know he'll want to hear this.

"What is it?" he growls. "I was busy."

"Don't ask me." Sei raises his hands defensively before leaning back and setting his boots on the table. "Ask Dex."

With a slow blink, Burlone turns his narrowed expression on me. "And?"

Licking my lips, I reveal the little slice of information I was recently gifted with. "Dominic Castello just called."

"So? Why would he call?"

"Seems he ran into someone a day or two ago."

"Get to the point, Dex. I'm not in the mood for foreplay."

Snorting, Sei covers his mouth before motioning for me

to continue. "Yeah, Dex. We all know how much Burlone likes to get right to the nitty-gritty, am I right?"

Burlone's mouth ticks up in amusement then he turns to me. "Yes. Let's get to the nitty-gritty. What'd Dominic Castello have to say that was so important that you felt the need to interrupt my free time?"

"Says he saw the queen out of her high tower."

Burlone's brows nearly reach his receding hairline as he asks for clarification. "What?"

"Regina Romano was sighted outside of the estate."

"How? No one's seen her since she was a kid." He doesn't look convinced.

"Apparently, before Gabriel Romano died, he was trying to set up an arranged marriage because he knew his health was failing and wanted to have the Romano family as strong as possible before he kicked the bucket."

With a wave of his hand, an annoyed Burlone spits, "We knew this, Dex. Get to the fucking point."

Clearing my throat, I continue, "He approached Dominic to see if he'd be interested in aligning forces––"

"By marrying Regina?" Sei interrupts, curiously. He plants his heavy boots on the floor and leans forward with interest.

"Yeah. But Dominic wouldn't consider it unless he saw a picture to prove she wasn't a five hundred pound elephant," I explain.

"So Gabriel gave it to him? A picture?" Burlone is humming with excitement, the whole room buzzing with the potential this news offers.

With a nod, I say, "Apparently."

"And where did he see her?"

"A mile or so away, near the Charlette."

"Did he describe her to you?" Burlone's tone is ice cold. Calculating. This was the piece of information he was looking for, and I know he's going to weave it into his plan flawlessly.

"No, but he asked for your private email to forward the picture."

"Why not send it to you?" Sei asks while stubbing out the butt of his cigarette in the ashtray sitting on the corner of Burlone's desk.

I shrug, though I know why.

Burlone answers for me. "Because he knows how to respect the boss, Sei. He knows who has the iron fist, and it sure as hell isn't Dex...or you." Turning to me, he continues, "And did you give him my email address?"

My gaze connects with his from across the room, a silent battle that I have no intention of fighting. "Yeah."

"Perfect."

28

KINGSTON

I'm exhausted. With a tug on my tie, I loosen the knot before knocking on Regina's bedroom door.

Stefan said this is where she is, though I'm not surprised when I'm greeted with silence.

"Regina?" I call out.

No answer.

Gritting my teeth, I pray for patience then try again. "Regina, I need to talk to you. Will you please open the damn door?"

A muffled sound echoes through the solid door before it squeaks open. "Yes, oh wise one?" She's in her pajamas with her hair pulled into a messy ponytail, confirming her plans to stay in for the night.

"Hey. I just wanted to check in with you."

"And why is that?"

"Because you're my baby sister, and I care about you."

She scoffs, unable to hide her disdain. "Or is it because Dad left you in charge of me, and you'd feel guilty as hell if you let his regime fall, including the itty bitty piece I play in it?"

I look toward the heavens, wanting to scream at her for acting so damn childish. I'd give anything to relinquish my rights as her protector. Not because I don't love her, but because it's so freaking difficult to keep her safe while staying in her good graces. Once upon a time, we were close. Then Dad started to get sick, and I was forced to step up while Regina was forced to remember her place. Neither of us has had an easy time accepting our roles.

My nostrils flare, but I somehow manage to keep my tone calm. "Don't go there, Regina. Not tonight. I have enough shit on my plate right now, and I really don't think I can add your daddy issues to the agenda, okay?"

"Fine." She spins in a circle with her arms raised at her sides. "As you can see, I'm doing just great, thanks for asking. You should definitely give Stefan a raise. He's been keeping me in tip-top shape. Won't even let me break a nail. Ain't that sweet?" Her sarcasm is potent, but I choose to ignore it.

Swallowing the need to strangle her, I channel my inner Gandhi and press forward. "Well, I'm glad it's been working out then. Thank you for being accommodating with the new rule of him shadowing you." Her brows furrow at my comment, and I have no doubt it's because I actually complimented her on something. Humility isn't exactly my strong suit. Edging closer, I add, "I actually wanted to talk to you about that."

"About him shadowing me?" With folded arms, Regina leans against the doorframe.

"Yeah. There's some shit going down tonight, and I need him with me, which means I need you to stay home."

For a brief second, her eyes dim before heating with fire. "Sorry, King, but I can't do that. I have plans tonight."

"Well, you're going to have to reschedule because I'm already going to be one man short, and I need Stefan. He has a particular skill set that we need."

"What do you mean, you're going to be one man short?" she inquires.

Surprising both of us, I reveal a minor piece of information. "Reggie. He's following someone for me who doesn't have the luxury of staying home tonight like you do, and I can't be in two places at once, which means I need you to stay home."

"What's going on tonight? And don't tell me it's family business, Kingston. For someone that's been cooped up my entire life, I'm not an idiot. If you want me to stay, then you sure as hell better fill me in."

Groaning, I let my head fall back on my shoulders before scrubbing my hands through my hair and tugging on the roots. The bite of pain is enough to clear my head.

Why does she have to be so damn difficult?

"I don't make the rules, Regina. I only enforce them, which includes leaving you in the dark. It is what it is. You want it to change? Get married so you can actually have some influence."

"I'm not going to be a pawn, Kingston. We've had this conversation a thousand times."

"And we're going to keep repeating it until you finally agree to grow up, accept your fate, and get married. You think I wanted this life, Regina? You think this is what I asked for?" I slam my hand against the wall. She flinches. "I can't change my duty, and neither can you. This might not be what you want to hear right now, but it's what Dad wanted, and I'm not going to let him down just because you're too fucking scared to do your duty."

Her eyes well with tears, but she doesn't let them fall, and I have to give her credit. She's one of the strongest people I know. When it comes to emotions, she *has* to be. Being born with a pussy instead of a dick in this world brings an entirely different set of issues, and I'm not naive enough to say it doesn't suck for her. But it's life, and the sooner she accepts it, the sooner she can move forward and live outside of this home that's always felt more like a prison to her.

"Am I talking to my brother right now or the boss of the Romano family?" she whispers, holding my gaze.

"Boss," I grit out.

"Then I guess that's that. Goodnight, Boss." The door slams in my face, and I squeeze my eyes shut in response.

Fuck.

29

ACE

I wake up to the sound of footsteps down the hallway. My hands clutch my chest as memories of my last encounter with Kingston in this apartment flutter to the surface. The only difference is the golden light shining through the curtains that tells me it's morning. For some reason, I'm not afraid like I know I should be. I can sense who it is before I set eyes on my intruder, and the only feeling wreaking havoc on my insides is overwhelming anticipation.

There's a light knock on my bedroom door, and I turn to see a sexy as hell Kingston leaning against the jamb with his arms crossed.

Called it.

"What are you doing here?" I ask. My voice is still rusty from sleep.

"That's not a very warm welcome."

I laugh. "No offense, but I wasn't exactly expecting you. I thought supervillains only came out at night."

With a dry chuckle, he strides into my room and sits on the edge of my mattress. The scent of his woodsy cologne follows him, wafting through the air seconds later, and I sigh in contentment.

Damn, he smells good.

"That's the reaction I was going for," he teases as his hand brushes along my bare forearm and up to my collarbone in a gentle caress. "I came to apologize. I won't be able to attend the tournament, but I wanted to wish you good luck."

I grin. "I kinda figured you wouldn't be able to make it, but for curiosity's sake, let's hear the excuse."

"Other than the fact you'll be in a casino owned by my arch enemy?"

"I knew you were a supervillain," I quip.

With another dark laugh, he snakes his hand around my throat and squeezes softly. That same swell of anticipation takes over, and I arch my back in response. He drops a lazy kiss to my mouth. Greedily, I open my lips and slide my tongue against his as my entire body starts to hum with need. I pout when he pulls away seconds later and whispers in a husky voice, "I *am* the bad guy, Ace. Don't ever forget that."

His heated stare pins me in place as a thought crosses my mind. *Truth.* But he's *my* bad guy. Or at least, I want him to be.

"I didn't just come here to apologize," he reveals. "I want you to be safe tonight."

"I will be. It'll be fine."

He continues as if I haven't even spoken. "There are too many paparazzi covering the tournament for Burlone to try anything in the casino as long as you stay in the public eye. Don't go anywhere that would leave you vulnerable, understand?"

I nod.

"Good. I have a guy who will be waiting for you outside the entrance as soon as you finish."

"Diece?" I ask, getting my hopes up.

"No, Reggie. You won't know he's there because he's very good at what he does, but I promise you, he'll keep you safe in case Burlone tries to mess with you." His nose runs along the column of my throat. "I have business to attend to, so I won't be able to visit until tomorrow. But after that, you're all mine."

"Is that right?" I quip with a teasing smile.

"Damn right it is. If I didn't have shit to do, I'd act on all the indecent fantasies that popped into my head as soon as I saw you lying in bed this morning."

Licking my lips, I ask, "And what fantasies did you imagine?"

"Well—"

The blaring sound of a cell phone ringing echoes from his front pocket, and he groans, dropping his forehead to rest against mine before pulling out the blasted phone and swiping his thumb along the screen.

"Yeah?"

Silence.

"I'll be there in twenty."

Hanging up the phone, he tangles his hands in my hair and gives me another panty-melting kiss. When he pulls away, he says, "Kick some ass tonight, Ace."

"You too."

He quirks his brow. "Why, Ace, I have no idea what you're talking about."

I laugh. "Sure, you don't. I'll talk to you later, King."

"You too."

Then he leaves me with a day full of thumb-twiddling as I wait for the tournament to start where I can finally exact my revenge on someone who deserves so much more than a public humiliation and a few dollars lost. But it's the best I can do, so I'll execute it with my dying breath.

Staring in the mirror at Dottie's Diner, I take a deep breath then lacquer my upper lashes with a bit more mascara. After an hour of debate, I finally decided on a simple black cocktail dress with my warm brown hair curled in loose waves and left hanging around my shoulders. I look like...me. It's a stark contrast to the personas I normally wear, and I still can't decide if it's a good choice or not. Regardless, I need to get moving, or I'll miss the tournament, and my wardrobe won't matter anyway.

After I put the mascara wand in the hot pink tube and twist the cap for good measure, I toss it in the bottomless pit I call a backpack when the worn deck of cards catches my eye. Before I can stop myself, I reach inside and grab the familiar cards. It's one of the only objects I still have from my childhood, and the sight makes me miss my mom more than usual. I run my thumb along the edge then lift the pack up to my nose and breathe deep. There's still a hint of smoke that clings to them, reminding me of my childhood trailer and the memories that accompany it. With shaky hands, I drop the deck back into my bag then swing the strap over my shoulder and head out into the seating area.

I don't have time for a walk down memory lane, especially right now when I'm about to confront the monster who stars in most of my nightmares.

"See ya, Dottie!" I call out, waving my hand in the air as I notice the majority of tables are occupied which is an unusual sight, but I guess it makes sense when I'm usually only here after hours.

"You comin' back tonight?"

"Yeah! I got a date with Gigi!" I wink.

She grins before tucking the pen in her curly, dyed hair and yelling, "Alright, then. See ya, doll! Good luck tonight!"

With a shaky breath, I nod then turn on my heel and make my way to Sin.

THE PLACE IS PACKED. THAT'S THE FIRST THING I NOTICE AS I enter the casino through a cloud of cigarette smoke. Holding my breath, I walk through the haze to the registration table where the same stuck-up concierge hands me my info.

"Head to the main poker table, give them this voucher, then they'll cash you in." He points to his right but doesn't bother giving me any other directions, barely deeming me worthy of a response in the first place. In any other circumstance, I'd probably give him some salty remark, but I'm too distracted by the flashing lights and heady anxiety pulsing through me.

I'm here. This is the moment. What if I lose? What if he recognizes me? What if I break down crying and curl into a ball on the center of the casino floor? With how nauseated I'm feeling, I'm going to say it's a definite possibility. I've done everything in my power to prepare for this moment, but am I ready? I don't think I've ever been so nervous in my entire life. Maybe I should visit the bathroom first and go puke. I mean, better there than all over the poker table, right? And what if I have to sit by him. God, I don't think I could handle—

"Ma'am? I haven't got all day. Take this and go." The concierge waves the voucher in the air, and I grab it with sweaty palms then move to search for my seat when Jack stops me with his hand on my arm.

"Hey."

Gaze narrowed, I bite out, "Jack? What are you doing here?"

"What? I can't show my support?"

My nostrils flare as I shake out of his grasp. "I can't do this with you right now. I need to focus."

"Look, you can focus in a minute. Right now, I need to talk to you about your boyfriend."

"He's not my boyfriend," I object.

"Fine. Call it whatever you want, but messing with Kingston Romano in any form is still a bad idea—"

"Will you shut up?" I hiss, looking around the casino. My pulse spikes when I see multiple sets of eyes watching our argument, including a particularly interested guy that I'm afraid to place, but the tiny diamond tattoo under his left eye is enough to make me shiver. *Shit.*

"Don't talk private shit in public, Jack. It's common sense."

He pushes me to a darkened corner a few feet away. "Is this better?"

"Not really," I counter, folding my arms across my chest.

I don't have time for this.

"Well, then maybe you'll take me up on it the next time I offer to go somewhere private instead of letting one of Kingston's big goons come to the rescue." Jack leans forward, getting in my face as his arms vibrate with frustration.

People are still looking in our direction, making my skin tingle with awareness, but I don't know how to get out of this.

"Look," I spit out quietly. "I didn't know Diece would be stepping in like that. But you should be glad it was him and not Kingston. You might think I'm the one who doesn't know who she's dealing with, but I think it's you, Jack. You need to back off, or you're going to get hurt."

With a scoff, Jack scrubs his hands over his face. "You're probably right about that, Ace. I'm risking my neck for you, and you aren't even grateful. From the shit I've heard about Kingston,"—he shakes his head—"you're gonna end up in a body bag."

I take a second to consider the likelihood of his comment coming to fruition. Is it possible? Would Kingston hurt me? Looking back on every individual interaction we've had, I almost want to laugh at the possibility. No. I don't see that happening. He might put on a facade with everyone else, but I know him. The *real* him. The one who wouldn't hurt a fly if it wasn't warranted. Sure, he can be scary, and I have no doubt he could hurt someone if the situation arose, but I don't think I have anything to be afraid of. I'm sure of it.

"Kingston wouldn't hurt me," I state as Jack studies me carefully.

"Well, if it isn't him, then it'll be one of his enemies, Ace. The guy has a rap sheet a mile long, and don't even get me started on the people he's connected to. You have no idea what you stepped in."

I'm so sick of this. Standing on my toes for an extra inch of height, I get in his face that's red with anger. "And you do?"

"Yeah, Ace. I—"

"The Sin Poker Tournament is about to begin. Remember,

there is no flash photography, and all cellular devices must be turned off. Thank you." The announcement echoes through the open floor plan of the casino, interrupting whatever Jack was going to say.

But it doesn't matter anyway.

"Look, Jack. I gotta go. Thanks for your concern, but I trust Kingston."

Stepping toward the crowd near the poker table, Jack's voice calls out, "Yeah, but are you sure you're trusting the right guy?"

I hesitate for the briefest of seconds before shaking off his comment and focusing on the tournament that I've been preparing for since I was a little girl. I can't worry about my future right now because I'm too busy avenging my past.

Jack and Kingston can wait.

ACE

The place is buzzing. As I look around, all I see are a bunch of little worker bees with their cameras or cell phones or beer bottles, humming around the black felt-top table with their eyes glued to me as I take one of the last available seats. With a sigh of relief, I notice I won't be sitting next to Burlone.

I've never played in a tournament, but I've watched plenty. I know the drill, but it doesn't stop the anxiety from nearly swallowing me whole as I shift in my seat. The man to my left is wearing a fancy brown cowboy hat with a flannel button-up shirt. All he's missing is a piece of straw hanging from his mouth, and he'd be straight out of a Western. I've never seen him play, but I doubt he'll be an issue.

Turning to my right, I study a man named Patrick "The Pat Down" Madden. He's a well-renowned poker champion. He's been on the circuit for years, and I've seen this guy play. He's good, but I've been able to pinpoint a few of his tells first-hand, so while I should be shaking in my proverbial boots, he's not the one who terrifies me. I'll leave that to Burlone.

Patrick must feel me staring at him because he casually turns in his seat and slides his sunglasses down an inch on his nose to get a better look at me.

"You in the right place?"

With a gulp, I shrug one shoulder as my nerves get the better of me. "I sure hope so."

Patrick laughs, offering his hand for me to shake. I take it with a shy smile.

"Me too. I'd hate for a pretty girl like you to be thrown to the sharks. I'm Patrick."

"M-Macey. Nice to meet you."

"So, Macey, what's a girl like you doing in a place like this?"

Again, I give him another casual shrug but let my cheeks heat for good measure. If I'm going to look nervous, I might as well play it up for all the spectators.

"Here to play a game of poker," I admit. "You?"

With a narrowed gaze, an intrigued Patrick takes his time inspecting me. "I haven't seen you around, and I feel like I'd remember you. Like I said, a pretty girl like you is hard to forget. Have you played professionally before?"

"Nope." I make sure to pop the 'P' at the end. "So, go easy on me, okay?"

I'd thought long and hard about what persona I was going to play for the evening, and innocent little poker novice seemed like a good route. Having a vagina means I'm instantly underestimated in everyone's eyes. Instead of trying to prove them wrong, why not embrace it and use it against them?

"Sure thing, Macey. Sure thing. Just watch and learn." With a wink, he turns to the front of the table as the dealer approaches and starts making small talk with him like a good little soldier.

Patrick is charismatic; I'll give him that much.

Unsure what to do with myself, I start to pick at my trimmed fingernails when the cameras start flashing. Looking up, I'm given a glimpse as to why. Burlone Allegretti swaggers up to the table. My stomach tightens, and a hefty dose of regret hits me with the fact that I forgot to run to the bathroom and puke my guts out before taking my seat. He's right there. Within five feet of me. I think I'm going to be sick. Placing my sweaty palms on my lap, I wring them anxiously beneath the table, grateful he can't see me fidgeting. The urge to run is so overwhelming that my feet start to tap against the ground, my knee bouncing a mile a minute until Patrick looks over at me curiously. Giving him another shy smile, I force myself to stop while recounting the plan.

Beat Burlone. Wound his pride. Take his money. You can do this, Ace. You're not the little girl he hurt. You're stronger than him. Smarter. You've been preparing for this moment since your mom disappeared. Now, don't screw it up. After you win? You can disappear without a trace, and he'll never be able to hurt you again.

I swallow as my mind conjures up an image of Kingston before leaving a stone in my stomach. If I beat Burlone...then what?

Do I still disappear? Do I leave Gigi? Dottie? What about Kingston? Would he even care if I left?

The questions assault me from all sides until all I'm left with is a heavy dose of unease until Burlone raises his hands to quiet the humming audience, and a hush falls over the crowd.

"Ladies and gentlemen, I want to thank you all for coming out tonight. It's going to be a great game filled with entertainment and finesse. As you all know, I enjoy dabbling in the art of poker from time to time, and I'm so excited you could join my fellow players and me as we participate in a little wager of wits. Let's get started, shall we?"

My nose wrinkles in distaste before I remember the

importance of Rule #6 in this very moment. Don't get personal. He might act like a big buffoon, but as I watch him scan his opponents, I know he's sharp as a tack, picking apart each of our weaknesses before the game has even begun.

When his assessing stare lands on me as he takes his seat, he pauses, tilting his head to the side for a second longer while I pray to everything that's holy that Kingston's meddling was enough to solidify my fake identity from his scrutiny. His eyes almost seem to spark with recognition, but I tell myself it's just my imagination playing tricks on me. Like Gigi had mentioned, the guy's an ass. It's definitely possible I was nothing more than a blip on his radar all those years ago, and he doesn't even remember me. Regardless, my breathing stops before I cover it with a dopey grin that I hope throws him off his scent.

Turning to Patrick, I whisper, "Why is he staring at me?"

Patrick follows my line of sight to see Burlone's inquisitive expression.

Leaning closer to me, Patrick whispers in my ear, "Seems he's distracted by that pretty face just as much as I am. It's a good thing I'm sitting next to you and not across from you like that poor sap, or I'm pretty sure I'd get my ass handed to me within the first hand."

With a breathy laugh, I shake my head then send a quick glance in Burlone's direction only to see he's moved on with his inspection. I sigh in relief, grateful my impromptu flirting with Patrick was enough to distract Burlone from placing me.

I think, anyway.

Shuffling a fresh deck of cards, the dealer's quiet voice commands the room. "Hello, everyone. As you can see, my name is Chance." He drops his chin to point out his name tag before continuing. "We're going to play some Texas Hold'em tonight with the standard rules. The player to my left,"—he motions to some hotshot in a designer suit—"will start with the small blind. Let's begin."

32

ACE

W ith a flick of his wrist, Chance deals the cards around the table until there are two in front of every player. Casually, I lift the corners of the cards I've been dealt and take a quick peek before my eyes dart around the table. Glancing back at my cards, my vision goes blurry, and I give myself a mental pep talk.

Okay, Ace. This is it. Stop freaking out about the asshat across the table and focus. If you want to put him in his place, then you need to win, which means you need to clear your head. Slowly, I let out the breath I've been holding and conceal my smile. *I've got this.*

After taking another look at my cards, I consider my game plan. I should fold, but I want to solidify my opponents' initial impression of me. I need to look like I don't really know what I'm doing. At least, not to play at this level, and this is a great opportunity to prove it.

Everyone places their ante in the center of the table, signifying they want to play the hand. When it's my turn, I toss a chip in. Chance then places three community cards face up––also known as the flop––in the center of the black felt table.

Watching the players around me, I search for their tells. Anything that will help me read them and give me an idea of what their hand is like. A twitch of the mouth, a touch of their shirt. A twist of their fingers. *Anything.* I don't notice that I'm avoiding Burlone's presence until I catch him smirking at me. Digging my fingers into the palm of my hand that rests against my leg beneath the table and hidden from his view, I let the bite of pain ground me while waiting for him to break our little staring contest. Seconds later, he turns his attention back to Chance, and I unclench my fist.

Mr. Suit is asked if he wants to bid, and he obliges by tossing a small stack of chips onto the table. Everyone follows suit, including me, even though it pains me to waste money when I know I'm not going to win.

Remember the big picture, Ace.

The hand continues when Chance adds another card to the community set. Now there are four in the center and two in our hands. We can use a total of five to create the best hand possible. Unfortunately for me, I still have shit to work with.

Again, the players are asked if they'd like to bet or fold. Anticipation rolls through me as I ignore Burlone and watch Mr. Suit throw his cards onto the table, folding, followed by Cowboy #1 and Cowboy #2. Oh, yes, there are *two* cowboys. Both from the South, and both with southern accents that remind me of Dottie, only more sophisticated.

Patrick, Burlone, and I are the only players who haven't folded yet when Patrick tosses another chip worth five thousand dollars into the center. Tucking my hair behind my ear, I smile nervously then follow suit, throwing a chip into the pot.

I can feel Burlone watching me as he does the same thing,

playing right into my hands, though I could do without his attention. Once everyone has placed their bets, Chance flips over the last card onto the table, giving us five community cards. Patrick checks by brushing his knuckles against the felt, and I follow suit, silently telling everyone at the table that I don't want to add anything to the pot.

Again, Burlone calculates my move and counters it by mirroring my action. Once we've all checked, we begin showing our cards. Patrick has a pair of tens, I have shit, and Burlone ends with a pair of jacks. With a triumphant smile, he leans forward and sweeps the chips in the center of the table toward him.

The hand cost me thirty thousand dollars, but I'm going to end up winning because of it. I can tell because as soon as the hand is played, Burlone writes me off as a formidable opponent. Exactly the way I wanted him to.

Game. Set. Match.

An hour later, we've weeded out the losers, and the only players left are Patrick, Burlone, me, and Texas. Glancing to my right, I offer him a friendly smile before noting his dwindling pile of chips.

After Chance deals the next hand, Burlone tosses down his cards immediately, followed by Patrick seconds later. I, on the other hand, have a pair of sixes. Texas gives me the side-eye as I throw in my ante, showing I want to play the rest of the hand. With a subtle mouth twitch, he does the same.

Chance lays down three community cards in the center of the table, displaying another six along with a two and a king.

Perfect.

I don't want to scare off Texas by betting big, so I decide to toss in two chips, praying he'll follow suit.

He does.

Another card is placed in the center, face up. It doesn't

matter what it is. I've got this. Three of a kind is hard to beat, and unless he has a pair of kings in his hand and plans to use the king on the table, then I've got this hand in the bag.

However, with another twitch of his lips, I know he doesn't.

If I want to cut him out of the game, then I need to guide him like a baby deer. Slowly. Patiently.

Licking his lips, he waits for me to raise the bet, call it, or fold. I take a long second to chew my lower lip before throwing a couple more chips into the pot before shifting my gaze to him and smiling tightly. My heart is racing like a jackhammer, but I keep my expression tense, as though I'm worried about what the outcome of the hand is going to be when I've already played the odds in my head and know my chances of walking away the victor are insanely high.

The combination is enough to convince him to stay in, and he meets my bet, raising me the rest of his money.

I'm so close, I can almost taste it, yet I try to stay calm. Instead of putting all of my chips in right away, I pretend to weigh my options before hesitantly following suit.

"Nervous, Macey?" Texas mutters under his breath. His entire body oozes confidence as he leans back in his chair and watches Chance flip the final card. Unless it's a king, I'm solid.

Come on, come on, come on, come on, I chant in my head.

It's a three.

I won! But he doesn't know that yet.

Chance has us show our hands, and his jaw nearly drops when he sees my pair of sixes combined with the six on the table.

With gritted teeth, a frustrated Texas throws his cards onto the black felt before shoving away from the table and storming off as an ever-professional Chance reaches for them and turns his hand over to reveal that Texas had a pair of kings.

My grin nearly splits my face in two as I stare at his losing hand while a round of applause echoes throughout the casino.

After soaking up the win for a few seconds, I drag my prize from the center of the table and start to stack the chips in front of me.

"Not bad," Patrick adds with an impressed smirk.

"Why, thank you," I quip, my pulse spiking with a fresh wave of adrenaline.

Another one bites the dust.

ACE

Poker can be draining. Really draining. A low throb at the base of my skull is making itself known as I continue tossing my antes into the pile, winning some hands and losing others. Patrick lost about thirty minutes ago in a brutal hand with Burlone. I was actually a little sad to see him go. He was pretty funny with his offhand comments and made this feel more like a game instead of a risky revenge strategy. He had a way of settling my nerves and distracting me from the man across from me, and I'll miss his interference. As he got up from the table after losing, he gave my shoulder a gentle squeeze before whispering, "Kick his ass, Mace. I'll be rooting for ya."

With a sympathetic smile, I replied, "I'll try."

And boy, am I trying.

Rolling my shoulders, I let out a brief yawn when Chance deals another hand. It feels like the thousandth one for the night. I've decided the adrenaline has worn off, and I need to recover from the rollercoaster of emotions I've been through this evening, but it's not over yet. In fact, it feels like it'll *never* be over.

"Getting tired, Ms. Johnson?" Burlone rumbles from his side of the table. I flinch when he addresses me, but cover it with another yawn to hide my fear. I don't think I'll ever get used to being so close to him, and I'm itching to run in the opposite direction.

But first, I need to win.

"Sure am." I take a look at my cards, ignoring Burlone's heavy stare.

"Care to make it interesting?"

With a sigh, I force myself to give him my attention while adding my ante to the pot. Over the last few hands, the ante has been raised to help end the tournament more quickly, but he and I seem to keep tugging the chips back and forth, depending on the cards that are dealt.

"And playing with hundreds of thousands of dollars isn't interesting?" I quip, maintaining my persona.

The crowd laughs while Burlone only looks mildly amused. "In a different game, I'd suggest playing with something other than money on the line, Ms. Johnson. In fact, I think I could have a great deal of fun with a different set of rules." His gaze slides over me, leaving a filmy residue on my skin that makes me desperate for a shower. "But in this particular instance, I meant something much more appropriate for the public eye."

My mouth floods with bitter acid, but I swallow it back. *I think I'm going to be sick.*

A hushed silence replaces the earlier lightness in the crowd. It's as if they can feel the same commanding presence as I can.

With another thick swallow, I force myself to stay calm. I've seen this side of Burlone. The charismatic, egotistical prick with double meanings woven into every syllable. The thought is almost enough to make me pause, but I press forward.

"What do you have in mind?" The smile I give him feels like plastic, but I think he's too self-absorbed to notice.

"Five hands. That's how many we have left to play. You can still bet or fold or whatever the hell you want, but we only play for five more rounds. That way, you won't miss your bedtime." He adds a wink for good measure, lightening the mood all over again. The crowd chuckles around me as he waits for my response.

"Sir," Chance interrupts. "That's against the rules."

"Not really, though. I mean, if we both agree to it, then what's the harm?"

Chance attempts to explain, "Well—"

"I'll do it," I say, surprising myself.

Both sets of eyes, along with every single one in the room, turn to me.

"Are you sure, miss?" Chance prods.

"Yup. Five hands. Winner takes all."

Burlone's arrogance is almost palpable as he zeroes in on me. "Perfect. Shall we start with this one, since we've already seen our cards or...?" His voice trails off, keeping his expression blank in hopes of preventing me from reading him.

It's interesting to be on this end. He thinks he's won, yet he's giving me exactly what I want. I knew I could make him bleed his chips slowly if I had no choice. But getting the opportunity to cut to the chase is exactly how I would play this if I had the chance. And he's giving me exactly that. The knowledge that I'm so close to getting what I want seems to supersede the anxiety that normally weighs around my shoulders whenever he's near. I savor the lightness that's been absent since the first time I found him sitting at our tiny kitchen table with a cigar in his hand.

I'm so close. I can almost taste it.

"Yup," I reply, reminding myself that I'm not that little girl anymore. "I think this hand sounds great. Since I don't want to miss my bedtime and all."

With a syrupy sweet grin, I push a thick stack of chips into the pot and wait for him to fold. Like a puppet, he does exactly that.

"Then I think I'll sit this one out." With a flick of his wrist, he tosses his two cards into the center table, then adds, "Four hands left, Ms. Johnson."

"Yup. I'm glad you can count."

34

JACK

This girl. I shake my head as the same question runs through my mind for the thousandth time in one night. *What the hell is she thinking?*

Four hands? There's over three hundred thousand dollars on the table, and she offers to win or lose it in *four hands*? My nostrils flare in frustration as I take a closer look.

The dealer, Chance, starts handing out cards to both Burlone then Ace. With a grin, Burlone tosses in his ante, and Ace does the same.

Chance moves the game along quickly as he places three cards face-up on the table. That same confident smirk is plastered on Burlone's face. He's not even trying to hide the fact that his hand is good. Ace, on the other hand, looks nervous. She's trying to hide it, but I can see it in her gaze, shifting from her hand, back to the community cards, then back again.

It's Burlone's turn to lead the bets, and he does so by throwing nearly half his stack into the center. He's either an arrogant prick who expects Ace to fold, or he's reading the situation the same way I am. Ace doesn't have anything, and instead of dragging it out, he's forcing her to the next hand.

Anxiously, Ace tucks her hair behind her ear then matches his bet before calling it, which means it stops Burlone from adding any more money to the pot before Chance can show another card.

Chance places another one onto the center of the table. There are now two aces, a king, and a jack laying face up. Watching Burlone's reaction, I can only assume he's holding a queen and ten in his hand, giving him a straight, because his face is nearly splitting in two from his reaction to the community cards.

Pushing the rest of his chips into the center pot, he boldly announces, "Your move, Ms. Johnson."

Again, Ace fidgets in her seat before brushing her hair with her hands and tucking a few of the strands behind her ear. It's the same motion she did at the beginning of the game when she bluffed hard and lost.

She's either an absolute idiot who doesn't know who she's playing against, or she's an utter genius. I can't decide which one is more accurate when it comes to the enigma of a girl I met all those nights ago.

Pushing the rest of the chips to the center of the table, she mutters, "Call. Obviously."

Chance turns the last card onto the table, completing the river before asking Burlone to show his hand.

Triumphantly, he turns over a pair of kings. "Three of a kind. King high. Sorry, Ms. Johnson. You put up a good fight, but I guess my undefeated title will have to remain intact for now."

Lifting his hands into the air, Chance stops Burlone from collecting the chips from the center pile.

"Ms. Johnson?"

Ace pins Burlone with her stare. It's filled with so much

animosity that I'm surprised Burlone isn't burnt to a crisp where he sits. As if in slow motion, she tosses a single card onto the pile of chips. An ace, which brings her to two pairs. Ace high. But it's not enough to beat Burlone's three of a kind.

As Burlone's grin widens, she finishes him off with another flick of her wrist. The entire room goes silent as if we're all holding our collective breath at once. Tossing a second ace onto the stack, she lowers her chin and watches in satisfaction as Burlone's grin slides off his face.

"Full house, Mr. Allegretti. But you put up a good fight." His jaw clenches as she continues, "I have to ask though, does defeating you come with a plaque or anything? Or maybe I can hire someone to make one. Ya know, since you were undefeated and all."

Hot. Fucking. Damn.

I've never seen anything more attractive in my life as she slowly drags the stack of chips toward her, her gaze never leaving Burlone's as fumes practically shoot from his ears. I know what he's thinking because the rest of the crowd is thinking the exact same thing. She just played him like a fucking fiddle in front of everyone, and he'll never be able to recover from the embarrassment. He just got his ass handed to him by a nobody because he underestimated her. A girl who hasn't played a single hand of professional poker before tonight just swept the tournament and dethroned the cocky sonofabitch who put it together in the first place.

Hot. Damn.

35

KINGSTON

MEANWHILE...

The air is calm, almost balmy as I wait near the safe house for D's arrival. Him and Stefan, along with a few other men, are spread throughout the city, strategically placed to prevent our plan from crumbling, no matter what curveballs are thrown our way.

Lou, a soldier and computer genius, stands at my side as we watch a white van roll down the street. Seconds later, a loud popping sound breaks the silence as Stefan uses a sniper rifle to puncture holes in the tires. With a squeal, the driver slams on his brakes and is ambushed by seven men with their handguns drawn.

The pussy surrenders without a fight as he raises his hands into the air for all of us to see before opening the door. Two of my men reach for him and grab his arms, twisting them behind his back. He whimpers in pain.

Tilting my head, I assess his strange behavior. It's out of character for a soldier to come quietly. However, as soon as he sees Diece saunter over, he starts thrashing in an attempt to get away.

This is the reaction I was anticipating.

With a single hit, Diece knocks out Burlone's man then tosses him over his shoulder as if he weighs nothing more than a feather. Walking toward me, he lifts his chin then stalks inside and gets to work strapping the lifeless body to a hard, metal chair.

My expression is stone cold as I follow him into the empty warehouse. It's the same one my father brought me to when I had my first kill. I can still feel the cold metal of the gun as he placed it in my hand and encouraged me to pull the trigger.

"Do you see what we do to traitors?" he asked. I was still shaking like a leaf from witnessing my first torture session, my stomach rolling with nausea. They had peeled back sections of his skin, ripped out toenails from his feet, broken bones with a hammer. It was gruesome. Unthinkable. Sickening. Yet, justified because he had lied to his family. He had given information to the Feds. He had earned every single amount of pain they inflicted and deserved the bullet I placed in his skull.

And tonight?

Tonight wouldn't be any different.

Sliding my black suit jacket from my shoulders, I hand it to Lou then approach the unconscious body sitting in a heap a few feet away.

A table is set up beside him with various tools necessary for making even the strongest of men sing.

And I'm in the mood for an entire album.

"Hey, Boss?" D asks, grabbing my attention. When my stare connects with his, he continues, "What do you want me to do with the van?"

"How many are in there?"

"Three."

Three innocent women who were on their way to be sold like cattle. I'd like to say my conscience is cleared with the knowledge I saved them from a fate worse than death, but I know how many I've turned a blind eye to. Girls just like them who were sold to the highest bidder, and I'll never be able to wash my hands of their blood.

"What kind of shape are they in?"

"A few cuts and bruises. Nothing broken," D answers gruffly.

"Then let them go."

With a nod, D passes along the orders, and I know shit will get handled as it always does when Diece is in charge.

"Now," I continue. "Let's begin."

Seconds later, Burlone's man comes sputtering to life when Lou tosses a bucket of ice water in his face.

"What the—"

He blinks quickly in an attempt to get rid of the frigid liquid clinging to his lashes.

"Morning, Sunshine," I offer with a grin.

The moment he recognizes me, his jaw drops, and absolute terror takes over his expression. "Fuck," he breathes as the smell of piss permeates the air.

"You're about to be," D jokes, slapping his big paw of a hand on my back before shoving me toward the table. "Get to work, Boss. I have a bet with Stefan to see how long it takes you to make him squeal."

"Come on, D. You're not supposed to tell him! That changes the odds!" Stefan interrupts from the doorway.

"He's right, D. Plus, where's the fun in that? Sometimes the foreplay is better than the main event."

D scoffs. "Says the guy who isn't getting laid."

"Watch it," I mutter under my breath. He's right, though. I need to get this shit done so I can figure out my next move with a certain brunette who's been the center of all my thoughts. I received a text from Reggie earlier tonight as she stepped onto Burlone's territory, but I haven't heard a word since. The thought makes my jaw tighten. The sooner I get this shit taken care of, the sooner I can find Ace and make sure she's still safe.

Gathering a small chisel and hammer from the table, I walk toward the guy I'm about to decimate and squat down so we're eye to eye.

"Hi. By your reaction, I'm going to assume you know who I am. Is that right?"

With a trembling lower lip, he whimpers, "Y-yes, sir."

"Good." I pat his knee. "What's my name?"

"K-Kingston, sir."

"Is that all?"

"K-Kingston Romano. The D-Dark King."

"Good. Now, social etiquette would suggest it's your turn to introduce yourself." When he stays silent, I squeeze his knee.

"M-Marty, sir. My name is Marty."

Again, I praise him. "Good. So tell me this, Marty. You seemed a little…," I pause, "*anxious* when you woke up and saw me. Why is that?"

With an audible gulp, a terrified Marty starts shaking. "B-because of the rumors, sir."

"And what rumors are those?" I push.

"That you're ruthless."

"And?"

"That you know how to hurt people."

Tsking, I say, "Many men in my line of work know how to hurt people, Marty. I think you're going to have to be a little more specific."

"P-please don't hurt me," he begs, turning into a blubbering mess right before my eyes.

"Now, now, Marty. Don't be a coward. I haven't even touched you yet. All we're doing is chatting. Isn't that right, gentlemen?" I address the rest of the spectators in the room.

A rumble of yesses echoes throughout the space in response.

"See? Just chatting, Marty. But if you don't keep talking, then we're going to have a problem. Understand?"

With his eyes squeezed shut, and a mumbled prayer on his lips, he nods.

"Good. Let's start easy, shall we? Who are you working for?"

When he doesn't answer right away, I lift the tiny hammer and slam it against the knuckles in his thumb. As soon as it connects, the bones surrounding his tiny joint shatter into pieces.

"Fuuuuck!" Marty yells with tears streaming down his face.

"No, I don't think that's the right answer. Try again."

"P-please—"

Again, I lift the hammer and hit it against his hand.

His screams are piercing as he shouts, "Okay! Okay! I'll talk! Please! Stop!"

"Answer the question, Marty. It really is that simple."

"Burlone. I work for Burlone."

I nod. "And what, exactly, were you doing on my grounds?"

With fascination, I watch his Adam's apple bob up and down in his throat. "I–I was told to come here."

"Why?" I grit out, my gaze narrowing.

His voice is stilted as if he can't quite get his tongue to move how he wants it to. "B-because. Because I was meeting someone."

"And who were you meeting?"

"I-I don't know."

Lifting the hammer, he squeals before I can drop it down to his hand for a third time, rambling everything I need to know like a fucking waterfall. "I swear, I don't know! I swear it! All I know is that it was supposed to look like I was working for you, and that the Feds were going to pick me up. They promised they'd take care of my family if I went along with it. They told me they'd pay off my debts if I told them I worked for you. If I told them the girls in the van belonged to you. That's all they said! I didn't know anything! I swear! Just please," he begs. "Please don't hurt me."

Looking over my shoulder to D, he gives me a short nod.

"Then it looks like we're through here." Stefan steps forward and shoves the barrel of a gun to his temple, pulling the trigger before Marty even has a chance to register that his life is about to end.

Bang.

"Well, that was anticlimactic," D notes. "He didn't even make it past ten minutes."

Stefan holsters his gun before pulling out a small roll of cash and handing it to Diece. "Yeah, yeah. Here's your damn money. Boss, do you think you could drag it out a little longer next time?"

With a smirk, I say, "I'll see what I can do. Get the cleaning crew here, and don't forget to grab the plates off the van."

"Already done," Lou confirms.

"Then let's get out of here."

DEX

W hen my phone sounds with a text notification, I'm almost scared to look at it. Burlone is vibrating with anger, pacing the small office like a caged beast. Curses flying, he chucks a book against the wall then continues tossing every threat he can think of at the girl who just schooled him in a game of poker, taking over three hundred thousand dollars with a single hand. It's not the money he's pissed about, though. It's his pride.

"That bitch has no idea what she's done," he spits. "She thinks she can embarrass me? That she can fucking take my money? I swear…. Who is she, anyway?"

Sei's dry laugh reverberates through the silent room. "Funny enough, I overheard her having a little conversation with someone before the tournament. Seems she has an interesting connection with a certain Romano prince."

With furrowed brows, Burlone voices the same question filtering through my mind. "Kingston?"

Sei nods, looking happy as ever.

"How the hell does she know Kingston?"

"Apparently," he laughs, "they're fucking each other."

My gaze bounces back to Burlone, waiting to see his reaction.

Scratching his jaw, a contemplative Burlone remains silent, letting the information marinate before stating, "I want her dead."

"You can't do that," I interject.

"Excuse me?" Burlone asks his voice brooking no argument.

"Yeah? Why the hell not?" Sei adds.

"Because it doesn't take a genius to figure out she's on your shit list for beating you tonight. The Feds are already up our asses, and you, yourself have been saying we need to lie low. Having the girl who embarrassed you on national television disappear isn't exactly discreet."

Burlone narrows his gaze but doesn't argue.

"Well," Sei offers, "At least you fucked over Kingston tonight, right? Which means the Feds will be backing off soon, and you should get the opportunity to teach her a lesson. Dex is right. I wouldn't kill her. That pretty little ass looks like a ripe peach, ready for the picking."

Their voices fade into the background as I pull out my phone and read a message sent from my contact. The guy who should be dead right now, or at the very least, in the FBI's custody. The guy who was supposed to have purchased the girls from Marty. *Thomas.*

Private Number: The fruit never ripened.

Fuck.

Looking over at Sei, I find him staring at me with pinched brows as Burlone keeps ranting.

I lick my lips then clear my throat gaining their attention.

"Yeah?" Sei asks, having lost his earlier amusement from the tournament.

"The fruit wasn't delivered."

When a heavy silence encompasses the room, I wait for the fallout, and I'm not disappointed.

"What?" Burlone's stare is like ice.

"Just got a text from the buyer. Marty never showed."

"Fuck!" Burlone bellows, shoving everything off his desk. The veins near his temple are throbbing with unrestrained fury. He looks as if he's ready to explode.

"First the tournament? Now, this?" A loud growl escapes him before he stalks toward me and shoves me up against the nearest wall.

When my back hits the blood-red surface of his office, I grit my teeth and try to calm the overwhelming need to shove him away from me.

I'm twice Burlone's size and half his age. I could kill him with ease, but I don't have a death wish. I know what happens to members who betray their family. Hell, I'm the one who executed Burlone's orders in the past to show them their place.

With a clenched jaw, I try to ignore the spittle as it flies toward my face. "I gave you one fucking job, Dex. One job. And you failed. I should bury you for this."

I don't bother responding. It wouldn't do me any good, anyway.

"Then where are the girls?" Sei interjects from his seated position in the corner. Lazily, he lights a cigarette and lets it hang from the corner of his mouth. Just like me, he's used to Burlone's outbursts.

"How the fuck should I know?" Burlone roars.

With my shirt tangled in his grip, Burlone leans forward with a wicked glare. "You gonna fix this, Dex?" His tone is hot with rage as I stare right back at him.

"If you let me go, I will."

Reluctantly, he does as I ask then continues his pacing

from earlier. Dialing Marty, I'm greeted with his voicemail which only confirms my suspicion.

"Marty isn't answering."

"Which means…." Sei's voice trails off, letting me fill in the blank.

"It means he's dead."

"What do we know?" Burlone grits out.

"We know Marty's missing, likely dead, the girls are absent, and that your plan to screw over Kingston fell through."

Sei interjects, "We also know his girlfriend was at the tournament tonight and beat your ass in a game of cards."

"And that we can't touch her," I add.

With a snarl, a pissed off Burlone collapses into his chair behind his oak desk, rattling the floor with his weight. Slowly, the seconds on the clock audibly tick throughout the room as we all search for a solution to get us out of this mess. Or namely, *Burlone* out of this mess because he doesn't give two shits about Sei or me.

"I have an idea," Sei's gruff voice breaks the silence that was slowly driving me mad.

"And what's that?" Burlone rumbles.

"I think we can all assume this has Kingston written all over it."

Both of us nod.

"And I think we can also assume there are too many eyes on the girl for her to disappear."

Again, we nod. We've already established this.

"But I know how badly you want to make Kingston hurt, right?"

This time, I turn to Burlone to see his lips pulling into a thin line as he tries to compose himself. "Get to the point, Sei."

"His sister."

Squeezing my eyes shut, I know that with those two simple words, an innocent girl's fate has been sealed. And if I'm being completely honest, I'm surprised Sei was sharp enough to think of it himself.

With a snap of Burlone's fingers, he smiles. "Get it done."

"The only problem is, we don't know who she is or where she likes to go. So, how exactly would you like me to proceed?" Sei has a point.

Burlone offers, "I'll forward the image Dominic sent."

The air in the room grows thick with possibilities; each of them swirling into a chaotic blur.

Rolling his shoulders, Sei comments, "Okay."

"And Sei?"

"Yeah?"

"I don't want anyone else to know who we have. We need to play our cards right." Tapping his nubby fingers against his chin, Burlone adds, "While you're at it, grab a few more apples."

"Done." Sei pushes himself up from his seat, and I follow him toward the door when Burlone stops me. "Dex."

Turning on my heel, I raise my brows. "Yeah?"

"Kingston's girl might not be able to go missing, but that doesn't mean she can't get mugged on her way home from Sin. The streets are dangerous for a pretty girl like that at night. Understand?"

My stomach turns, but I don't argue. "Yeah, Boss."

"Good. I'll be on the floor doling out congratulatory ass-kissing for the rest of the night. Good luck, gentlemen." His lips quirk up mischievously before waving me out the door. Without a backward glance, I exit with the intent to follow orders that I know will make me sick.

Isn't the first time.

Won't be the last.

37

ACE

Cloud. Nine.

That's what I'm on. I'm practically skipping down the street with my backpack swinging from left to right in time with my steps when I round the corner and take the stairs two at a time before swinging the door open and stepping into Dottie's.

"Hey, Dottie!"

As soon as she sees me, a wide grin spreads across her face. "If that's your poker face, darlin', then you should look into a different profession."

Giggling, I let my smile nearly split my face in two but don't deem her comment worthy of a response.

Thankfully, she doesn't need one before rushing over to me and wrapping me in a giant bear hug. "You won! I can't believe it, doll! Tell me everything! Right now! I wanna hear every detail!"

I pull away with throbbing cheeks from smiling so hard and begin to scan the diner. "Trust me, I'm about to explode from excitement. Where's Gigi? You can take a break, and I'll tell you guys everything."

With a pitiful look, Dottie pats my shoulder. "I'm sorry, doll, but I ain't seen Gigi tonight. She must've gotten held up. Why don't ya grab a seat, and I'll bring your order over. Then you can eat while ya wait for her to get here. Sound alright?"

A swell of disappointment threatens to take over, but I shake it off.

"Yeah. Sounds great. Thanks, Dottie."

An hour later, I find myself still very much alone in my booth. Dottie has filled my coffee multiple times and has pulled as many details from me as she could about the tournament, but it just isn't the same as whenever I tell Gigi stuff.

Looking up at the clock on the wall, I see the time and rub my eyes. I'm exhausted.

Dottie must sense my fatigue too as she comes over and asks, "Are ya alright? Need anythin' else?"

I shake my head.

"I'm sure she just got caught up with somethin'. Come back tomorrow, and you can tell her all about it."

A pathetic smile graces my lips as I throw a couple twenties onto the table then throw my backpack over my shoulder.

"Yeah. I'm going to call it a night. Thanks for listening to my rambling, Dottie. I'll see you tomorrow."

"You sure you should be walkin' home tonight?" she asks with her brows pinched in concern.

Memories of my conversation with Kingston come to mind, but I'd still rather be safe than sorry. "No, I think I'm going to call a cab. Mind if I use your phone?"

"Anytime, doll."

"Thanks."

Walking over to the pay phone, I dial the number for a cab and am told he'll be here in a few minutes. I wait inside the diner until a yellow car pulls up to the curb, and I head outside with a final wave to Dottie.

"See ya, Dottie!"

"See ya later, doll."

~

THE STREETS ARE STILL QUIET AS I HAND THE DRIVER MY money and get out of the cab. The road is blocked near my building, but I can see the entrance only a hundred yards away. I've walked this route a thousand times, but it doesn't stop the hair on the back of my neck prickling with awareness. Releasing a slow breath, I remind myself that everything will be fine before heading toward the empty parking lot.

Other than the occasional squeal of tires in the distance, my feet scuffing against the damp pavement is the only sound accompanying me on my lonely walk.

Kingston wasn't kidding about his men being discreet, I note to myself with a quick peek over my shoulder. I haven't seen anyone all night. Breathing in deep, I look up at the dark sky that promises morning in a few short hours when I feel like someone's watching me.

I look over my shoulder, but the parking lot is still empty. Rule #3 screams at me to make a run for it. But I don't. Keeping my head down and my senses on high alert, I scan the dark shadows lining the street while tightening my grip on my backpack that holds a cashier's check for more money than I could have ever dreamed of winning.

Why the hell do I live in such a crappy neighborhood?

After squeezing my eyes shut in self-deprecation, I pop them open and scan my surroundings again before picking up my speed to a fast walk. The light near the entrance has been broken for months, so I'm not surprised to see the main door blanketed in darkness, but it doesn't stop my palms from sweating.

Usually, I sneak through a back alley and between a chain-link fence that's close to where Eddie likes to hang out, but I was dropped off by the main road which means I'm on my own.

With another glance behind me, I listen for the sound of footsteps but only hear my own. Gripping the straps of my backpack like it's my lifeline, I keep a clear gap between me and the bin that's tucked away near the front of the building.

A soft scratching up ahead sounds like a siren, and my heart jumps in response. I lick my lips and search the area casually as a prickling sensation races down my spine.

A damn cat pops up out of nowhere, followed by a dry laugh from me at how ridiculous I'm acting.

"Come on, Ace. It's a parking lot, not a horror movie," I mutter to myself in an attempt to point out how outrageous I'm being.

Still, it doesn't stop me from hastening my steps as I approach the front door and tug it open with as much strength as I can muster before darting up the stairs until I'm out of breath.

Digging through my backpack, I grab my key and place it in the lock before twisting the doorknob and slamming the door behind me.

Phew. You're safe.

I flip the switch on the wall then round the corner into my tiny kitchen in search of a drink. Reaching onto my tiptoes, my shaky hands grab a glass from the cabinet when that same prickling sensation slides down my spine. My entire body freezes as I turn around to see a dark figure emerge from the shadows. The glass slips from my hand, shattering into a dozen pieces on the tile floor beneath my feet as I lurch backward and fall on my ass.

"Shit. Shit. Shit."

As I scramble like a sand crab against the old flooring in

hopes of escaping the nightmare stalking toward me, every damn rule flickers through my mind for a solution to the shitstorm I inadvertently just walked into. Unfortunately, I come up empty. When a shard of glass pierces the palm of my hand, I collapse onto my elbows in agony. The sharp sting from the laceration shoots up my forearm, spreading like wildfire as that same dark figure inches closer.

Rule #7: Never leave something of value out in the open. And this time, in my own apartment––*alone*––I'm reminded that I just failed epically. I might not have left something of value out in the open, but I'm still going to pay dearly.

"Please," I beg, cradling my injured hand to my chest. "Please don't hurt me."

"Sorry, darlin'," the shadowed behemoth mutters under his breath. The sentiment does nothing to calm the adrenaline racing through my veins. Bending down, he tangles his fingers in my loose curls. The bite of his hold as he hauls me to my feet is enough to elicit a panicked scream from my lips.

"Help! Please! Somebody help me!"

I know my plea is meaningless. In this building, you keep your head down and your nose out of other people's business. But I have to try.

Hastily, he grapples for my mouth, covering it with his giant hand as I claw the exposed skin on his forearm. When the familiar X tattoo comes into focus through my blurred vision, I know I'm done for.

Like Kingston said, I screwed with the wrong guy, and I'm about to pay dearly for that mistake too.

With tears streaming down my cheeks, I beg for my life, mumbling against my attacker's palm in an attempt to convince him to show mercy. I doubt he can understand a single syllable, but it doesn't stop the words from tumbling past my lips. Seconds later, he releases his hold on my hair, but his other hand is still covering my mouth, preventing me from pleading for my life. His grasp is brutal as his fingers dig into my jaw and cheeks. If there's any chance of me surviving this encounter, I know that his punishing grip will leave bitter purple bruises on my pale skin.

Wiggling back and forth, I try to find a way to break free, but it only seems to bring him closer. The harsh light from the lamp beside my couch reflects off his face, making him appear almost demonic as he raises his fist. My breath catches in my throat as I watch him. However, it's his eyes that haunt me. They show the potential for another life. An alternate reality where he could make his own choices instead of being forced to fulfill someone else's desire with an iron fist. He's in as much of a prison as I am. And it's all because of Burlone. In this instant, I feel sorry for him because he's not a big, strong man. He's Burlone's bitch as much as I am. Hell, he's nothing but a coward who's been given the task of hurting an innocent girl who happened to bruise Burlone's ego.

My body goes limp in his hands as if I'm a ragdoll, giving up the fight he expects. With pinched brows, my attacker shows his confusion for a split second before remembering his purpose. I just hope it doesn't end with me in a body bag.

But maybe that's just wishful thinking on my part.

I don't see it coming. The angry knuckles as they connect with the side of my face, tattooing themselves in my memory as pain blossoms from my cheekbone to the back of my skull. The hit is like a freaking wrecking-ball that makes the back-hand from a week ago feel like child's play. When black spots start dotting my vision, I'm given one more apologetic look from my attacker before he throws another punch and the darkness finally takes over.

KINGSTON

I n my family's estate, there are three floors with an array of bedrooms spread throughout. When my dad died, I took over the master suite, but only because it was expected of me. In the bathroom that connects to his bedroom––*my* bedroom––I forcefully scrub my hands with a bar of soap. After my first kill, my father warned me it wouldn't get any easier. And even though I didn't pull the trigger this time, Marty's blood is still on my hands. But without his death, there would be so many more. Besides, he chose to take on the Romano family. And that was a fatal mistake.

Rinsing the suds off, I grab a towel and dry my hands. After replacing it on the rack, I unbutton my white dress shirt, one loophole at a time before gliding it down my shoulders and tossing it in the hamper.

Reggie isn't answering his fucking phone. I don't know how else to reach Ace, but I saw the results from the tournament. She won. I'm so damn proud and shocked she pulled it off in the first place. Pulling out my phone, I reread the last text from Reggie.

Reggie: At the diner. Eating eggs. No threats.

Rubbing my hand across my face, I head to the bedroom in hopes of getting some sleep when a loud knock pounds against my door.

With furrowed brows, I open it to see Stefan's ghostly complexion.

"What is it?"

"Regina's missing."

My fingers dig into the doorjamb in hopes of it keeping me grounded as I see the remorse shining in his eyes. There's no way. We talked. I told her she needed to stay home. This isn't possible. She has to be here somewhere. We just need to look.

"What do you mean she's missing?" I argue. "She's been here the whole night."

With a shake of his head, an apologetic Stefan continues, "No, sir. She snuck out. I checked the GPS on her phone, but it only led me down the block before I found her cell in the bushes. She's gone."

She disobeyed my orders. I'm terrified. Pissed. Frustrated. And so many other emotions I can't even comprehend them all.

What the hell were you thinking, Regina?

"Fuck!" I yell as I tug on the roots of my hair with so much force I'm sure they'll fall out in seconds. *I have to fix this.* Storming out of my room in nothing but a pair of black slacks, I head down the hall to the security room. The door is usually locked as a precaution, but Lou must already be aware of the situation because the door is propped open, ready for my entrance. Computer keyboard in hand, Lou's prepped and ready to help.

"Pull up the feed from tonight. I want to see everything," I order.

"Yes, sir." Lou starts tapping away until he finds what I'm looking for and starts displaying the videos on the screens that line the walls.

When I see Regina hidden in the shadows on one of the televisions, I point to it. "There." Lou resumes his typing, blowing up the video and playing it in slow motion.

I watch as my baby sister sneaks out the front door without a backward glance before moseying down the driveway then turning left. That's it. That's all I'm given.

"Do we have any footage of where we found her phone?" I grit out. My tone is like steel.

Clearing his throat, Lou shakes his head. "Sorry Boss, but we don't have shit. We'll find something, though. I'm going to keep looking."

I open my mouth to voice another question when I hear the slamming of heavy footsteps in the hallway coming closer.

Diece appears in the doorway, almost out of breath as he says, "Your office phone is ringing."

With sweaty palms, I sprint to my office on the first floor, taking the stairs two at a time before throwing open the door and answering the call.

"Yeah?" Quietly, I calm my breathing as I wait for a response. There are only a handful of people who know this number, and Regina's one of them.

"Kingston?" a feminine voice crackles through the speaker, but it sounds forced.

A second ticks by as I try to register who I'm talking to.

"Ace?"

She's not who I was expecting, but something feels off.

"Um. Yeah. Yeah, it's me."

Her labored response sets off the warning bells in my head.

"What's wrong?"

Silence.

"Ace, talk to me."

If it were anyone else on the other end of the line, I'd hang up and go searching for my sister, but it's *Ace*. And she doesn't sound right. My senses are on high alert, knowing something is wrong.

"I didn't know who else to call," she confides.

"Talk to me. Now."

I hear a soft sniffle before her raspy voice echoes through the speaker. "One of Burlone's men came to see me—"

"What'd he do?" I cut her off because the possibilities are made of nightmares. I need to find out how much she knows, and who's going to pay for hurting her. This call pushes me over the edge, and my grip tightens against the phone until I'm sure the plastic will crack from the pressure. My chest tightens as I wait for her response. The sooner I have names, the sooner I can slice their skin from their pathetic bodies. Inch. By inch.

She sniffs again but doesn't reply.

I check the time on my wristwatch and keep my tone even as I ask, "Where are you, Ace? I'm going to send someone to come get you."

With a soft whimper, she says, "Yeah. Um...I think that might be good. I'm uh, I'm at the liquor store by my apartment. On the corner of—"

"I know the one," I interrupt. "Be there in ten."

Hanging up the phone, I bark my orders to Diece who seems to have followed me.

"Where the hell's Reggie?"

I don't know why I bother to ask; I already know the answer.

D forces a swallow. "His phone is dead."

"Fuck!" I scream, finally snapping and hitting my fist against the desk. Reggie's dead. I have no doubt in my mind, though it makes my stomach churn to think about it. Death might be a relatively common occurrence in my world, but it doesn't get any easier when it's my own family.

Reggie. Ace. Regina. What started out as a successful night just turned catastrophic, and I don't know if I'm strong enough to carry the weight of it all. Then I remember who I am.

I'm the only one who can.

"Send someone to track him down with the GPS on his phone. If they find a body, have them call in the clean-up crew." He nods as I continue, "And I need you to go pick up Ace. *Now*."

A brief rap of his knuckles against my desk is all I get before he disappears down the hallway and to the garage. How the hell did everything get so screwed up?

And how am I going to fix it all?

.

39

KINGSTON

I feel like this night is never going to end. There are so many questions and not enough answers. With my elbows on the desk, I rest my head in my hands, scouring my memory for any information I might have to Regina's whereabouts when my office phone rings. Looking at the screen, I can see I'm being paged from the security room. Answering it, I hear Lou's voice echo through the speaker in my office.

"Hey, Boss?"

"Yeah?"

"D's back with your girl."

My girl. I open my mouth to deny it but finally accept the truth. If the knots in my stomach are anything to go by, then yeah. I'm going to say that she's my girl. I just need to convince her of that.

"She looks pretty bad, Boss. Just wanted to give you a heads up."

Swallowing the bile as it burns down my throat, I rub my face roughly.

"Thanks for the update. Any news on Regina?"

A heavy silence is all I get as a response before Lou hesitantly answers me. "Not yet. But we'll find her."

"Is there a possibility that she left her phone there for a reason? That she didn't *want* to be followed? I mean…it's possible, right?" Stefan's voice echoes through the phone, and I assume they've put the call on speaker. He's been working as diligently as Lou to find Regina, but I'm afraid I already know the answer.

"It's possible," I admit. "But I think the odds are stacked against us, considering how we screwed up Burlone's plans last night. Keep looking. And keep me updated. I need to deal with Ace right now."

A couple of, "Yes, sirs," echo throughout the room before the line goes dead.

Standing from my chair, I head in the direction of the garage when I see a girl who looks nothing like the one I've grown accustomed to seeing. With her arm cradled to her chest, she whimpers as soon as she sees me.

"Hey." A pitiful smile accompanies her weak voice as she limps closer with D by her side. She looks like she got ran over by a fucking truck. A fat lip that's begging for some ice, dried blood crusted beneath her nose, and two swollen eyes that are nearly swallowed whole from the dark purple bruising surrounding them.

I've seen a lot of shit in my life, but nothing has crippled me the way the broken girl in front of me has.

Rushing toward her, I wrap my arm around her shoulders then guide her down the hall and to the couch in the family room. Without protest, she follows before collapsing onto the cushions. She looks so tiny. So frail. My knees hit the ground so I can take a closer look.

As gently as I can, I touch each side of her face to examine the damage. My blood boils at the sight.

"You sure this was Burlone's men?" I grit out.

Her chest rises and falls slowly as a single tear slides down her cheek. "Yeah. You were right, Kingston. I messed with the wrong guy. I'm so sorry."

Sorry? She's apologizing?

I press a gentle kiss to her forehead then move to sit beside her on the couch. Pulling her into my lap, I hold her close and rock her back and forth. Back and forth. She melts into me a little more with each movement.

"Shh,...it's okay, Ace. You have nothing to be sorry for."

"I do, though," she whimpers. "I didn't know who to call. You didn't sign up for this. You have no obligation to help me, yet here I am." Raising her arms, she motions to the family room of my estate. A place that very few people have ever really been invited into.

"All I wanted was to take something from him the way he took something from me. But, instead...,"—she shudders in my arms—"all I won was a living nightmare I'll never be able to erase."

My hands tighten around her tiny waist, and it takes everything in me to loosen them. She doesn't need to see Dark King right now. She needs the tender King. The one only she's ever been privy to.

"You're right," I offer. "I didn't sign up for this. Neither of us did, yet you fell into my lap anyway, and I wouldn't change it. Listen to me, Ace." Carefully, I raise her chin with the pad of my forefinger until I have her full attention. Or at least, as much as she can give me when her entire face is smashed in. I grit my teeth, but push my anger aside and focus on how I can harness it. "You're mine now. Do you know what that means?"

She shakes her head.

"It means I'm going to burn every single one of them for what they did to you. And I'm not going to let you go."

The feel of a cold compress is pressed against my bare

shoulder. Diece is hovering over us like a mother hen as I take the offered ice pack and give him a nod of thanks.

He returns it with one of his own before addressing the wounded girl in my arms. "Hey, Ace?"

"Yeah?" she mumbles, pulling away from me then looking up at D.

"I'm sorry to interrupt, but I think we need to take a look at that hand."

I had almost forgotten about the way she cradled it against her, and I feel like an ass for not addressing it sooner. Lowering my head to get a better look, I gently wrap my thumb and forefinger around her wrist then pull it away from her protective embrace. Blood drips down her elbow, staining the black cocktail dress covering her tiny frame.

"Shit, Ace. What the hell happened?"

A fresh wave of guilt hits me harder than a sledgehammer. I should've been there for her. I should've protected her.

"It's just glass," she murmurs. Her whole body tenses at my examination.

Glancing up at D, I don't need to utter a word before he offers, "I'll go get the first-aid kit." We have doctors for this shit, but we both know that Ace needs me right now, not some stranger.

With a hesitant smile, Ace whispers, "Thanks, Diece."

"Anytime." He reappears seconds later with a decent sized plastic tote we use for quick fixes. Anything other than surgery can be handled in-house, and Ace is about to learn that firsthand.

"Thanks, D. Will you go check on Regina's situation?" I need some privacy with Ace. I need to know she's going to be okay. Physically and emotionally.

"Sure thing, King." He leaves without a backward glance.

Turning to Ace, I can almost see her soul losing its luster as she tries to process her experience. There will be time for that later. Right now, she needs a distraction before I lose her to the darkness. She needs the suffocating weight to be lifted for a few minutes, and I need to help her carry it. I gently slide her off my lap and back onto the couch before moving to kneel in front of her. Opening the kit, I give her my best doctor impression with a side of cocky superhero.

"Usually, I let the doc take care of these things, but I'm feeling generous tonight."

With a quirked brow, she returns, "Is that right?"

"Sure is." I start rifling through the bandages, gauze, and antiseptic in search of some tweezers. When I find them, I set them aside then grab a few other things we'll be needing. Needle. Thread. A sterile syringe and a vial of lidocaine to numb the skin, along with a few other items. Ace's face is filled with fascination as she watches my every move, and I know I've officially distracted her. Epic meltdown averted. For now, anyway. There will be time to process things later.

"Have you done this before?" The awe is clear in her tone.

"Maybe a time or two."

"Really?"

I laugh, dryly. "I learned how to give stitches by the time I was nine and could feel the difference between a sprain and a break long before that."

"Really? I just...I can't imagine that kind of life."

"Says the girl who learned how to count cards when she was...twelve?"

Pursing her lips, she corrects me, "Ten. But that was mainly to pass the time. This? This is crazy, Kingston." It seems our conversation is distracting her from the fact that she got the shit kicked out of her, and I'm happy to see the real Ace come back to the surface.

"Nah, just a part of life. Now, bring your hand over here. I want to see it better in the light."

She does as I ask, placing her hand palm up in mine as I

take a look at the damage. The wound is almost three inches long and looks angry as hell, surrounded by inflamed, red skin. The bravest of men would be feeling a slice like this. A swell of pride spreads throughout my chest for being able to claim Ace as mine.

"Damn, Ace. This is a good one."

With her mouth tilted up on one side, an amused expression paints her face.

"A good one?"

"Yeah. Growing up, we'd always refer to our injuries on some fucked-up scale. *That's nothing,* was a scratch or a bruise. Something that didn't even deem the attention of bringing it up in the first place, and if you did, you'd get shit for days. But *a good one* means it's likely going to scar and requires stitches or a cast. This,"—I gesture to her hand—"is a good one, Ace." Leaning closer, I place a soft kiss against her busted lip and nose, being careful not to hurt her.

"So are these."

She looks so vulnerable right now with my big hand cradling her bruised face, and her big doe eyes peeking up at me. I'd do anything to take away her pain. To steal the burden of her recovery and carry it by myself. But the only thing I can do is hold her and tell her it's going to be okay. I just wish I knew if it was the truth or not.

"Thank you, King." Her voice is nothing but a whisper, quiet enough that it could easily get lost in the intimate ambiance if I hadn't been paying attention.

With a brush of my fingers against the silky skin on her forearm, I pull her closer.

"Anytime, Ace. Now let's fix this hand."

40

KINGSTON

After digging into the laceration in search of any more glass then sewing it up, I wrap her injured hand with some clean gauze. Those same vulnerable eyes watch every meticulous movement in a daze as if she's waiting to snap out of a dream. Unfortunately, this is life. *My* life. And she just got thrown into the middle of it. The remorse that accompanies this fact is crippling.

Once I'm finished, I move to sit next to her on the couch once again, pulling her back onto my lap and cradling her injured hand, rubbing my thumb along the fresh bandage.

"I'm so sorry, Ace."

Peeking up at me and looking confused, she whispers, "Why?"

"That I didn't protect you. That you were dragged into this. That I asked you to give me information. Everything." Part of me wants to add that I would take it all back if I could, but I'm too selfish. She'd call me out for lying, anyway.

"This,"––she motions to her face––"had nothing to do with you. It was my fault because I was stupid enough to cross Burlone. And if I had never met you, I would've had no one to turn to when I needed them most. I would've been on my own, and it gets pretty lonely not being able to rely on anyone."

Wrapping my arm around her, I lean in and gently press my lips to hers.

"Yeah. It does. But you don't have to feel that way anymore, Ace."

With her eyes still closed from our kiss, she murmurs, "What are you saying?"

"I'm saying I want you. And I promise that I'm going to take care of this."

"You don't have to—"

"It's already done." Again, I brush my mouth against hers when the sound of footsteps distracts me.

"Boss?" D calls from down the hallway.

I answer as he rounds the corner. "Yeah?"

Stepping into the room with his hands at his sides, he looks at Ace who's huddled against me with her palms cradled in her lap.

"Can we talk for a second?" *In private.* He doesn't say the last part, but that doesn't mean I can't hear his message loud and clear.

As gently as I can, and without jostling Ace too much, I slide out from between her and the couch, making sure she's comfortable before I stand to my full height.

"Hey, Ace. I need to go have a chat with D. You gonna be okay here?"

"Yeah. Of course." Lying back, she rests her head against the armrest. "Are you okay if I stay? I mean…I can go if you need me to."

Did she not hear a single word I just said?

I brush away a stray hair that lays against her forehead and press a kiss to her temple. "Stay."

"You sure?"

"I already told you that you're mine now, so don't bother leaving, or I'll just come find you. I'll check on you in a few."

With a nod, she gingerly rolls onto her side and closes her eyes, sighing softly. My chest can finally expand to its full capacity when I see the peace written on her face. Yet, there's a slight pinch too, and I pray to whatever gods might be watching over us that I don't squander the trust she feels in my home. The trust that appears to be keeping her nightmares at bay for her to get some much-needed sleep.

D's subtle attempt to grab my attention by clearing his throat is heard loud and clear, making me pull my gaze from an already unconscious Ace. Turning, I wipe my palms against my slacks and head to my office with D following behind. Once inside, Diece tosses a shirt at me, nearly hitting me in the face with it. Under normal circumstances, I'm sure he'd be giving me shit for walking around with my shirt off all night but now isn't the time.

"Any update on Regina?"

His gaze darkens. "Yeah, that's what I wanted to talk to you about. We think Burlone might have her."

Fuck. How did I not know? If D is right, then we're in for a shitstorm. First, Reggie missing, then Ace's face being busted in, and now he has my sister? If this isn't a call for war, I don't know what is. Clenching my fists at my sides, I weigh my options and know I don't have many. The Romano family is strong. We can handle anything. But there's already turmoil from Vince's betrayal, and I don't want to rock the boat any more than I already have with the transition of power.

"What evidence do we have to prove this?"

It needs to be concrete if his men are going to pay for it with their blood.

D collapses into the chair across from my desk. "Lou hacked his email and found a picture of her."

"How the hell did he get a picture of her?" I growl low in my throat. My blood is boiling. That isn't possible. Regina's identity has been on total lockdown since my mother was murdered. Only a few select individuals in the Romano family would be able to recognize her in a lineup, and I trust each and every one of them with my own life.

"Remember Dominic?"

I pause, searching my memories for the specific Dominic that D's suggesting.

"That asshole my dad was trying to work with?"

"Yeah." With gritted teeth, he expands. "From what we can gather, your dad offered Regina as a consolation prize before coming to his fucking senses."

I shake my head. "That's not possible. My dad wouldn't work with Dominic."

"Your dad wasn't all there in the end, King, and we both know it. Regardless, he sent a picture to Dominic, who then forwarded it to Burlone a few nights ago."

Squeezing the back of my neck, I voice my confusion. "Why would he do that? Regina has basically lived her entire life in a prison to keep our enemies from recognizing her."

He lifts his shoulders. "My guess? Dominic's a superficial asshat who wanted to see his potential bride before he agreed to anything. Then your dad came to his senses after he sent the photo and backed out of the deal. Remember how paranoid he was about her in the end? Didn't even want to let her leave her room, for Christ's sake."

With a groan, I drop my head back and look to the ceiling. "Fuucckk..." I drag out the word, recalling how insane my dad went right before he died. The medication was rotting his brain until he was almost unbearable to be around. "Yeah. I remember. So Burlone has her photo. At the very least, we can assume he's looking for her. At the most, he's already found her."

"Yeah. That pretty much sums it up. I think it's time you give Burlone a call, King. See what he has to say."

Pacing the office, I consider my options only to find I don't have many.

His suggestion is...unconventional, to say the least. There are unwritten rules in our line of business, and one of them is keeping our noses out of other people's shit. We don't call each other up to chat. We don't call each other up for favors. And we sure as hell don't call each other up when someone goes missing.

Calculating, I weigh the pros and cons before voicing them to D. "If I call Burlone, and he doesn't have her, it'll become an all-out race to find my little sister."

"Yeah, but if he *does* have her, you might be able to find something he wants. To figure out how we can get her back," he counters.

And I need to get her back.

I'm her big brother. I'm supposed to protect her, and I've already failed her once. I won't let her down again.

Shifting my gaze between D and the phone sitting ominously on my desk, my nostrils flare. "Then it looks like I have a call to make."

41

KINGSTON

After Lou got me Burlone's contact information, I sat in my chair for a solid five minutes, staring into the empty space of my office like it just might hold the answers I'm looking for.

Unfortunately, Regina didn't appear from thin air, no matter how hard I wished she would. My entire body is vibrating with tension that I'm anxious to release as soon as I know who to project it on, though I think we might already know.

Steeling my shoulders, I dial Burlone's number and wait for him to pick up. I put the call on speakerphone as D, Lou, and Stefan are all sporadically positioned in the office, listening in on the conversation to stay up to date. I'm grateful for their presence because, whether I want to admit it or not, I need them right now.

A soft click cuts off the foreboding ringing on the line, only to be replaced with Burlone's voice.

"I was wondering when you'd call. To be honest, Kingston, I'm a little disappointed. It's been nearly four hours. Four hours where your baby sister could've had *anything* happen to her." He tsks, and the sound grates on my nerves, making my knuckles turn white as I grip the pen on my desk, strangling it while simultaneously wishing it was Burlone's sausage neck.

I've always hated the guy, but I've never loathed anyone with every fiber of my being until this moment.

"I mean, what would your father think?" he pushes.

"My father's dead, so he isn't your concern anymore. Now you get to deal with me. I appreciate the condolences, though. *Very* thoughtful." My voice is confident, lackadaisical. Exactly what I need it to be, no matter how hard it kills me to talk about my deceased father with so much forced ease.

In response, Burlone laughs deep and hard. D's jaw clenches.

"Aw, Kingston. I've missed these conversations. We should have them more often."

"Sure, we should. Unfortunately, I'm a little busy at the moment but would appreciate if you could help me out by returning my sister."

Again, that deep laugh. "I'd love to, Kingston. Really, I would. But you see, I'm a big fan of games. There's just something about the competition and the strategy that brings out the worst in people. And you see, if I hand over your gorgeous little sister, then where will that leave me?"

With gritted teeth, I offer, "With more time and a few less gray hairs?"

And maybe even alive, I add to myself, forcing a slow breath between said gritted teeth.

"I never pegged you for a funny man, Kingston. Are you saying your sister is a bit of a handful? Because I'd have to agree with you. She's given my men quite the treatment since she's been in our custody. Don't worry, though, we've dealt with many…," he pauses in search of the right word. "Sei, what's the right word?" he calls to someone on the other end of the line. "Undisciplined? Naughty? Stubborn? Feisty? Yes, I like that one. We've dealt with our fair share of *feistiness*. But we've long since understood how to transform those behaviors to more favorable ones. Isn't that right, Regina?"

Hearing him address my sister makes my heart stop and my breathing stilted while the rest of my men lean closer, being pulled into the conversation even further. Unfortunately, our straining ears can't hear whether or not she responds.

I need to get her out of there. The question is…how?

"So, my sister's there with you?" I prod, distracting him from any further contact with Regina.

"Obviously. My associate had a grand old time this evening as he picked her up, along with a handful of other girls to keep her company. That is, until we find them more suitable homes…for the right price."

My stomach bottoms out at the prospect. *No. Not her.*

Narrowing my gaze, I probe, "So, that's your plan then? To sell my sister?"

He tsks. "Kingston, Kingston, Kingston. I don't sell women. I sell fruit, and your sister's as sweet as they come."

The promise in his voice makes my skin crawl, finally pushing me over the edge.

"Don't fuck with her, Burlone. I swear to God, it'll be the last thing you do."

"Maybe you should've thought about that before you fucked with me first, Kingston. I had a plan that was supposed to come to fruition last night, but someone intervened, and one of my men disappeared. You wouldn't happen to know anything about that, would you?"

Marty.

My gaze shifts to D then glides over to Stefan and Lou, but I keep my mouth shut.

"I'm sure you recall him," Burlone continues. "But let's stay on topic, shall we? We were talking about your pretty little sister with her pretty little face, her pretty little body, and her pretty little virginity. Am I right, King? Is that precious little hymen still intact? Dominic said that was your dad's favorite selling feature for her. *She's a virgin! Don't you want a virgin?*" he mimics my dad's voice. "I can tell you from personal experience, Kingston, a virgin can go for a pretty penny."

I bite my tongue, tasting the tangy metallic flavor of blood to keep from yelling at him.

"You asking for money, Burlone?" I'm done dancing around with this shit.

A loud, obnoxious scoff greets me. "I always want money. But, no. That's not what I'm asking from you. All I'm asking is for you to play a little game with me."

My suspicion spikes, but I press forward with my gaze zeroed in on that damn pen being squeezed to death in the palm of my hand.

"And what kind of game is that?"

"As I'm sure you know, I played a little tournament last night with your girlfriend. Low blow, by the way. Sending her to take my money? Not what I was expecting, but I've got to give you credit for your balls. With how much you say you respect women, putting her in such a risky position was bold. Stupid, but bold. Has she told you yet that I had one of my men say hello? She really is a pretty thing—"

The last thread of patience is severed the moment he brings up Ace. I'm seconds from cracking a molar and can't take his voice for much longer. "You're awfully talkative tonight, Burlone, but maybe we could get to the point."

"See? This is why I like you. Your father never would've spoken to me like that. But you? Your generation? You don't care about disrespect, and I find it...*refreshing*. Yet, you must understand why I feel the need to put you in your place."

"I'm sure you do. Is my sister there? I'd love to talk to her."

A strange echo bleeds into the speaker seconds later, and my brows furrow in confusion.

"Sorry about that, Kingston. I had to put you on speaker. I've got a handful of ladies in my office now, but your sister is definitely included. Ladies, can you say hello for me?"

A chorus of sobbing ensues, followed by my sister's expletives that bring a soft smile to my face, along with the rest of the guys in my office.

The strange echo is cut off seconds later, bringing me back to a more private conversation between Burlone and me.

"See what I was saying about that feistiness? It's just so...*refreshing*. Both of you are exactly that. Now, back to what I was saying. Your girlfriend beat me in the tournament last night, and my ego's a little wounded, so I was thinking... what if I throw another one? Only this time, I'll invite my associates who also deal in fruit, and we'll have a unique buy-in. You might be too young to remember, but in the good old days, I used to throw these things quite often. What do you think?"

As a child, I remember my dad mentioning Burlone's tournaments. They were vile. Despicable. Depraved. They were something my father wouldn't touch with a ten-foot pole, and I don't plan on changing that any time soon. Pinching the bridge of my nose, I try to pull myself from the past and focus on the conversation at hand.

"I don't play poker, Burlone."

Recognizing a soft creak from the call, it makes me assume that Burlone just took a seat in his chair, his weight testing the strength of the furniture.

"But you should," he argues. "It's all about reading people.

And you're good at that, aren't you? I've been told it's one of your most unique assets, and I'd love to see it firsthand. Anyway, play if you want. Or don't. But if you want to get your sister back, then you'll want to come. Meet the gang. Have a beer. Consider this my grand invitation. However, like I mentioned before, there's one minor catch."

I'd give anything to rip the office phone off my desk and throw it against the wall to end this conversation, but I can't. Not if I want to save my sister. I feel like I'm in the middle of a bullfight but wasn't given a sword or red flag to defend myself. And now, the damn psychotic bull is racing toward me full speed ahead, and I'm helpless to fight him off.

"And what's the catch?" I voice, mimicking my casualness from earlier when my blood is boiling.

"I'm afraid you'll need the proper buy-in."

The tension spikes, followed by a sense of foreboding that's so thick, I'm afraid I'll be suffocated by it.

Shifting my gaze to D, I ask, "And what's that?"

I'm afraid I already know.

"Your little girlfriend." The smile on his face is clear in his voice. And I want to slit his throat for it.

"Cut the shit, Burlone," I spit, my wavering patience from earlier obsolete. "I don't mess with women. I leave that enterprise to you, remember?"

"Yes, just like your lack of interest in gambling. But I'm afraid this tournament will be your *only* opportunity to see Regina before she's out of my hands––and into someone else's. So, for her sake, I think you'd be wise to reconsider."

You'd think my father's office was an exhibit at the Met with how silent everyone is. Hell, my men are practically made from marble as they digest Burlone's terms, feeling as squeamish as I do.

"If you touch one fucking hair on her head—"

"Two weeks, Kingston. I'll try to remind the men to keep

their hands to themselves but…you know how they are. Boys will be boys, am I right?"

Seconds later, the call ends with a soft click that sounds louder than a damn blow horn.

Two weeks.

42

KINGSTON

My dark voice fills the silent office. "Ace doesn't leave the premises 'til I decide what to do with her."

"You really gonna do this?" D asks.

Shifting my scrutiny to him, I narrow my gaze. "Any other suggestions? 'Cause it didn't really sound like I had much of a choice."

Lou pipes up, "Well if we know where it'll be located, we can just go in guns a blazing and get her out."

I shake my head, my shoulders sagging from the weight of the situation.

"Burlone crossed a line by taking Regina, and we could probably find a relatively good backing if shit hit the fan, but to intentionally pick a fight with half the mafia when we're on neutral territory would be a suicide mission."

"What do you mean, neutral territory?" D interjects.

Searching my memory, I try to explain. "My dad used to tell me about Burlone's tournaments. The underground ones. There's a pact in place as soon as you enter the location where the tournament is being held. All weapons are left at the door, and if a single hair is hurt on anyone's head, it's a death sentence for the perpetrator's entire family. They will wipe us out like the plague if we go in guns blazing."

D adds, "And even if we do slaughter every asshat who attends the tournament, their men will find out who was involved, and we'll be screwed."

"Exactly."

Resting my elbows on the desk, I lay my head in my hands and search for a solution. Anything that could bring back Regina, not piss off the entire mob and half the cartels, and keep Ace out of this screwed up situation.

D interrupts my brainstorming with a defeated sigh, reading my mind.

"What are you gonna do about Ace?"

I glance over at him. "I haven't decided yet."

"You can't put her in that situation," he argues. "She's innocent in all of this, and Burlone is just wanting to fuck with her head the same way she messed with his. Using her as a pawn? There's got to be another way."

With a slam of my hand against my desk, I give him a cold, hard stare. "You think I don't know that, D? You think I *want* to sacrifice her for my sister? Sacrifice them both? I don't play poker, and Burlone is undefeated with the exception of last night. I know I can't risk Ace, but I can't let my sister be used, either." D has the decency to look contrite as I let the words rush out of me. "Not only is she my flesh and blood, but as soon as the other families find out she was taken from me and traded like fucking cattle, I'll be seen as laughing stock, and our enemies will try to wipe us out. All of our lives are on the line. Not just Regina's. Not just Ace's. *All of us* if we can't put Burlone and his men in their place. We just need to figure out how."

"Isn't that the million-dollar question," D mumbles under

his breath, leaning against the wall and staring into the distance.

I feel like a juggler right now with so many balls tossed into the air that it feels inevitable one or more will fall to the ground. But I can't let that happen. I won't. I just need to figure out a plan of action and set it into motion. If I can just—

"I'll do it," a feminine voice murmurs from the doorway. All heads snap to attention at the foreign sound in a room full of men. When I see her tiny body framed in the doorway, I bristle.

"Ace?"

She steps into the light with her freshly bandaged hand hanging at her side. The sight of her bruised complexion is enough to remind me of the severity of the situation and to cut her some slack for eavesdropping. If it were anyone else, they'd be reminded of their place, but she's as much a part of this as my sister.

Clearing her throat, she pushes her shoulders back and rushes out, "I'll do it. That bastard took my mom, beat the shit out of me, and apparently stole your sister too. He needs to be put in his place."

"Ace." Her swollen eyes hold my own, as I tell her, "This is family business. Go back to the couch. We'll talk in a minute."

With a shake of her head, a very determined Ace crosses her arms and goes head to head with me. "No. It might be family business, but this involves me too. I have a right to be here and talk about it." Patience gone, I grit my teeth even though her feistiness is sexy as hell.

"Careful, Ace. You forget who you're talking to."

"I haven't forgotten, but I won't be pushed around. Not even by you."

"Lou," I bark, ignoring her pathetic argument. "Take Ace to the guest room across from mine. I'll deal with her later."

"Excuse me?" she says in disbelief as Lou approaches her. Taking a step back, she glares at him. "Don't you dare touch me."

Lou looks over his shoulder at me, silently asking if I'm being serious.

I am.

After giving him a single nod, I hear Lou mumble under his breath, "Sorry," before reaching to grasp her arm. She shrugs away from him but keeps her attention on me. The anger radiating from her tiny body could burn down an entire city.

"I'm not your prisoner, Kingston."

Lou drops his arm to his side, looking helpless as his gaze bounces between the spitfire a few feet from him and me.

My voice is like ice as I answer, "Right now, you're whatever I need you to be. Go with Lou. Now. I'll come see you later."

"Kingston––"

"Lou, get her out of here."

Nostrils flaring, Ace shakes her head before spitting, "I can walk on my own."

Then she turns on her heel, marching down the hall. Lou trails behind to fulfill my request, whether she wants him to or not, leaving me alone with Diece and Stefan.

"She's pissed," D states the obvious while staring at his cell in the palm of his hand. The bright white glow from the screen bounces off his face, showcasing his bored expression, though I know he's just as invested in the conversation as I am.

"She'll have to get over it. Ace might not know how the mafia runs, but she's about to get a crash course in it––

whether she wants to or not." My tone screams indifference, though my conscience is rearing its ugly head.

I shouldn't have barked at her like that.

"Be careful, King," D cautions. "Her life might've hardened her, but she's still soft."

Stefan interjects, "I'm still reeling that she offered to help in the first place, instead of running in the opposite direction."

"Especially with her history, and the fact that she just got the shit kicked out of her," D adds with a hint of pride.

Pinching the bridge of my nose, I shove aside my guilt and focus on the task at hand. "Doesn't matter. We're going to do what's best for the family, not what Ace thinks will help."

"Then what do you suggest?" Stefan inquires. The expression painted across his face is a mixture of determination, respect, and trust. I know that he'd go to Hell and back for our family. And he might need to. We all might need to.

"We need to get Regina back and make the Allegrettis pay."

"Seems to me, all they did was piss off the wrong family." D slides his phone into his front pocket, giving me his full attention.

"Yeah. And we're going to educate them about what happens when you cross the Romanos."

Even if I have to sacrifice Ace to do it.

43

ACE

Every inch of my body aches, but it doesn't stop my blood from boiling. Pacing the opulent room across from Kingston's like a caged beast, I let my anger take hold.

Asshole. Sonofabitch. Rat bastard. Motherfucker.

I can't believe he sent me away. That he doesn't trust me. That he won't let me talk to him. I only offered to help, and he doesn't even have the decency to let me do that much!

Jaw clenching, I continue marching back and forth along the thick, padded carpet beneath my bare feet when I hear the distinct sound of the door handle twisting.

As soon as Kingston comes into view, I begin my verbal assault.

"You sonofa—"

Kingston raises his hand, and my mouth snaps shut.

I hate the control he has over my body, but I remain silent even though my inner bitch is clawing to get out.

"I need your help," he begins, leaning his shoulder against the doorframe and giving me the space I desperately need.

His comment makes me pause. Tilting my head, I assess

him closer. His short, dark hair is messy as if he's been running his fingers through it. He looks like he hasn't slept at all, and the dark, silk tie that is usually tied to perfection around his neck has been loosened hinting at his anxiety. He's usually so put together that seeing him this way lessens the anger pulsing through me.

With a defeated sigh, I surprise myself when I murmur, "What do you need, King?"

"I need you to teach me how to play poker."

My brows raise, and my eyes widen as I point to my chest. "You want *me* to teach you how to play poker?"

His mouth quirks in amusement before he takes a hesitant step into the room and closer to me, sensing the icy barrier I'd built between us slowly melting.

"Yeah, Ace. I want you to teach me how to play poker. You're the best. And we need the best if we're going to beat Burlone at his own game."

"We? As in the *precious* Romano family?" The bitterness seeps into my voice as I recall how he chose his family over me, even though I'm the one who offered to help in the first place.

Raking his fingers through his hair, he tugs at the roots before scratching the scruff on his chiseled jaw. "It's nothing personal, Ace. It's just the life of a made man. But when I said *we*, I meant you too. Earlier, you offered to put your life on the line to save my sister. You still up for that?"

I don't miss the way he actually asks for my input, even though the minor twitch by his right eye lets me know how much it kills him inside to request something instead of demanding it. Memories of my childhood assault me, quickly followed by the knowledge that his sister is experiencing the same hell I had no choice but to survive. Am I willing to put my life on the line to save his sister? Am I being impulsive by even considering it? I don't know. But I do know that I hate

Burlone. I hate him with every fiber of my being. If I had a gun in my hand and Burlone was in the same room with me, I wouldn't even hesitate to pull the trigger. I'd give anything to erase him and the memories that haunt me.

After a few seconds, I come to a conclusion and take a cautious step toward Kingston. When I'm within reach, his large hands grab my hips and tug me into him until our fronts are plastered together. Closing my eyes, I rest my head against his chest and let his warmth seep into me before murmuring, "Yeah. I'll do whatever it takes to help your sister. But you need to promise me something."

"And what's that?" His chest rumbles against my ear.

"That you never let Burlone touch another person ever again."

"What are you suggesting, Wild Card?"

He knows what I'm suggesting. He's not dense, but a small part of me is aware this is a test. Kingston wants to see if I'm bold enough to request something so despicable.

And I am.

Pulling away from the warmth of his chest, I look up at him, my gaze on fire.

"I want you to kill him."

44

ACE

Waking up in King's bed is nothing short of surreal. Last night, he picked me up, carried me to his bed, and laid me down on his mattress, then dropped a quick kiss to my head, telling me to get some rest and that he'd be back in a little while.

With tired eyes, I look around the expansive room with its gorgeous furniture and open windows. Dark wood. Dark sheets. Dark curtains. It's gorgeous. Just like the man who lives here. Attempting to sit up, I collapse seconds later. My whole body is sore from my encounter with Burlone's guy, but the silky sheets enveloping me are almost enough to compensate for the pain.

I turn on my side to see the other half of the giant bed empty. Reaching over, I feel the sheets to see if they're still warm, but the cool sensation confirms my suspicion. He didn't come to bed last night, and I can't blame him. Not when his sister is in the hands of a monster like Burlone. My gut swirls at the thought as memories of my childhood resurface for what feels like the thousandth time in the last twenty-four hours. Releasing a slow breath, I try again, sitting up and scooting my legs over the side of the bed.

My ribs are throbbing, but King confirmed nothing's broken, saying that whoever beat the hell out of me took it easy.

Still hurts like hell, though.

I roll my eyes at the thought and touch my feet to the floor before making my way down the hall in search of the elusive Kingston.

As I approach his office, I overhear him and D talking about me in muffled voices. Hesitating, I lick my lips then knock on the open door to grab their attention.

Two pairs of eyes dart to me, and their conversation ceases.

"Hi." Awkwardly, I wave my bandaged hand at them.

With a laugh, an amused Kingston motions me to come in. "How'd you sleep?"

My feet pause in their pursuit. Before, I'd been escorted from his office as if I were trespassing, and now I'm being invited inside? I shrug off my confusion and shuffle across the threshold.

"Better than you. Did you come to bed at all?" If the bags under his eyes are anything to go by, I'd say no.

"I needed to finish up some stuff and get a game plan together."

"And what's your game plan?"

D grimaces but doesn't say anything, leaving Kingston to fill me in. His dark green stare pins me in place before he offers a half-assed apology. "Sorry, Ace, but it's family business."

So help me...I thought we'd already discussed this.

Feeling a headache building, I rub my temples and squeeze my eyes shut.

"It's my life on the line here, remember? No offense, but I think I have a right to know what I'm getting into."

I can't believe he'd even consider keeping me in the dark on this. Does he even know me at all? I can't help if I don't know what the plan is.

"You'll know what we need you to, I promise. Which reminds me, you're going to be staying here for a while."

My brows furrow, and my annoyance spikes. "What do you mean *for a while?*"

"For a long while," Kingston clarifies. "I can't keep you safe if you aren't here, Ace."

"Yeah, but if Burlone wanted to do something to me, he would've already done it." I motion to my face. "Exhibit A."

I watch as his Adam's apple bobs up and down in his throat while assessing the damage done to my face. "And it kills me every time I see it."

The remorse is clear in his voice, but it doesn't stop my hackles from rising. I've been taking care of myself for as long as I can remember. Yes, I needed his help the other night, and I'm grateful he was willing to step in and take care of me, but I'm not about to uproot my entire life for him. I can't.

Taking a deep breath, I explain, "Look, nothing's going to happen, and if you're that worried, why don't you just put a guard on me or something like you mentioned in the past? That'll fix the problem, and I'll still be able to do whatever the hell I want. See? Win-win."

With a shake of his head, D interjects, "We tried that. Found his body stashed in a dumpster."

I gasp, covering my mouth as his words register. "What?"

I was so certain I'd been alone that night. That if Kingston hadn't called off my guard, none of this would've happened. I didn't blame him. I just knew something must've come up, and he'd assumed I'd be safe. I clutch my chest; my heart feeling as though it's been splintered at the knowledge that an innocent man is dead. Because of me.

"We *did* have a guard tailing you, Ace. We did, and he failed. I can't let that happen again. I can't risk that. I can't risk *you*."

"So, what are you saying?" I whisper, feeling like my entire life is spinning out of control, and I can't do anything to stop it.

"I'm saying that you'll be staying here for a while," he repeats. His tone brooks no argument, but I can't help myself.

"And I don't get a say in the matter? It might be a shitty apartment, King, but it's still my home."

His jaw appears to be made of stone when he looks me straight in the eye and says, "Not anymore, it's not."

There's a callousness to his comment that burns. It pisses me off, making me feel like what I want doesn't matter. And part of me hates him for it. I'm not going to be owned by someone who doesn't take my feelings into account. In fact, I'm not going to be owned by anyone.

Looking at D, I plead with my eyes for him to step in. To say something––anything––that will change Kingston's mind. I'm not ready for my entire life to be turned upside down any more than it already has.

D shakes his head, then casts his eyes to the ground, sealing my fate.

Asshole.

I turn to Kingston and fold my arms in an attempt to contain my anger.

"Well, do I at least get the chance to grab a few of my things? It's not like I can wear your wardrobe, King."

Lazily, his eyes scan me up and down, taking in his dress shirt he let me borrow last night that reaches my knees.

"King!" I snap my fingers to get his attention.

Looking up at me, he smirks.

"I'm serious. I need to go to my apartment, and I need to talk to one of my friends who will be worried about me if I don't explain where I am." King opens his mouth to argue when I cut him off, my eyes shooting daggers at him as I stare him down. "You can't just lock me up and throw away the key. If you do, then you're not any better than Burlone."

As soon as the insult is thrown, I wish I could take it back. Kingston flinches like my verbal assault is a physical one before turning to D with a blank expression.

"Help her get her shit from her place, but be back within an hour." Turning to me, he adds, "If you try anything, I will find you, and I will bring you back here. I don't care if you're kicking and screaming the entire way. We're done playing by your rules. Now, we're playing by mine."

Then he looks down at the paperwork tossed haphazardly across his desk, officially dismissing us. But the guilt and anger tag along too.

45

ACE

"Didn't think you'd have a bitchy side," D notes as we walk side by side to his car.

Bristling, I ask, "Excuse me?"

With a tilt of his chin toward the house, he responds, "That back there? Kinda bitchy." Somehow, he finds a way to sound amused yet disappointed at the same time. And I might've detected a hint of pride too, but maybe that's wishful thinking on my part.

When we get to his black sedan, he opens the passenger side, letting me slide in. Before he can close the door, I defend myself. "I wasn't being bitchy. I was being honest. He doesn't own me, D."

He doesn't. I'll never be owned or controlled by anyone again. I refuse to. Even when it hurts someone I'm really starting to care about. Someone who dropped everything to take care of me. Who let me sleep in his bed last night. Who wants to keep me safe.

Dammit, I'm kind of a bitch for snapping at him.

With a look of pity, he shakes his head. "Trust me, Ace. He knows that, I know that, and you know that. If anything, I'd say it's the other way around." He closes the door before I have a chance to reply then walks around to his side and gets behind the wheel.

Exasperated, I continue the conversation he's clearly trying to end. "Then why would he try to use his authority on me like that? He can't just order me around. It hits too close to home and how I was raised. I won't step into another relationship like that. I can't."

He starts the car then backs out of the driveway and pulls onto the main street while I anxiously wait for his response.

"You're not the only one that was affected by their upbringing, Ace. His mom was murdered when he was a little kid. Collateral damage for a deal gone wrong. After that, his dad locked Regina up, never letting her out of the estate because he was so terrified something would happen to her too. Then he died, and King took over the role as the head of the family. The first thing he did was give Regina some space. He wanted to give her the freedom she was craving and look what happened. She's been taken too. You can't blame him for being scared to let you out of his sight." He glances over at me and scans my face before turning his eyes back to the road. "Especially when you look like *that*."

Raising my hand, I gingerly touch the inflamed skin, flinching when I put too much pressure on my cheekbone.

"See what I mean? It doesn't feel good to have your face beaten to a pulp, and it doesn't feel good to look at it and know it's your fault, either."

"It's not his fault," I argue. "If anything, it's mine. I shouldn't have entered that tournament."

With a sigh, he gives me the side-eye. "No. You shouldn't have. Kingston warned you it was a bad idea, but don't beat yourself up about it. We can't change the past."

"You're right. We can't. How did Burlone find out King and I were a thing, though? I thought we'd been careful." I voice the question out loud as I stare blankly through the passenger window. Then it hits me. Before the tournament, Jack confronted me about my relationship in the middle of Sin, Burlone's casino. Jack blew Rule #8 into tiny little pieces. Don't discuss private shit in public. It's bound to screw you over. And it did.

Diece's gruff voice brings me back to the present. "I don't know how he found out, but it doesn't really matter now. What matters is keeping you safe. That's all Kingston is trying to do. Can you cut him a little slack?"

Digging my teeth into my lower lip, I watch as the trees whirl by in a blur. I don't think D understands what that slack would mean for me, but I try to look at it from Kingston's perspective.

Hearing about Kingston's mom breaks my heart. I can't even imagine the guilt that would accompany his sister's disappearance with a history like his. And D might have a point about Kingston feeling guilty for Burlone's little goon's visit with me too. I know it isn't his fault. But I also know that Kingston doesn't excuse situations like that without taking responsibility for every minor detail, regardless of his part in it. He knew the risks as much as I did, and we both underestimated our enemy. If Kingston was hurt and there was a possibility that my actions played a factor in his pain, you better damn well believe I'd be beating myself up for it. And I can only imagine he's doing the same for me.

After a few moments, I whisper, "Yeah. I can try to cut him some slack."

"Thank you."

My eyes widen in surprise as the sentiment leaves his lips. I'm slowly learning how hard please and thank you's are you to come by with these two men.

After soaking it up for a few seconds, I murmur,

"Speaking of thanks...I want to thank you, again, for coming to my rescue last night."

Maybe I'm imagining things, but I swear I can see his olive skin turn a shade redder under his stubbled cheeks. "Don't mention it."

We pull up to the side of the building near the decrepit parking lot of my apartment building, and D puts the car in park.

As I grab the door handle, I say, "I'll be out in ten."

"Nope. No deal. I'm coming in."

I roll my eyes before giving D a pointed stare. "Seriously? It's not like the bad guy is still hiding in the shadows. It'd be highly unoriginal if he tried the same thing twice."

His mouth quirking at my terrible joke, D opens the driver's side door and explains, "Consider me your very own shadow any time you're out of the estate. Wherever you go, I go. You argue? I tie you in your room. Capiche?"

"You mean King's room?"

"Yeah. Hell, I could kill two birds with one stone and say it's his birthday present."

Snorting, I open the door and toss over my shoulder, "Whatever."

~

PACKING IS FAST. I DON'T OWN MUCH, AND I'M A LITTLE surprised how few things I really need. Within ten minutes, I have a small duffle bag thrown over my shoulder as we make our way back to the car.

When I start walking across the parking lot in the opposite direction of D's sedan, he calls out, "Where are you going?"

"I need to talk to someone real fast."

Within seconds, he's already caught up and matches his pace with my own, striding up next to me. "And who's that?"

"My friend," I offer. *Or one of them, anyway.* I still need to figure out how to reach Gigi and tell her what's going on while demanding an explanation from her too.

Looking around the empty parking lot, his brows furrow, but he doesn't comment as I approach the heap of human curled into a ball near the dumpster. I squat down and shake him softly.

"Hey, Eddie."

Eddie startles before his weathered face makes an appearance, peeking up at me. "Hey, Ace. Where you been? I was worried 'bout you. Stayed up all night waitin', but ya never came home. I'm sure sorry I dozed off. I just couldn't keep my eyes open for a second longer."

The remorse in his voice makes me smile.

"It's fine, Eddie. You need your rest. I just wanted to tell you that I'm going to go away for a little while, okay?"

Eddie glances around me, noticing the giant bear a few feet away with his arms crossed over his chest.

"Who's that?" Eddie asks, suspiciously. "And what happened to yer face?"

He might be a crazy old man, but I kind of love the protective part of him that insists on looking out for me. Resting my hand against his hunched shoulder, I try to calm him down before he tries to go all Rambo on a man twice his size.

"That's my friend. His name is Diece. Don't worry, Eddie; he's a good guy."

"He looks familiar. Have I seen ya 'round here?" he calls to D.

D takes a step closer to keep Eddie from shouting, then answers, "I don't think so."

With squinty eyes, Eddie continues his assessment. "Nah,

I think I've seen you around. Wasn't you here the other day lookin' for Ace?"

"No." D's gaze bounces between Eddie and me as he voices his response with a sudden bite I'm not used to.

"I coulda sworn—"

"It wasn't me. But if you see him lurking around again, give me a call." D hands him a business card and a few quarters before turning toward his car and calling, "Come on, Ace. We gotta go."

I watch his back as he retreats before waving at Eddie. "He's right. I'd better get going. I'll see you later, okay?"

"Sure thing, Ace. Sure thing."

J ogging to catch up to Diece's massive strides, I'm almost out of breath by the time I reach him.

His demeanor is ice cold as he opens the passenger door and directs me inside. Once both our seat belts are buckled and we're on the road, I turn to face him while paying attention to every minor movement.

"Who was lurking around my apartment?"

"I don't know," he grits out, the lie clear on his tongue.

"Lie," I call him out, even though he's not privy to Kingston's and my game.

Quirking a brow, he glares at me before returning his attention to the road.

"Excuse me?"

"I said, that's a lie," I reply simply. "You *do* know, and now, it's time for you to divulge the truth."

I watch as his forearms bulge with pent-up frustration, his knuckles turning white as they grip the steering wheel with both hands on ten and two like a good little driver.

"Talk, D," I push.

With flared nostrils, he distracts me by asking a question of his own. "Did the guy who hurt you have any tattoos?"

I take a second to think about the question, feeling a little whiplashed from the topic change but feeling generous enough to let him get away with it. "Um, yeah. A giant X on the inside of his forearm. Why?"

The words are barely out of my mouth before D slams his hand against the steering wheel and yells, "Fuck!"

I wince, confused by his response. "I take it you're familiar with him?"

"Something like that," he mumbles under his breath.

The silence in the car is deafening as I tilt my head and study a man I barely know, yet somehow trust. And that's when I finally piece together the conversation with Eddie and D's unusual reaction. Same eyes. Same mouth. Same strong jaw.

Holy crap.

"Eddie's right," I murmur. "You *do* look like him."

Again, D glances toward me then back to the road but doesn't say a word.

"So, who is he?" I press.

"He's no one."

"Lie. Tell me the truth, D."

The silence that follows is more telling than anything he could say, but I don't let him off the hook by changing the subject. Instead, I continue to stare a hole in the side of his head, channeling my inner Kingston in an attempt to turn up the heat and make him crack under the pressure. I'm sick of always being kept in the dark. It isn't fair they get to weed out all my secrets, and I'm left trying to piece things together on my own.

After a few seconds, I watch his Adam's apple bob up and down as he swallows thickly. "He's my brother."

My mind reels as I try to make sense of the screwed up truth. "How is that even possible?"

Like for real. How the hell is that possible? I thought family lineage was kind of a big deal in the mafia. Maybe I'm crazy, but I could've sworn that brothers couldn't be on opposite teams. I almost snort as the thought crosses my mind because let's be honest, it's not like they're playing kickball during recess. Well, unless it involves drugs, racketeering, smuggling, and more. Still…Diece having a brother? And said brother beating the crap out of me last night? What the hell? There's got to be a good story there.

"It's a long story," he hedges, looking uncomfortable.

Called it!

"Yeah, I don't give a crap if it's a long story or not. I've got all day, D. Now, spill. How the hell did you each end up working for different families?"

Exasperated, he gives in to my prodding. "Technically, he's my half-brother. My dad and mom got divorced before I barely turned two, then she ran off, and he got stuck with me. He had a habit of visiting…*prostitutes*." He forces the word out as if it leaves a bitter taste in his mouth. "And got one of them pregnant. She ended up owing Burlone a shitton of money, so she gave him her only son then disappeared. Some people suspect that he killed her or sold her through the skin trade, but no one knows for sure."

The car goes quiet as I try to wrap my head around the information he just divulged. Damn, that sounds like a pretty crappy upbringing. I almost feel sorry for the guy.

"Why would Burlone want a kid to take care of?" I probe, confused.

He shrugs but gives me the best answer he can. "Rumor has it that he can't have kids and was wanting an heir. He took two boys in within a few months of each other, and they've been fighting for his attention ever since."

"But how do you know he's your brother? Other than the uncanny resemblance?"

"Because my dad found out before Dex's mom disappeared. She came to the Romano estate begging for money, but he sent her away. In the passenger seat, he saw Dex, did the math, saw the resemblance, and the rest is history. He even approached Burlone a year or two later asking for his son back, but Burlone refused." The sadness in his voice is potent, making my heart hurt for him and the brother he never knew.

"You have a brother," I mumble before reaching over and squeezing his forearm in an attempt to be supportive.

Looking over at me, he confirms, "Yeah. I have a brother."

"Does he know about you? About his past?"

With a shake of his head, a somber Diece goes quiet. Patiently, I wait for him to gather himself as we turn down Kingston's street.

"Honestly? I have no idea. Part of me wishes he knew so that we could meet. I could take him under my wing. I could teach him everything I know. The other part knows how much it would kill him to know his mom gave him up to pay off her debt and that his dad turned him away without knowing the repercussions. That's pretty fucked up, ya know?"

I nod, taking a second to step into his shoes and feel his pain, which only makes my cheek and nose throb. Looking in the side mirror, I assess the damage and grimace. My entire face is purple and blue.

"Does he usually hit women?"

Slowly, D looks over at me, taking in my busted lip, swollen nose, and raccoon eyes, just like I had. His gaze shines with pity as he softly shakes his head. "I don't think so. Last I checked, he would collect Burlone's debts and rough up a few people on occasion, but he didn't hurt innocent women."

I don't know why, but D's answer seems to relieve the tension in my chest. Maybe there's hope for him after all.

"Do you think he knows that Burlone's into human trafficking?"

Gritting his teeth, he admits, "It'd be impossible for him to *not* know. It's Burlone's entire business. He leaves the drugs and guns to other families. But women? Those are all him."

I can excuse a lot of things, but knowingly being part of something as sinister as human trafficking is inexcusable. Diece must have all the redeeming qualities in the family because his brother seems to have misplaced his humanity.

"Then you're better off without him." I turn back in my seat as we pull into the driveway.

D leans his head back against the headrest and lets out a soft sigh.

"Yeah…but is he better off without me?"

47

ACE

I raise my hand and tap my knuckles against King's open office door. His head is down, and his eyebrows are pulled low as if he's concentrating really hard. As soon as he hears my soft knock, his head snaps up, and his gaze connects with mine.

"Hey." My voice is rusty from lack of use.

"Hey," he replies just as softly.

"Can I come in?"

He nods.

Stepping inside, I head to the opposite side of his desk and sit on the very edge of the chair in an attempt to get as close to Kingston as I can while not knowing how close he *wants* me to be.

Warily, he watches me, making my heart break.

"I'm sorry," I start. "I'm so sorry I said those things. It wasn't okay to compare you to Burlone, and it was a hit below the belt. You're nothing like him, Kingston. I know you just want me to be safe, and you're feeling spooked right now. I was a brat, and I don't know how to make it better."

My apology hangs in the air for a few brief seconds

before he stands and walks around his desk. With him at his full height, and me sitting with my back ramrod straight, I feel smaller than an ant.

Peeking up at him, I wait for him to decide whether or not he'll accept my apology, praying that he does. Whatever is going on between us isn't just surface-level crap. I care about him––a lot. And I can't believe I was so callous to screw it up.

"Truth," he murmurs. "I'm sorry I didn't give you a choice. I'll try to take your past into consideration and talk things through with you instead of giving you orders as if you're one of my men. Okay?"

A soft smile tugs at my lips as I watch an unbendable man bend. For me.

"Truth."

As I push myself up from my chair, he reaches for my waist and drags me closer until I'm standing between his legs while he leans against the desk. With my hands resting on his broad chest, I soak up his innocent touch when he smiles. It's soft but real, reminding me of a ray of sunshine peeking through the clouds after a storm. I return it with one of my own, trying to hide my awe that the man in front of me could give me a smile like *that*. One that holds an edge of promise to it that makes my heart beat a little faster. The warmth in his eyes is a balm to my soul, which is both terrifying and exhilarating. And it scares me with how much I'm starting to rely on it. His warmth. His touch. His heart. I slowly rub my hands along his pecs and up to his shoulders. *His soul.* I need all of him, and I pray that I'm not the only one getting lost in this relationship.

Lacing his fingers through my messy waves, he accepts my apology with a panty-melting kiss that makes my knees weak. The realization that I *really* like this man is staggering but glaringly accurate as I open my mouth to him and show him how sorry I really am.

The thought of losing him brings tears to my eyes, but I push them away and slip my tongue into his mouth. I'm being dramatic. We weren't even really in a fight or anything. Hell, I can barely call it a disagreement, but the situation still brought feelings to the surface I hadn't addressed before. Ones that made me question what I'd do if he didn't care. If he didn't want me around. If he didn't show a gentleness around me that he usually reserves for...no one.

After he pulls away from our kiss, he drags his hands down to my waist and laces his fingers at the small of my back to keep me close. I'm grateful when he changes the subject and brings a lightness to our conversation that lets me hide from the ins and outs of our relationship a little longer.

"How was getting your stuff?" he asks.

"It was okay. D told me something, though."

He quirks his brow. "And what's that?"

"That he has a brother. Or a...half-brother, I guess?"

I still can't fully understand what that means.

"Wow." The surprise is clear on Kingston's face as he takes a second to digest the information.

I laugh softly. "Wow? What's that supposed to mean?"

"I'm just surprised he told you that. Only a small handful of people know about D's little brother. And by small, I mean *small*. He must like you."

Looking back on our conversation in the car, I feel a sense of peace and camaraderie that is rare in friendships. One I plan on cultivating with Diece if he'll let me.

"I hope so. I really like him too."

"Not too much, I hope," he grumbles.

With a flirtatious smile, I press my luck. "Is someone jealous?"

His bright green eyes turn darker, and a playful Kingston leans forward then bites my neck, sending tingles straight to my toes.

"Maybe," he returns. With our fronts plastered together, Kingston starts planting slow, open-mouthed kisses along my neck and jaw, leading back to my mouth where he slips his tongue between my lips. He tastes so damn good, it's not even funny, and I suck him deeper into my mouth, savoring his unique taste like aged whiskey.

"Mmm," I moan, tilting my head up as he breaks our mouths apart and continues his assault on my body. "I think I like jealous Kingston."

With a soft, deliberate roll of his hips, I can feel his excitement on my stomach, and I hold my breath in response, squeezing my eyes closed and soaking up the elusive moment I was afraid I'd never have again after my screw up from earlier.

"I think he likes you too," Kingston breathes huskily.

Throwing my head back, I let out a breathy laugh before Kingston grabs the back of my head with one hand and kisses me like it's his dying wish. My amusement from seconds ago is replaced with heated lust as I let my instincts take over. The feel of his rough hands tangling in my hair. The sweet taste on my tongue. The powerful muscles pressed against my chest––the need oozing from every pore on Kingston's body.

It makes me feel powerful. Wanted. Needed.

And those damn feelings from before are back with full-force, refusing to be ignored.

With one hand still tangled in my locks and holding me in place, his other hand slides down my back and grabs my ass, squeezing the muscle until I'm sure it'll form bruises in the shape of his fingertips. Bruises that I'll wear like a badge of honor. But the physical contact only leaves me wanting more. And when his fingers graze the apex of my thighs, I gasp on contact.

Pulling away, he looks down at me with a wicked grin. "Do you like that, Wild Card?"

I roll my eyes and tug him closer. "And here I thought you were the smart one. Didn't think I'd need to walk you through this, but—"

He cuts me off with another kiss before pressing his fingers against my core all over again. A little rougher this time. My smartass response disappears into thin air, and a low growl escapes King when he unbuttons the top of my jeans and slips his hand beneath my cotton boyshorts to find me hot and ready.

"Shit, Ace," he murmurs against my mouth.

"Don't stop," I beg, grabbing his wrist and urging him to continue.

With a slow curve of his fingers and a quirk of his lips, he mutters, "Not a chance in hell."

As his calloused finger slips between my slick folds, I squeeze my eyes shut. Then he presses into me. And I'm lost.

In.

Out.

In.

Out.

Each rhythmic tease only spurs on my erratic breathing and makes every nerve in my body feel like a livewire. I squeeze my eyes shut and rest my head on his broad shoulder. His lips brush against my neck before he growls, "Look at me, Wild Card."

I moan and tilt my head to the side, giving him better access to my sensitive skin while ignoring his demand.

His fingers pick up their rhythm as another order leaves his lips. "Now."

Forcing my heavy head up, I hold his dark gaze for barely a second before I fall. Hard.

"Fuuuuck," I breathe. The orgasm rushes through me like a tsunami, hitting everywhere at once and spreading like wildfire along with a flurry of emotions that leave me breathless.

"Good girl," he praises as I slowly come back to earth, though the blissful haze refuses to dissipate. Once the waves of pleasure have subsided, and I'm busy gasping for air, he pulls his hand from my jeans and licks his fingers, his gaze still heated with lust. And maybe something else too, but I can't quite place what the emotion is, though I'm afraid it's shining in my eyes as well.

I watch in fascination, speechless until he puts his freshly cleaned fingers into the belt buckle loops around my waist and jerks me closer, planting a soft last kiss against me.

Whatever this is? It's real, and I think I'm sick of fighting it. He says that I'm his, and I think I'm ready to admit that he's mine too.

"Good talk?" he jests.

With a laugh, I joke, "Yeah. Good talk."

48

ACE

I sleep in a spare bedroom. I don't know why, and it probably has something to do with the fit I threw about needing my own life and space, but Kingston ordered Diece to put my stuff in a room across the hall from his. Maybe it's a good thing. I mean, moving in together when I've barely admitted to myself that I'm okay being owned by him? I'm pretty sure that's the definition of moving too fast.

But it didn't stop me from tossing and turning all night, wishing he was there to hold me and keep my nightmares of Diece's brother at bay.

After showering and getting dressed in a white tank top and shorts, I head to Kingston's office. I haven't been here long, but I've already learned where Kingston spends the majority of his time.

"Hey." I knock against the doorjamb, and he glances up at me before his mouth quirks.

"Hey. How'd you sleep?"

With a shrug, I step over the threshold and take a seat across from him. "Fine, I guess."

"Lie. What's going on?"

"Nothing. I just missed you," I admit, surprising myself with my vulnerability.

The truth brings a smile to his lips before he leans back in his office chair and lifts his chin. "Come here, Ace."

Pushing myself up from my seat, I walk around the desk, and he pulls me into his lap. The scruff from his beard scratches my neck as he nuzzles into me and places a kiss along the column of my throat, making me close my eyes.

"I have some work to get done today," he admits. "We have a lot of shit going on, and I'm trying to keep all of it moving in the right direction while also keeping Regina's disappearance under wraps. But how about I take the night off, and we'll grab a bite to eat?"

I don't miss how he states it like a question instead of an order, and I have to bite my lip to keep from grinning.

"I'd like that. Would you be okay if I go to the diner today?"

Kingston's brows pinch as his hand rubs up and down my back, making my muscles melt under his touch.

"That place you used to always go?"

"Yeah, Dottie's. I have a friend there. A pretty close friend, actually. I wanted to let her know that I won't be coming around for a little while because of everything that's going on. I don't want her to be worried or anything."

Reaching around me, he grabs his phone off the top of his desk and dials a number before waiting for the other person to pick up. When he does, Kingston barks, "D, I need you to take Ace to a diner."

The room is silent as Kingston listens to his right-hand man on the other end before answering, "Yeah, I know. She'll be thirty minutes, tops."

More silence until Kingston looks me up and down as I sit in his lap. "Yeah. Sounds good. She's ready to go."

Hanging up the phone, Kingston lifts his chin. "D will be here in five. You can go with him. He's got shit to do though, so you'll have to be quick."

I smile then wrap my arms around his neck and plant a loud, smacking kiss against him.

"Deal."

"THE FOOD ANY GOOD HERE?" D GRUNTS, EYEING THE PLACE.

"Yup. Their eggs and hashbrowns are amazing, but my friend loves the pancakes, waffles, and French toast too."

With his lips tilted up in amusement, D offers, "So pretty much everything on the menu then."

"Pretty much," I laugh, swinging the door open.

Dottie comes rushing over and throws a big hug around me. "Oh, thank the Lawd!"

My arms hang awkwardly at my sides as she squeezes the crap out of me before putting me at arm's length and assessing the damage to my face that's still an angry purple and blue.

"I was so worried 'bout y'all!" she adds while fretting over me like a mother hen.

I look over at D to see the same confusion painted on his face. Even he can tell this greeting is unusual.

"Everything okay, Dottie?" I ask, sensing her anxiety.

"Haven't y'all seen the news? About all those missin' girls? And then y'all didn't come in for breakfast and...and..." Her lower lip quivers as her eyes gather with tears. "What happened to your face, doll?"

I knew she'd ask questions. Part of me wanted to wait until I'd healed before showing my face here, but I was too anxious to talk to Gigi. Still, the horrified expression painted on Dottie's face makes me feel guilty for causing her any added stress.

With a shake of my head, I clear my throat. "Nothing, Dottie. It's all taken care of. Promise."

She continues fussing over my busted lip, staring at it like it's a third eye before wringing out her hands and taking a small step back.

"Well, alright, then. As long as you and Gigi are sure you're okay."

"Speaking of G, is she here?" I begin searching for her throughout the diner but come up empty as Dottie's breath catches. Her wrinkly old hands cover her open mouth in surprise.

"You haven't seen her?"

"No? You know this is the only place we ever meet. I was hoping I'd see her today."

"Honey, I ain't seen her since she rushed out a few nights ago. I don't know where she is." Her tone is worried and laced with sympathy as her eyes bounce from me to D, then around the diner before landing on my bruised face all over again.

D eavesdrops on our conversation from a few feet away, shifting awkwardly from one foot to the other with his hands in the pockets of his slacks. I look over at him in hopes that he holds all the answers, but his stone-cold expression doesn't give anything away.

Turning back to Dottie, I force a smile, though it feels about as fake as they come. "Okay. Well, I think we'd still like to sit and order and maybe wait to see if she comes by. Is that all right with you?"

"Of course, of course." She waves her hands in the air, motioning to the booths and tables scattered throughout the diner. "Just find a place anywhere. I'll bring your usual."

"Thanks, Dottie. Make it two. I just got done telling Diece

how amazing the food is since his stomach was rumbling the entire way over here."

"I can fix that. I'll bring it over when it's ready." She winks at Diece, making his cheeks turn pink from her innocent flirting before going on her way.

D follows behind me as I lead him to a corner booth then sit down, tucking my backpack beneath the table with one leg on each side of it out of habit.

Rule #7: Never leave something of value out in the open. Even if there isn't much in it nowadays.

"What's with the bag?" D asks with a quirked brow.

"What do you mean?"

"Well, I don't ever see you without it, and you get weird if it leaves your sight."

I grimace at his observation because I always thought I was more subtle when following my rules, but apparently, I was wrong.

Chewing my lower lip, I admit, "It kind of holds my whole world."

Instead of scoffing like I would expect, he casually leans back in his seat and rests his hands behind his head with a smirk.

"Then I guess you'll have to let me take a look inside one of these days."

"Doubtful, my friend. Very doubtful. Speaking of friends, though…" I sober instantly. "Do you have any idea where mine is?"

Bringing up Gigi is enough to put a halt on the innocent teasing from only a moment ago. D scratches the side of his face while staring into the distance like he's debating something with himself. "Tell me about your friend."

I shrug. "What do you want to know?"

"Who is she? Does she have family who would report her missing? Tell me everything you know."

Well, crap. I search through the conversations Gigi and I have had over the last few months and don't find much information that would be useful, but I divulge everything I can.

"Umm…let's see. Her name is Gigi. She has a pretty rich family but hates them. Owns a house in the Hamptons…I think? Or maybe that was a joke? Umm…"

D stares at me, confused.

"What?" I ask, defensively.

"How long have you known her?"

"A few months? We met here at the diner and clicked, but we didn't really talk about our personal lives, which is probably why we got along so well." I laugh. "Our backgrounds are so screwed up that we decided to connect over things like bacon and eggs."

"Sounds like a pretty good friendship," he admits, surprising me with his sincerity.

"It is." I smile. "But I'm sorry I can't give you very many details that would help find her."

Shifting in his seat, he releases a sigh. "I'm afraid that whatever information you could bring to the table might not help anyway. I have an idea of where she could be, but you're not going to like it."

There's something about his apologetic voice that makes me nervous.

"Tell me, D," I push. "I need to know."

"Do the math, Ace. If she was close to you, then I'm going to say it's possible Burlone or his men knew that."

My knee starts to bounce beneath the table, my palms growing sweaty, and my eyes welling with tears. "How possible, D?"

Leaning forward, he puts his hand on mine as it rests on the table.

"Pretty fucking possible."

Burlone wouldn't...would he? Drag an innocent girl into human trafficking all because she knows me? The answer is glaringly obvious and serves its purpose by acting like a dagger to my chest.

He would. And I think he did. The realization is crippling.

I want to cry. I want to hit something. I want to run away. And I want to hurt Burlone all over again. My emotions are all over the place as tears well in my eyes, and I brush them away angrily before grimacing when my cheek throbs in pain.

I hate him. I hate him so much. He needs to pay for so many things. The knowledge that Kingston's sister is enduring terrible things at the hand of Burlone was unbearable. And now there's a possibility of Gigi enduring the same treatment. I need to fix this. How the hell do I fix this? I've never felt so helpless in my entire life as I'm transported back to when I was a little girl, and he would hurt me just for the thrill of it. Stomach rolling, I remember all the things he put me through while recognizing that there's a giant possibility that he's doing the same things to my best friend.

And the only reason she's in this position is because we regularly sat together in a diner and ate breakfast at two in the morning.

I squeeze my eyes shut, another salty tear rolling down my cheek.

"Ace. You okay?"

It's a stupid question. Diece knows that. I know that. But it seems to pull me back from my fucked-up past long enough to help me get hold of my emotions. I release a shaky breath before staring blankly at the empty table in front of me, speechless.

Dottie still hasn't come around with our food, but it doesn't matter, anyway. There's not a chance in hell I could swallow a single bite.

"I'm not so hungry anymore," I admit.

"Then let's get you home, Ace." D opens his wallet and tosses a few twenties onto the table before sliding out of the booth and waiting for me to join him. When I do, we walk side by side back to the car with a Texas-sized stone in the bottom of my gut.

49

KINGSTON

The garage door slams, tugging at my curiosity. I walk down the hall to see my right-hand man following behind a petite blur who just disappeared up the stairs. When D looks at me, I can see the helplessness written across his face. The overwhelming need to follow her drives me to step toward the base of the stairs, but I stop myself and turn to the only man who knows what's wrong.

"What happened?"

With a look of sheer exhaustion, he murmurs, "Her friend is missing."

"And do we know where she is?"

His laughter has a sharp edge to it as he looks toward the ceiling. "We have an idea."

Fuck.

It doesn't take a genius to figure out where her best friend disappeared to. My blood starts to boil. *I'm going to kill him.*

Taking the stairs two at a time, a sense of need pulses through me. I need to fix this. I need to make her feel better. I need to make this right. I need to find my sister and Ace's friend. And I need to put Burlone in the ground.

I stop my pursuit when I reach the door, finding myself in a foreign situation. Do I knock? I raise my hand to do so before dropping it to my side.

With a twist of the handle, I call out, "Ace?"

Sniffles greet me.

The hinges squeak slightly as I push the door the rest of the way open and step into the room across from mine where Ace slept last night.

Sitting on the edge of the bed is a distraught Ace with her head in her hands, her entire body racked with sobs.

My chest tightens, and my lungs struggle to expand as I watch as the girl who's been through too damn much...breaks.

"Ace?" I rush over and wrap my arms around her, holding her tight as she completely loses it.

"She's gone. She's gone. It's all my fault. I can't do this. I can't take it anymore."

The sound of her gut-wrenching cries is like a knife to my chest. I slowly rub my hand up and down her back because I honestly don't know what else to do. She's hurting, and it's killing me. I'd give anything to fix this. I just wish I knew how. Her fingers tighten their grip on my shirt, twisting the material back and forth, wringing out her agony through her hold.

"Shh. It's okay." I try to comfort her the only way I know how, but I can tell it isn't working by the way her back continues heaving as she keeps beating herself up.

"I never should've talked to her. I never should've entered the tournament. I never should've tried to get back at him for what he did. This is all my fault, but she's the one paying for it. All because we were friends."

"It's going to be okay, Ace—"

"You don't understand!" She cuts me off. "I know what she's going through. I know what he's forcing her to do. I know all of it." Another sob escapes her ruby red lips as she looks up at me with tear-stained cheeks before dropping her head back to my chest and burrowing deep. Like I might have the power to save her from her past, and I'd give anything to do exactly that. Still, I need to know the truth. All of it.

"What do you mean, *you know?*"

She doesn't dare look up at me as I voice my question, keeping herself tucked against my chest. Warning bells are ringing in my head, but I don't want to believe them, and I pray I'm wrong.

"Because I got to experience it first-hand as a little girl." Her voice cracks on the last word, my heart following right after.

"Ace—"

She shoves away from me, shaking her head back and forth over and over again in an attempt to scatter the nightmare of memories that were her childhood.

And I want to flay the bastard who hurt her all over again.

"I can't. I can't let that happen to her. I can't let that happen to your sister. I can't do any of this anymore." Collapsing into my arms once more, she rests her forehead on my shoulder as she mourns for the little girl she once was and the experiences she had to suffer through while knowing her best friend and my little sister are likely suffering the same fate at the hands of a monster. One who puts men like me––men who have murdered and maimed––to shame.

I don't know how long we sit like this, and in all honesty, I don't care, either. All that matters is Ace. All that matters is finding a way to let her heal and to keep her safe. All that matters is killing the sonofabitch who hurt her.

When the sobbing has stopped, and the tension in her

body melts away, I whisper, "I'm going to get your friend back, Ace. I'm going to get my sister. And I'm going to kill Burlone for what he did to you."

Ace backs away a few inches and dares to look up at me, her eyes still swollen from crying and from taking a beating a few nights before. But it doesn't make her any less beautiful. In fact, I'm not sure I've ever seen a bluer set of eyes.

With a pitiful squeak, she replies, "Truth."

Gently, I drag her closer and lay down onto my back, the mattress dipping beneath me.

Nuzzling into my side, she breathes a quiet sigh before asking, "Tell me something good, King? Anything."

My fingers lazily drag up and down the exposed skin on her arm as I search for something good to tell her. Something that might make her smile after the horrific day she's had.

Clearing my throat, I whisper, "When I was little, my mom and I would cook together."

She shifts onto her elbow and looks up at me, her long, dark hair cascading over one shoulder, and I'm taken aback at how gorgeous she truly is.

"Really?"

"Yeah. I'd sit on the counter and watch her cook all day until my dad would come get me and teach me manly things." My voice drops an octave, making her laugh.

"And what would you both make?" she asks, intrigued.

"Pasta, of course."

"You Italians. Do you ever eat anything else?" She rolls her eyes.

Patting my stomach for good measure, I tell her, "I definitely do. Do you think I get this physique from carb-loading twenty-four seven?"

"Physique? What physique?" With her chin propped on

my pec, an amused Ace nearly brings me to my knees with her beauty, but I don't let myself get distracted.

"Don't act like you weren't checking me out when I sewed up your hand," I tease.

A coy little grin is firmly in place as she argues, "I don't know what you're talking about. I was a little too busy getting stitched up to be ogling you. But sure, whatever helps your ego."

With my hands under her arms, I drag her up until she's fully on top of me, and we're nearly nose to nose.

"Want to know what else would help my ego?" I shift my hips beneath her to give her a hint.

Her gaze dims slightly as her teeth dig into her lower lip. "You sure you still want me after…?"

After knowing that Burlone used her. Abused her. Took something that didn't belong to him. That he didn't deserve. That she didn't *want* to give him.

The thought brings a bitter taste to my mouth before I remember the girl lying on top of me with so many insecurities she should never have had to carry.

Lacing my fingers through her long hair, I tug her closer and place a gentle kiss against her mouth. Her lashes flutter closed, and she almost melts into me before I stop her.

"Ace, I've never wanted anything more in my entire life."

Opening her eyes, she takes her time deciding whether or not I'm being honest with her. After an eternity, she whispers, "Truth."

s I'm reading a book in the library, the unusual banging of pots and pans being tossed around piques my curiosity. King's been busy working for the past few hours, so I found my respite in the form of a book. However, the clanging coming from the kitchen grabs my attention. I set the worn novel on the side table then walk down the hall.

A giant smile nearly splits my face in two when I see Kingston in a black apron with his back to me and his head in the fridge. The view is pretty damn appetizing, but the curiosity still seems to have gotten the best of me as I get his attention.

"Whatcha doin'?"

Turning around, he gives me a megawatt grin that would melt the panties off a nun. But it's meant for me. Somehow, that only amplifies its effect.

"Hey. Just thought I'd make some dinner."

"You cook?"

"I told you I did. Mama Romano taught me," he explains.

"Well, yeah, but I assumed when you said she taught you,

you meant you watched her cook and stole nibbles here and there."

With a laugh, he shakes his head and corrects me. "If I ever stole a taste without helping, I'd have gotten smacked with the spatula. Never underestimate a Romano chef in the kitchen. Now, get over here and help me."

There's something about the way he bosses me around. Maybe it's his voice that sends tingles down my spine. Maybe it's his quirked brow that begs me to challenge him. Regardless, my body obeys without a second thought. Making my way around the island, I stand with my arms at my sides and wait for my orders.

With a tomato in one hand and some garlic cloves in the other, Kingston wraps me in a warm hug and plants a soft kiss against my temple. "You look amazing today."

"You don't look so bad yourself. I like the apron, by the way. Very manly."

He scrunches up his face teasingly before releasing me from our embrace and tossing the tomato at me.

When I catch it, he explains, "Red is a bitch to get out of white. Gotta cover up, Ace. It's rule number one in the kitchen. Now, grab the cutting board over there and the knife from the knife block. Chop, chop."

He smacks my butt for good measure, leaving me with teeth marks in my lower lip where I bit them in an attempt to keep myself from smiling so damn hard.

I like playful Kingston. I like him a lot.

I'm not sure I've ever seen this side of him before, but I'm pretty sure I'd do anything to keep him around, which is why I ask, "So you have rules, eh?"

After reaching for the cutting board, I put the tomato and garlic on top of it as I wait for his answer.

"Huh?"

"You said. 'rule number one, gotta cover up in the

kitchen.'" I mimic his voice, dropping mine down a few octaves which only makes him laugh.

"Is that what I sound like?"

I shrug before grabbing the knife and getting to work on this tomato, along with the three others he's added to the stack.

"Pretty much but with a bossier tone. You should probably work on that."

"But if I lost my bossy tone, how would I get my men to listen to me?" he counters.

"Good point. You'd probably have to look for a different profession. And let's be honest...,"––I point the knife toward his covered torso––"I don't see you pulling off the apron long-term."

In retaliation, Kingston grabs a dish towel and whips it at my butt, snapping it against my jeans and making me squeal.

"Bullshit," he argues. "We both know I pull off the apron like a master chef."

"Maybe Betty Crocker," I tease with a wink.

He laughs, throwing his head back and giving me a decent view of the long column of his throat along with a nice peek of his chest since the first two buttons on his shirt have been undone after a long day at work.

The normalcy of the moment is almost enough to make me forget the shitstorm we're in. Right now, I can pretend we're an ordinary couple making dinner after a day at the office. The thought makes me pause, and Kingston must notice my lack of contribution to the dish because I find his arms around my waist within seconds.

Resting his chin on my shoulder, he asks, "You okay?"

The sincerity seeping out of him makes me hesitate and search for the truth. I haven't dared to ask myself if I'm okay because I've been too afraid of the answer. As his embrace tightens, I melt into him.

"No. I'm not okay. But I will be as soon as we kill Burlone. I want to thank you for tonight, though. For this." I turn my head to look at him over my shoulder, and he smiles softly as I add, "This normalcy is exactly what I needed."

"Anytime, Wild Card. So, what were you saying about my rules? Were you making fun of me?" He goes to tickle my sides when I stop him.

"No, never! I was just going to tell you that I have my own set of rules too."

His hands drop from my ribs and press into the cool granite on either side of me instead.

"Oh, really? I'm intrigued. Let's hear them."

Setting down the knife, I turn around in his arms until he's caging me against the center island.

"Rule number one: Keep your head down and your eyes up. It makes you invisible but not stupid."

"Truth. What's rule number two?"

"Always be aware of your surroundings."

He grabs the knife still sitting behind me and moves it a couple of feet away before picking me up and setting me on the counter. I grab onto his shoulders to keep myself balanced as a breath of laughter escapes me.

"Number three?" he probes.

"If something feels fishy, it probably is. Trust your instincts."

His gaze drops to my mouth.

"And what are your instincts telling you right now?"

Sliding his hands to my lower back, he drops them to my butt and pulls me closer until I have no choice but to wrap my legs around his waist or drop to the floor.

"Rule number five," I whisper, ignoring his question. "Be a machine. Don't allow distractions. They'll only break you."

"Am I a distraction?"

With a smile, I murmur, "Only the best kind."

He leans closer and nuzzles into my neck. The friction makes me sigh, and I tilt my head up to give him better access.

"Rule number six: Don't get personal," I continue as the buzz from his kiss sends tingles racing down my spine.

"This feels pretty personal to me, Ace."

With my heart pounding in my chest, I chuckle at the ludicrousness of the situation. *Yeah. I'd say this is pretty personal to me too.*

"Any more rules I should know about?" he breathes, the words tickling my sensitive skin.

"Rule number seven: Never leave something of value out in the open."

He picks me up and tosses me over his shoulder. "Good point. Let's take this to the bedroom."

My laughter follows us down the hall until we reach his destination. With a slam of the door, my feet are on the ground, then his hands are on me and roaming every inch of skin on display. Clearly unsatisfied with the lack of accessibility, he grabs the hem of my shirt and tugs it over my head.

"You skipped rule number four," he notes.

"Never say never."

This one makes him pause, his gaze zeroing in on my mouth.

"Truth," he murmurs. My dark hair cascades around my shoulders before his hands are tangling into my locks and holding me in place. With a growl, his tongue dips into my mouth, and a soft moan escapes me from the unexpected intrusion. There's no messing around with Kingston. He takes what he wants. And his kisses prove exactly that. When he's satisfied I won't move, his calloused hands glide down my back before unhooking my bra. Breasts free, he tosses the flimsy black material to the ground at my feet before cupping my breasts and squeezing. My head drops down to see his rough palms touching me so intimately.

Shit, that's hot.

With a wicked grin, he nudges my head with his, and I look up to see his eyes glowing with mirth.

"You like that, Ace?"

"You know I do," I counter, both annoyed and embarrassed at his blunt assessment.

"Let me show you what else you'll like."

His touch skims down my bare stomach before he unbuttons my jeans and grabs my ass, lifting me with ease until I have no choice but to wrap my legs around his taut waist. My arms follow suit as I use his shoulders to balance myself. Eyes narrowing as I assess my bare skin against his clothed torso, I decide he's wearing way too many clothes right now, and I fumble with the buttons on his pristine white dress shirt.

"Anxious, Wild Card?" He smirks when he sees my struggle.

I motion to the damn shirt that refuses to cooperate. "Micromanaging, King?" I return with a scowl. "You try it. These things are stubborn."

His amused lips drop a quick kiss to my nose before he lays me down on the bed, and I'm surprised by his gentleness. As my weight presses into the mattress, he grabs the waistband of my jeans and tugs them off in one quick yank, nearly taking me with them. The action pulls a fit of giggles out of me.

So much for being gentle.

"Careful, King! Or else I'll end up on the floor!"

"Would you land on your knees?" he razzes, quirking his brow in interest.

"Shut up and get your shirt off before I change my mind."

With ease, his fingers triumph in the battle between

buttons and man as he finally starts to take off his shirt. My mouth waters as more and more skin is put on display for my own personal view. Yes, I've seen him without a shirt before, but it never fails to impress me. The muscles of his chest tighten, and his abs flex, showcasing a six-pack that is damn near edible before the white material slides down his thick biceps. My hands itch to reach out and touch them when his voice distracts me.

"Yeah, I don't see that happening," he comments.

"Huh?" I ask, confused but refusing to look away from his hot, tan skin that's on full display.

He laughs. "You changing your mind. I don't see that happening. Not when you're looking at me like that."

If I had any sense of pride, I might prove him wrong, but I'm a helpless mess right now, and I need him. I need him so damn bad it's not even funny. So, instead, I give him a half-assed glare before sitting up and hooking my fingers into the belt loops of his slacks. Then I tug him toward me. He catches himself with his hands as I find myself on my back being caged in by a strong, powerful man who could squash me like a bug if he wanted to.

But instead, he looks down at me as if I'm more valuable than the Mona Lisa. And I kind of love it.

"I'm going to make you mine now, Ace," he murmurs. It isn't a question, and he sure as hell isn't asking permission, yet I know he'd stop if I asked him.

And I kind of love him for that too.

Snaking my arms around his back, I drag my fingers up to his shoulders and pull him down until his weight is sandwiching me between his muscular frame and the mattress. The heat from his skin brands me, making my nipples harden as his chest brushes against mine. But I'm not scared. The realization is staggering, and spurs me on. I comb my fingers through the back of his hair as he bends down for another kiss. And once again, I find myself lost to him. He nibbles on my lower lip before peppering kisses along my throat and chest, slipping my nipple into my mouth and running his tongue along the small bud as his hand massages my other breast.

I open my thighs, cradling his chest and rocking my hips back and forth as my desperation threatens to consume me. I can feel his smile against my heated skin before he lets go of my breast with his mouth and slides lower, continuing his torture until I'm nothing but a bundle of nerves and anticipation.

"King——"

"Shh," he murmurs, dragging his gaze away from my core to focus on my heated cheeks. "Let me taste you."

Again. It isn't a question. It's a demand. One that I'm terrified to give into, yet helpless against it.

He's right. He *does* own me. And he's about to prove it.

His fingers dance along my inner thighs as he appreciates the most intimate piece of me before his tongue darts between his lips. Then he leans closer and breathes me in. My muscles tense, but his hands keep me in place. When his tongue slips between my folds, my jaw drops.

"Shit," I curse, squirming beneath him. I just can't decide if I'm trying to get away from him or pull him closer.

His chuckle vibrates against my core, and loosens the vice around my heart. Or maybe it tightens it. Honestly, I'm not sure. The only thing I can focus on is his touch. His tongue. The way his scruff tickles my inner thighs. The way his hot breath fans against my center. All of it is enough to send me spiraling in an instant. My back arches as he pulls an orgasm from me before climbing back up my body. I can taste myself on his lips when he captures my mouth with his, but it doesn't disgust me. It only spurs me on, lighting another fire to replace the one he'd just let consume me.

"You okay?" he whispers, resting his head against mine.

My chest rises and falls as I catch my breath before giving him a nod.

"Good girl."

Satisfied, Kingston slips his hand between us and lines himself up with me. This is it. The moment I'd been positive would wreck me. But I'm not scared. Not anymore. Because it's King. My King. The head of his cock nudges against my center.

"You ready?" he rasps.

I look up at him and nod.

Then he presses into me. Stretching me. Making me his while erasing every memory from my childhood that convinced me I was ruined. That I was nothing but a chewed up piece of used gum that no one would ever want. Because *King* wants me.

He needs me.

And I need him.

My toes curl and my lips part before he captures my mouth with his and slides his tongue into me, mimicking his movements as he slowly pumps his hips.

Back and forth.

Back and forth.

As the minutes tick by and the anticipation builds, his thrusts get more desperate, and so do I. Because it's too much, and somehow not enough at the same time. Too much lust. Too many feelings. Too many nerves that are threatening to explode. And yet, I want more. I *need* more. I need him. All of him. My fingers scrape along his back and I hook my ankles around his waist.

"Faster," I breathe.

He picks up his pace, and swallows my moan as he hits the perfect spot inside of me. His grunts mirror my gasps.

Then my eyelids slam shut and I finally give in. I let myself fall. For the man. The life. The unknown. All of it.

And in this moment, as he takes a piece of me that I've finally given willingly for the first time in my life, I feel normal. And maybe even a little loved too while my rules take a backseat, and Kingston steals the spotlight, promising me that it's okay to fall.

And that he'll catch me.

KINGSTON

"**A**lright, Mister. It's time we get to work." Ace is in nothing but my dress shirt from earlier. The hem almost reaches her knees, but she's left the top few buttons undone and looks nothing short of exquisite.

We've just finished cleaning up dinner, and I watch in fascination as she heads for her backpack and comes back with a worn deck of cards.

"You ready?" She quirks her brow, shuffling the cards like a pro even though her hand is still lightly bandaged to keep her stitches from getting infected.

I groan but pull out a chair across from her. "Am I allowed to say no?"

With a light laugh, she shakes her head. "Sorry, Mister. It's time for Bossy Ace to make an appearance. You have a lot to learn and not a lot of time to learn it. Now, tell me what you know."

Clearing my throat, I go over the different types of hands and their strengths. "There's a two pair, three pair, four pair, full-house—"

"Which is?" she interrupts, waiting for me to reply.

"A two-pair and a three-pair in the same hand."

"Good. Go on."

I laugh at her praise before following her orders to proceed. "There's a straight, which is all the numbers in order such as two, three, four, five, and six. And there's a flush, which is all five cards having the same suit."

"Good." Her face lights up with pride, and my chest swells with it too as she presses forward. "So, you're familiar with basic strategy, then?"

"I know how to get through a hand and what the little blind and big blinds are, but that's about it."

"So...you're familiar with basic strategy," she teases. "Alright, there's a lot that I could teach you, but I think one of the biggest things you need to learn is the importance of seating placement, and how it can affect *how* you bet. A lot of players raise the same hands no matter the position. That's not what you should do. For example, if you're in UTG, you should open twelve to fifteen percent of hands at equilibrium. But, when you're on the button, which is the dealer, you now need to open fifty percent of hands at equilibrium. The reason for this is the number of players who will play after you."

My eyes glaze over instantly. "I'm sorry, what?"

With a soft laugh, she sets the cards on the table and grabs a notepad and pen. After drawing an oval that represents the table, she begins to scribble out different seating positions, definitions of what they are, and the statistics I'm supposed to consider with each hand I'm dealt based on the seating placement.

My jaw nearly hits the floor as I say, "You're a smart little shit, aren't you?"

Ace grins then playfully shoves me. "Don't sound so surprised, King."

"I'm not. I'm just…" I hesitate, searching for the right word which only makes her gasp in outrage.

"Whatever! You can't be *that* surprised I know what I'm talking about."

"I'm not surprised you know what you're talking about," I correct her. "I'm surprised there's so much strategy based on shit I never would've thought about. And I'm not going to lie; it's sexy as hell hearing it delivered from your pouty little mouth."

That same pouty mouth tilts up in amusement. "You think I'm sexy when I talk poker?"

"Fuck, yes. I knew you were gorgeous, Ace, but brains too?" I lift my arm and wrap it around her neck, pulling her in for a slow kiss. She sighs and leans into me, almost melting into a puddle at my feet. "That makes you the perfect package."

"You've already gotten into my pants, King. There's no need to keep laying it on so thick," she argues sarcastically before wiggling out of my grasp and shuffling the same deck of cards from earlier. I know she's full of shit by the way her cheeks are tinged pink, so I decide to keep arguing. She's cute when she gets all riled up.

"Lie."

Rolling her eyes, she changes the subject. "Stop distracting me. We have work to do."

"Then let's get started, oh wise one. Consider me your star pupil."

Deck in hand, she deals the cards between us and goes over a few more strategy techniques. A couple of hours later, my brain is swimming with new information, and I feel like I need a tumbler of whiskey to soothe the headache that's starting to pound behind my eyes.

"Alright, King. That was a good hand to end on. Next

time, we'll play with chips and bring a few of your guys in here to help mix things up. Do you have any questions?"

"Just one." I drop my chin to the tattered cards in Ace's hand. "What's with the cards?"

She shrugs, trying to act innocent. "What do you mean?"

"They're Allegretti cards. The same ones they play with at Sin."

"Yup. They sure are," Ace acknowledges, her eyes bouncing around the room like a pinball.

"And why do you play with Allegretti cards? Looks like they're pretty worn." I'm not sure why I'm pushing this, but it seems curiosity is getting the best of me.

Her fumbling fingers screw up the shuffle, scattering a few cards along the table before she sets the rest down. Part of me wants to back peddle and let her out of the impromptu interrogation, but the other part of me needs to know. I need to see the real her. *All* of her.

"Tell me, Wild Card," I push, keeping my tone gentle.

With a look that guts me, she says, "They're *his*." Her voice cracks at the mere mention of him, and I don't need to ask who it is she's talking about––just why she cares.

Placing my hand against her knee underneath the table, I probe, "And?"

"And they were left on my kitchen table the night I woke up to find my mom missing."

Shit.

"I learned how to play on these cards. I would spend night after night in my foster homes, flipping them over and using the moonlight to master card counting." With a soft laugh, she adds, "I used to have dreams where all I would see were the faces of the kings and queens in my head, only to wake up and start all over. These are the cards that I've carried in my bag for forever. They're the only connection I have to my past that helps me remember the nightmares were real." Her eyes are glassy as she looks at me. "It's kind of screwed up that I carry them around, isn't it? I mean…who in their right mind would want to remember that shit?"

Squeezing her knee, I really look at the situation from her perspective. She was so helpless. So young. Yet she did what needed to be done, and I couldn't be more proud to call her mine.

I let go of her knee and raise her chin to make sure I have her full attention.

"I think you keep them to remind yourself of all the things you've overcome. You're a survivor, but you're a fighter too. Facing Burlone and beating his ass was the only revenge you could inflict on him, and the cards were your weapon."

With a nod, a speechless Ace stays motionless beside me as I realize she's the strongest person I know. Instead of running from her past, she embraced it and swore not to let it break her. I know a lot of men who would've crumbled under easier circumstances. But not her.

Releasing her chin, I tuck a stray piece of her soft, brown hair behind her ear and cup her jaw. "You're strong. And smart. And so fucking gorgeous. I'm glad you've kept these cards, and I'm glad you've told me about your past. I'm in awe of you, Wild Card."

Sealing my declaration with a kiss, she returns it with so much passion and fire I'm surprised we don't both combust from its heat. When she pushes away from the table and tugs me toward my bedroom, she whispers, "Truth."

And I couldn't agree more.

"**A**ny chance you'd let me go to the grocery store today?" I ask, hating how desperate I sound as I hover near the entrance to Kingston's office.

Looking up from his computer, King states, "We have food. Go check the cupboards and the fridge."

"Yeah, but—"

"No. I have too much going on to take you, and it's not safe for you to go by yourself."

To say I've been going stir crazy since the night I got beaten up is a massive understatement. I don't know how much longer I can take it. It doesn't matter how opulent his home is, staring at the same four walls is slowly driving me mad.

Walking toward him, I bypass the chair across from his desk and sit on his lap before wrapping my arms around his neck. His eyes widen in surprise, but he doesn't ask me to stand up, so I'm going to take it as a win.

"I need some normalcy. Please, please, please?" I beg, sticking my lower lip out for good measure. With a soft laugh, an amused Kingston leans forward and sucks my lip into his mouth before giving it a playful bite. Giggling, I shove him away and wait for my answer.

"Fine. Go buy your groceries, but take D with you."

My shoulders slump at his attempt to compromise. "I feel like D is getting sick of playing my babysitter. I'm pretty sure he has better things to do than tag along on my errands, Kingston."

"He does have better things to do. But you want to go out, and I'm too busy to take you. D is the only guy I trust. If you go, then he goes. Once things calm down, it'll be me escorting you to the grocery store, but for now, Diece will have to do."

Caving to his demands, I give him another kiss. This one is softer, slower. It's more intimate than playful, and I love it to my core.

"I'm excited for this shitstorm to pass," I whisper against his mouth.

"Me too," he confides. "We'll get through this. I promise."

My heart stalls at his assurance, and I don't miss the way he says *we*, either. I know he's told me that I'm his. I know he's shown me that I matter to him. I know Diece has assured me that Kingston's feelings for me are the real deal. But still, none of the evidence seems to quiet the voice inside my head that tells me to be careful. Dreams are dangerous for a girl like me, and they're slowly starting to revolve around the man in front of me and the future we can build together.

"You sure you won't get sick of me by then?" I whisper.

With a teasing grin, he smacks my butt then lifts me to my feet.

"Not a chance. I've already told you that you're mine, and I don't get rid of things once I've claimed them. Now, get out of here. You're distracting me. I'll send D a text, and he'll meet you in the garage."

I blow him a sweet kiss, nearly skipping to the door as I call out, "Thank you!"

～

TWENTY MINUTES LATER, I'M PERUSING THE GROCERY STORE with a red plastic basket hanging from my arm while D trails behind me like a sad little puppy.

"Shoot! I forgot the cauliflower. Will you go grab me one in the produce aisle? I'll meet you by the milk."

With a grunt, Diece follows orders with the promise to meet me in a few.

As I reach for a bag of Twizzlers, a familiar voice surprises me from behind.

"Ace?"

Turning on my heel with my mouth open wide and my hands raised defensively, I see him. "Jack?" I clutch my chest and release a sigh of relief. "You scared the shit out of me!"

"You scared the shit out of me!" he returns angrily. "Where the hell have you been? You fucking disappeared, Ace. I've been worried sick about you."

A familiar sense of guilt churns in my stomach as I see the distress written across his face that I've clearly caused. Dropping my gaze down to my shoes, I dig my teeth into my lower lip before offering an apology because even though I don't want to admit it, he deserves one.

"I'm sorry, Jack. I didn't mean to freak you out. I've just been…"

Shit. What have I been? Busy? Running for my life? Shacking up with the head of the Romano family? I'm at a loss for words, and he can sense it.

"You've been *what* exactly?" he probes, his voice dripping with accusation.

Wincing, I mutter, "Preoccupied?"

"With what?"

"Life?" It's a question, not an answer.

He runs his fingers through his short, blonde hair, and I can feel the frustration radiating from him. It seems to intensify my guilt, and if I were a dog, I can guarantee my tail would be tucked between my legs.

"I went by your apartment the other day," he tells me. "Some homeless guy was loitering in the parking lot and mentioned you'd moved. I thought he was full of shit." With a dry laugh, he shakes his head in disbelief. "I thought you were dead, Ace."

"Nope. Definitely not dead—"

"Just mixed up in some shit with the mob?" he finishes for me with a look of disgust. I don't blame him, but he's got it all wrong. He doesn't know Kingston like I do. He doesn't know what Burlone has done or the situation we're all in. He knows nothing.

"Jack—"

"Look, I know a hell of a lot more than you think I do. When those girls went missing, it scared me. You…" Groaning, he rubs his hands against his face before scrutinizing me with bloodshot eyes. "You're messing with the wrong people, Ace."

I can see how much this is killing him, seeing me with Kingston when he's probably heard rumors of what a terrible person he is. But Kingston isn't like that with me. And I just wish I could relieve his worries or explain that he doesn't need to be stressing about my well-being. That I'm okay. Or at least, I will be once we get everything taken care of.

"Jack, we've had this conversation before."

"And we're going to have it again," he replies sharply. "I can help you if you let me."

"You can't help me, Jack. And honestly? I'm not so sure I want to be saved. Kingston isn't a bad guy."

"You don't know him," he grits out while scanning the empty aisle for any ears that might be listening.

"I do know him."

"And what about Burlone, huh? Do you know him too? What he does to women? What I thought he did to you?"

"Yeah, I do," I bite out, bristling at his comment. "Trust me, Jack. I learned about Burlone a long time ago, and I'll never forget what a scumbag he is, which is why I'm helping Kingston take him down." I pull my lips into a thin line to keep from spewing anything else in the middle of a freaking grocery store.

"Wait…what?" Jack probes, reaching for my wrist.

I pull away from him to keep a decent amount of space between us. "I gotta go, Jack."

"Wait." Sticking his hand into his pocket, he removes a small business card and gives it to me while looking over my shoulder. "Don't let anyone see this, Ace. It could literally kill me."

I take a peek down at the cardstock, my heart racing as the words register in my head. *Jack Connelly, Federal Bureau of Investigation*. I freeze.

Shit. Shit. Shit.

"I gotta go. Call me if you need anything, okay? Despite what you think, I'm one of the good guys." Jack rounds the corner and disappears from view, leaving only a trace of his cologne and the sharp cream paper in my hand as a reminder he was really here. With as much discipline as I can muster, I squeeze my eyes shut and count to three before daring to open them again.

Yup. Still says Federal Bureau of Investigation.

Stunned, I slide the business card into my back pocket while my heart pounds against my chest. Jack's an agent. A *freaking* agent. A freaking agent that I'm connected to. While dating the head of the Romano family. What the hell does this mean for me? Would Kingston think I was working with the Feds? Am I in danger because I was associated with him? Diece has seen us together before when we were at the Charlette. Does he know about Jack's real identity?

My mind keeps spinning as I stand there, unable to move in the middle of the candy aisle because I don't know what else to do. I don't know what to say. I don't know who to tell. I know nothing. Yet way more than I should.

"Ace, where have you been? I was waiting by the damn milk." D's husky voice shakes me from my reverie, and I reach for the bag of Twizzlers then put it in the basket hanging on my arm.

Poker face on full display, I turn to D. "Hey, sorry. I couldn't decide what treat I wanted after dinner."

D reaches for the peanut butter M&M's, tossing a giant bag into the basket with a wink. "Peanut butter M&M's, Ace. Always."

"I think you're right." Laughing, I shake my head, smile, and pray he can't see through it to the nerves that are threatening to expose the card that's in my back pocket.

After we grab a gallon of milk and pay for our groceries, D and I are driving home when he asks me something that makes my blood turn cold.

"So, I saw your little friend. The one from the Charlette a few weeks ago."

My palms start to sweat as I twist them in my lap. "Oh?"

"Yeah. What was his name again? Jack?"

"Oh, yeah. He came and said hi in the candy aisle."

"Yeah, that's what I figured. King would kill me if he knew I let you out of my sight."

I roll my eyes, trying to pretend like I'm not having an epic meltdown inside. "Your secret is safe with me."

"Did he say anything else?" D continues his innocent prodding from the driver's seat, and I watch for any kind of clue that might tell me what he's thinking. If he knows about the business card that's currently burning a hole in my back pocket. If he knows that I have a connection with the FBI that would make me look really freaking incriminating to anyone, let alone to someone who works for the Romano family.

But as I look for any hint that I'm in danger, I don't find any. Just a regular bodyguard who has slowly turned into a friend that's making casual conversation on the way home from the grocery store.

For a girl who was craving normalcy, I can't tell if I'm truly experiencing it right now or if I'm seconds away from being interrogated.

After a beat of silence, I offer a quiet, "Nope," and D decides to throw another curveball, raising goosebumps along my arms.

"That's good, Ace. Because until things calm down, I'd be wary of testing Kingston's patience."

"What do you mean?"

Giving me the side-eye, he explains, "You know Kingston is the head of the Romano family."

"Yeah?"

"And you know what the mob does, right?"

Not really. I mean, I've seen movies and read a story or two, but that's about it.

"Umm..."

D laughs. "Damn, you're innocent. Sometimes I forget what that's like. Anyway, you don't need to know the details, just that Kingston has a bit of a reputation."

"What kind of reputation?" I prod, leaning closer to the center console curiously.

"Honestly? Kingston is ruthless, Ace. He's cold. Lethal. And exact. The guy he is when he's around you is the complete opposite of the one everyone else sees. They call him the Dark King because when it comes to interrogation, he's the best."

I've heard that nickname before. I think it was Jack that used it the first time when he was warning me to stay away from Kingston. I'd thought he was full of crap, but apparently, his cautiousness had merit.

Licking my lips, I ask, "What do you mean *interrogation?*"

"Kingston specializes in getting information from people. He can pull anything out of anyone. And he does it slowly and with as much pain as possible. Hell, you've seen it. He can read people like a fucking book and knows when they're hiding something. If he thought Jack was sniffing around you too much or was too curious about you or what our family does, he'd take him in and start asking questions, and it wouldn't be pretty."

My breathing quickens, but I try to control it by forming a small 'O' with my mouth and releasing the pent-up oxygen slowly.

"Do I need to be worried?"

"Only if you see Kingston pull out a knife," D jokes, turning on his blinker and pulling onto a side road close to home.

My blood turns to ice as I try to connect the man I know and am falling for with the guy D just described while ignoring the business card that feels like a ticking time bomb.

"Noted," I choke out.

We spend the next ten minutes in a quiet standoff because I don't know what to say. I don't know what to think. I'm not sure I really know anything anymore.

With a heavy silence in the car, D asks, "Why are you being so quiet?"

Why am I being so quiet? Because I'm freaking out! That's why!

Desperately, I search for an explanation that would dismiss my weird behavior.

Shrugging, I reply, "I don't know. I guess I'm just a little surprised, that's all. King has always seemed so...*not* what you described."

"That's because you're you. Kingston is softer around you."

I laugh, awkwardly. "You say that like it's a bad thing."

"Normally, it isn't," he consoles. "But when dealing with Burlone, we need ruthless Kingston. We need the one who can think outside the box and bring him down without worrying about what his girlfriend thinks."

"Girlfriend?" My voice cracks, but he waves me off.

"You know what I mean."

Digging my teeth into my lower lip, I look out the window because honestly? I don't really know what to say to that.

"Would it bother you if ruthless Kingston came out to play?" he presses. "If you knew he was only doing it to protect you?"

I think about the Kingston I know. The one who gives me soft kisses and makes me homemade pasta when I'm feeling down. The one who brought me into his home and gently took care of my bumps and bruises. But then I picture Burlone and his ruthlessness, making me squirm in my seat at the memory. I can't be like my mom and wind up with the wrong guy. Then again, I just don't see any similarities between the two.

"I don't know," I reply honestly.

"Well, you better figure it out, Ace, because we need the Dark King. And we might need you to pry it out of him if he keeps fighting his instincts when he's around you."

KINGSTON

The email from Burlone is enough to snap the last of my restraint. It's one week until the tournament, and I can't believe he'd pull this shit. As I scan it for the thousandth time, my eyes glaze over the picture of my half-naked sister along with four other innocent girls. I pick up my phone and dial Lou.

His voice crackles through my cell. "Yeah, Boss?"

"Did you see the email?" I growl, my knuckles turning white.

There's a heavy silence for a split second before he murmurs, "Yeah."

"Have you tried tracking it so we can get a better idea of everyone who's going?"

The sound of fingers touching a keyboard greets me before it stops, and Lou answers, "Yeah. I'll send you the list right now."

"Forward it to Diece too."

"Done."

Pressing the end button on my phone with more force than necessary, I refresh my email and see the list pop up in my inbox. As I peruse the information, my mind searches for a possible solution to the shitstorm that's brewing. I can't get the image of my sister out of my head. A man was touching her. He was toying with her bra, and her eyes were glued to his giant hands. The stark comparison between the captor's tattoos and my sister's pale skin was enough to make my stomach roll. I have no idea if she's okay. If she's being hurt. I know nothing, and I can't stand being out of control. Therefore, I need to find a way to change that.

Picking the phone back up, I begin to dial D's number when he appears in my doorway.

"Speak of the devil. Did you check your email?" I ask him as he swaggers in and takes a seat across from me.

"Yeah. Figured you'd want to talk face-to-face. Should we discuss the original email you forwarded to me or just get right down to the assholes who are attending?"

"Burlone has never auctioned girls via email," I start.

"Yeah, and why the hell would he add a picture of your sister? I thought she wasn't for sale?"

I search for a possible explanation, but nothing feels concrete.

"I don't know. A silent threat, maybe? He could also be trying to squeeze an extra hundred grand out of his buyers by having someone else purchase her then use her for the buy-in only to lose when Burlone dominates the poker table like he's expecting. Or he could be toying with me. He didn't say who she is. He had her lined up with the rest of them as another Jane Doe."

D counters, "Yeah, but that could be because no one would buy her if they knew they'd be stepping into a war with the Romano family as soon as they did."

"That's true," I agree, leaning back into my chair and scratching the five o'clock shadow growing on my jaw. "And what the hell was that greeting for my debut participation in the body of the email? Who the fuck does he think he is?" I bristle at the knowledge that Burlone just screwed me over. Again. Yet, for some reason, I need to hear my right-hand man confirm it out loud.

"He's putting a target on your back, King. Not only will your enemies know your location in a week, but you're now officially linked to Burlone and the underground gambling ring with a side of human trafficking. If any Feds come sniffing around and he gets caught, he now has incriminating evidence against you. He played you, King. And now you need to decide what you're going to do about it."

"Yeah," I sigh, squeezing the bridge of my nose. "I think you pretty much hit the nail on the head."

"So, what *are* you going to do about it?"

"I have an idea. It'll still be a gamble, but if it works, we'll be able to make Burlone burn the way he deserves. Hell, if I could get my hands on him…"

"Yeah, yeah. We know what the Dark King would do with an opportunity like that," D smirks. "Do you think Regina's okay?"

"I don't think I have a choice but to convince myself she's surviving. She's been through a lot of hard stuff in her life. She can overcome this too."

My sister might be a bitch sometimes, but she's smart. And resourceful. She'll do whatever needs to be done to survive until I can rescue her. And I won't let her down.

"She's a tough little shit, isn't she?" A slow smile spreads across D's face as the memories of Regina filter through his mind, making me join in.

"Yeah. I think that's pretty much the perfect way to describe her. Did you see the other players?" I ask, bringing us back to the task at hand and the second email Lou had forwarded. Reminiscing is nothing but a waste of time, and right now, the clock is ticking.

He catches my drift and clears his throat. "Yeah. Do you think it's a coincidence the head distributor for the Eastern human trafficking ring is attending? Or that Dominic, the pussy who ratted out Regina's identity will be going too?"

"It was another slap in the face because there's no way that bastard won't be revealing Regina's identity to the table as soon as we sit down. It's a distraction tactic. Burlone is wanting to get me flustered—"

"Is it working?" D interrupts, his gaze focused solely on me.

With a swallow, I admit something I never would to another soul. "Yeah. I think it is."

"Don't let it. Keep your head in the game. Keep practicing. Be ready to beat Burlone at his own game. At the felt-top table as well as off it."

"That's why I want to get Plan B in place. Will you figure out as much information as you can on the other players along with everyone you suspect will be in the room during the tournament?"

"Yeah."

"Good. I think I need to send an email of my own."

"To Burlone?" D probes.

"No, to his associates," I reply as the wheels in my head start turning.

"Then let's get it done. Go see your girl. Let her put a smile on your face. You look too fucking serious, Kingston."

I laugh dryly while shaking my head. Count on D to make a smartass comment that would somehow make me smile when all I want to do is grab a torch and start burning things. D stands, tapping his knuckles against my oak desk then heads to the door.

"One more thing," I say, stopping him.

He turns around. "Yeah?"

"Have you heard anything else from our men?"

"About...?" His voice trails off, showcasing his confusion.

"About me taking over the Romano family."

Sighing, he shakes his head. "I've already told you, King. From what I can tell, Vince was the only guy who was distressed about the transition. Everyone else seems content. You're a good leader. Don't second guess yourself."

I'm not second-guessing myself, but there's something that nags the back of my mind, hinting that someone else might be. My father always told me to trust my instincts, and even though there isn't any proof, they're blaring like a damn fog horn.

With a single nod, I dismiss Diece. "Keep me updated."

"I will."

What's wrong?" I ask the shadow near the door to my bedroom. Under normal circumstances, I'd be scared out of my mind to have a stranger watching me in the shadows. But the presence is familiar, and I know that it's Kingston with every fiber of my being. The situation reminds me of my apartment when I'd be anxiously waiting for him to visit me, and a fresh wave of butterflies assaults my stomach as I wait for him to answer me.

His husky voice sends tingles racing down my spine. "Nothing."

"Lie," I return, sensing his frustration. "Talk to me, Kingston. It's almost two in the morning, and I heard shouting downstairs. Why don't you come to bed?" He's been sleeping with me here in the guest room across the hall. I've loved feeling his embrace in the middle of the night but wake up convinced it was all a dream. Why? Because he's always missing by the time my eyes peek open in the morning.

When his dark shadow doesn't move, I threaten, "Don't

make me get out of bed to come get you, Mister. It's freezing. Come warm me up."

The teasing in my voice is enough to get him to edge closer. As he finally reaches me, his weight sinks into the mattress and makes me roll toward him. Lifting onto my elbow, I continue to watch him in the moonlight that's filtering in through the window.

"Talk to me, King. I'm right here."

Silence.

"Please?" I beg. I can see his torment. The purple bags under his eyes. The pale skin. The scruffier beard that's usually trimmed. Something is bothering him, and it kills me that he refuses to open up to me. I want to help him carry his burdens the same way he carries mine, but he needs to let me.

"It's family business."

"Is that supposed to mean something to me?" I laugh lightly as another blinding example of the different worlds we've been raised in comes to light. I'm not naïve. He's made it apparent on multiple occasions that family business means it's none of *my* business. But that doesn't lessen the sting that accompanies it every time he makes it obvious that he can't trust me.

With a dry laugh, Kingston finally looks down at me and starts to play with my long strands of hair that are spread across the pillow like a messy web.

"Family business means it's for the men only. We can't talk about it with anyone else."

"Lie."

"It's not a lie," he argues, but I interrupt him.

"It is, Kingston. You can talk to *me*. You can talk to me about anything."

His fingers stop playing with my hair as if I've shocked

him before he continues his exploration. The tender touch feels exquisite, and I close my eyes at the gentle tugging.

"You want the truth?" His voice is hushed, vulnerable, and so freaking heartbreaking. "I'm scared, Ace."

When a big, brooding man like Kingston admits he's scared, you know there's trouble. And I also know there isn't anything I can do about it but stand by his side as he faces whatever demons are haunting him. Haunting *us*.

"Me too," I breathe.

Looking down at me, he continues to play with my hair, and the rhythmic action seems to calm me.

"Why would you agree to be part of this insanity? Why would you let me use you to save my sister?"

"You're not using me—"

"That's exactly what I'm doing, Ace. And it guts me every time I think about it."

"I trust you."

"So?" A furious Kingston pushes off the bed and starts pacing the floor like a caged lion. I'd be scared if I didn't know him like I do. "Your trust doesn't mean I'm going to beat Burlone. It doesn't counter the fact that I'll likely get killed as soon as I step foot in there regardless of the rules set in place to prevent that. I just put a plan in motion that's a huge risk, Ace. And if it turns bad, then I won't be able to protect you. I won't be able to save my sister." He digs his fingers through the roots of his dark hair. "Sometimes, I feel like I should've never intervened with Burlone's plans to frame the Romano family for human trafficking. I'd rather rot in prison for a crime I didn't commit than let the people I care about get caught in the crosshairs."

"Kingston. You are not going to let this family down. You are not going to fail. And you sure as hell aren't going to let Burlone touch your sister, or me, or even Gigi. I know you. And I know that whatever plan you've set into motion is going to work. It might be risky, but it's going to knock Burlone on his ass. I guarantee it."

Looking down at me as I lay on the mattress, he remains silent, so I push a little harder. "I'm smart, King. You've said so yourself. Do you really think I'd put my life on the line if I didn't know you'd be able to keep me safe?"

The look in his eyes says it all, and I know without a doubt that I'm right. The man in front of me would do anything to protect the people he cares about. And that includes me.

I slide out from beneath the sheets in nothing but a t-shirt and boy shorts like a woman on a mission as I approach him––the man who swept into my life unannounced and turned it upside down. His gaze eats me up as I saunter toward him with swaying hips. Slowly, my fingers begin unbuttoning his dress shirt from top to bottom, revealing inch after inch of tanned muscles I want to lick. Once his chest is bare before me, I peek up at him, dragging my hands against his warm skin then wrap my arms around his neck and whisper, "In fact, I think it's about time I thank you for it."

"I haven't saved you yet, Ace," he growls, grabbing my wrists and preventing their pursuit.

I run my lips against the scruff of his jaw. They pull into a smile when his facial hair tickles the sensitive skin, and I realize how happy this man makes me. How safe I feel, despite the shitty circumstances, when I'm with him.

Sighing in contentment, I murmur, "That's where you're wrong. You *have* saved me. From a life full of loneliness, rules, and paranoia. You don't know how often I used to look over my shoulder, wondering if I was being followed. If I was safe. If Burlone was going to hurt me again."

"Babe—"

I tug my wrist from his grasp and rest my finger against

his mouth as his lips pull into a thin line. "Shh...let me finish."

With a gasp, I feel his tongue swirl around the tip before he gives me a single nod that grants me permission to continue.

I laugh. "So bossy. All I'm saying is that I know you'll keep me safe. I know you'll figure this shit out. I know that you can talk to me when you're hurting or afraid. And I know that I'm starting to fall for––" My mouth snaps shut. Nope. I think that's enough honesty for one day, and I sure as hell am not going to be the first to reveal my feelings in this relationship. He might've claimed me as his, but we haven't said any words. And that won't be changing anytime soon.

With a growl, he wraps his arms around my waist and throws me onto the bed. I'm squealing as soon as my feet are lifted from the ground, but it's quickly transformed into a laugh when my back hits the bed, and Kingston joins me by using his body weight to press me into the mattress.

Caging me in with his arms while lying on top of me, he starts running his nose from my jaw up to my temple then whispers, "You're pretty irresistible when you're honest. Did you know that?"

I keep my lips zipped.

"Come on, Ace. You were doing so well. Maybe you could stroke my ego for just a *little* bit longer by finishing that statement."

"I can think of one thing I'd be willing to stroke," I offer, batting my eyes innocently at him.

With a chuckle, Kingston bites my earlobe enough to make me squeak. I wiggle beneath him in an attempt to get away from his delicious torture. But I don't get very far before he stops teasing and starts playing me like a damn violin, making me hit every note he wants with ease.

Moaning, I spread my legs and let him take the lead, pleasuring me in the way only he's capable of. I watch as he drifts down my body before sticking his thumbs into the hem of my boyshorts and sliding them down my legs. Once I'm bare to him, he peppers kisses along my inner thighs, spreading me wide.

I don't fight it. I couldn't if I wanted to. Especially when I know what his mouth is capable of.

Again, he takes his time teasing me with a touch of his tongue and a flick of his fingers until my back is arching off the mattress, and my hands are tangled in the sheets.

"Please, Kingston. Please. I need you," I whimper as he continues his assault with his mouth.

He shakes his head, and the scruff along his jaw tickles my skin. "Not until you stroke my ego."

"I already offered to stroke your dick if you'd just bring it up here!" I screech. His hot breath fans across my sensitive flesh teasingly.

"No deal, Wild Card. Tell me what I need to hear."

I'm so freaking close it's not even funny before I wrap my legs around his shoulders and buck toward him, desperately guiding him to the spot where I'm needing relief.

"Please," I beg.

"Uh-uh," he tsks, pinning me in place with his calloused hands on my lower stomach.

A groan of frustration slips out of me before I drop my head back to my pillow and stare up at the ceiling.

Nostrils flaring, I grit out, "Fine. I'm falling for you, Kingston Romano. I'm falling hard. Happy now?"

Within seconds, he pushes me over the edge, making me scream and somehow tapping into my frustration and turning it into absolute bliss and euphoria. I'm panting like I've run a marathon as I look down to find his gaze glued to mine before he says with an arrogant smirk, "Yes. Now was that so hard?"

"Asshole," I mutter before pulling him up and wrapping my legs around his waist. "You owe me two of those for that."

"Deal."

He pushes into me with ease, and we both tumble over the edge minutes later before I tell him the truth. Willingly, this time. "I really am falling for you, Kingston, and I know you'll take care of me. And your sister. And the entire Romano family. Even if it's the last thing you do."

Nestling into my neck, he mutters one word.

"Truth."

"Good game, guys! Thanks for helping out tonight!" I tell Lou, Diece, and Stefan as they tuck in their chairs around the dining room table. We've just finished a couple rounds of poker in hopes of it helping Kingston get a better feel for the importance of table position and how to implement the strategy.

He's been kind of lackadaisical about the whole thing, and I can't decide if it's because he's discouraged, or if he's just counting on his new plan to work out and doesn't need to put as much effort into learning the game. Regardless, I think tonight helped.

As I gather the cards, I catch D stretching his arms over his head then tapping his knuckles against the table. It's one of his familiar quirks, and the action makes me smile.

"Thanks for having us, Ace. That was interesting as hell. We're going to call it a night, though. You're getting better, King. Ace is a good little teacher." He winks at me then leaves the room. Lou and Stefan follow after, murmuring their goodbyes.

Kingston, however, is still at the table, staring at the chips as if they hold the key to solving world hunger.

"Hey." Trying to grab his attention, I throw a card at him, and it does its job, bringing him back to me.

He blinks. "Hey, sorry."

"How do you think it went?" I ask.

"It wasn't bad, but they also can't compete with Burlone so…"

"So you don't think that you can compete with Burlone, even though you cleaned up during tonight's game?" I finish for him.

With a shake of his head, a vulnerable Kingston admits, "I don't know what to think anymore. And this might be a moot point, anyway. If my other plan works out then…"

"Will you tell me your other plan?"

"Babe—"

"I know, I know. You and your stupid rules." A breath of laughter escapes me as I remember Gigi saying the same thing to me. Setting aside my frustration, I add, "Want to know something interesting, King? I had my rules, too, yet they don't even really enter my mind anymore. Not since I found you and moved in here. I trust you, King. With everything. And I think one of these days, you'll realize you can trust me too and that you can tell me anything. Including what your plan is and how I can help."

He opens his mouth to say something, but I cut him off. "*But*…since you're not ready, and I don't want to push you, let's focus on poker, shall we? You've already gotten the basics down, and you've learned some strategy techniques that can be really valuable––as you saw with tonight's outcome. You cleaned up, and you need to give yourself a little credit. But I think it's time we start talking about Burlone, in particular. What do you think?"

"Yeah." He sits up a little straighter with a fire in his eyes that's pretty freaking attractive. The determination is sexy as hell. "I think that's a good idea."

"Okay." I set the cards down and reach for his hands, linking our fingers together and squeezing softly. "First, you're already at an advantage because you're a master at reading people. You've always been able to tell if I'm lying or telling the truth, and I know you've done the same thing with the men you interrogate."

Kingston opens his mouth to refute my comment, but I press on before he has a chance to argue. "I've heard a bit about your specific set of skills, and I think you should tap into them."

His eyes cloud for a split second before sharpening. "How the hell do you know about that?"

I brush his question aside. He doesn't need to know about my heart-to-heart with D.

"Do you think I'm blind?" I joke. "I might not have had front row seats to your...extra-curricular activities, but that doesn't mean I haven't noticed the blood-stained shirts on occasion or the bruised knuckles. And don't even get me started on the knife you keep strapped to your ankle. I'm not an idiot, and I'm not a naïve little girl who doesn't know who she's sleeping with. To win the tournament, all you need to do is know the rules, know the strategies, and know your opponents. And you have all of that mastered. The only difference between poker and your interrogation techniques is that with poker, your cards are your weapons instead of a knife."

A heavy silence hangs over us as Kingston stares at me, appearing to be made from stone. Brushing aside my entire comment, he repeats, "You didn't answer my question, Ace. How do you know about my specific set of skills?" His voice is like ice.

"I did tell you—"

"I want the whole truth. Not half of it," he bites out. The man in front of me transforms into a stranger in the blink of an eye. The usual warmth that I feel around him is replaced with a frigid glare that seeps into my bones and makes me desperate for a scalding shower.

I cringe. Sometimes I hate how well he can read me. Praying he won't cut off any of Diece's fingers, I admit, "D."

"And you still want me?" he pushes, though his tone is indifferent. "Knowing all the blood that's on my hands?"

I don't bother to tell him I don't know any real specifics. It doesn't matter, anyway. Nothing can change how I feel about him. How I see him as a protector and not an adversary. Standing, I lean across the table then kiss the back of his hands in hopes of comforting him and putting him at ease.

He doesn't move an inch, but he *does* watch me with his dark, scrutinizing eyes. I can feel him pushing me away. I can feel his walls sliding into place. I can feel the distance between us, even though we're inches away from each other. I can feel it all.

With a deep breath, I hold his stare. "I don't care what you've done. I don't care who you are when you're the Dark King. I care about you. The real you. I care about who you are when you're around me. I care about how you treat me. You make me feel precious. Cherished, even." I smile. "D says you're different when you're around me. He thinks you're softer and sometimes more hesitant like you're afraid to show your true self. Like you're afraid I won't understand the real you." Licking my lips, I sit back down and tell him the truth. "I love that you're trying to protect me, but if you want to win this tournament, then you need to stop holding back. You need to be *you*. You need to be ruthless. You *need* to be the Dark King."

"And what if you don't like the man you meet when I let him loose?"

"Not possible." I shake my head, trying to imagine a world where I don't love him. Where I don't understand he was made for me.

His hands squeeze mine, but he doesn't say anything, so I decide to leave that battle for another day. "Now, I'm going to tell you all I know about Burlone and his little ticks, and you're going to take notes. You ready?"

He grabs onto the subject change without a backward glance. "Ready."

I smile. "First. If Burlone is anxious, he makes a point to *not* touch his chips unless absolutely necessary. If he's pretty laid back then he'll fidget with them on occasion. That doesn't really tell you what's in his hand, but how he feels about his hand, which is just as important. Also, if he doesn't take a second look at his cards, he's confident he's going to win, and you should fold. But, if he looks at them every time the dealer lays a community card, then he still has something but isn't quite as confident. This is when he's most dangerous because he isn't sure of the outcome, either. It makes the hand a wild card, and you don't want him to suck out. Do you remember what that means?"

Nodding, he explains, "Being sucked out means you were losing at the beginning of the hand, but by the time the last community card is shown, it gives you the edge to win the pot. For example, let's say I go all-in with two kings, and I'm called by an opponent who's holding two aces. Then the dealer lays a king among the community cards, thus enabling me to *suck out* and win the hand despite having been behind when the chips went in."

I clap my hands dramatically, my face showing my pride. "Not too bad, King. I'm impressed."

"I learned from the best," he jokes. "Does he have a tell for when he's bluffing?"

"He'll look you straight in the eye when he bets. He'll

ooze arrogance as if you'd be an idiot to question him, to take him on. That's when you know he's full of shit."

"Good to know. And what are my tells?" he probes.

With a sly grin, I admit, "I don't think I'm ready to reveal them quite yet."

"And why's that?" he laughs.

"Because I might want to get something out of you one of these days, and if I tell you your little idiosyncrasies, then you'll try to cover them up. It'll throw off my entire strategy, Kingston, and where's the fun in that?"

Kingston opens his mouth and tugs his hands away from me with feigned outrage.

"Is that a challenge, Ace?"

With that same sly grin firmly in place, I reply, "Only if you're not too scared to take me up on it. How else will we know if you're ready or not?"

"Game on, Ms. Mezzerich. I have one condition, though." His gaze heats with lust, making me squirm in my seat. To hide my reaction, I stand up and raise my hands over my head to stretch then yawn for good measure.

"And what's that?"

"We play strip poker."

Giggling, I shake my head then start walking down the hall before tossing over my shoulder, "How did I know you were going to say that?"

"Is that a yes?" he yells back.

"Maybe. Now, come to bed. You got me all hot and needy with all that poker talk."

His laughter echoes back, and I'd be willing to bet all my chips that he'll be joining me in a minute or two. The bastard might like to make me beg, but I'm glad I was able to put a smile on his face.

Even if it's just for a little while.

56

ACE

Nearly skipping down the stairs and toward Kingston's office, I rap my knuckles against the doorframe.

"Yeah?" His voice sounds annoyed, but I know that'll change. Sure enough, his eyes light up when he looks over at me.

"Oh. Hey."

I grin. "Hey, Mr. Romano. Are you ready for a challenge?"

Kingston's brows crinkle. He's been cooped up in his office all day, and I'm ready for him to put away his work and have some fun with me. The pressure to keep the Romano family intact while the tournament looms closer has been eating him alive, and I want my playful, fun Kingston for a few hours.

Sensing my need, he clicks a few buttons on his computer before scooting his chair back and swaggering toward me. The pheromones must be oozing from his pores because I'm seconds away from throwing in the towel and begging him to do me right here, right now, which would completely ruin my plans for the evening.

"No offense, Ace. But with the way you're looking at me right now, I don't really sense a challenge."

I turn on my heel before I can prove him right and yell over my shoulder, "Whatever, young Padawan. Follow me."

Cards in hand, I walk to the kitchen table, take a seat, and begin shuffling the Allegretti deck. A curious Kingston sits across from me, pressing his back into his chair and casually undoing the top button of his shirt to reveal the long column of this throat.

I know he's simply getting comfortable after a long day at work, but he's totally distracting me with a glimpse of his olive skin. Damn him and his ruggedly attractive face.

"Okay, Yoda, let's see what this challenge is."

It takes every ounce of concentration to remember my game plan for the evening, but I dig deep and somehow spark my memory about tonight's lesson.

"Plain and simple. I believe you promised me a game of strip poker, and I'm calling to collect."

Throwing his head back, he laughs loud and hard. The sound makes my heart sing, and I join in, giggling right along with him.

"Well, alright, then. Let's see whatcha got, Wild Card."

I begin dealing the cards and watch his demeanor for any little twitch that might tell me what he's thinking as he looks at his cards. But he's like a steel vault, not revealing a thing.

Three community cards are placed face-up in the center of the table when he glances up at me.

"So, what are the rules? How does this work? You'll have to forgive me for not being strip poker savvy." Narrowing his gaze in suspicion, he adds, "And you better tell me you had to Google this shit, or I'm going to have to hunt someone down."

With a grin, I explain, "No hunting necessary. The rules are pretty simple. If you fold, you automatically lose a piece of clothing––victor's choice. However, if you play the round and lose, you can choose your own article of clothing to discard. Other than that, it's the same rules as normal Texas Holdem without the betting in between. And…to see how well you can read your opponent––aka me––we're going to add one more rule. If you're able to guess what my hand is before I show you, then I have to take off two articles of clothing. But if you're wrong, you have to remove two pieces of your own clothes. Understand?"

"Yeah. So, pretty much you'd be an idiot to fold because even if you know you're going to lose, you still have the chance of guessing what cards the other player is holding, which makes them discard two items of clothing, right?"

"Yup."

"Well, then…I'm not folding this hand. Are you?"

I take another peek at my cards, seeing I have nothing, but I decide to play along anyway because, like he said, I'd be an idiot to fold.

"Nope."

Placing another card face-up in the center of the table, I school my features. If we were playing with chips, there's no way I'd stay in, but I'm curious to see how he plays against me when there's something he wants on the line.

After a fifth card is placed next to the other four, I look up to find Kingston watching me closely.

"Would you like to make a guess at what I'm holding?" I ask, batting my eyes.

"Two of a kind?"

I flip my cards over to show he's wrong; I've got nothing. "Nope."

With a shrug, he slides his arms out of his jacket then tugs his tie over his head before showing me his cards. "I still won the hand, Ace." He shows me a pair of sixes. "Now take off your shirt. There's way too much clothing covering that beautiful skin."

Tsking, I shake my head then take off my shoes. "Sorry, Kingston. I didn't fold, which means you don't get to choose what I take off."

"Fiiine," he whines before winking at me. "Deal another hand; we need to get you naked."

Laughing, I do as I'm told and give us our cards then put three in the center.

"Folding?" I ask.

"Fuck, no."

My mouth lifts, but I add a couple more cards to the community pile to move things along.

"I have a guess," I say, pinning him with my stare.

"And?"

"Three of a kind."

A mock-outraged Kingston tosses his cards into the center of the table before throwing his hands into the air. "How the hell did you know that?" he laughs.

"Lucky guess." I wink. "But maybe you should try *not* grinning like a loon when the cards are flipped over."

"Good point." He slides his belt through the loops and drops it to the ground. "One of these times, I'm going to fool you, Wild Card. And you're going to rue the day you ever challenged me."

Again, I just laugh, soaking up the easy connection we have and how much lighter I feel when I'm around him. "Not likely, but I appreciate your work ethic."

Shaking his head, he gathers the cards and begins shuffling. "One day, Ace. One day."

We continue playing, laughing, shouting in outrage, and licking our lips as more items of clothing disappear from our bodies until we're in nothing but our underwear.

I have to give Kingston props; he's getting better. He's

learning what to look for and how to hide his emotions even better than before. Although part of me wonders if his true feelings come to the surface anytime we're around each other, and that he'll have an easier time keeping them in check when he plays against Burlone. Especially when I consider what Diece mentioned when we went grocery shopping––how Kingston is different around me. Softer.

But maybe that's just wishful thinking.

When I look at my cards, I pull my lips into a thin line to keep from smiling. Two kings. Effortlessly, Kingston lines up three cards onto the table face-up. Two aces and a six, which gives me a two-pair. We don't bother asking if either of us is folding because we haven't the entire evening.

I can feel King watching me as he flips over the final two cards. Another ace and a seven which gives me a full house.

"I have a guess," Kingston says with a confident grin.

"You look awfully sure of yourself."

"Because I am. I'd bet all in if we were playing with chips."

"Because you're sure your hand can beat mine, or you're sure you know what's in my hand?"

"Both. You have a full house, and I have four of a kind. Now take off the rest of your clothes and come sit on my lap."

My jaw hits the floor at his confidence combined with his accuracy. "You have four of a kind?" He flips over his card to show me an ace and a queen.

"Seems like I'm good at collecting aces," he teases, winking for good measure.

"But...how did you know what I had?"

"Because you're right. With a little effort, I can read you like a fucking book. Now get over here. Don't make me ask again."

Reaching behind my back, I unclasp my bra and drop it to the floor, leaving my underwear on as I walk around the table, taking my time. The way his gaze heats as he eats up every inch of skin I have on display is pretty much the best confidence boost a girl can ask for, and my heart feels like it just might burst at the realization I get to call him mine. Shaking off the very real and serious turn my thoughts just took, I hook my thumbs around the flimsy material at my hips and tug them slowly down my legs.

"You got lucky," I quip as I watch him tug down his black boxers.

With a grin, he razzes, "Never took you for a sore loser, Ace."

"Then maybe you're not so good at reading me after all."

He laughs before reaching forward and tugging me closer. His hot, needy hands grip my ass before he situates me so that I'm straddling his lap.

"Now ride me, Wild Card. I've been dying for you since you challenged me in my office, and I think we both know how impatient I can get." With a light slap to my butt, he leans back and lets me take the lead. I give him a coy smile before following his orders like a good little girl while knowing who's really in charge in this very moment.

Me.

And I love him even more for giving me that power.

His thick erection is hot in my palm as I rub my hand up and down it. Slowly. Teasingly. Until a bud of precum glistens at his tip. I lick my lips and drag my thumb across it before bringing the drop of moisture to my lips. Kingston's gaze darkens. I suck it into my mouth, and smile.

"You like that?" he rasps.

"Maybe."

His gaze darkens, daring me to tease him further, but I'm too turned on to toy with him anymore.

Maybe later.

Rising onto my tiptoes, I line him up with my center then

slowly take him inside of me. The familiar stretch makes my brows pinch before Kingston tangles his fingers into my hair and slams his mouth against mine, erasing any discomfort from his cock that's buried deep inside of me.

Shit, he tastes good.

After a few seconds, I roll my hips. Finding my own rhythm, I'm determined to leave King a mess like he always manages to do with me. And it works. As I speed up my pace, his grip on my hair tightens, and I smile against his mouth, using his shoulders for balance.

His grunts only spur me on as we both race to our orgasms like it's a cure for our sanity when we both know it'll only feed the chaos of emotions. And need. And lust. And above all. Love.

But I'm okay with that.

And as he lets himself go, I know he's okay with it too.

57

KINGSTON

Voices echo through the house and down to my office as I finish typing an email. It's going to be sent to a few choice cartels who will be participating in Burlone's tournament with me, and if things go according to plan, it'll help solidify my strategy.

"Wait here," D murmurs from the hallway before popping his head around the doorframe in my office.

"Hey. You have a visitor." His voice is cryptic, piquing my curiosity as I look up.

"Who?"

"Dex." My eyes open wide, showing him my absolute surprise as he continues, "I think you need to hear what he has to say. He also gave me this."

Stepping forward, D hands me a folded piece of paper.

What the hell?

"Where did you get this?" I ask in disbelief. Regina's swirling cursive is written across the front, and the sight puts all my senses on high alert.

"I told you; Dex gave it to me. He reached out and asked if we could meet."

"And you went?"

He has the decency to look sheepish. "Yeah, I went. I didn't want to stress you out or anything, and I know it was selfish of me to risk my life just to see my long lost brother but--"

"You just couldn't help yourself," I finish for him.

"Yeah. And it's a good thing too." Dropping his chin, he motions to the letter. "Read it. Then you can decide what you want to do with Burlone's right-hand man."

"Is that how we're classifying him? Or should we address the fact that he's your brother?"

With a sigh, he nods. "And my brother."

Satisfied, I unfold the cream piece of paper and start reading. My breath gets caught in my throat as I scan the message a dozen times, confusion knotting my stomach.

Hey King,

It's me. First– I'm so sorry I snuck out. I screwed up, and that's on me. But I want you to know I'm okay. Please don't shoot Dex! He's been watching over me. He's been taking care of me. He's been really good to me, King. He's not like the other men. I know you'd kill me if I were in front of you right now, but I really care about him, and I'm begging you to give him a chance. He wants to get BOTH of us out of this situation and has information from Burlone that the tournament is a trap. I'm sure you've already been able to guess that would be the case, but Dex can confirm it. You can't go. I don't care if I'm sold or...whatever the plans are for me. Burlone is going to kill you if you show up, and I can't let that happen. Especially because if I had listened to you, I wouldn't be in this position in the first place. Just be careful, okay? And listen to Dex. He's the only shot we have.

Love you,

Regina

Looking up at my best friend with my heart in my throat, I ask, "Did you read this?"

"Yeah."

"And do you believe it?"

"It's her handwriting, King. And let's be honest, no one could make that girl do something she didn't want to do. Plus, remember the picture from Burlone's email? Her expression didn't make sense. But now—"

"Now that she's admitted she's fallen for her captor?" I shake my head. Count on Regina to screw up so monumentally that I don't even know what to do with the situation. However, the image of her from Burlone's email comes to mind, and I try to analyze it from a different perspective. My fists tighten at my sides, crumpling the paper into a ball as I realize that my sister did indeed write the letter, and she did indeed fall for him as well.

Shit.

Apparently, I need to Google Stockholm Syndrome. Fan-fucking-tastic.

Reading my expression, Diece grimaces. "Yeah. It makes sense why she wouldn't look terrified, ya know?"

"Do you think Dex cares about her, as well? Or is he just after her virginity? Or is this just a trap, and you're playing right into his hands?"

"Give me a little more credit, King," Diece seethes. "It makes sense why Dex would approach us to save her. Why he'd risk his own life––along with Burlone's retribution if he ever found out––to keep her safe."

Tapping my finger against my chin, I look at my right-hand man. "Do you trust him?"

"I don't know," D responds gruffly. "He seems genuine, but maybe my judgment is clouded because I've wanted him to be a Romano since I was twelve and saw him drive off with his mom. Maybe it's just wishful thinking on my part that he's changed. Regardless, I think you need to hear him out and decide for yourself."

With a wave, I motion for him to invite Dex inside.

Seconds later, a man who looks eerily similar to my best friend steps into my office with his hands tucked into his slacks and his shoulders hunched.

"Take a seat," I offer, dropping my gaze to the chair adjacent to my desk.

"Thanks."

"What do you know about me?"

"Enough."

"Enough to know that I'm pretty fucking good at being able to tell if someone is telling the truth or not?"

He holds my stare. "Yeah. I may have heard that."

"Then let's cut the shit, shall we? Did you fuck my sister?"

With a slight flinch at my derogatory term, he murmurs, "Yes."

Truth.

So, apparently, that rules out the I-want-her-virginity theory.

"Do you care about her the same way she cares about you?"

"Yes." He's more confident this time. A hint of pride laces his tone as he admits it.

Truth.

"Am I walking into a trap?"

"Yes." This time, I see him almost deflate with guilt right before my eyes. And I know the situation is killing him. He doesn't want me dead, but only because he knows it would gut my sister.

Truth.

"Are you willing to betray the Allegretti family by giving us confidential information that, if linked back to you, will guarantee the skin being flayed from your body by Burlone?

And that if we find out the information you give us is faulty, then we'll do it ourselves?"

He swallows but doesn't break my gaze, which only emphasizes his resolve. "Yes."

Truth.

"And what do you want in return?" I almost want to laugh when I realize how similar this conversation is to a hand of poker. We're both watching the cards unfold in front of us in little pieces of honesty and trust. And are now about to place our bets on each other, praying it'll pay out in the end.

"I want your sister to be safe."

My suspicion spikes, sensing a lie, or half of one anyway.

"Tell me the *whole* truth, Dex. I told you to cut the shit, remember?"

Bristling, he drops his head back in defeat and stares up at the ceiling. "You want the whole truth, Kingston? Fine. I want her to be safe. But I also want to keep her for myself because she already owns me. I didn't ask for it because I'm not stupid enough to think it's a possibility. I'm a fucking Allegretti who'll be dead by the end of the week as soon as my men find out that I'm the traitor who screwed up Burlone's plans by squealing to the enemy." Dragging his hands from the top of his head and down his face, he brings his gaze back to mine. "So, yeah. If I can ask for one thing, then I want her safe. That's it."

"And you're not going to ask for your own protection?" I push curiously.

"I'm not naïve enough to think I'd get it, Kingston. I've been in the game long enough to know you never really trust someone who's always been your enemy, even when they show up at your front door to help you."

"No. You're showing up at my front door to help my sister. You don't give a shit about me because of what your dad did to you as a kid. Or *didn't* do, in his case. However, you haven't always been an enemy to the Romano family. You're a victim of an old man's wrong decision, and I think we can both come to an agreement––if you're willing to prove your loyalty."

The man in front of me goes deathly calm, the anxiety from moments before vanishing into thin air as he comprehends what I'm offering. Little does he know, I'm not doing it for him. I'm doing it for his brother and for my baby sister. I'm righting the wrongs that should've never happened in the first place. I just pray I'm not going all-in on the wrong hand.

"And how do I prove my loyalty?"

Scratching the five o'clock shadow on my jaw, I tell him, "We'll be in touch."

58

JACK

Running my hand through my hair, I tug on the roots before shifting my phone to my other ear.

Gritting my teeth, I spit, "Yeah, I understand. I haven't found shit on Burlone recently. His entire operation has been silent since the night of the poker tournament at Sin." Ace's face flashes through my memory before my boss's voice pulls me back to the present.

"Three girls were reported missing that night. *Three*, Connelly. That number doesn't include all the women from the last fifteen years that we can link to Burlone. Do you want me to get you the headcount?"

"No, sir." I already know the answer by heart and don't need a reminder.

"Then, where the hell are they?"

"I stayed at the casino all night. I was on Burlone the entire evening just like you told me to be. He disappeared into the elevator for about thirty minutes after he lost the tournament then showed up on the main floor and spent the night toasting opponents and having his ass kissed. You told me to watch Burlone, and I did. I can't be in two places at once, sir." With my hand clenched at my side, I picture Ace's face a few days later while knowing it was partially my fault for not following her that night and protecting her. I'm just grateful she didn't end up missing, but I know Burlone's smarter than that. He's too smart.

"Did any of his men leave through the front door?"

"Of course they did," I grit out. "It's Burlone's fucking casino. They come and go as they please."

"Watch your tone, Connelly."

Releasing a heavy sigh, I offer my apology. "I'm sorry, sir. I'm as frustrated as you are. Like I've already told you, one of my guys was outside watching the front, but apparently, he didn't see anything."

"Sounds like laziness to me."

With flaring nostrils, I search for an ounce of patience but seem to be running low. "It wasn't laziness. His men know how to blend in when they want to. They know how to fly under the radar. Why do you think they're always slipping through our fingers?"

"Not our fingers, Jack. *Your* fingers. And if you can't bring me something soon, I'm pulling you off the case."

I slam my hand against the wall in my shitty apartment, but it does little to ease my frustration. "That's bullshit, and you know it."

"One more curse from your mouth, and there'll be consequences," my boss returns.

I sigh and release my clenched fist before sitting on the edge of the mattress in my room. "Look, I'm sorry, sir. Again. We just need a break in this case. Soon."

"Finally, we agree on something," my superior murmurs, grating on my nerves. "Every day you come up empty-handed is another day those women aren't afforded their revenge. It's another day scum like Burlone are left on the streets and continue the shit they do. I've got my superiors breathing down my neck for justice, and I'm sick of telling them that we don't have shit, Jack. Sick and tired."

"Me, too," I add as the ever-present weight of my job digs into my shoulders a little more.

"Then get me those bastards, and get me those innocent girls."

"Yes, sir."

I hang up the phone and lie back onto the bed while staring up at the popcorn textured ceiling.

The question is…how?

ACE

It's been hours since D drove his brother home then holed himself up in Kingston's office. The two have been going at it with the door closed, trying to work the final kinks from their plan. Pacing the hall in front of his locked door, I finally slam my hands against it.

"This whole no-women thing is bullshit! Open up, Kingston! Let me help!"

Resting my head against the solid oak door, I wait for their verdict. The muffled voices go silent for a solid thirty seconds before the thick piece of wood squeaks on its hinges, and an amused smirk appears on D's face.

"Why, hello, Ace. Fancy seeing you here."

With a roll of my eyes, I shove him aside and step into the man cave. "So, what's going on? What's the new tidbit of information? And how can I help?"

A stressed Kingston crooks his finger at me, and I saunter over before plopping in his lap and kissing him lazily.

"You okay?" I can feel his stress as if it's my own.

His fingers squeeze softly against my jean-clad thigh.

"Yeah. We've been working on something. We just need to play our cards right."

"Speaking of which," D interrupts. "King, what does she know?"

"Not much," he admits, appearing contrite. I turn in his lap and stare him down.

"I can help. You just need to fill me in. Plus, if we're talking about playing cards, then I'm your woman," I tease in an attempt to lighten the mood.

Leaning forward, King gives me another soft kiss before releasing a sigh against my lips. "We've been having discussions with a few of the men who are invited to the tournament. These men are scum, Ace, but they're also superstitious fuckers who don't trust anyone. For the past week or so, D and I have been proposing the possibility of Burlone working with the Feds."

With my jaw on the floor, I screech, "Burlone is working with the Feds?"

No freaking way.

"No." D's laughter echoes throughout the room. "We're just hinting at it."

Wait. What?

"But why? And how the hell would you get them to believe you over Burlone?" I inquire, my attention switching from Kingston to D, then back to Kingston, begging either of them to fill me in.

"Because Burlone's been acting batshit crazy lately," D remarks matter-of-factly.

Kingston laughs dryly then gives me the details I'm craving. "The Feds have been sniffing around Burlone for the past couple of years, but Burlone was pretty good at dodging them until about six months ago. Burlone was getting desperate and decided to set up the Romano family in an attempt to throw the Feds off his scent."

The tournament at Sin flashes through my mind along with memories of the first time I met King at the Charlette, piecing together my part and how I gave Kingston the date of Burlone's plotting.

Kingston continues, "The only problem was that we found out about it and screwed up his plan. Instead of letting him frame us for all of the trafficking going on in the area, we picked up the guy he'd paid to drop off the girls on our property before the Feds could flag the operation. The buyer was ready and waiting at the pick-up site, but Burlone's guy never came. However, the Feds were there to pick up the buyer anyway, which ended up making Burlone look shitty for not giving the buyer a heads-up. Since then, everyone's been hesitant to work with him. All we've been doing is whispering the possibility that Burlone has been working with the Feds and set up the buyer. Unfortunately, we need to find something that will tip them over the edge and convince his colleagues that the rumors are true. If we can give them some kind of solid evidence that Burlone's a snitch and has been turning in people to the Feds, then Burlone will lose his backing at the tournament."

My forehead wrinkles in confusion as I process the information before stumbling on his last sentence. "What do you mean, *his backing at the tournament?*"

D answers my question while leaning against the doorframe of Kingston's office looking like a stone-cold killer. "He's planning on raping you and Regina in front of everyone before putting a bullet in Kingston's skull at the end of the night. Burlone thinks the men coming to the tournament are all on his side since he's worked with them in the past while the Romanos have always stayed far away from trafficking. He thinks they won't care if he doesn't honor the protection rules that are set in place for these very circumstances. If we can cast doubt on their relationship and prove Burlone's a snitch, then they'll back us instead."

"And if they do back the Romano family?" My voice is shaky, and I'm sure my eyes are the size of saucers, but I swallow down the fact he just mentioned the possibility of me getting raped in front of a bunch of men before killing Kingston. Nope. We're going to pretend that little tidbit doesn't affect me at all.

Kingston's chest rumbles with his response. "Then we pull the rug out from under the Allegretti family and put Burlone in the ground."

If it were anyone else, I might flinch at the prospect of burying someone, but with a man as wicked as him, I feel almost giddy at the promise in King's voice.

"Is that possible?"

"Don't look too excited, Ace," Kingston teases with a smile. It's clear he's pleased with my response to the glimpse of darkness he just gave me. "Yeah. It's possible. *If* it looks like he's working with the Feds. The rumors aren't enough to wipe out an entire family, though, and if we take down Burlone, then we need to take down the entire Allegretti family. It helps that his right-hand man can vouch for the lie, saying he's overheard conversations and shit, but we don't think it's quite enough. We need something concrete, which isn't possible because he's not a rat."

"Rock, meet hard place," D pipes up sarcastically.

Digging my teeth into my lower lip, I turn to King as a thought reveals itself to me.

No, it's a terrible idea. But maybe...

A burst of adrenaline rushes through me, but I force my mouth to stay closed. Voicing a possible solution to our problem might end with a bullet in my own skull if the wrong person were to find out. But I also know I can't risk that bullet winding up in Kingston's skull, either, and if I don't tell him my idea, then one might. Sensing my unease, he tilts his head and assesses me.

"What's going on?"

I continue to chew on my lower lip.

"Ace?" he presses.

On shaky legs, I stand up and shuffle a foot away from Kingston to give us both some space.

"Do you trust me, King?"

"Of course, Wild Card. But that look is freaking me out." He laughs, though there isn't any humor in it, and I have a feeling he can feel the same foreboding as I can. Swallowing thickly, I reach into the back pocket of my jeans and pull out a business card. *Jack's* business card.

"I have an idea."

His brows furrow in curiosity before taking a closer look. "And?"

"Do you remember—"

"What the fuck is that?" King explodes, eyeing the small piece of cardstock in my hand as if it were a ticking time bomb. I jump from his outburst as D looks over his shoulder toward the empty hallway then rushes to close the office door. His chiseled jaw hardens, and I know exactly what he's thinking. He thinks I lied to him. That I lied to both of them.

Under their scrutinization, my tongue fumbles over the words, "It's not what it looks like."

"Better not be what it looks like, Wild Card, or you'd put me in a pretty messed up situation," Kingston spits, his gaze narrowing in suspicion.

"Boss," D murmurs, his tone heavy.

I look over at him to see his hand resting near the Glock I know is tucked behind his suit jacket.

Shit. Shit. Shit.

"Start talking, Ace. Now." The steeliness in Kingston's voice surprises me, making me flinch.

"Do you really think I'd betray you?" I whisper. My feet seem to have lost all desire for self-preservation as they take a cautious step toward him. If I can just touch him. If I can make him see that it's *me* he's glaring at, and not the enemy, then I might be able to bring my Kingston back to the room instead of the stranger who's glaring at me like I'm a double agent.

With his spine made of steel, he watches me warily but doesn't move a muscle. "I told you to start talking, and I suggest you don't make me ask twice."

My feet stop their pursuit. *Shit.* He's pissed. As I release a shaky breath, I look over my shoulder and address Diece. "Do you remember the grocery store?"

Fists clenching, he gives me a jerky nod.

"You saw Jack there. He approached me—" The news pulls a roar from Kingston's chest, and I raise my hand in a silent plea. After shaking his head in disgust, he quiets down long enough for me to continue. "I didn't know he was going to be there. I promise, Kingston. I need you to trust me right now." Roughly, the palms of his hands rub against his face, but he remains silent, so I press on. "Jack thought I was in danger and gave me his card. I promise you that I had no idea who Jack was, or that he's been undercover. I met him at Sin, and then he just…started popping up places. For some reason I still don't really understand, he was trying to look out for me, and when I disappeared, he lost it. Then he saw me in the store with D––which was completely coinciden-tal––and gave me his card. He told me that if I ever need anything from him, he's here to help, but I promise you that I would never tell him anything, Kingston. Ever. Not unless I spoke with you first, and we both agreed it was in our best interest, and after what you've just told me, I think it might be."

The silence in the room is so thick that my lungs struggle

to breathe, my chest constricting in agony as I watch the man I've fallen for observing me so coldly.

With a tense voice, he continues his interrogation. "Why didn't you tell me before?"

"Because he's only doing his job, and I didn't want him to get hurt. A-and I didn't want you to look at me the way you're looking at me right now," I confide before dropping my gaze down to my bare feet.

"D," Kingston barks. "Out. Now."

"But—"

"Now."

The door opens then closes with a soft click seconds later, and I'm left with the most powerful man I've ever met who's making me feel like his enemy when I'm supposed to be on his team.

"Sit." My neck snaps up to see him leaning against the desk with his ankles crossed and a frown firmly in place.

I gulp before taking a seat on the chair opposite him. With my butt on the edge, I wait for him to say something. Anything.

"Do you know what a connection like this looks like?" he asks in a lethal tone.

Peeking up at him, I nod.

"Do you know what kind of position this puts me in?"

Again, I nod.

"Do you know what I should do with this information?"

I squeeze my eyes shut only to hear his hand slam against the top of his desk, making me jump for the third time in five minutes.

"Answer me," he growls.

"Yes."

"Then tell me why you think I shouldn't. If it were anyone else in this room with a card like that, they'd already be dead. Why should I treat you any different?"

The image he paints steals my breath. If I ever wanted to truly see how strongly he feels about me, it seems like now is the perfect opportunity.

Licking my lips, I chance another glance up at him. His eyes are hooded and pitch black. His fists are tight in barely restrained anger. And his muscles are bunching beneath his shirt like a damn tiger who's been cornered. *This* is the Dark King. And I'm challenging him.

"Because I'm trusting you."

"Or you're using me," he counters.

"Do you really think I'd use you like that, Kingston? Think about it, and I mean really think about it. I'm putting my life on the line in hopes of finding a solution, and one fell into my lap. You can't blame me for that. I didn't go out looking for Jack. I didn't know who he was. But if you could just…trust me. I think I have an idea. One that can fix everything."

"You've said that already. Better keep talking, Wild Card."

Clearing my throat, I dive right in.

60

KINGSTON

I t isn't easy to gain my respect, but as Ace goes toe-to-toe with me, I can't help but admire her determination.

That doesn't stop the overwhelming suspicion from taking hold, however.

"I said talk," I bark.

I watch as her pink tongue darts out between her lips before running along them. "You need evidence that Burlone works for the Feds. I know a Fed who might be willing to help."

Tapping my finger against my chin, I say, "You said *might*. Do you know what happens if he *doesn't* want to give us the fabricated documents we're asking for?"

"He'll give it to us," she counters. There's an edge of determination in her voice, but it isn't enough to convince me.

I scoff. "How do you know, Ace?"

"Because he knows what a terrible human being Burlone is just like we do."

A wave of frustration mixed with defeat rolls through me. Leaning forward, I ask, "Ace. Who am I?"

Ace's brows pinch in confusion. "Huh?"

"Who am I?"

"You're Kingston?" It's obvious she doesn't know where I'm going with this, so I spell it out for her.

"I'm Kingston Romano. Head of the Romano family. I'm a made man, Ace. I'm a *bad* man."

"Well yeah, but—"

"What makes me any different than Burlone in Jack Connelly's eyes?"

With a huff, she crosses her arms. "You don't have multiple women at your disposal for a quick buck. That's the difference. If we can offer him something he wants in return—"

"And what if we can't find something he wants? You're suggesting we approach a Fed, Ace. If he refuses to help us, then I'll have no choice but to kill him to protect ourselves. To protect our family. Are you okay with that?"

"It won't come to that," she argues, though I can see the doubt in her eyes.

"It might," I return. "I need to know whose side you're on. Because right now, you could still walk away. You could still disappear into the night. Your name hasn't been tainted by the mafia yet, but if your connection with a Fed is discovered, and then that Fed goes missing because they refuse to cooperate with us, it won't take a genius to figure out the part you played. Do you want that?"

Gaze steely, she stands from her seat before nudging my legs apart and pushing between them. I feel her soft palms cup both sides of my face, and the intimate touch surprises me. Especially when I just finished giving her an ultimatum I'd never planned on voicing aloud.

Pulling me down until my forehead rests against hers, she whispers, "I'm in this, King. I'm *all* in. If Jack doesn't go along with this, then we do what needs to be done to protect the family. There's no going back for me...no matter what."

I watch for any sign of a lie, even if she's hiding the truth from herself as much as she's hiding it from me, but I don't see it. The resolution in her eyes is clear, and my chest squeezes in anticipation.

"Truth," I murmur, my lips hovering an inch from hers.

"Then let me ask you again. Do you trust me?"

I nod.

"Let's do this."

I DON'T LIKE THIS. I DON'T LIKE THIS ONE FUCKING BIT. I watch Ace dial Jack's number with a clenched jaw, convinced we're all going to end up dead or in prison. But she asked for my trust, and after hearing her side of the story, I grudgingly told her she had it.

Those big doe eyes got to me as she explained what had happened, and her logic behind following this path was enough to convince me she's right. I assessed every movement as she laid out her plan. I couldn't detect a single lie in her absurd story concerning how she received that damn card. Watching her closely, I still can't find a single bone in her body that whispers betrayal. Either I'm going soft, or she's telling the truth. I just pray that my feelings for her haven't clouded my judgment. But I guess we'll just have to wait and see.

"Um, hey," her soft little voice murmurs into the receiver. "Yeah, it's me, Ace."

Silence.

Her gaze darts over to me before looking down at her sneakers. "I'm fine, I promise. Look, do you think we could meet somewhere?"

Silence.

"Umm...there's a diner? Dottie's? It's on—" She pauses. "Okay, good. See you then."

Her hand that's holding the phone to her ear drops to her side, and she gives me the thumbs up. "Looks like we're meeting him in thirty minutes at Dottie's."

"Thank God. I'm starving," D adds, rubbing his stomach dramatically. As soon as I told D that I trust Ace, he jumped on board without any questions, and I appreciate his support. Ace laughs at his antics before walking around the desk and planting a kiss against my mouth.

"It's going to be okay," she promises, her eyes shining with sincerity.

"And if it isn't, am I allowed to kill him?"

Messing with the Feds is unheard of in this business. Well, unless you want to end up dead like Burlone is going to be. *If* everything goes according to plan.

Hesitantly, she leans forward and drops another kiss to my mouth. This one is slower. Sweeter. And so damn addictive I have to force my hands to stay at my sides when they're begging to wrap around her tiny waist so that I can press myself against her. The tip of my tongue brushes against the seam of her mouth as I hear D clearing his throat. I'd almost forgotten he was in the room, though I don't really give a shit. With a sigh, Ace pulls away and rests her head against my forehead. "Come on, King. Buy me some French toast, will ya?"

D interrupts. "French toast? I thought you were an eggs kind of girl?"

Looking over her shoulder at him, she shrugs. "Yeah. I guess it's my own little tribute to G. Have you heard anything about her?"

"She's a ghost, Ace," he replies. "We haven't been able to find anything."

Her face sobers, but I press forward because she needs to know the truth.

"Your friend vanished, and we think it has something to do with Burlone. But we'll find her. I promise."

With a nod, a somber Ace wraps her arms around herself before I press my hand against her back and lead her to my black Audi parked in the garage. I open the passenger door and help her inside. Once she's situated, I climb behind the steering wheel. D sits in the back, and we head to Dottie's.

THE PLACE IS EXACTLY WHAT I EXPECTED. FIFTIES DINER. THE smell of grease. The booths tucked along the walls. It's... quaint. And clean. I've gotta give the owner some credit for keeping it in pretty decent shape, especially in a neighborhood like this. I scan the area for the man of the hour.

As soon as I see the guy sitting in one of the booths near the back of the diner, my steps almost falter.

"This is Jack? The asshole who grabbed you in my casino?" I spit angrily.

Ace has the decency to look apologetic before placing her hand on my bicep and giving it a soft squeeze.

"He's our only shot right now to get the concrete evidence we need, King. Can you please play nice? For me?"

With a clenched jaw, I dig deep and find some semblance of control before putting my hand against the small of her back and pushing her forward. "I think it'd be best if he saw you first, Wild Card. Because if he sees us swarm him, he might have a heart attack."

Laughing awkwardly, she takes a step toward the booth before turning on her heel. "Come over in two minutes. I'll try to prep him, but I don't want to give him a chance to actually leave, ya know?"

Both D and I nod before D jokes, "We'll be right over by the hostess table. But don't make us wait long. I wasn't kidding when I said I was hungry."

Giving D a playful wink, Ace says, "I'll place your order when Dottie comes over. Eggs, sausage, and breakfast potatoes?"

His stomach growls. "Yes, please. And order some for Kingston too. I don't want him getting handsy with my sausage."

Snorting, she waves us off. "See you in a few."

With the confidence of a runway model, Ace approaches Jack and sits down across from him before a waitress comes and takes their order. I watch as her mouth forms my name, quickly followed by the douche slapping his hand against the table angrily, his posture turning rigid. My nostrils flare when I see Ace put her delicate little hand on top of his to calm him down.

Sensing my frustration, D grabs my forearm. "Give her a second, King. It's all good. She's taking care of it."

"I don't like her touching him," I grit out.

I don't like it at all.

"You don't own her, man. Pretty sure it's the other way around."

Giving him the side-eye, I see an amused smirk on his face, and if we weren't in public, I'd wipe it off with my fist.

I don't bother responding to his remark because I'm afraid he might have a point. How else would a girl off the streets be able to convince a mob boss to meet with the Feds?

Cracking my knuckles, I mutter, "It's been two minutes. Time's up."

Casually, I walk over to the booth then slide in next to Ace without waiting for an invitation. I don't need one, anyway. Not after everything she's put me through. D grabs a chair from a nearby table. The legs scrape against the tile floor as he drags it toward us then plops into it lazily and rests his elbows on the table. Once we're situated, I assess the man I've been told I should rely on. The only problem? With the way he looks at Ace, I know my judgment will be clouded, and I won't be able to trust my gut.

Which means I'll have to put my trust in the girl beside me, instead. Looking over at her, she gives me an innocent smile then rests her hand against my thigh beneath the table. Her touch immediately calms me, and it only confirms D's comment from earlier. She fucking owns me.

Our food is being placed in front of us seconds later by an older woman with short dyed-red hair and a no-shit attitude that I admire.

"I see the way y'all are lookin' at each other," she starts. "I spent way too much of my time and money to see my diner ruined by a brawl or a pissin' contest. If things get crazy, take it outside. That ain't negotiable, ya hear?"

My mouth quirks up on one side. "Loud and clear. Thanks for letting us borrow your establishment. We'll take good care of it."

"Good answer. I'll be over there if y'all need anything." Her forefinger points to the other side of the diner before she turns on her heel and goes on to help the next customer, leaving us to ourselves.

"Ace said you wanted to see me?" Jack breaks the tense silence with a sarcastic tone that immediately grates on my nerves. His frustration is clear but unnecessary.

D pops a breakfast potato into his mouth then jokes, "Don't get your panties in a twist, Jack Connelly, FBI agent. We're only here to talk."

"Sure you are," Jack mumbles under his breath, his eyes narrowing on Ace.

"Look," Ace says. "We need your help."

With a scoff, Jack shakes his head. "And what kind of help

329

would a mafia king need from an FBI agent? I'm not going to cover up the shit you've done. I'm not going to go crawling back to the academy empty-handed, and I'm not a dirty cop. So what the hell do you think you can get from me?"

"Let me ask you something, Jack." My voice is like ice; my demeanor is confident, bordering on arrogant. I know Ace can see the change in me compared to the man she's always seen by the way her breath catches in her throat. Her hand shakes as it rests against my leg, but she doesn't remove it. Instead, her head does a tiny bob of approval, encouraging me to be the man I need to be and to get shit done.

Which is exactly what I intend to do.

Clearing my throat, I press forward. "What would you do if you were given the opportunity to take down the entire human trafficking ring in the Midwest?"

His eyes nearly bug out of his head before he schools his features. "I'd say you were full of shit."

"And if I wasn't?"

Gritting his teeth, he asks, "How?"

"Despite what you think you know, I don't deal in the skin trade. It's despicable. Vile. The lowest of the low. My father used to always believe in ignoring that side of the business and those who dabble in it. But since I've taken on his role, I can't see a benefit to keeping them around."

"Are you saying you want to work for the good guys?" Jack probes in disbelief.

D laughs loud and hard, throwing his head back and slapping his hand against his knee until tears are in his eyes. "I'm sorry, you have to be joking, right? Work for you? Bullshit. We're talking about a fucking trade, Jack. Plain and simple."

"And what are you wanting to trade, exactly?" a skeptical Jack returns.

"I need you to give me evidence that Burlone Allegretti is working for the FBI."

His brows pinch in the center before looking between Ace, me, and D. "But he's—"

"Shh," I tsk as if I were talking to a little kid, an arrogant grin firmly in place. "If you can get me the evidence I need, I'll deliver the top four human traffickers to you in a handbasket."

"Four? I thought there were five."

"There won't be by the time I'm finished with him."

With a shake of his head, Jack leans back into the booth and crosses his arms over his chest. "I can't be involved with murder."

"You're already involved with murder by not helping us. And rape. And kidnapping. And every other despicable crime out there. It really is that simple."

He swallows, his skin turning slightly pale while I spell it out for him. D keeps taking bites of his breakfast, munching happily on his breakfast potatoes and eggs while we wait for Jack to say something.

Rubbing his brow, Jack admits, "I don't know what you want me to say right now. I'm not a traitor."

Ace leans forward, her soft voice hushed but urgent. "We're not asking you to be a traitor, Jack. We're asking you to help us weed out an evil man who has hurt too many people during his measly existence. And if I'm being totally honest? I'm not asking; I'm begging. Please. If you don't do this, I'll never find my best friend, and Kingston's sister will be lost forever in a torturous hell that should never exist. *Please.*" Her eyes are shining with unshed tears that nearly buries the heartless bastard I've become. This girl is the strongest person I've ever met, and I hate that I wasn't there to protect her from experiencing the hell she just described firsthand.

Jack continues to stare at my girl from across the table until breaking his gaze and turning to me. "I need Burlone."

"You can't have him."

"You don't understand," Jack argues. "My entire operation has been to bring Burlone down."

"He'll be taken care of, and I can assure you it'll be with a hell of a lot more justice than the judicial court can offer," I add with a cold, hard stare.

My comment makes him pause. I can see the wheels turning in his head as he considers his options. Ace's leg bounces beneath the table, and I smile when my hand brushes against her skintight jeans, instantly calming her.

Shifting in his seat, Jack rests against the tabletop and leans closer. "You can get me the other four?"

"Yes."

"When do you need it?"

"By tomorrow morning."

Jack fails to hide his surprise. "And you think I can work that fast?"

"You'll have to," I reply, staring him down.

"And when will I get my handbasket?"

D laughs again, but I ignore him and answer Jack's question. "Tomorrow night."

Our eyes remain locked as I watch Jack weigh the pros and cons for a solid minute. He's close to cracking. I can feel it. From my periphery, Ace's attention bounces between the two of us, waiting to see what the verdict will be.

"Then it seems I have some work to do. Obviously, you know how to reach me if you need anything else." Jack's lips form a thin line, not too pleased with the way we used his feelings for Ace against him.

"We will," Ace says, apologetically.

With a nod, Jack slides out from the booth and adds, "Thanks for breakfast," then walks to the diner's exit without a backward glance, making D laugh even harder.

"I like that guy. Will you pay for my breakfast too?"

Ace's grin is hesitant before she playfully nudges me in the ribs and rests her head against my shoulder.

"Put it on his tab," she answers for me.

"See? I knew I liked you too." Fork in hand, D winks then shovels another massive bite of scrambled eggs into his mouth, feeling the same relief I am that we might actually be able to pull this off.

61

KINGSTON

The next evening, I adjust my tie while staring into the mirror as the weight of the world feels heavy on my shoulders. After leaving the diner, we cracked open a bottle of wine for Ace, and I poured myself a few fingers of whiskey. We sat on the balcony overlooking the city without exchanging more than a handful of words. And today, I've spent my time preparing for going head to head with Burlone the best that I could. Now? Now, it's go time.

I feel like I'm already in one of Ace's damn poker games and have pushed my entire fortune into the center of the table. With the cards I've been dealt, I've played the best hand possible. But there aren't any real guarantees it's good enough until I see it all play out. The problem is that I'm not dealing in cash. I'm dealing in lives. Multiple lives. If it were just mine, I'd keep my chin raised and a cocky smile firmly placed on my face. But it's not *just* my life. It's Ace's. Regina's. Possibly my men. And countless innocent women who have all unwittingly bet on me too.

With a snap of D's fingers, I shake my head and eye him in the mirror.

"Everything ready?" I ask, clearing my throat.

"As ready as it can be."

"Did Jack pull through?"

A confident smirk tugs at his mouth and he hands over his cell with an image pulled up on the screen. Looking at the picture, I see a screenshot of a piece of paper with Burlone's ugly mug shot printed in the right-hand corner with the official Federal Bureau Investigation letterhead scrawled across the top. I zoom in and begin reading the police jargon typed in Times New Roman before reaching the end where I find Burlone Allegretti's signature written in blue ink.

Grinning, I hand the phone back to Diece then grab my suit jacket from a hanger and slide it on. "Gotta hand it to him. Looks like he held up his end of the bargain."

"I'll say." D's tone is enthusiastic. "I already forwarded it to the rest of the poker attendees."

"And?"

"And they're in. Or at least they say they are. There are no real guarantees in this kind of situation, though. Are you sure you want Ace to go?"

Grimacing, I tighten my jaw and grit out, "I don't think I have much of a choice. If I don't show up with her, Burlone's men won't let me in the door. And if I don't get in, I can kiss Regina and the rest of the plan goodbye." My chest tightens. "We've worked too hard to let that happen."

"So you're going all in."

"And praying I'll suck out and beat that bastard at his own game," I finish.

With a heavy pat on my shoulder, D ushers me out the door. "We've got him, King."

We better.

"And what about Dex?" I probe, mentioning his half-brother. We haven't really discussed his part since he showed up in my office courtesy of Diece. "Is he going to step up and play his part?"

"I sure as hell hope so. He's a gamble, King, but you saw the letter from Regina too. You saw how he acted at the mention of her getting hurt. In a way, I think he has just as much at stake as us. So yeah, I think he'll back us."

"Well, let's pray like hell that he does because, without him, our story loses most of its validity. And we can't let that happen."

"No." He shakes his head. "We can't. Jack said he'll leave the back entrance to the estate unattended so Dex can get Burlone and Regina out of the building without being flagged. He also said you and Ace have immunity, so you can walk out the front door without being touched."

We're walking down the hall toward the garage as I scan for Ace. She had wanted to have a glass of wine before we left to settle her nerves, but I don't appreciate the anxiety that gnaws at my stomach with her absence.

"Perfect. I don't need this coming back to bite us in the ass," I mutter.

"It won't. It's going to play out the way we need it to, King. We got this."

Rounding the corner, I see Ace through the patio doors that lead to the balcony. It's cool for this time of night, and I watch from a short distance as she enjoys it firsthand. A gentle breeze sways her long, silky hair, and a soft smile graces her lips while she takes in the view of the whole city painted in darkness and the golden lights twinkling. Her skin is almost glowing a soft ivory from the alabaster moonlight as she lifts the nearly empty glass of wine to her cherry red lips and takes a final sip.

"Lucky bastard," D mumbles next to me. "Go tell her it's time to go and keep me updated. Me and a few of the men will be hanging out near Burlone's place in case anything gets out of hand."

I nod, unable to take my eyes off my Wild Card.

With a pat on the back, D adds, "We've been in stickier situations before, King. We'll get out of this one too."

"It's not me that I'm worried about."

He follows my gaze as it lands on Ace as she stares up at the full moon hanging in the cloudless sky.

"She's strong, King. The other men in that room need to fear you, and you need to make them. You can't let her presence soften you tonight. You need to be the Dark King. Do you think you can do that with her there?"

"I don't think I have a choice."

"You don't. But I can guarantee she'll still love you after. Even if she does end up getting a front-row seat to the Dark King in action. Understand?"

With a nod, I take a step toward my girl and toss over my shoulder, "Yeah. I got it."

THE NEED TO HOLD ACE IS OVERWHELMING. IT'S AS IF I'M missing a limb anytime she isn't near, and right now, the ache is staggering. I felt like I almost lost her when she admitted her connection to the FBI. And, though I'd chosen to trust her, I still wasn't sure if I'd regret it when she convinced me to meet Jack. But now that everything is set into motion, and the future is imminent, I can't help but feel like I need to cherish every moment with her because I don't know if it'll be our last.

"Hey, Wild Card," I murmur as a gust of wind nearly topples her over. Her fingers run against the frayed Allegretti cards in her hand, and I have no doubt she was lost in her memories before I interrupted her.

"Hey, you." She smiles before tucking the worn deck into her clutch and wrapping her cool arms around me. Her skin has pebbled from being out here too long, and I rub my hands up and down her bare arms to heat her up.

"You're freezing. How long have you been out here?"

"A while," she admits, her cheeks turning rosy. "But I feel like as soon as I step inside, it'll be time to go. And I'm not ready."

My eyes seek out the clutch that now holds those same weathered cards, and I sigh.

"You scared, babe?"

I don't know why I ask. I already know the answer. Of course, she's scared. She'd be a fool *not* to be. She's willingly putting her life on the line. For me. For my sister. For the Romano family.

Laying her head against my chest, she takes a slow breath as a horn blares in the distance. I take the opportunity to pull her closer, linking my fingers against her lower back.

"I don't want you to get hurt," she admits on a sigh.

"Me?" I laugh, dryly. "You're worried about me?"

"Of course, I'm worried about you," she argues into my suit with her head still tucked against me. "I love you, King. Imagining a life without you is…" She sniffles. "It's crippling."

The three words hit like a sucker punch, but I restrain myself from falling on my ass. It's funny. I didn't think I was capable of love. Sure, I care for my sister and my men. But *love?* My muscles tense as I squeeze her tighter.

"Then don't imagine it, Ace. Picture this as a poker hand. We're all surrounding the table and have placed our bets, but Burlone doesn't know about the final card we've slipped to the dealer that guarantees a royal flush. He doesn't know that his cocky little grin is about to be wiped off his face tonight by the time the final card is played. I've put all the pieces in place, Ace. Now we just have to stay strong and not fold. Even if it's scary as hell."

With her arms resting against my chest, she looks up at me and whispers, "You're sexy when you talk poker."

I laugh, remembering the first night I'd told her the same thing. "Is that right?"

"Uh-huh. Now kiss me, King. Let me steal a little of your bravery."

Leaning closer, I whisper against her lips, "Anytime, Ace." Then I kiss her. It's soft and slow. A reminder to her that I'm not the monster she's likely to meet tonight. I'm King. *Her* King.

When I pull away, she sighs with her eyes still closed. Then, blinking slowly as if awaking from a dream, she smiles up at me. "Thank you."

"For what?"

"For everything."

I almost snort but stop myself at the last second. "No offense, Ace, but you have a twisted way of looking at things. Since the moment we met, I've screwed up your life in more ways than I can count. You've been followed. Beaten up. Twice, I might add." I raise my two fingers, and she grimaces. "And you're now being used as a human buy-in for a poker tournament any sane person would want to stay a thousand miles away from. And what do you say to me? Thank you." I roll my eyes and shake my head, feeling amazed that I get to call her mine when I have no right to. She and I have been through a lot, and if we can just make it through tonight, everything will be okay.

"Well, I *am* grateful. Without you, I'd still be the same lonely girl in search of a home. You...you *are* my home now."

Tugging her into me, I place one more kiss against the crown of her head then guide her to the patio door.

"Come on, Ace. We have somewhere we need to be."

"And then you owe me some scrambled eggs and sausage," she quips by my side.

"I'll give you some sausage," I joke, pinching her ass.

With her head thrown back, she laughs full and loud before smacking me in the chest and winking. "Only if I can take a bite out of it. I'm starving."

I shiver and toss my arm around her tiny frame. "No deal. I'll get you your damn sausage."

She takes advantage and puts her head on my shoulder as we open the door to the garage and go to the car. "Yeah, you will."

62

ACE

The closer we get to Burlone's house, the more tension accompanies our car ride. King and I are practically robotic in our movements as we walk up the steps leading to an immaculate front door that's got to be twelve feet high with a giant brass handle and a knocker that reminds me of medieval times. The exorbitantly priced cars that line the driveway hint that we're one of the last to arrive. Just like Kingston wanted.

He raps his knuckles against the monstrous door, then we wait.

When it opens, I see a guy with a diamond tattoo below his eye, and I instinctively curl into King's side. He tightens his hold around my shoulder, silently grounding me when all I want to do is disappear. Glancing up at the man in front of me, I try to place how I recognize him.

There's just something about him.

After a second, it hits me. I remember him from when I first overheard Burlone mentioning his alibi, then again when I saw him eavesdropping on my conversation with Jack before the tournament. He must be the one who

341

revealed to Burlone that King and I were together. And I instantly hate him for it.

"Come on in." The sketchy guy waves his arm with a flourish before bowing dramatically as we step over the threshold. He seems like a thug. A jerk. An ass. I secretly wish someone would slam his hand in the door or make him slip on some ice and fall on his butt. A ghost of a smile graces my lips as I imagine witnessing it.

If only.

"Play nice, Wild Card," Kingston whispers in my ear, trying to contain his smile. He moves to lead me farther into the house when the guy stops us. "Excuse me, but your…"— he looks me up and down hungrily— "*guest* will need to wear these. It's standard procedure, of course."

Grinning wickedly, he lifts up a silver platter for Kingston to view. On it are a pair of handcuffs and what appears to be a collar. My nose scrunches in disgust while my heart stalls in my chest.

No, no, no, no.

"Are you fucking kidding me?" King spits, tightening his protective hold around my waist. His grip is almost painful, yet not hard enough at the same time. The stark bite from his touch is enough to remind me he's here. He's got me.

"Sorry, sir, but like I said, it's standard procedure. If you plan on participating in the tournament, then your buy-in needs to be properly handled. However, if that's a problem, you're welcome to leave." The asshole has the audacity to open the front door with his right hand while still balancing the platter with his left.

Gritted teeth on display, King takes the collar and handcuffs but hesitates to put them on me. I can see his reservations in his eyes as they connect with mine. I never thought I'd see the man in front of me hesitate. But right now? He is. I can see him at war with himself. I can see the wheels turning in his head as he weighs his options. Unfortunately, I know he'll come to the same conclusion I have. We don't have a choice.

Keeping my feet firmly planted, I stare at the objects dangling from Kingston's hand as if they're a snake waiting to strike. My gaze turns to the guy who answered the door, then back to Kingston. He looks about two seconds away from storming out with me in tow, throwing our whole plan out the window. And I can't let that happen.

"It's okay," I reassure him under my breath while praying the asshat from a few feet away can't hear me. My eyes dart to said asshat before returning to Kingston. "Promise."

"Where are the keys?" King barks to the spectator who's getting way too much enjoyment out of King's reluctance. Without a word, he picks them up from the platter and lifts them into the air.

"Here you go. Once you reach the main room where the tournament is being held, you'll place the keys in the center pot for the final winner to collect at the end of the night."

With a final glare at Burlone's thug, King turns to me reluctantly, looking way too helpless for his own good. I raise my arms toward him and shrug one shoulder.

"It's fine, King. I'll be out in no time, remember?"

My comment is meant to soothe him but only seems to rile up the guy who answered the door. Thankfully, another firm look from King is enough to shut him up.

King grasps my offered hands as if I'm a helpless bird and brushes his thumbs against the inside of my wrists before lifting the cuffs. The intention is clear in his apologetic eyes while the metal is cold against my skin, making me flinch when the locks click into place.

A satisfied grin is plastered on the asshole's face as he says, "Best get going. Burlone is *very* anxious to get started, and you're the last to arrive, so chop chop." He claps his hands for good measure before dangling the keys in front of Kingston's face. With a cold, hard stare, Kingston takes them from him, tucks them into his suit jacket, then guides me across the marble tile with his hand on my lower back.

As I look around the expansive foyer, my mouth opens slightly. The space is immaculate. Not a thing looks out of place, yet there aren't any personal touches anywhere. Rich golds and deep reds suggest an opulence I've never even dreamed of.

"Is this Burlone's house?" I ask, my voice coming out squeaky and mouse-like.

"Technically, no. It's registered under an alias, but, yes. He owns it."

"It's huge."

"Yeah. Take a left up here."

"How do you know where you're going?"

"They explained it in the email with a small disclaimer that if you're not where you're supposed to be, you'll be killed without a second thought."

I gulp. "That sounds promising."

His deep chuckle reverberates through me as we round the corner. "No worries, Ace. We got this."

I sure hope so, I think to myself, but I keep my lips zipped.

I wish his confidence was contagious because the only thing I'm feeling right now is that I'm about to puke.

When we reach the open ballroom, a smoky fog makes my eyes water. Or at least I think that's what it is. A gaudy chandelier hangs from the ceiling, and beneath it is a fancy poker table with black felt and six cushioned chairs surrounding it. Five of the seats are taken by men while breathtakingly gorgeous women stand next to them with the same collars around their throats and handcuffs around their wrists as I'm currently wearing. The sight is nothing short of a nightmare.

The fight or flight instinct hits me full-force, and I have to use every ounce of self-discipline to keep my feet from running in the opposite direction.

My eyes take in each individual girl, focusing on their discomfort instead of my own. If we can pull this off, then they'll all be safe. Some have tears streaming down their faces. Others appear to be numb from trauma. I nearly stumble when I see Gigi in a tight, red dress and a swelling bruise against her cheekbone.

"No. No, no, no, no," I mumble under my breath, my eyes glued to my best friend as my entire body goes into shock. I'm shaking like a leaf when Kingston catches me at the last second and shushes me quietly so only I can hear. "It's okay, Ace."

"You don't understand." My voice cracks, and my eyes well with tears as I choke out, "Gigi's here."

I knew it was a possibility. Hell, I knew the odds were pretty damn likely, but it still doesn't stop the reality that she's been living an absolute nightmare from nearly taking me down to the floor. And it's all because of me. Because we sat together and bonded over breakfast foods. Because we were friends.

He tosses a quick glance over his shoulder at the table before looking down at me, and I know he can feel my pain as if it's his own because I feel the same way.

"We'll get her out. But I need you to be patient, okay?"

The metallic taste of blood explodes in my mouth as I dig my teeth into my lower lip to keep from having a complete meltdown. The tangy flavor is barely enough to keep my emotions in check. For now, anyway.

He's right. If we're going to get out of this, then I need to chill out and be patient.

Nodding, I follow Kingston to the last vacant spot at the table then place my hand on his shoulder like the rest of the girls. The odd behavior makes me feel like I'm nothing more than an object--a pretty piece of meat for all the men to look at. And boy, are they looking. I can feel their eyes on me. The way they observe me like a cut of prime rib from the butcher, inspecting me for their own sick use. My stomach rolls at the thought, and my fingers dig into Kingston's shoulder. Since he's made of solid muscle, he doesn't even flinch as I take a bit of my frustration out on him. The collar feels like it's slowly shrinking around my neck, making me swallow thickly.

Calm down, Ace.

With effort, I loosen my hold on him while reminding myself that Kingston needs a strong woman by his side so he can focus on Burlone. If everything goes according to plan, the slimeball is about to have his world thrown on its axis. And I've never wanted something more in my entire life.

I take a deep breath and try to calm my nerves then take the opportunity to get a closer look at the girls around the table. When I find Gigi looking at me with the same shock written on her face as I'm sure is written on mine, I want to cry all over again.

"It's okay," I mouth to her in an attempt to appear unfazed by the entire ordeal. I have no doubt she can see right through me.

She blinks rapidly in response, holding back a fresh set of tears. But she doesn't say anything. Who knows? With the hell she's been through, maybe she's too afraid to try.

63

ACE

"**G**entlemen, I'm glad you could all make it," Burlone starts, distracting me from Gigi's terrified expression. His voice brings back haunting memories every time I hear it, and I have to fight my knees from buckling as the horrific memories hit for the thousandth time since this whole thing started.

"Now, as you all know, the rules are a simple winner takes all format. However, while I've been gracious enough to prepare your women for you, none of you have compensated me for my efforts in acquiring them. Instead, you requested to pay in person this evening before the official tournament started. As you all know, this is highly irregular, but I've been generous enough to comply. Well, gentlemen, the time has arrived. Now, if you will…" His voice trails off as he motions to the table, silently asking the slimy assholes willing to sell and buy women sitting around the table to pay up.

No one moves a muscle.

With my heart racing, I wait to see Kingston's move. This is the moment we've been waiting for, and the ball is officially in his court. *Our* court. When Kingston doesn't do anything, curiosity gets the best of me, and I look around the room to find I'm not the only one anxious to see how this is going to play out. Every man is staring at Kingston too. I'd give anything to see his face right now, but I can't, so I'll have to settle for Burlone's.

His big, bushy eyebrows are furrowed as he looks at his associates who are all frozen in their places.

"I'm sorry, were those instructions confusing? I mean, I know there's an open bar and all but--" He chuckles awkwardly at his pathetic joke while the rest of the room stays motionless.

"You're awfully insistent we pay up," one man mutters under his breath. If it'd been in any other situation, I'm sure he could've kept his comment to himself. Unfortunately for him, the room is so silent that his quiet voice is easily understood.

With his salt and pepper hair slicked back, the stranger is busy fiddling with his hands as his gaze springs around the room in search of backup before landing firmly on Kingston who still hasn't moved a muscle. Clearly, he's biding his time. I just don't know what he's waiting for, but I trust him enough to know that when the opportunity presents itself, he'll step forward and state his case. A swarm of nervous bats ravages my stomach as Burlone's eyes darken.

"Excuse me?" Burlone scoffs. "Dex, escort Mr. Carbonne from the premises. It seems he's misunderstood the dynamic of our relationship. But don't worry, I'm sure we can find a way to rectify that as quickly as possible with a little persuasion." The threat is clear, especially since Dex has always been the muscle for Burlone. The one to *educate* Burlone's enemies with his fists. Two weeks ago, I got a lesson firsthand, and the recovery was a bitch. Gingerly, I touch my rib cage that's still slightly bruised and hurts when I breathe in too deeply. I know he's supposedly on our side, but it doesn't stop the shiver from racing through me at the memory of our one-on-one encounter. I'm not sure if I'll ever truly trust him, but Kingston has chosen to, and I'll trust *him* with my life.

Mr. Carbonne, however, gulps loudly before tugging on the collar of his button-up as if it's choking him. I want to laugh at the irony since the girl behind him is literally wearing a collar too, just like the rest of us women in the room.

Asshole. Kind of sucks being threatened, doesn't it?

I place my sweaty palm back on Kingston's shoulder. His muscles tense beneath his shirt as he waits with bated breath to see how Dex responds to Burlone's orders. I catch myself holding my breath too. This is the moment. The one that tells us if we're going to be slaughtered tonight, or if we have a chance to pull this off. Because without Dex? We're screwed.

From the shadows, I hear his gruff voice that makes me break out into a sweat from the first time I met him. "Apologies, Mr. Allegretti. But I'm afraid I can't do that."

"Excuse me?" Burlone turns in his seat with a glare, searching for Dex around the perimeter of the room.

Digging my teeth into my lower lip, I find Dex in the corner with a handgun resting by his side and a casual *I-don't-give-a-shit* expression painted across his face. It's still hard for me to look him in the eye when the last time I saw him, his fist was connecting with the side of my face. Over and over again. But Kingston reassured me we could trust him, so I'm here, praying it isn't a mistake. By the look on his smug face, I'd say we made the right choice.

"What the fuck are you doing?" Burlone grits out with a narrowed gaze.

"Nothing." Dex shrugs. "Just making sure to keep everything in check, which means Mr. Carbonne gets to stay here for a bit longer."

"Have you forgotten your place, Dex?"

"No, I've found it," he returns, looking at Kingston for a split second. But it's long enough for Burlone to start piecing things together. His mouth opens in disbelief.

"Sei!" Burlone shouts. His neck snaps to the front as he searches for his other loyal soldier.

"I'm afraid Sei's not available at the moment," Dex adds conversationally. "And neither are the rest of your men."

"What the fuck did you do?"

"Just taking out the trash, Burlone. And those that didn't need my assistance in disappearing were generously compensated. I'm sure you understand," Dex replies before motioning to Kingston. "Boss, I think now would be a great time to step in."

Kingston chuckles darkly, gaining the attention of everyone in the room as the spotlight shifts from one man to another. I don't miss the way Dex calls him boss, and I'm positive everyone else here heard it loud and clear too.

"I dunno, Dex. I think this is rather entertaining, don't you?" Kingston finally voices. I know this isn't the time or the place, but the confidence he's exuding is sexy as hell. My fingers trail along his neck before finding their place back on his shoulder, my spine straightening.

We can do this. We can do this.

The rest of the people in the room stay silent as they watch the situation unfold with rapt attention.

"What the fuck is going on?" Burlone bellows angrily. Droplets of sweat are starting to cling to his forehead. His face is slightly purple from frustration, and part of me wants to take a picture to remember this moment. Unfortunately, I know it would probably be used as evidence against us if it made its way into the wrong hands.

Especially when I know the potential outcome of tonight. It won't end pretty for him. For any of them.

"Alright, alright. I'll step in," Kingston interrupts. I can hear the smile in his voice, and the sound calms me enough to think this might turn out okay.

"Dex came to me recently. Can you believe that, Burlone?" Kingston asks though he's addressing the whole room. Hell, he's commanding it. "Your own right-hand man? I thought it was a little out of character too, but Dex felt the need to voice a suspicion he had about his dear old boss. Secret meetings. Intentionally botched drop-offs. I found it fascinating, so I decided to do a little research of my own. What I found was...*interesting,* to say the least."

Burlone shakes his head in disbelief. "What the hell are you talking about, King?"

"I'm talking about your association with the FBI, and your plan to incriminate everyone at this table tonight as soon as they handed over their money for the beautiful women you've *found.*" The way King says the word *found* is enough to insinuate the opposite.

Burlone sputters, "What the fuck does that mean?"

"Dex," King calls while ignoring Burlone completely.

Gun at his side, he steps out of the shadows. "Yeah, Boss?"

"Were the women in this room handled differently than usual?"

"Yeah."

"Care to expand?" King laughs, dryly.

Dex joins in before explaining, "The men were explicitly told *not* to touch them. In fact, Burlone brought me in and ordered me to keep them from being spoiled before they were officially purchased, which he's never done before. If we're being honest, he's usually one of the first to break them in."

The men around the room all laugh, like that little tidbit

isn't one of the most despicable things Dex could've said. My stomach clenches when Kingston's own chuckle joins in before he continues his probing.

"And why do you think they were being protected?"

"Because he didn't want any incriminating evidence on the Allegretti family. Only his associates."

"And why is that?"

"Because he cut a deal with the Feds," Dex finishes. His tone is matter-of-fact and almost lazy. If I weren't in on the ruse, I just might believe him myself.

Outraged, Burlone shoves his chair away from the table a few inches but stays seated as he argues, "That's bullshit, and you know it. Gentlemen, why would I talk to the Feds? It's not logical."

"It is if they've got incriminating evidence against you like your former soldier just stated," Mr. Carbonne pipes in while crossing his arms over his large, round chest. "It makes sense for you to work out a deal with the Feds to help them gather evidence against your associates instead of arresting you. Selfish, Burlone. But smart. *If* you hadn't been caught."

With a roll of his eyes, Burlone shakes his head. "That's the most ludicrous thing I've ever heard. What kind of evidence do you have? You can't honestly believe the high and mighty Romano family over one of your own?"

Another man interrupts from my left. He's got to be almost sixty years old and looks like an old bulldog, his jowls hanging off his face. "Interestingly, I would normally agree with you, Burlone. But then I heard from one of my associates who informed me of a little incident a few weeks ago. One where you had set up a drop off on Kingston's turf but didn't show up with the women. However, the Feds *did* know where you were meeting and were there to greet him. The only reason my associate didn't get caught was because the Romano family stepped in and fucked up your plans. I assume that's why you personally named Kingston Romano in the email invitation to this tournament. To incriminate him when we all know he's never been one to dabble in the skin trade. You wanted to use the email against him in a court of law."

"This is all hearsay. There's no proof." Burlone's defense falls flat on his audience, and I know I'm not the only one feeling the tides turn in Kingston's favor. However, the push and pull are definitely still there. I know we haven't won yet.

"And if there was proof?" Kingston interrupts the conversation, taking control of the room with a simple question.

My breathing quickens, and I shift my weight between my feet, the need to run still very much present as the testosterone in the room––along with the accusations––intensifies.

Burlone's face goes splotchy and red. His mouth opens and closes like a fish out of water, playing right into our hands. "I-it's not possible."

"I'm going to have to respectfully disagree, my friend."

64

KINGSTON

With a snap of my fingers, Dex stalks closer and puts the gun to Burlone's head, ensuring he doesn't move. I lift my hand and cover Ace's as it rests on my shoulder before murmuring, "Hey, Wild Card. Can you excuse me for a minute?"

She smiles nervously then takes a slow step back and lets me scoot out of my chair. Rounding the table, I rest my hip against the black felt top and tower over Burlone while feeling every single eye in the room watching my every move. If I was anyone else, I might crumble from the pressure, but I bask in it.

"Do you know what we do to traitors, Burlone?"

"I'm not a fucking traitor, Kingston," he spits.

No, you're not, I think to myself. A cocky smirk finds its place on my face. Even though I haven't gotten away with this yet, I need to appear like I have.

"Well, let's see what our fellow associates have to say then, shall we?" I look around the table. "Gentlemen? If you think this man deserves to die a slow and painful death, raise your hand. If you don't, then I'll let him go, you'll pay for your women, and we'll play the tournament as if this never happened."

I keep my face straight and indifferent when, in reality, my heart is pounding against my chest like a jackhammer. The hand has officially been laid out for all to see, and now, I have to find out if they bought it. If I've won. Slowly, one after another, hands are raised into the air.

All except one.

"There a problem, Mr. Russo?"

The man in question has the eyes of a snake and the history of one too. My father always hated him, and so have I. I'd give anything to see him and his entire organization burn.

Mr. Russo clears his throat and looks pointedly at me as if I'm the one about to be wiped from the earth instead of Burlone.

"I've seen your evidence," he begins. "I've seen the official FBI letterhead with his picture on it. But I know Burlone, and I'm having a hard time believing what you've shown me. I think you'll need to give me a bit more proof before I can condemn someone I once considered a friend to a traitorous death."

Fuck.

My mind scrambles for a Hail Mary that might help us pull this off, but I can't figure out what to do. Dex goes to open his mouth to interject when a feminine voice to my right distracts me.

"Burlone?"

All heads swivel in the same direction where a girl with soft blonde hair stands in a tight dress that leaves little to the imagination. Her shoulders are back, and her fiery eyes are set on Burlone. I don't know their history, but it doesn't take a genius to figure out the likelihood that he screwed up her life the same way he screwed up Ace's. He doesn't bother to answer her, not deeming her worthy, but she persists anyway. "Do you know what the FBI does to traitors?"

The room is deathly silent, and I don't move a muscle other than chancing a glimpse at Dex. *What the hell is going on?* I'm given a mirage of a smile before it disappears into thin air, and he looks back at the girl.

She continues with a glare at her captor. "We toss them back to their own kind, letting them fend for themselves."

Burlone shifts in his seat before gritting out, "What the fuck are you talking about, bitch? Shut your filthy mouth before I make you."

"Shhh," she tsks as if she were talking to a toddler. "I'm an undercover agent for the Federal Bureau of Investigation, and we had a deal. As soon as you found a buyer for me and the transaction went through, we'd storm the castle, throw your friends in jail, and you'd be off the hook. However, there was one condition I had. Do you remember what it was?"

Burlone opens his mouth to answer, but Dex slams the butt of his handgun into the back of his head, making his neck snap forward and his chin drop to his chest. In a daze, he shakes his head, so the girl answers for him.

"You guaranteed my protection. You told me I wouldn't be touched. But I was...countless times. And now, your associates know the truth. You're a fucking traitor, and I hope they make you pay for it slowly and in the most painful way possible."

Burlone sputters, "I-if you were an FBI agent, why would you out yourself in a room full of mafia bosses?"

She shrugs. "I'm dead, anyway. Might as well take one asshole who's a liar down with me for what he did. Mr. Russo, you said you wanted proof. Now, you have it. He's a traitor who was plotting against all of you with my team to save his own skin. If I weren't guaranteed to be dead by the end of this conversation, I'd give you physical evidence as a nice little cherry on top. But for now, you'll have to take my word for it."

An onslaught of questions attacks me at once as I stare at the girl in front of me. Who is she? What the hell just happened? Did Jack know? Is this a ruse? A trap? It can't be.

Mr. Russo straightens his tie then looks to me. "And now, you have my vote. Gut the poor bastard. And she's right. Make it slow. Make it hurt. Make him pay for being a rat."

"With pleasure." I smile, feigning confidence when all I feel is confusion. "Unfortunately, my utility bag is at home, and we don't know how long we have until the Feds storm the castle, as the undercover agent so eloquently stated, so I think we'll be going. Dex?"

"Yeah?"

"I'm going to need you to escort *her* to my car too." I tilt my head toward the FBI agent, putting the rest of the room at ease with the promise of her demise, as well. In reality, I'll be returning her to Jack after he answers a few of my questions because her presence wasn't part of the plan. However, I'm not going to say I'm ungrateful for the part she played.

If she hadn't stepped in, Mr. Russo would've never been swayed, and the people I care about would've never left this room.

"Done." Raising his hand in the air, Dex slams the gun against Burlone's head again, harder this time. His body slumps in his chair instantly before Dex reaches into his suit pocket and retrieves a set of zip ties, placing them around Burlone's slackened wrists and ankles. Then, he turns to the blonde girl and asks, "Do you want to do this the easy way or the hard way?"

With tears in her eyes, she whispers, "I'm done fighting. It never did me much good, anyway."

There's something about the defeat in her voice that

brings a fresh wave of pity. Maybe she can talk with Ace for a few minutes before we return her to Jack. Seems to me that she could use a listening ear for all the shit she's been through. I can't even imagine, but I *can* guarantee Burlone will pay for it with his blood.

Nodding, he tosses an unconscious Burlone over his shoulder then reaches for her handcuffs. As he tugs her toward the exit, the rest of us watch in fascination because none of us expected that turn of events––not even me.

"What about the rest of them?" Mr. Carbonne asks, eyeing the cuffed women with collars around their necks cowering in the corners.

"They've all been tagged by the Feds and are being watched. I'll take care of them. But, just to confirm, if I were to be able to wipe their identities, would you be interested in purchasing?" The words taste bitter as they leave my mouth, but I keep my expression indifferent.

Mr. Russo adjusts himself through his pants. "With pleasure."

"I understand, Mr. Russo. And the rest of you?"

Jack made it clear that we'd need evidence on tape if he had any hope of arresting them, and I want to make sure we don't leave any loopholes for them to slip through.

A chorus of yes's echo throughout the room, and I respond with a wicked smile.

"Good. Gentlemen, it's been great doing business with you." Placing my hand on Ace's lower back and leading her to the exit, I add, "We'll be in touch soon."

Once our feet hit the driveway, a swarm of FBI agents disperse from the trees, rushing the house with weapons raised and dark masks covering their faces. Ace nuzzles into my side for protection as a satisfied Jack approaches us.

"Did we get what we needed?"

A recording device is tossed to him by Ace with her hands still linked together.

"Yup. You'll have to pardon the glitches, though." She smirks. "Very finicky little piece of equipment. But we got the evidence you needed of all the men agreeing to purchase the women."

"Finicky, huh? Funny…it was working just fine when I taught you how to use it."

With a shrug, she lifts her hands for me to unlock. "Right? Weird. Hey, King, wanna help a girl out?"

"I dunno. I kind of like you all tied up," I tease, fetching the key from my jacket pocket. I wasn't stupid enough to put them into the center pot. If anyone is going to put my girl in cuffs or take them off, it'll be me.

Shuddering, Jack takes a few steps back toward the house. "Aaand, I think that's my cue. Thanks for your help. You've saved a lot of women from a pretty shitty future."

"Hey, Jack," I call out before he disappears with the rest of his men.

"Yeah?"

"You never told me you had an undercover agent in that house."

Dumbfounded, Jack says, "We don't."

Then who the hell was that girl? Seems I have a few more questions to ask, but they won't be directed at Jack. We might've found a truce for a short period of time, but it isn't going to be a long-term thing. I don't mind him taking out the trash for me, but I'm not a rat, and our lives will always be at odds with each other.

I wouldn't have it any other way.

A beat of silence follows before I wave him off. "Yeah, you're right. Forget I said anything."

"See you around, Jack," Ace adds, ending the conversation.

"You too, Ace."

This time, Jack really does leave. If there wasn't an undercover agent in that room, then who was the girl who pretended to be one? And what was her motive?

A dainty little cough brings me back while Ace quirks her brow and raises her hands in the air.

"A little help, King?"

Sliding the key into the cuffs, I unlock Ace's hands first, then her collar before peppering soft, open-mouthed kisses along her skin. A tender smile in place, she looks up at me with a sense of ease even though her hands are still shaky in my grasp.

"You okay?" I murmur. I know she's strong. But she's also precious. And tonight, she just came face-to-face with her childhood nightmare for a second time. That's gotta mess her up...at least for a little while.

Sighing, she admits, "I will be. I think I'm still processing everything, ya know?"

Yeah. So am I, I think to myself.

"Let's get you home." I open the passenger door, and she slides in without protest. Once she's situated, I round the front then get behind the wheel and back the car out of the premises. Turning around in the passenger seat, Ace watches the massive house fade into the distance before asking, "What about your sister, Dex, and Gigi?"

"What?" I ask, hitting the brakes. "Gigi?"

"I told you she was there!" Ace shouts, obviously freaking out that I didn't instantly reassure her that Gigi's being taken care of. "The girl in the red dress with the bruised face. We can't leave her with all those men and all those agents. Please, King. We need to turn around or something."

She's losing her mind, so I place my hand on her bare thigh as my mind searches for the girl in question.

"There was only one girl in a red dress," I murmur.

"Yeah. Gigi."

On a laugh, I mutter to myself, "No fucking way."

Turning in her seat, Ace gives me a puzzled expression before reaching over and shoving my shoulder. "What's so funny? I'm not kidding! We need to go back for her."

"I should've known," I mumble under my breath before voicing a little louder. "When did you first meet Gigi?"

Pinching her brows together, she thinks about it before answering. "I don't know. A few months ago? We met at the diner in the middle of the night after I got done counting cards and Dottie said she looked like we could both use a friend, pretty much setting us up on a blind *friend date*. We hit it off, and I guess it became a tradition."

"So, you'd never go anywhere else? Do anything else?"

Ace looks confused, and maybe a bit annoyed too, as she tells me, "What else was there to do? Before you, my life revolved around counting cards, eating, and sleeping. That's about it. Why do you ask? And what's with that sneaky smile on your face?" She shoves my shoulder again, begging me to put her out of her misery.

"My mom used to call my little sister Gigi when she was a baby. Regina means Queen in Italian, which my dad found fitting, but Mama Romano thought Regina sounded way too grown up, so she gave her that nickname. She used it until the day she died, but Regina was only three or so. I never would've thought she'd remember something like that."

The color drains from her face.

"What are you saying, Kingston?" she whispers.

"I'm saying my sister fooled us all. The alias she gave you was her childhood nickname, and I was too preoccupied to put the pieces together."

Digging her teeth into her lower lip, Ace clarifies, "So Regina is Gigi? *My* Gigi?"

Again, I cackle. "Yup. Sneaky little brat."

Ace joins in before adding, "No wonder she loved seeing me steal money at the Charlette. Seems you two had a rocky few months there."

"Yeah." I sober, remembering all the fights and slammed doors. "We did."

She laces her fingers through mine before bringing the back of my hand up to her lips and placing a gentle kiss against it.

"I'm here for both of you. If you need anything, let me know."

Leaning across the center console, I meet her in the middle and give her a quick peck on the lips. "I will. Love you, Ace."

The grin that nearly splits her face in two is contagious, and I find myself smiling right back. I never thought I'd say that to anyone. But with her? It just slipped out, and I don't regret it in the slightest.

"Love you too, King."

JACK

"Connelly, get your ass in here," I hear from down the hall. With another slap on the back from one of the men on my team, I head to my superior's office.

Poking my head through Agent Reed's door frame, I ask, "Yes, sir? You wanted to see me?"

"Yeah. Get in here."

I follow his orders and take a seat across from him. Jonathan Reed is as put together as always in his crisp, white shirt and black slacks. Hell, even his shaved head looks freshly polished. My mouth tilts up in the corner before I smooth my features. The asshole has had it out for me for as long as I can remember, and he's never been one to congratulate me for my successes––even when it benefits him personally.

Once I'm situated, he continues, "I wanted to congratulate you on the bust." *Bullshit.* "We've been chasing Carbonne, Russo, Biancci, and Moretti for a long time, and I'm impressed you were able to bring them in."

I cross my arms over my chest and lean back in my chair. "Thanks. Like you said, it was a long time coming."

"It was. Do we have enough evidence to make it stick?"

"Yes, sir. We have multiple eyewitnesses, the suspects' voices on tape admitting their intent in purchasing a girl or having purchased one in the past, and enough DNA on the premises to keep them in jail for the rest of their lives."

"Good."

A tense silence follows his comment, and I shift in my seat.

There's something in the way he's staring at me that confirms my earlier suspicion. He's still an ass, and a congratulatory conversation was *not* on the agenda for our little visit.

I can feel the *but* coming. My anxiety spikes.

"But,"—*there it is*—"we're still missing a very important piece in your case. Wanna tell me who?" With his fingers steepled in front of him, an unamused Agent Reed stares at me pointedly.

Gritting my teeth, I mutter, "Burlone Allegretti."

"That's right. Your anonymous tip brought in four of the five. The problem is that there's still someone out there, and that's unacceptable."

"Yes, sir."

"Celebrate tonight, then bring me my final man." He waves his hand in the air, clearly dismissing me. There's just one problem.

"And if I can't find him?" I ask.

Bringing his gaze back to mine, he answers, "Then you still failed, and I can't close your case. Is finding Burlone going to be a problem?"

Yeah. He's dead.

I clear my throat. "No, sir."

"Good."

ACE

When I see Dex's car pull up to the house, I rush toward it and swing the passenger door open before practically tackling Gigi with hugs.

"G! I've missed you so much! I can't believe you're Kingston's sister! I had no idea. Neither of us did. Your brother thought it was hilarious, by the way. Are you okay? I couldn't find you. I've been freaking out. I'm so glad you're here." The words keep tumbling out of me as I squeeze the crap out of her.

With a soft laugh, Gigi returns my embrace. "I'll be okay, Ace. And I'm glad my brother doesn't want to shoot me for putting all of you through the wringer."

I wave her off. "You'll be fine. Promise. Come on." Grabbing her hand, I try to pull her into the house when she stops me.

"I'll be right there. Do you think you could take Q in for me?"

I tilt my head in confusion before registering the under-cover FBI agent in the back. Her skin is pale; her hair a tangled mess hanging around her hunched shoulders.

There's a cut on her lower lip and bruises scattered along her arms. Whatever she's been through, it's been hell. She looks lost. And alone. And in much worse shape than Gigi. Glancing back at her, I see the need for a minute alone with Dex written plainly across her face. I'd be a terrible wing-woman if I didn't give it to her. With a knowing smile and a final squeeze, I turn my attention to the stranger in the back.

"Oh. Hi," I start. "I'm Ace. And you're Q?"

The girl stares blankly out the window, not bothering to respond. My heart breaks for her.

Tossing a wide-eyed look of helplessness toward Gigi and Dex, I wait for them to tell me how I can help, but they both stare blankly back. They're as lost as I am. Hesitantly, I slide out of the passenger seat where I was practically sitting on top of Gigi then open the back door.

Offering my hand, I state, "Come on, Q. Let's get you inside and out of those cuffs and dress."

The promise of freedom is enough to get her moving. She slides out of the car and slowly follows me inside Kingston's estate.

The silence is deafening as I open the front door and motion to the house. I assume she's harmless since Dex left her with me, so I ask, "Would you like a tour?"

Silence.

Chewing my upper lip, I try to think of something I can say to help her. Her shoulders are hunched, and there's a clear leave-me-alone vibe that she's radiating, but I can't help myself.

What would I have wanted someone to tell me?

"Hey." I stop her with a gentle touch on her forearm. She jumps back but doesn't run, so I take it as a sign that I'm okay to continue.

I look closer at the girl in front of me before taking a quick look around to confirm we're alone. Rule #2: Always be aware of your surroundings. I smile as the rule flashes through my mind. It's funny how they've all but disappeared since moving in with King. But as I look at the girl in front of me, I know I need to implement them right now. She needs the rules. The structure. The foundation to build her new life. Because she'll never be the same. Not after everything she's been through.

Thankfully, the open entryway is empty, reminding me of Rule #8: Don't discuss private shit in public. It's bound to screw you over. While the family might know my private shit, that doesn't mean I enjoy discussing it in front of them. In front of *anyone*, actually. However, as I look at the ghost of a girl in front of me, I have a feeling she needs to know too.

"I want you to know something," I start as she stares back at me. "I've been where you are. Not exactly...but close enough. I had my first run-in with Burlone when I was a little girl, and he broke me. I don't know how many times Burlone hurt you, but—"

"It wasn't Burlone."

Digging my teeth into my lower lip, I hesitate before asking a question I'm not sure I want the answer to. "Then who was it?"

The broken girl looks over at me with absolute hatred and fury shining in her gaze. "Sei."

I don't recognize that name, but it doesn't matter anyway because his outcome will be the same.

"Then we'll make sure Sei gets taken care of," I promise somberly. "But until then, I need to figure out where the keys to your cuffs are, and then we'll get you showered and find you a place to sleep. Does that sound okay?"

"Hey," Stefan calls from the staircase, interrupting our little heart-to-heart.

I try to hide my annoyance. "Yeah?"

"Kingston wants to see everyone in his office right now.

We have some shit to talk about, and Diece is dying for a recap."

"Okay. We'll be right there."

I dismiss him by giving him my back only to find Q a quivering mess, making my heart hurt.

"Look at me, Q."

She swallows bravely before tugging her gaze from the floor and holding my stare.

"Everyone in this house is a good guy. They would never hurt a girl the way you've been hurt. I promise. Let's go have this little talk, and then we'll get that shower and bed, okay?"

"How do you know they're not going to kill me?"

"Why would they kill you?" I ask, confused.

"Because I said I worked for the FBI. That doesn't exactly sound promising to men like that."

The girl makes a good point.

Though I don't miss the way she worded her comment. *I said I worked for the FBI.* Not that she actually does.

"*Do* you work for the FBI?" I press, unable to hide my curiosity. Jack didn't know what the hell Kingston was talking about when he brought Q up. So who the hell is she?

She doesn't respond, so I shake my head and remind myself that we have somewhere we need to be.

"It doesn't matter. Let's go."

Gently, I start guiding her down the hallway, and by some miracle, she follows. I can't blame her. I wouldn't want to talk, either. When I'm sure my question will go unanswered, Q surprises me by reaching for my hand and holding on for dear life. The action makes me want to cry, but I restrain myself because right now, she needs me to be the strong one, and it's the least I can do for her.

A C E

I grab Q's hand and bring it into my lap in an attempt to help her feel like she's not alone. She returns it with a tight squeeze. We're sitting in Kingston's office as we wait for everyone to join us. Well...when I say everyone, I mean Dex and Regina. Kingston is sitting behind his desk, Stefan is looking at his phone, and Diece has been busy staring at Q like she's a damn steak for the last five minutes. There's no way Q can't feel his gaze eating her up, but she's been handling it like a champ when all I want to do is smack him upside the head. Does he not know what she's been through? How terrified she is? Peeking over at her from the corner of my eye, I study Q from a man's perspective. She's absolutely stunning. I can't even imagine what she'd look like if the bruises were absent and a smile graced her lips instead of the constant frown that's been crippling her. Regardless, Diece needs to know what he's dealing with and how to keep his hands to himself. After everything she's been through, it's going to take a special man to help her open up. I glance over at her again. And I doubt it'll be any time soon.

The sound of footsteps down the hall distracts me from

dissecting Diece's obsession any further. Gigi appears in the doorway, and seconds later, Dex follows behind.

Jumping up, Diece wraps Gigi in his arms, and they start whispering to each other.

Taking advantage of the privacy, I pull Q closer and murmur, "You doing okay?"

She nods, but her face is blank.

"Diece is harmless."

With a quiet scoff, she rolls her eyes. "No one's harmless."

I open my mouth to argue when I'm interrupted by Diece as he asks Dex, "Hey. How'd it go?"

"Good. Burlone's still in the trunk. Where do you want me to put him?" He shifts his weight between his feet, looking awkward as hell. And I don't blame him. Until Kingston gives him the okay, he's still *technically* the enemy.

"We have a shed out back," Diece offers. "But let's catch up with King first."

"Speaking of which, way to steal my thunder, D. She's my sister, remember?" King argues, marching toward Regina and tugging her close. Apparently, he doesn't like being second. I smirk.

Again, Gigi is busy whispering, but I think I hear apologies on both ends before Kingston finally releases her. Tears are streaming down her face as she hastily wipes beneath her eyes and returns to Dex's side. The movement makes me anxious. Dex might've pulled through, but I still know what his fists can do. Without a word, he wraps his arm around her waist and kisses the top of her head. I look over at Kingston in concern to see him glaring at the exchanged affection.

"Well, since we're all here and we've had our little reunion, I figured it'd be best to get everyone caught up. Dex," he barks. "Where's Burlone?"

"Still in the trunk. D said he'd show me the shed in a few," Dex answers.

Stefan interrupts, "I'll do it. Just give me your keys."

Dex digs into his pockets then tosses them through the air before Stefan catches them and disappears out the door. Seconds later, Dex throws another key at me, making me jump in surprise. Untangling my hand with Q's, I pick it up from my lap as he motions to Q's cuffs. Finally understanding, I start unlocking them while Kingston gets to the next order of business.

"As far as your loyalty goes, you've earned your spot in the Romano family. I'll make an announcement tomorrow."

The relief in Dex's expression tugs at the knot in my chest, lessening the pressure that usually accompanies it whenever I lay eyes on him. Maybe I can learn to trust him one day too.

Maybe.

Clearing his throat, Dex looks to his brother quickly before dropping his gaze to Regina.

"And what about her?"

The room is so quiet, Dex's heavy breathing is the only sound that can be heard as he waits for Kingston's approval.

"Let me ask you something, Dex," Kingston says carefully, lifting his chin to his sister. "Do you know who she is?"

"Of course."

"Tell me."

Confused, Dex explains, "She's Regina Romano."

"And who is Regina Romano?"

Dex opens his mouth to throw out a guess when Kingston cuts him off. "She's the princess to the Romano family. She's the daughter of Gabriel and Emilia Romano and sister to Kingston Romano, the head of the Romano family. Now let me ask you this. Who. Are. You?" Each word is as sharp as a knife, revealing his verdict without bothering to say the words outright.

I watch as Dex's jaw flexes, and I can tell he's biting his tongue.

"Answer the question," Kingston pushes, his eyes laser-focused. This is the Dark King. The heartless King. The one that's ripping his sister's heart out with his callousness but doesn't give a shit. I look over at Regina to see a single glistening tear slide down her cheek. Angrily, she wipes the moisture away, anxious to see how the situation plays out. And if I'm being honest, so am I.

Regina's captor grits out his name. "Dex."

"Just Dex?"

"Yes," he confirms, refusing to be intimidated by Kingston.

Tapping his chin, Kingston leans forward. "And why is that?"

"Because my father didn't claim me," Dex growls.

"No. He didn't. You're nothing but a bastard. Regina Romano is so far out of your league that you'd be lucky to clean the shit off her shoes."

"Kingston, please—" Regina interrupts, but Kingston cuts her off with a cold look.

"Regina, I know you have feelings for him, but have you ever considered the possibility that those feelings are based off who you perceived him to be when you didn't have anyone else? You barely know him."

"It doesn't matter, King. I know that I—"

"Stop!"

Her quivering lips pull into a thin line, and Dex tenses beside her. I can tell he's close to snapping, and part of me wonders if that's what Kingston wants. We've seen his loyalty to the Romano family, but was it for Regina or Kingston?

"Regina, you're dismissed," Kingston orders. "Go to your

room and wash up. Dex, if you'd still like a place here as a soldier, I'll give it to you. You've earned it. However, if you plan to pursue my sister, I'll tell you right now that you'll be gutted for it. Understand?"

Regina storms off without waiting for Dex's response, and my eyes widen in shock.

"Kingston—" I interrupt in an attempt to soothe him. He gives me a pointed look that dares me to continue, so I keep my mouth shut.

"Not now, Ace. I'm not going to change my mind, but if you'd like to discuss it further, we'll discuss it in private. Understand?"

That's something at least.

I nod.

"Good. Now, next order of business. You." He points to Q who's still busy clutching my hand like it's a lifeline. "What's your name?"

She doesn't answer, still frozen in shock at his sharpness, so I do it for her. "Her name is Q."

"I thought her name was Gigi?" Diece interjects, giving me a puzzled look.

With a roll of my eyes, I try to clarify everything for him. "Regina is my friend who went missing. She's my Gigi." My heart hurts that she was dismissed to her room by Kingston, but I press on, knowing I'll get a chance to talk to her when this is over. "We met at Dottie's one night and bonded over coffee and breakfast food. Q is just an innocent bystander who got caught in Burlone's crosshairs and ended up saving the day."

Gaze narrowing in suspicion, Kingston addresses Q. "Speaking of which, what the hell happened in that room, and why did you do it?"

She stares blankly ahead, lost in the memory for a few seconds before I nudge her softly.

Clearing her throat, she answers, "You needed my help, and I was dead anyway."

"But why help me?"

With a quick look at me, Q mutters, "I saw her walk in with you. I saw the way she willingly touched you. I saw the way you spoke to her. The way you treated her."

"And that was enough to put your own life on the line?"

"What life?" she sneers. "I was in the middle of being sold as a sex slave. My life was already over, and it didn't hurt that I could take out Burlone by backing your story."

Her blunt honesty hits like a bull, making all of the grown men in the room pause to get their bearings.

After a few seconds, Kingston continues his questioning. "And what about now? You're free, yet you've put a giant target on your back. Those men are all being arrested for human trafficking, but that doesn't mean they don't know people who are still on the outside. They assume I'm going to kill you because you outed yourself as an agent, but Burlone sent your pictures to a lot of bad men. Men who possibly already had another buyer set in place in case they won the tournament. Men who could recognize you. Who could place you as a fucking agent. Do you know what will happen if they find you?"

Her eyes are glassy, but she doesn't bother to respond. Instead, she keeps staring straight ahead as if King isn't five feet in front of her. As if he isn't reaming into her for her mistake when, in reality, she brought our plan to fruition. Without her help, we could all be dead. Hell, I have no doubt that we would be.

Kingston keeps going. "If they find you, the last two weeks of your life will have been a walk in the park compared to what they'll put you through. Understand?"

A single tear slides down her cheek, dripping off her chin. She doesn't bother to wipe it away. And the sight kills me.

"Enough," Diece barks, surprising me and everyone else in the room. I've never heard him talk back to Kingston. I've never heard him interrupt him or even question his methods.

All heads turn to him.

"Excuse me?" Kingston grits out.

"I'm pretty sure she gets the picture, Boss," D says, his chest puffed up. "I think it's time you mention the solution now."

Anxiously, I wait to hear what the solution is too. Q's hold on my hand tightens until I'm sure my fingers are purple, but I'm too invested in the conversation to look down and confirm my theory.

"My solution is for you to watch her, D. To take care of her until things calm down. Do you think you can do that? Keep her in hiding? Change her appearance? That kind of thing?"

Diece nods mechanically, his attention shooting to Q beside me. Ignoring him, she simply keeps staring blankly at the wall. Numb. As if her future isn't being discussed a few feet in front of her. As if she doesn't care what the outcome of her life will be because she's already given up on it.

"Good. Ace," Kingston addresses me. "You're still living with me. Don't bother arguing."

I open my mouth to do exactly that before narrowing my eyes and crossing my arms. "Who says I'm arguing?"

With his lips tilted up in amusement, Kingston teases, "Good girl. Will you take Q up to the guest room across from us and make sure she's comfortable? D and I have a visitor we'd like to have a little chat with."

"Wait!" The mention of Burlone seems to light a spark in Q as she jumps to her feet. Her jackrabbit move scares the shit out of me, making me flinch. Placing my hand on my racing heart, I try to figure out where her burst of energy came from, and what she's so passionate about.

Kingston tilts his head and assesses her. "Need something, Q?"

She swallows thickly as the wheels in her head start to turn. Hands shaking at her sides, Q boldly says, "I need a baseball bat and five minutes with the asshole who stole my life."

"Me too," I add, feeling as if I've found another soul sister. We both deserve retribution, and the possibility of being able to hurt Burlone is too good to pass up. Seeing him in that room refreshed all my childhood memories, and I want to make him pay for each and every one of them.

Snapping his fingers, King turns to Diece. "Take Q to the shed. Give her a bat. I'll be over in fifteen. Ace, I need you to stay with me. You'll get your time in a few."

With his hands raised in the air in surrender, Diece approaches Q as if she's a scared little deer. "Come with me. Seems you have some frustration you need to work out of your system."

Then it's just me and King.

As soon as the door closes behind Q and Diece, leaving me alone with Kingston, his voice rumbles, "You're mad at me."

Licking my lips, I consider my feelings before shaking my head. "I'm not mad. Just confused."

"About what?"

Frustration blooms in my chest that he would even feel the need to ask me that. *He can't honestly be that dense.* Quirking my brow, I explain something that shouldn't need an explanation.

Stupid men.

"Why would you do that to Regina? Why were you so harsh with Dex? I just don't understand."

With a sigh, he pats his lap, and my mouth threatens to tug into a smile, softening my annoyance. Like a good little girl, I do as I'm told and walk around his desk before sitting on his knee.

"That better, Santa?" I tease.

Laughing, he drags me down for a deep, long kiss that

makes my toes curl. Once he's practically turned me to putty, he pulls away. "Much better."

"Good. Now, answer my question. Why won't you let Gigi be with Dex?"

His attention shifts to the closed office door as his index finger trails along the slit in my dress. The intimate touch is almost enough to distract me. *Almost.* As I squirm in his lap, he gives me a cocky grin before asking a question of his own.

"Do you trust him?"

I place my hand on top of his as it rests on my upper thigh so I can focus. "It doesn't matter if I trust him. Gigi trusts him, and she knows him better than both of us."

"Does she, though?" His eyes darken. "He was her captor, Ace. Yes, he protected her. And yes, he pulled through tonight. But he's still a stranger. Until I know I can trust him fully, I can't give them my blessing."

"But why couldn't you just tell them that? Give them a little hope? You didn't just shoot down the possibility of them being with each other; you freaking blew it up."

Again, that same cocky smile makes an appearance before he sobers. And it's the sobering part that makes me nervous. I know that whatever he's about to say is something that's bothering him. I just don't know what it is.

Raising his hand, he brushes a strand of my dark hair away from my cheek before cupping my jaw. The intimacy is overwhelming, and I lean into his touch.

His warm, minty breath fans across my face as he releases another sigh. "I have reason to believe there's a rat in my organization." I gasp, but he keeps me close as he continues, "What better way to uncover him than by giving the rat a potential ally? Dex was once the enemy. He's extremely pissed off at his new boss right now, and he has connections with a shit ton of men who have a grudge against the

Romano family. If the rat is looking for a new friend, I just delivered one in a handbasket."

I'm shocked that he just revealed his plan to me. It's *family business*, yet he's trusting me with the confidential information. Confidential information that could make--or break--the family. Still, that doesn't mean I don't have reservations about his arrangement, and if he trusts me enough to disclose the information to me, then he needs to hear them.

"So, you're using him?" I probe.

"No. I'm testing him."

"And there's a difference?"

With a smile, he pulls me down for another kiss, dragging his tongue along the seam of my lips before murmuring, "Yes. One that gives him the prize of my little sister at the end if he succeeds."

"And if he fails?" I whisper, terrified of his answer.

"Then he'll only receive death."

"You sure you want to do this, Wild Card?" King asks as we walk toward the shed fifteen minutes later. After our little chat, Kingston stood up and suggested we relieve Q of her...duty. He wanted to give Q privacy to do what needed to be done. He could see her need for revenge as much as I could, and I wanted to give her the same thing.

"Yeah," I answer. "I'm not the delicate little flower you paint me as, King. I've been wanting to make him hurt since the moment he entered my life. And I want answers too. I want to know what happened to my mom."

"You might not get your answers, Ace. I just want to make sure you'll be okay if you don't."

I take a second to really consider the possibility that he might not remember me or what he did. That he might not remember my mom or what happened to her. That my existence really was so inconsequential to him that he honestly can't recall how he ruined it. How he ruined me.

"Honestly? I'm done being hurt by him. I just want to move forward, but I want to do it with a clean slate. As soon as I find out the truth--whether it's what I want to hear or not--I'll move on."

"You can move on, but only after I put him in a body bag," he growls, putting a protective arm around me. His reply makes me smile.

"Can I ask you something, Kingston?"

"Yeah."

"You say things like that, but I haven't really seen that side of you since we first met, and even then you were pretty tame."

He tugs me closer. "I've kept that monster locked away, but after seeing how strong you are, I'm not afraid to unleash him on your worst enemy."

"Good. Because you couldn't scare me if you tried. I love you, Kingston Romano. All of you."

"You too, Wild Card. You too." He leans forward and gives me a soft kiss before tugging me the rest of the way to the shed.

Looking down at me, he pauses at the door. "You ready?"

"As I'll ever be," I return.

"Then let's finish this."

With a swift tug of the handle, Kingston gives me a view of the shed. I gasp when I see Burlone tied to the chair, blood pouring down his face and the smell of pee lingering in the air. Covering my mouth, I turn to King who looks over my head at D.

"What the hell happened here?"

I follow his gaze and find D with his arms wrapped around Q as she burrows into his chest with her eyes squeezed shut. He continues rubbing her back as he states, "Q happened. Looks to me like she's a natural at torture, King. She might be able to give you a run for your money."

King chuckles under his breath in amusement before motioning to the door. "Well, get out of here. I promised Ace a few minutes before I started asking my questions, and with how bad he looks, I'm not sure I'll have much time before he passes out again."

Burlone groans in pain, making King smile even wider before he adds, "Thanks for warming him up for me, though."

Diece rolls his eyes and carries Q out in his arms. My concern for her spikes when she doesn't protest and doesn't bother to look my way, either. Burlone broke her. Just like he broke the little girl I once was.

And now he's going to pay for it.

Once they're gone, I step toward the back corner where I see a cabinet tucked away.

"Is this where you keep everything?" I ask. My nose wrinkles in distaste from the rank stench permeating the air as I look around the room. It isn't very big. There's a single light hanging from the ceiling and cement flooring with a drain in the center that happens to also be right below Burlone's unconscious form. The walls are bare other than the cabinet that is now within reach.

Kingston chuckles darkly. "Yeah. I would say go crazy, but I'm selfish and want a turn too for all the shit he put us through, so maybe take it easy on him."

With a dry laugh, I grab a switchblade and say, "No guarantees."

Shaking his head, he pulls up a folding chair and takes a seat. "Fine. But only because I love you."

I had changed into a t-shirt, jeans, and sneakers before coming here. When I take in all the blood and other fluids I'd rather not label, I'm grateful I did. As King had mentioned once before, blood is a bitch to get out of clothes. Clearing my throat, I tap my shoe against the bottom of Burlone's loafers. "Hey. Time to wake up, Sunshine."

Again, he groans.

Leaning closer, I snap my fingers in front of his nose. "Come on, Burlone. I have a few questions for you, and I'm going to need you to answer them for me."

Slowly, he blinks his eyes as if his swollen lids weigh a thousand pounds. "There ya go. The more you talk, the less I hurt you, okay?"

Those are a few words I never thought I'd say.

Another groan.

"I'll take that as a yes. Do you know who I am?"

The asshole mutters something, but I can't understand what the hell it is, so I lean a little closer.

"I'm sorry, what was that?" I press.

An annoyed Kingston steps forward and digs his thumb into an open wound along his forearm. Blood flows out of it freely, dripping onto the splattered cement floor and is quickly followed by a scream from our captive.

"Kingston's girlfriend," he slurs once Kingston relieves the pressure. I have to really focus to understand what he's saying.

"Do you know who I was before that?"

"A bitch who conned me."

Kingston snorts, and I turn to give him a smile before giving Burlone my full attention. "Yeah. That too. Do I spark your memory in any other way?"

He lifts his head and looks at me. Really looks at me. But his eyebrows stay pulled low in confusion.

"Let me give you a hint. Picture me with blonde hair...just like my mom."

A spark of recognition shines through his gaze.

"Now we're getting somewhere," I murmur. "Do you remember my mom, Burlone?"

With a cough, he mutters, "Yeah. Crack whore who liked it dirty and would do anything for her next fix."

My nostrils flare, but I push forward. "And do you remember her daughter?"

"Of course I do. Pretty little thing too. It's a shame you—"

I slam the switchblade into his thigh, turning his demeaning comment into a tortured scream.

"Don't ever talk about that little girl again, understand?"

"You asked, you crazy bitch!" he shouts, spewing spittle with his words.

I twist the switchblade in his leg, making him scream even louder before I calmly say, "I have one more question."

"What? What is it?" he cries.

"Do you know where my mom is?"

"She's dead! Didn't even make it to the buyer. My men used her up and spit her out before I could make a dime off her."

Releasing my hold on the switchblade, I leave it embedded deep in his leg then turn to King.

"You're up."

The pride swells in my chest as Ace admires her handiwork before stepping away from her victim and toward me. Unable to control myself, I wrap my hand around the back of her neck and tug her into my chest before dropping a hard kiss to her pouty lips.

"You sure you don't have any more questions for this fucker?" I mutter against her mouth.

She nods. "Yeah. He was nothing but a monster. And now my very own supervillain gets to defeat him while I have a front-row seat."

After a breath of laughter, I ask, "You wanna stay?" I can't hide my disbelief. I'd assumed she'd retreat to our room to clean herself up while I get a few more answers I need before putting a bullet in his skull.

"Positive," she breathes, peeking up at me. There's no fear. No hesitation. Just trust. Anticipation. And an overwhelming need for peace.

Pressing my mouth against hers for a second time, I murmur, "Then let's get this over with."

I turn to Burlone to see him watching our interaction with open hatred, but he's smart enough to hold his tongue.

"Never knew you were such a softie," he notes. "She tastes pretty sweet, doesn't she? You should've seen her when--"

My fist connects with his already bruised jaw, causing his head to swing to the side as red-tinged spittle flies from his mouth.

Apparently, he's not as smart as I'd assumed.

"Careful, Burlone," I warn as the deep ache in my knuckles centers me. "The Romano family let you get away with too much for too long. But not anymore."

"Fuck you," he spits, more saliva flying. "If you honestly think I'm not going to walk out of this room, you're more dense than I thought."

With a dark laugh, I give him my back and begin sorting through a few items tucked away in the cabinet. However, there's something about the switchblade lodged into Burlone's leg that calls to me. I shake my head. It won't work for the specific techniques I have in mind. Sighing, I reach for one of my favorites--a six-inch blade with a polished ebony handle that fits perfectly in my grip. My mouth pulls into a grin.

At a lazy pace, I circle the poor bastard who's strapped to a chair in the middle of my interrogation room--one slow step at a time.

"I find it interesting that you actually think I'd let you go after everything you've done. Let's just put a pin in the fact that you tortured my girlfriend. That you raped her. Sent one of your men to beat the shit out of her. And scarred her in more ways than you could ever imagine. Don't worry, though; she's stronger than you could ever imagine. Not only did she beat you at your own game; she did it *twice*." My pride swells a second time as my attention shifts to her. She nods softly, encouraging me to continue. Clearing my throat, I try to focus on the task at hand instead of the brunette bombshell who's about to see a whole new side of me. And for once, I'm not terrified she'll run in the other direction.

"Let's focus on the fact that you took the princess of the Romano family, shall we?" I pause when I'm behind him, enjoying the way my presence makes him squirm. He cranes his neck to keep me in his view as I watch tiny goosebumps pop up along the back of his head before disappearing beneath his stained white shirt.

"You've had your fun, Kingston," he argues.

I laugh before tightening my grip around the knife in my right hand. "No. I think I'm just beginning." Pressing my right forearm against his left temple roughly, he has no choice but to rest his right ear against the top of his shoulder. I angle his head until the entire left side of his neck is exposed toward the ceiling.

"Wait, wait, wait, wait, Kingston. Be reasonable. You've had your fun. I've learned my lesson. Besides, no one touched your sister. I kept her safe--"

His words morph into screams as I grip the shell of his left ear then slice through the skin with exact precision. Even though the blade is wicked sharp, I have to saw at the carti-lage as Burlone's blood oozes down his neck.

His arms tug against their restraints, his head jerking back and forth, but I don't release him until his ear is in my hand. Lazily, I toss it in his lap.

"Apparently, you weren't listening to me very well, Burlone. Maybe now you'll try a little harder to cooperate. Capiche?"

The tears are streaming freely down his face, his lower lip quivering pathetically. But the hatred in his eyes? That's giving me the information I need. He wants me to burn for my actions. Now, I need to find out if it's possible that I might.

"Good boy." I wipe the blood from my left hand along the top of his head, smearing it into his hair while treating him like a dog.

Hell, like a little bitch. I smirk at the thought.

"You're never going to breathe air outside of this room. Ever. Again," I divulge. "The sooner you realize that, the sooner we can get the answers we need. And the sooner we can put you out of your misery. However, if you don't feel like being helpful, I'm more than happy to persuade you a little more. Any questions?"

"Motherfu––"

"Careful, Burlone," I tsk, raising the crimson-colored blade into the air. "I still need your tongue, but you have plenty of other appendages that I don't find necessary to getting the answers I want. Nod if you understand."

His swelling jaw is clenched tight, and his beady eyes hold so much hatred, I'm surprised I'm still standing.

"Nod," I bark.

And like a good little boy, he does.

"Good boy," I repeat, condescendingly. "Who knew about the tournament? Anyone else that wasn't on the email list?"

He remains silent. That is until I grab his wrist and drag the edge of the knife along his middle knuckle.

"Fine!" he squeals like a little pig, struggling against my firm grasp. "Fine, I'll tell you!"

Releasing him, I stand to my full height and cross my arms, being careful of the blade in my right hand. "Start. Talking."

"I can only speak for the Allegretti family."

"And what did they know?" I press in a cool tone.

"That I was throwing a tournament together."

"Did you have any buyers lined up for the girls?"

He laughs. "You mean the fruit? Of course." At the mention of his favorite conquest, he brightens. "Any good businessman would have a buyer lined up for fresh merchandise. Don't you?"

"Have a buyer? For the girls? No. I don't believe in selling women, remember?"

"I meant I'm sure you always have a buyer lined up for the drugs. The guns. The...*information.*" With a smirk, his cloudy gaze moves from mine to Ace's. "Do you know who you're screwing, Pretty Girl? Because if you did, I think you'd be running in the other direction. Sure, I'm not a good guy, but he isn't a saint, either."

"I know exactly who I'm sleeping with," Ace replies indifferently from behind me. "But thanks for your concern."

"If I'd have known you'd slip into bed with someone of our caliber willingly, I'd have——"

"Careful," I interrupt. "I have a few more questions that I need answers to, and I'm afraid if you keep talking, I won't be able to control myself."

"Then get to the point, Kingston. I'm afraid I've grown bored of your little game."

"I thought you loved games, remember?" With a sarcastic laugh, I wave the knife through the air. "But you're right. I've got more important shit to do today than let you breathe much longer. Who were the buyers?"

Annoyed, he mutters, "You already know. They were in the process of purchasing before your lie swayed them——"

"I meant the buyers you'd lined up for after you won the tournament. We both know you're too much of a cocky sonofabitch to not have assumed you'd come out the victor."

"Touche." He smirks. "Unfortunately, I don't know the names off the top of my head."

"Lie. Who were they?"

"Why does it matter?" he argues. "They're not getting the girls."

"Yes. But they're likely looking for them. Answer me."

"No."

Impatient, I turn back to the cabinet and grab a set of pliers with the intention of ripping out a few of his fingernails. When he sees them in my hand, he shakes his head back and forth rapidly.

"Fine! I don't know the names off the top of my head, but we corresponded through email. I'm sure your tech gurus can take it from there. J-just put it down." He stares at the pliers as if they're a damn viper that could strike at any second.

Interesting.

Once Lou breaks into his email, we might be able to find out the location of Q's buyer and can keep her far away from him to avoid any chance encounters. We can't let anyone recognize her, or she'll end up in a casket.

Satisfied, with his previous answer, I say, "Last question. Was Vince the only guy you were in contact with in the Romano family?"

I keep my expression indifferent, though my entire body is vibrating with anxiety.

The asshat gives me a sinister smile. The blood from his internal bleeding––I think I can thank Q for that––stains his teeth, making him look like something straight out of a horror movie.

"I'd heard about Vince's disappearance. It's a shame. I didn't even have to work for his intel. He gladly handed it over in a handbasket."

"Answer the question."

Beady eyes narrowing, he assesses me. I know what he's looking for. Weakness. Uncertainty. Fear.

I show him nothing.

"Watch your back, Kingston," he divulges cryptically. "Someone has a target on it."

"Who." It's a question, even though I've voiced it as a statement.

He sneers. "Who doesn't?"

Patience obliterated, I grab the handle in his leg from Ace's switchblade and twist it deeper into his thigh muscle.

His curse is loud and shrill as he drops his head back and looks toward the ceiling.

"I don't know who it is! I don't know!"

"What do you mean, you don't know?"

"He never reached out to me," he pants, breathing through the unbearable pain. "I only heard Vince mention him once, but he never said a name. That's all I know. I swear that's all I know!"

Satisfied with his response, I withdraw the switchblade and toss it onto the cement floor near the corner of the room. The clang of it hitting my target echoes through the room before an eerie silence replaces it.

"And what did Vince say?"

"Not enough. Obviously."

"Tell me." I step forward, and the bastard flinches in response.

"Your shipment dates. Your contacts in Congress. Little things."

"And what were you going to do with the information?"

"Nothing."

My face stays blank, while my mind reels. "Nothing?"

Shaking his head, he divulges, "I didn't ask for the information. I had no use for it. Well, other than the location of your warehouses. But that plan didn't exactly pan out the way I'd planned, now did it? Regardless, you and I have never been competition. You were merely an inconvenience for me."

"And getting rid of your body will be an inconvenience for me," I quip. With my shirt soaked in crimson from another hour of torture, I roll up my sleeves then pick up a Glock from the cabinet.

"Any final words, Burlone?"

"Go to hell," he spits through a mouthful of blood. The bruises around his eyes nearly swallow his beady pupils, and the image is nothing short of perfection.

"See you there." Pressing the gun to his forehead, I pull the trigger without hesitation. Ace watches me end Burlone's life, looking numb until I drop my gun-wielding hand to my side. Rushing toward me, she wraps her arms around me and takes a few slow, steady breaths before whispering, "Thank you. Thank you for saving me. For ending him. For everything."

Gently, I lean forward and press a kiss to her lips. She's never tasted sweeter.

"You're welcome, Ace."

Ushering her outside, the sun glowing brighter and brighter, I pull out my phone and send a quick message to Stefan.

Me: Need a cleaning crew.

Stefan: Done.

"So, what now?" Ace asks, snuggling into my side.

"Now? Now, we let your past stay in your past and focus on our future. Together. Think you can do that, Wild Card?"

"Yeah. In fact, I think it should be a rule."

I roll my eyes. "You and your rules. Which one is that now?"

"Number one."

"But I thought—"

"Nope. The rest don't matter as long as you're by my side. What do you think?"

"I think you're sexy when you talk like that." Grinning, I bend down as she rises on her toes, meeting me in the middle for a long-overdue kiss. I find it funny that she doesn't care I'm dripping in Burlone's blood or that I'm a monster to most. She loves me for me, and I'm a lucky bastard to call her mine.

I agree with her. As long as she's by my side, nothing else matters.

I'm all in.

***

Thank you for reading Wild Card! I hope you love Ace and Kingston's story.

Regina and Dex's story continues in <u>Little Bird</u>

***

Two Weeks Earlier
Regina

I don't know how I got here. Not really. I remember walking down the street before a strange set of arms wrapped around my waist, and the burning prick of a needle pressed into my neck. After that? Darkness.

That is, until I woke up in an office surrounded by naked women who were just as beaten--just as bloodied--as me. When I saw Burlone behind the desk, my pulse spiked, and my breathing grew shallow before I remembered the importance of not letting them *see*.

I can't let them see the real me or my real emotions.

No.

I need to be numb.

Fifteen minutes later, I was dragged into an empty room with a twin-sized bed in the center of it. Then I was left alone in nothing but a black bra and matching bikini cut underwear, which is where I find myself now.

Looking around the space, I notice a pair of handcuffs attached to the metal bed frame and struggle to pull my eyes away from the promise they hold.

I never thought I'd find myself here. Although, now that I think about it, I'm not sure anyone really does. Still, my entire life has been spent in a different kind of prison to keep me from a fate like this. My eyes gather with tears when I realize he was right. My father. My brother. Everyone. A girl like me will never be safe. She'll never be normal. She'll never be anything at all.

Inhaling a shaky breath, I hold it for ten seconds then release it through my mouth. But on the next inhale, the lingering scent of pee that clings to the stained mattress burns my nostrils, making me cough.

I'm in so much freaking trouble.

Panicking, I force my eyes closed and squeeze them shut as tight as I possibly can.

I'm screwed. I'm so screwed. I'm so freaking screwed.

The mantra continues over and over again before I drive my fingernails into the palm of my hand, hoping that the bite of pain will ground me. With another deep breath, I dig deep and search for the courage to look around the rest of the room. Opening my eyes, I do another quick scan of my prison. Other than the bed and a medium sized Home Depot bucket tucked in the corner, it's empty. The walls are made from cinder blocks, the floors are nothing but a slab of cement, and there aren't any windows. As soon as I come to that realization, I feel the walls pressing in from all sides.

I think I'm going to be sick.

Read Little Bird Now

Sign up for Kelsie's newsletter to receive exclusive content, including the first two chapters of every new book two weeks before its release date!

Dear Reader,

I want to thank you guys from the bottom of my heart for taking a chance on Wild Card, and for giving me the opportunity to share this story with you. I couldn't do this without you!

I would also be very grateful if you could take the time to leave a review. It's amazing how such a little thing like a review can be such a huge help to an author!

Thank you so much!!!

-Kelsie

ABOUT THE AUTHOR

Kelsie is a sucker for a love story with all the feels. When she's not chasing words for her next book, you will probably find her reading or, more likely, hanging out with her husband and playing with her three kiddos who love to drive her crazy.

She adores photography, baking, her yorkie, her boxer, and her devon rex. Now that she's actively pursuing her writing dreams, she's set her sights on someday finding the self-discipline to not binge-watch an entire series on Netflix in one sitting.

If you'd like to connect with Kelsie, follow her on Facebook, sign up for her newsletter, or join Kelsie Rae's Reader Group to stay up to date on new releases, exclusive content, give-aways, and her crazy publishing journey.

ALSO BY KELSIE RAE

Advantage Play Series

(Romantic Suspense/Mafia Series)

Wild Card

Little Bird

Bitter Queen

Black Jack

Signature Sweethearts Series

(Contemporary Romance Standalone Series)

Liv

Luke

Breezy

Jude

Rhett

Sophie

Marcus

Anthony

Skye

Saylor

Wrecked Roommates Series

(Contemporary Romance Standalone Series)

Model Behavior

Forbidden Lyrics

Messy Strokes

Stand Alones

Fifty-Fifty

Drowning in Love

Hired Hottie

Crush

Bartered Souls Duet

(Urban Fantasy Series)

Gambled Soul

Wager Won

Sign up for Kelsie's newsletter to receive exclusive content, including the first two chapters of every new book two weeks before its release date!